Three irresistible,

She Can't Say No to the Greek Tycoon

Three passionate and enticing love stories from
three beloved Mills & Boon authors!

She Can't Say No to the Greek Tycoon

DIANA HAMILTON

KATHRYN ROSS

ANNIE WEST

MILLS & BOON

All the characters in this book have no existence outside the imagination of
the author, and have no relation whatsoever to anyone bearing the same name
or names. They are not even distantly inspired by any individual known or
unknown to the author, and all the incidents are pure invention.

First published in Great Britain 2011
by Mills & Boon, an imprint of Harlequin (UK) Limited,
Eton House, 18-24 Paradise Road, Richmond, Surrey TW9 1SR

SHE CAN'T SAY NO TO THE GREEK TYCOON
© by Harlequin Enterprises II B.V./S.à.r.l 2011

The Kouvaris Marriage,The Greek Tycoon's Innocent and *The Greek's
Convenient Mistress* were first published in Great Britain by Harlequin (UK)
Limited in separate, single volumes.

The Kouvaris Marriage © Diana Hamilton 2006
The Greek Tycoon's Innocent © Kathryn Ross 2007
The Greek's Convenient Mistress © Annie West 2006

ISBN: 978 0 263 88434 0

05-0411

Printed and bound in Spain
by Blackprint CPI, Barcelona

THE KOUVARIS
MARRIAGE

BY
DIANA HAMILTON

Diana Hamilton is a true romantic, and fell in love with her husband at first sight. They still live in the fairytale Tudor house where they raised their three children. Now the idyll is shared with eight rescue cats and a puppy. But, despite an often chaotic lifestyle ever since she learned to read and write Diana has had her nose in a book – either reading or writing one—and plans to go on doing just that for a very long time to come.

PROLOGUE

Done!

Maddie Ryan straightened, hot and sweaty beneath the sun that blazed from a cerulean sky, and rested her grubby hands on her curvy hips. Every leaf and bloom was perfect, the terracotta planters were arranged in attractive groupings around the arcaded courtyard. The ancient central stone fountain was beautifully restored and finally working, sending a silvery plume of water dancing skywards, then falling back into the shallow stone basin, creating lovely water music.

Everything was ready for tonight's party and her first important commission as a landscape gardener was successfully completed, a commission given by her best friend since schooldays, Amanda.

Thinking of Amanda, she grinned. It was an unlikely friendship—everyone had said so—the tomboy and the fastidious, delicate blonde beauty. But it had worked. On leaving school, Amanda had made her mark as a top model and led a truly glamorous lifestyle. But Maddie, working her way through horticultural college, hadn't been envious, just happy for her—especially when she'd fallen in love and married a fabulously wealthy Greek tycoon.

Then, three months after the wedding, she'd phoned one chilly spring day. 'How do you like the idea of a well-paid working holiday? Cristos has bought this fabulous villa just outside Athens. The house is perfect but the grounds are a neglected mess—especially the courtyard. I fancy something Moorish. Could you take the commission? Cristos said money no object.' A breathy giggle. 'He'd do anything to please me. He's not like your normal Greek male; he treats women as if they have minds of their own!'

Tomorrow Maddie would be returning to England with a fat cheque, a tan, and a bunch of happy memories—and the hope that her mother had fielded at least a couple of responses to her adverts in the local press while she'd been away.

Turning to make one final check on the discreetly hidden irrigation system that kept the planters watered, she noticed the stout wooden door that led from the courtyard to the lemon grove swing open. Thrusting out her lower lip, she huffed away the strands of caramel curls that were tangling with the thick upsweep of her lashes and got an unimpeded view of the hunk—no other description fitted—who had sauntered into the courtyard.

Like her, he was dressed casually. Almost threadbare faded jeans, against her skimpy cotton shorts, and an ancient black vest top that except for size matched her own. One of the locals, she deduced as he strolled towards her, looking for casual work. But, unlike the late adolescents she'd hired to help with the heavy stuff, this guy looked older—thirty-four or -five at a guess.

Out of work, with a wife and a brood of young children? Looking to pick up a few days' pay? What a waste. With looks like his he would never want for work as a male model: tall, dark and gorgeous, his face crafted to guarantee weak knees in the female population. Strong bones, a firm, commanding mouth with just the right hint of sensuality, she listed to herself. Adding, as he came nearer, an intriguing pair of warm golden eyes fringed with sinfully long dark lashes.

Those fascinating eyes held a question as he halted in front of her, and Maddie had to swallow an annoying constriction in her throat as she apologised with genuine sincerity. 'The project's finished. We're no longer hiring. I'm sorry.'

'Is that so?' He didn't look disappointed. He actually smiled. And the effect was electrifying. Fresh perspiration broke out on her short upper lip. A dark eyebrow quirked. 'And you are?'

'Mad.' Qualifying that quickly, in case he thought she really was, she went on, 'Maddie Ryan. Project designer.' Christened Madeleine because her mother, having given birth to three boisterous boys, had longed for a daughter she could dress in pretty clothes and bring up to be ultra-feminine. But Madeleine had refused to answer to anything but Mad—or Maddie, at a pinch—and could clearly remember back to the age of three or four, when her poor mother had tried to dress her in something pink and frilly for her birthday party. She had gone stiff as a board, screaming her head off as she'd refused to wear anything so girly.

She adored her parents, but she idolised her big brothers, and had always set out to prove she could do anything they could do—from climbing the tallest trees and tickling trout to paddling a home-made raft across the lake on the estate where her dad was employed as head groundsman. Eventually her mother had resigned herself to having a tomboy daughter—freckle-faced, permanently grubby, sticking plasters adorning her coltish legs, untameable curls—and loved her more than she'd thought possible.

'So you are English?' The sexy golden eyes wandered over her, and, nodding the affirmative, Maddie felt her flesh quiver as his eyes swept back up to fuse with hers. In all of her twenty-two years no man had ever had this effect on her, and the unaccustomed and scary stinging sensation of intimacy shook her rigid. 'Do you speak my language?' he asked, on a throaty purr that sent something hot sizzling through her veins. Then his eyes dropped to her wide mouth, lips parted as she puzzled over why he should ask that. His attractively accented voice had implied more than mere politeness. 'I am interested to know how you relayed your wishes to your workers.'

'Oh—that!' Maddie relaxed. Friendly question. Friendly she could handle, no problem. She'd had plenty of male friends, both at school and at college. Been best mates with most of the village boys. But never a serious boyfriend. None of her male friends had ever picked her as his special girl. They'd treated her as one of them— come to her with any problems, discussed stuff—but when it came to romance they'd picked the sort of flirty girlies who could simper and giggle for England.

Speedwell-blue eyes smiled. 'No, I don't speak Greek. I picked up a few words from the casuals—' her smile broadened to a wide grin, her neat freckle-banded nose wrinkling '—but I sort of guessed they're not words one would use in polite company! Nikos—the permanent gardener Cristos hired—is pretty fluent in English, and he translated for me.'

Her voice tailed off. Flustered, she noted that he didn't seem to be listening to her side of this strange conversation. Had he simply asked the first thing to come into his too-handsome head just to keep her talking? Because he was back to making that slow, thoroughly unsettling inventory of her too-bountiful body again, his eyes lingering too long for her comfort on the smooth golden thighs directly beneath the ragged hem of her skimpy shorts.

Pressing her knees close together, to guard against a decidedly perverse instinct to shift them apart and tilt her hips towards that gorgeous, power-packed rangy body, she decided to get rid of him. Aiming for repressive, her words emerged in a husky tone she didn't recognise as her own. 'Did you want something? Can I help you?'

Worryingly, he moved just that little bit closer. His broad shoulders lifted infinitesimally, the bronzed skin gleaming like oiled silk, as it made her wonder what that skin would feel like beneath her fingers.

He gave no answer, but the silence sizzled with something unspoken and his slow smile made her tremble, made her wonder what was happening here—because as sure as hens laid eggs no male had ever made her feel this strange before. This—this what? Expectant?

She swallowed thickly just as he said, 'I think that for now you should find shade.' With lazy grace, the lightest of touches, he brushed a strand of damp hair away from her hot forehead. 'You are hot. Very hot!' Golden eyes danced. 'I'll see you around.'

Not if I see you first, was Maddie's wild unspoken thought as she took the hint and scurried away from his unsettling presence, heading for the wide door that led to the cool interior of the villa. Her skin was still tingling where he had so lightly touched it, sending responsive quivers down her spine.

Typical Greek male, she fumed. Most of the casuals had been the same. Unable to stop strutting their stuff when a female was around. She'd been able to overlook them, no trouble at all. She didn't *do* flirting. Didn't know how. Didn't want to know how. Hadn't had any practice.

But the stranger had been different. And how! It had made her feel uncomfortable. An extra large dose of charisma, she decided as she reached the sanctuary of the suite of rooms she'd been given. A knock-out dose that would make him irresistible if he had seduction in mind.

Seduction? She wasn't going to go there. No way! No doubt he acted that way with any female under ninety. So snap out of it, she scolded herself.

Getting out of her work clothes, she headed for the shower and put him quite brutally out of her mind. Or tried to. With little success, she conceded with vast annoyance.

The party was going with the sort of discreet swing that only serious money could contrive. Ultra-glamorous guests wandered out from the lavish buffet to the courtyard, wine glasses elegantly in hand, murmuring congratulations for the romance of the strategically placed uplighters, the plants Maddie had chosen for their perfume, the pale roses and sweetly scented jasmine festooning the pillars of the arcade. And because Amanda and Cristos, bless them, had made sure everyone present knew *she* was the creator of the lush loveliness, Maddie kept her fingers crossed that some of the guests might remember her if they needed any work done in the future.

Amanda joined her on the secluded stone seat Maddie had retired to to get her breath back after answering so many horticultural questions, a glass of chilled white wine in her hot hands.

'It's going perfectly. Everyone's impressed. You never know—you might get one or two commissions.'

'I hope so!' Maddie grinned at her friend. 'I'd love to work here again—I've fallen in love with the country! And I'll never be able to thank you enough for thinking of me.'

'Who else would I think of, dolt?' Amanda's lovely face dimpled with affection. 'And take my advice—if you *are* offered a commission, charge top dollar. These people come from the top layer of Greek society— money coming out of their ears—they *expect* to pay mega-bucks. Offer them cut price and they'll come all over squeamish and run a mile!'

'I'll remember that slice of cynicism!' Maddie took a grateful long sip of wine and pushed her untidy fringe out of her eyes with her free hand, her dancing blue eyes wandering between the groups of beautiful people who were slowly circulating, chatting, the women discreetly pricing and placing each other's jewels and designer dresses.

Dressing for the party, Maddie hadn't even tried to compete. Heck, how could she? Willowy she wasn't, and her wardrobe was as sparse as the hairs on a balding man's head. So she'd got into the only dress she'd brought with her—a simple blue shirtwaister, plain but presentable.

She immediately wished she didn't look so ordinary when she saw him.

An uncontrollable something made her heart leap and her stomach perform a weird loop. The guy she'd tagged as a casual worker—magnetic in a white tuxedo, urbane, elegant—was obviously one of the super-wealthy beings her friend mixed with now she'd married into the highest stratum of Greek society. All his attention was being given to the dark, fashionably skinny beauty clinging to his arm as if she'd been grafted there.

'Oops—latecomer. I'd better do my hostess thing.'

Amanda, noticing the unmissable, rose to her feet, and Maddie, because she couldn't help it, asked, 'Who is he?'

'He's gorgeous, isn't he?' Amanda smoothed the ice-blue silk of her skirt and giggled. 'Dimitri Kouvaris—the shipping magnate and a near neighbour. He walked over this morning to discuss a business deal with Cristos—but he's taken! The clinging vine is Irini—some distant family connection, I believe—and the general consensus is that wedding bells are soon to be tolled! So you have been warned!'

Great! Maddie thought bracingly. And the warning was unnecessary. Seeing him in this exalted milieu provided the metaphorical bucket of cold water she'd needed—because despite all her good intentions she hadn't been able to get him or his final words out of her mind. Or the way he'd looked at her, the sexual interest demonstrated by his body language—and what a body!

She had to put a stop to the unwanted and repeated invasion of the totally stupid thought that he might be the one man capable of making her break her vow of chastity. A vow made to herself because her burgeon-

ing career meant far more to her than any romantic en-
tanglement, and because of her need to prove herself to
her parent, who seemed to think that a woman needed
a man to look after her, to make her whole.

Codswallop!—as she'd inelegantly informed her
mother when she'd aired that outdated view.

But she couldn't help watching the latecomers and
noting the way that the hand that wasn't around the
beautiful Irini's waist lifted in a salute of recognition as
he glanced beyond Amanda to where she was sitting on
her stone bench.

Her face flaming, Maddie refused to respond, and
tried to wriggle further back into the shadows. The last
thing she wanted or needed was for him to saunter over,
clinging vine in tow, and humiliate her by reminding her
how she had mistaken him for a casual worker.

If that had been his intention she was spared, when
a group of guests headed by Cristos joined him. But she
squirmed with embarrassment and uncomfortably
strong frissons of something else entirely when his eyes
kept seeking her out. Narrowed, speculative eyes.

A huge shudder racked its way through her. Enough!
She wasn't going to sit here like a transfixed rabbit
while that man stared at her! Clumsily, she shot to her
feet, and headed briskly back to the villa, where his
eyes couldn't follow her, making for her room and the
calming, sensible task of packing for her departure back
to England in the morning.

It was beginning to grow dark when Maddie parked her
old van at the side of the stone cottage that had been her
home for all her life. It had been a tight squeeze with

four children, but her mother had made it a comfy home. Too comfy, perhaps, she reflected wryly. Only Adam, the eldest, had moved out, when he'd married two years ago. He and Anne had been lucky to get a council house on an estate a mile away, his job as a forestry worker providing for his wife and the next generation of Ryans— a toddler of eighteen months and twins on the way.

Sam and Ben still lived at home. Their joint market garden business—supplying organic produce to local pubs and hotels—didn't make enough profit to allow them to move out. Not that they seemed in any hurry to turn their backs on their Mum's home cooking and laundry service.

Taking the key from the ignition she huffed out a sigh. At nearly twenty-three she should be leaving the nest, giving Mum a break. And she would—as soon as her business took off.

The profits from the Greek job were earmarked for new tools, a possible van upgrade and wider advertising—because the local press had only brought in one enquiry for the make-over of a small back garden in the nearby market town. The clients, recently moved in, wanted the usual. What they called an 'outdoor room', with a play area for a young child, the ubiquitous decking and a tiny lawn. Bog standard stuff which she'd completed in five days, and nothing else on the horizon.

Normally optimistic—a bit too Micawberish her dad sometimes said, but fondly—Maddie felt unusually down as she locked the van and headed for the side door that led directly into the warm heart of the house— the kitchen. Mum would be beavering away, preparing the evening meal for when her ravenously hungry menfolk returned. Friday night, she usually made a huge steak pie. Maddie would prepare the massive amount of vegetables as soon as she'd got out of her muddy work boots and shed her ancient waxed jacket.

Fixing a bright smile on her generous mouth—dear old Mum had better things to do than look at a long face—Maddie pushed open the door and her smile went. Her mouth dropped open and her heart jumped to her throat, leaving her feeling weirdly lightheaded.

He was there. Dimitri Kouvaris. In the outrageously gorgeous, impeccably suited flesh. Sitting at the enormous kitchen table, drinking tea, and being plied with shortbread by her pink-cheeked chattering parent.

He looked up.

And smiled.

It was a perfect spring day. The day after his bombshell arrival on the scene. Her blue eyes narrowed, Maddie watched him saunter ahead along the narrow woodland path.

Dressed this morning in stone-coloured jeans that clipped his narrow male hips and long legs, and a casual honey-toned shirt that clung to the intimidating width of his shoulders, he dominated the surroundings. The sea of bluebells, now in promising bud, didn't even merit a glance. She had eyes only for him. And deplored it.

Last night, at Mum's invitation, he'd stayed for supper, integrating easily with her family. He had explained that he'd met her in Athens through a mutual friend, and that as he was in the area on business he'd decided to look her up.

And she might, if she'd tried hard, have believed it.

But not after the way he'd turned up this morning. All bright-eyed and bushy-tailed, smoothly imparting that as he had a free day and Maddie, as he'd discovered—prised out of someone, more likely!—had no work on, he'd appreciate it if she showed him some of the surrounding countryside. He had tossed in the invitation that they all dine with him that evening at his hotel, erasing Mum's tiny questioning frown at a stroke.

But Maddie was still questioning.

Why should a drop-dead handsome, rotten rich Greek tycoon with a gorgeous fiancée take the trouble to 'look up' an ordinary working girl and her ordinary family? A stranger to male sexual interest, she wasn't so green as to fail to recognise it when it came her way. She'd registered it on that first day back in Athens. She chewed worriedly on her full lower lip. Trouble was, it was mutual, and she was drawn to him when common sense dictated that she should be running a mile.

Turning as the narrow path debouched onto a wide grassy meadow, Dimitri waited for her, his heartbeats quickening. Glossy curls surrounded her flushed heart-shaped face, her sultry lips were parted; her lush body was clothed in faded jeans and a workmanlike shirt. She was as unlike the elegant designer-clad females who threw themselves at him on a tediously regular basis as it was possible to be.

Testosterone pumped through his body. Self-admittedly cynical about the female half of the population, who looked at him and saw nothing but spectacular wealth, this immediate and ravaging physical awareness had never happened to him before. And no way was he

about to knock it. He wanted her and would have her—
would fight to the death to claim her!

'Why are you here? What do you want?' She sounded
breathless. She *was* breathless. Yet the pace he'd set
hadn't been in the least taxing. All part and parcel of the
effect he had on her, she conceded uneasily, and
quivered as he took her hand and raised it to his lips.

The warmth, the firmness of his mouth as it trailed over
the backs of her fingers, took what was left of her breath
away. And when he murmured, 'You want the truth?' it
took an enormous effort of will to look him in the eyes.

'What else?' she said.

Meeting those spectacular, mesmeric golden eyes had
been a big mistake, she registered, as her knees went
weak and simultaneously her breasts peaked and thrust
with greedy urgency against the thin cotton of her shirt.

As if he knew exactly what was happening to her, his
long strong hands went to her waist, easing her against
his body, making her burningly, bone-crunchingly
aware of the hard extent of his arousal.

Feverishly torn between what her mind was telling
her and what her body craved, it took some moments
before she registered his, 'I need to get back to Athens
within the month. And when I go I will take you with
me. As my wife.' When it did, her mind took over with
a vengeance.

Pulling away from him, she squawked, 'Have you
gone crazy? How can you want to marry me? It's
madness. You hardly know me!' Then her eyes narrowed
to scornful slits. 'Is that the way you usually get into a
girl's knickers? Promise to marry her?'

Shaken by his sudden peal of laughter, she could

only splutter as he folded his arms around her and vowed, 'I knew I wanted you in my body and in my soul the first time I saw you. And if that is crazy, then I like being crazy. Tonight, at dinner, I will ask your father's permission to court you. And then I will do everything in my power to persuade you to accept me.'

At her shaky accusation, 'You *are* mad!' he lowered his head and kissed her. And all the niggling questions as to why a guy like him, who could pick and choose between the world's most beautiful women, should earmark *her* as his future bride disappeared for the next earth-shattering couple of hours.

CHAPTER ONE

His face like thunder, Dimitri Kouvaris strode down the first-storey corridor of his sumptuous villa on the outskirts of Athens, hands fisted at his sides, his wide shoulders as rigid as an enraged bull about to charge.

Eleni, the youngest member of his household staff, flattened herself against the wall at his approach, and only expelled her pent-up breath as he shot down the sweeping staircase two treads at a time.

The soles of his handmade shoes ringing against the marble slabs, he crossed the wide hallway and after a cursory rap entered his aunt's quarters.

'Did you know about this?' he demanded on a terse bite, lobbing over the piece of paper crumpled into his fist. And he watched, the gold of his eyes dark with inner fury, as the thin pale fingers of his father's elder spinster sister smoothed the creases out.

The few words burned like acid into his brain.

Our marriage is over. My solicitor will be in touch regarding our divorce.

Three months and she said it was over! No explanation. Nothing but a note left on the pillow of their opulent marriage bed. How dared she?

'She dishonours the Kouvaris name!' he bit out, and the silvery head rose from her prinked-lipped perusal. The sharp black eyes were disdainful as his seventy-year-old aunt dropped the note on the small table at her side and fastidiously wiped her fingers on a silk handkerchief.

'You dishonoured our family name when you made her your bride,' Alexandra Kouvaris pronounced, with a profound lack of compassion. 'A common gold-digger with her eye obviously on a handsome divorce settlement. A high price to pay for an abortive attempt to get an heir, nephew.' She settled back in her chair with a rustle of black silk and reached for the book she'd been reading, dismissing him. 'No, I didn't know she'd gone. I am not in her confidence and I have not pined to be in that position. I suggest you check the contents of your safe to see how much of the jewellery she persuaded you to lavish on her she's taken with her.'

His mouth flat with distaste, Dimitri swung on his heels and left. He couldn't verbally flay his aunt for voicing what everyone would be thinking—although he'd had to bite his tongue to stop himself from doing just that. In the mood he was in he'd lash out at anyone who dared to breathe in his presence, he conceded savagely. In scant seconds he was back in the bedroom he'd shared with his bride, dragging open hanging cupboards and drawers, eventually standing, brows clenched, staring out of one of the tall windows that gave a partial view of the distant Acropolis.

She seemed to have left in just the clothes she was

wearing, her passport and handbag her only luggage. Not one item of designer clothing or jewellery was missing. Was she, as his aunt had stated, going for the much larger prize? Aiming to reach a divorce settlement of half of his vast wealth, making him a laughing stock?

His strong teeth ground together. Over his dead body! Prick a Greek male's pride and the wrath of the gods would descend in dire retribution!

Hadn't he given her everything a woman could possibly want? An enviably beautiful home, unlimited funds, servants to cater to her every whim, great sex. His tight features turned dark with temper as too-vivid memories of the way his pre-marriage largely ignored lunch-breaks had turned into sheer paradise between the sheets with his wife, because the hours before night-time had always seemed impossible to get through without availing himself of the delights of her luscious, responsive body.

Had her generous response been nothing but an act? His lovemaking something to be endured to keep him sweet and unsuspecting until she sneaked away and petitioned for divorce?

No one did that to Dimitri Kouvaris! *No one!*

Turning in driven haste, he used his mobile to instruct his senior PA to cancel all meetings for the next three days. He stuffed a few necessities into an overnight bag with his free hand. Then, ending the call, he keyed in the number of the airport and finally, on receiving the information he needed, contacted the pilot of his private jet.

Tears welled in Joan Ryan's tired eyes as she turned to slide the kettle onto the hotplate of the ancient Aga. That dratted inner shaking had started up again, and over the last twenty-four hours she had drunk enough tea to float a battleship.

Nevertheless, she had to be sympathetic and helpful, put her other problems aside, because no sooner had Joe, her husband—who should by rights be resting, according to doctor's orders, following his heart scare, not getting himself stressed out—together with their three sons walked out of the door than her son-in-law had walked in. And dropped another whopping bombshell.

Maddie had walked out on their marriage.

Maddie wanted a divorce.

It couldn't be happening, she thought on a spurt of uncomprehending agitation. She couldn't for the life of her understand how that marriage had gone so wrong, so quickly. Her daughter had looked radiant with happiness when she'd made her wedding vows in the small parish church just three months ago. She and Joe had been so happy too. Just fancy—their tomboy daughter, who'd never even had a proper boyfriend, marrying such a handsome, wealthy, generous dream of a man. Their adored Maddie stepping ecstatically into an assured future.

And now this!

Dimitri looked strained—as any man would after such a shock, not to mention a headlong dash from Greece and driving up here in a hired car. So a nice cup of tea…

She turned, carried the pot to the big old table, and noted that he had sat himself in Joe's chair, his finely made yet strong hands clenched on the pitted pine tabletop.

'I wish I could help,' Joan mourned, feeling useless. 'For the life of me, I can't understand it. She's never given the smallest hint that anything was wrong in her phone calls. But then, she wouldn't.' She dredged up a sigh. 'That's Maddie for you. She's always had a streak of independence a mile wide.' Hand shaking, she covered the pot with its padded cosy. 'I've heard nothing since her last call a week ago. She hasn't turned up here.'

With an effort, Dimitri forced his hands to relax, flatten against the grainy surface. Joan Ryan was obviously as much at sea as he was.

Forget the acid burn of anger inside him. Clearly the poor woman was worried sick. He liked Maddie's parents—admired their capacity for hard work, their honesty, their love for their family. He couldn't bring himself to tell Joan that her beloved daughter was a sly, scheming gold-digger, marrying him only for what she'd decided she could screw out of him!

He wouldn't have believed it himself until today. Women had been coming on to him since he'd hit his late teens, and he'd learned to suss out gold-diggers from a hundred paces. He would have staked his life on Maddie being genuine, wanting him only for himself, wanting children as much as he did. Had his brain gone soft that first time he'd seen her, wanted her as he'd never wanted any other woman, his heart and soul telling him that here was the one woman in the world he could trust implicitly?

But what other explanation could there be? Colour scorched across his angular cheekbones. Until today their marriage had been fantastic. Not a cross word, just soft words and smiles. Laughter, joy. She'd been just that little bit quieter of late, he'd noted, and once, when he'd gently asked if there was anything wrong, she'd turned that lovely smile on him, reached for him, and assured him that everything was perfect.

An obvious and utterly devious truth—because everything had been going to her greedy plan. He truly didn't want to believe that of her—not of her. But, lacking any other explanation, he had to face it.

Joan pulled out a chair, sat heavily, and poured the tea with a shaking hand. Compassion for her distressed state forced him to say, 'Try not to worry. She'll turn up. She would have taken a scheduled commercial flight, so it would take her much longer to get to Heathrow and then make her way here than it took me. Where else would she go?' He'd checked the departure times of flights to the UK, guessing she would be heading for home. 'Can you think of anywhere else?'

Unable to speak for the lump in her throat, Joan shook her head. The lump assumed monumental proportions as Dimitri supplied reassuringly, 'She'll turn up here. I'm sure of it. But should she phone ahead I must ask you not to tell her I'm here. I need to talk to her, to sort things out.'

Carefully, keeping his tone gentle, schooling out the anger, the outraged pride of the Greek male, he covered her workworn hand with his own—because Joan Ryan was a patently good woman, and none of this was her fault. 'You mustn't worry.'

Kindness was her undoing. She'd genuinely had no intention of burdening him with her family's problems—certainly not while he was so upset over Maddie's desertion. But Joan couldn't stop the torrent of sobs that racked her comfortable frame, and then her handsome, caring son-in-law fetched the box of tissues from the windowsill, slid it in front of her and put a compassionate hand on her shoulder.

'What's wrong, Joan?' he asked. He'd expected her to be puzzled and upset by her daughter's behaviour, but not to the extent of breaking down entirely. 'Tell me. I might be able to help.'

It all came pouring out.

It was late, and as dark as a country night could be. The taxi driver was grumbling under his breath as he negotiated the twisting, narrow, tree-hung lanes. Maddie, leaning forward, had to give him directions.

'It's about a mile ahead,' she told him as he took the left-hand fork she'd just indicated. 'I'll tell you when we get there.' She subsided, stuck with her own thoughts. And they weren't pleasant company.

The journey from Athens had been a complete nightmare. She wasn't going to think about her broken marriage—it hurt too much—so she'd think about the trials of her flight to freedom instead. Her departure from Athens had been delayed by a couple of hours. Eventually reaching Heathrow, she'd queued for ages to get her euros changed to sterling, then headed for Euston and sat over a cup of what was supposed to be coffee while she'd waited for a train to Shrewsbury. She had phoned home to say she'd be arriving—probably at midnight at this rate, after the difficulty of finding a driver willing to take her way out to the sticks.

Mum had sounded a bit odd on the phone. Maddie hadn't told her that her marriage was over—that would have to be done face to face. It would upset her parents; she knew that. They thought she'd made the perfect marriage.

And it could have been so perfect. She'd loved him so very much. Enough to push her doubts as to why he should want to marry so far beneath him out of her mind. Doubts that had trickled slowly but inexorably back on her return to Athens as his bride. Her insides twisted painfully, and she had to stiffen her spine and remind herself that she would not be used. That she would never regret walking out on him, that she would not weep for him.

Did he think she was without pride? Did he think that she was too stupid to discover the truth? That she was too besotted with him, too enthralled by his magnificent body, his lovemaking, the things he could give her, ever to go looking for it?

As the headlights picked out the driveway to the small stone house she rocketed thankfully out of her pointless mental maunderings and stated, with feeling, 'You can drop me here.'

Tears of weak relief blurred her eyes. Home at long last! To the beginning of a new and independent life. Apart from starting divorce proceedings, she need never allow a single thought centring on Dimitri Kouvaris into her head again.

Stumbling with fatigue, she headed up the short track after paying off the driver, and in the total darkness bumbled into the rear of a car parked beside the two beat-up Land Rovers belonging to her father and brothers.

Muttering, Maddie bent to rub her bruised shins. She registered the slam of a car door, and looked up to find the dark, strangely intimidating figure of Dimitri blocking her path.

'Get in the car.'

The terse command sent a shiver prickling down her now rigid spine.

Her mind was a chaotic jumble of shock. What did he think he was doing here? Didn't he understand a simply written statement that their marriage was over? Her throat worked convulsively, and her, 'I'm not going anywhere with you!' emerged on strangled, breathless tones that made her cringe at her seeming indecisiveness. She spoke more firmly, with effort. 'I am going home. Let me pass.' This because he had pinioned her arms in strong, masterful hands, and his touch still had the power to melt her.

'Your family have retired for the night,' he relayed. 'We have discussed the issue and have agreed that it is best that you go with me to my hotel. We need to talk.'

'No!' Maddie bit out in mutiny. 'There's nothing to talk about.'

As she knew from painful experience, he could talk her into believing black was white, and despite her staunch intention to put him out of her life she knew that as yet she was too raw and hurt to keep to that resolve if he decided to use his devilish charm to make her change her mind. For his own despicable ends.

'You can't make me go anywhere with you,' she flung in challenge.

'No?' Still sounding measured—conversational, almost—he parried, 'I have been waiting in that car for over half an hour now, and patience is not my strong point. I have never forced any woman to do anything against her will. But—and this I promise—should you refuse, your family will be homeless by the end of the month. You have the power to stop that happening. It is your choice.'

CHAPTER TWO

WITH deep reluctance Maddie approached the passenger door Dimitri was holding open. Even in the darkness there was no mistaking the grim, forbidding cast of his bold features.

She swallowed convulsively. It was the first time she'd been on the receiving end of his displeasure. The first time he'd shown his true colours. The rest—the smiles, the softness, the warmth and indulgence of the past three months—had been nothing but one huge act, she reminded herself firmly.

Feet dragging to a halt as she reached the open car door, she sucked in a deep breath. She wasn't looking at him now. She could feel his icy rage. It penetrated her layers of clothing, prickled her skin.

'I'm waiting.' Then his voice softened. 'I will take you to your parents first thing in the morning, I give my word. Until then it is best they relax in the belief that we are sorting our own problems out.'

'Why? They're not children in need of fairy tales!'

'I will explain.' His voice hardened with impatience. 'But not here.'

The line of Maddie's mouth grew stubborn. Used

to having his every whim catered to immediately, Dimitri Kouvaris didn't *do* waiting. Well tough. It was time he learned.

Ignoring him with some difficulty, she managed to get her mind back on track. She had two options. She could stick to her guns—walk on up to the cottage, rouse her parents, and ask them what the hell her soon to be ex-husband was talking about. How could he threaten to make them homeless? He was talking rubbish, surely?

Only he didn't make idle threats, she acknowledged with an inner shudder. He had a reputation in business for ruthlessness. What he said, he meant, and pity any person who got in his way or tried to pull the wool over his eyes. She had never seen that side of him before, but it had been there, hadn't it? Cleverly hidden, but there, in a marriage that had had one purpose only. To get an heir. That cold ruthlessness was out in the open now, she recognised, and resignedly plumped for the second option.

Her chin defiantly angled, Maddie slid into the passenger seat, her heart jolting as the door at her side closed with force. If there was the slightest chance that he could carry through with that threat then she owed it to her parents to fall in with his wishes.

For now. Only for now, she promised herself.

The drive to the nearby small market town was accomplished in tight silence. Unlike her journey with the taxi driver, Maddie had no need to give Dimitri directions through the tangle of narrow lanes. The Greek drove and navigated as he did everything else—exceptionally well—and he would have exact recall of the tortuous route between her home and the hotel he'd been using just over three months ago, when he'd embarked on his sneaky campaign to persuade her to marry him.

Unwilling to give headroom to the thought of how absurdly gullible and bird-brained she'd been back then, Maddie clamped her teeth together until her jaw ached, and made herself think of the present.

It was blistering her mind. His totally unexpected presence. His weird threats. If she, loving him with a depth that had shaken her, could take the sensible course, end their marriage and walk away then why couldn't he? It would be so much easier for him, given that he had never loved her in the first place, had seen her only as a walking, fertile womb.

Her smooth brow furrowed as she tried to find an answer. She had genuinely believed that, knowing her decision to end their marriage, he would have shrugged those impressive shoulders and consigned her to history. A swift divorce—made simpler because of her firm intention not to ask for any financial settlement—followed smartly by a marriage to another such as she—a gullible little nobody from an ordinary, fairly simple but prolific family. The sort who wouldn't know how to stand her ground against the mighty Kouvaris empire when she found herself in the divorce courts, her child given into his custody.

Her face flamed with a mixture of outraged pride and humiliation. She should have cottoned on—at least suspected his motives all those months ago. It had been there right under her nose if only her starstruck eyes had been able to see. His questions, which had given him the information that she came from undeniably fecund stock. Their—what had his snooty aunt called it?—their hole-and-corner wedding. And the lack of anything as romantic as a honeymoon. Not that she'd minded that. She had assured him that she understood perfectly when he'd pleaded that pressure of work meant he had to be in Athens, soppily saying that where he was was where she wanted to be. She'd been too blinded by love to read anything into any of it.

Her hands clenched, her fingernails cutting into her palms. Looking back, she just didn't believe herself! How could she have thought, for one insane moment, that a man as knock-'em-dead gorgeous, charismatic, sophisticated, rotten rich and frighteningly clever would want to tie himself for life to an ordinary-looking, low-status nobody like her?

As he brought the car to a halt in front of the small town's only hotel Maddie made herself a set-in-concrete promise. If her devious husband tried to make her change her mind, because he'd decided he didn't want the delay of even a quickie divorce and then the tiresome chore of hunting down another sucker, with the tedious expenditure of all that seemingly effortless charm to get her to marry him, and had decided he'd be better off sticking to the brood mare he'd got—which, thinking about it, was the only motive possible for him being here at all—then she would resist all his attempts to her very last breath!

With scarcely controlled impatience Dimitri fisted the ignition key and exited the car, reaching the passenger side in a handful of power-driven strides.

He wrenched the car door open and ordered, 'Come.' He had to use every last ounce of self-control to stop himself from hauling her to her feet. In the space of twenty-four hours his wife had changed from a voluptuous, adoring wanton to an ice-cold stranger. And he didn't know why—although he had strong and utterly distasteful suspicions. It was driving him insane. And no one, not even his wife, would be allowed to do that!

As if she sensed the stirrings of his volcanic anger, Maddie moved. Slowly swinging her feet to the ground, she exited the car and stood, facing the timber-framed façade of the hotel. The light from above the main entrance illuminated her. She was wearing jeans and a lightweight jacket, a leather bag clutched in one small hand, a mutinous twist to her mouth.

Dimitri cupped an unforgiving hand beneath her elbow and headed to the main door. If he bent his head he could tease the mutiny away, feel those lush lips tremble beneath his own, flower for him. The gateway to paradise. She liked sex, more than met his demands. But no way would he oblige—now, or in the foreseeable future. That would be part of her punishment!

No, the sex hadn't been feigned. Everything else in their marriage had been, though. Starting with her wedding vows, uttered with her eye on the main chance. He was ninety per cent sure of it. Three months of her life in exchange for a settlement that would keep her in luxury for the rest of her days. Logically, it was the only scenario that remotely fitted in with what she had done—and, heaven knew, he'd racked his brain to try and find another, coming up with a big fat zero.

She would not do that to him!

He removed his hand from her arm as if even that connection was poisonous.

Maddie shivered as the heavy main door swung closed behind them and he strode away from her. She hadn't wanted this confrontation; it had been forced on her. No wonder her nerves were going haywire, adrenalin pumping through her veins. He was rigid with anger, she recognised. And she could understand it.

He was a busy man, a driven man. Amanda had told her, in one of her long, chatty phone calls after Maddie had returned to England that first time, that Dimitri Kouvaris had pumped her for information. About her, about her family. Stupidly, the knowledge had excited her, made her feel almost special. How he would hate the waste of his time. Not that it had taken much of that, she recalled with a sickening lurch of her tummy. Five days later, after having gathered the necessary information from her unsuspecting friend, he had charmed her into a state of besotted adoration with very little effort.

No, he would view the three months of their marriage as an unforgivable waste of his time and effort. And it *would* have taken an effort on his part to treat a peasant as if she were a princess, she decided with a resurgent cynicism. As for the other—the sex—trying to get her pregnant at every opportunity with no result, while thinking of the time when he could get rid of the wife he didn't love and marry the woman he *did* love, must have infuriated him.

He'd hidden it well. She had to give him that.

But now it was showing.

Thing was, was she brave enough to handle it? Discover what he meant by those threats? And the answer was, she *had* to be.

At this late hour the hotel foyer was deserted, the

lights low, adding another layer of atmosphere to the heavy exposed beams and oak panelling of what had once been a coaching inn. The night porter had emerged from his cubby-hole behind Reception and was handing Dimitri a key. A few inaudible words were exchanged, and then he swung round on his heels and faced her, his stance disdainful, coated in ice.

Sucking in her breath, she obeyed his curtly expressive hand gesture and made herself move towards him, her head high. True, she wasn't here of her own free will—but she'd be damned if she was going to let herself down and act like a victim.

'We can talk in the lounge.' Her voice as firm as she could make it, Maddie gestured towards a partly open door. The steel grille was lowered over the bar, but there were comfy lounge chairs grouped around the tables, and the light from the foyer gave sufficient illumination.

Totally ignoring that sensible suggestion, just as if she'd never spoken, Dimitri started up the uncarpeted broad oak staircase, and Maddie, biting back a howl of fury, followed.

Arrogant low-life!

Still seething, Maddie caught up with him as he opened a door and reached in to switch on a light.

'In.'

Her stomach clenched painfully. This icily intimidating side of him was alien to her. But she was going to have to get used to it—at least for as long as it took him to spell out what had to be, surely, his groundless threats.

Slightly comforted by that slice of common sense, Maddie stepped into a room that looked as if it hadn't had a makeover since the sixteenth century. And all the better for it, she approved, making an inventory of the jewel-coloured rugs laid over wide, highly polished oak boards, the ornately carved four poster bed and linen press, the tapestry-like curtains. It took her weary mind off being here with the husband she had loved to distraction and now hated with a vehemence that made her bones tremble.

An overnight bag stood at the foot of the bed. So he must have checked in here before driving out to her parents' home. To wait. Somehow he had known that she must contact her folks on her arrival back in the UK, stay with them or in the vicinity until the divorce came through, she deduced tiredly—though the reason for his precipitate actions escaped her. And how had he arrived ahead of her?

She would have already been waiting for her delayed flight when he'd returned at lunchtime, making for the bedroom as usual and more of the sex he was so good at—the hoped for end result his son and heir—and finding her note instead.

And yet he had been ahead of her, waiting for her. His private jet—of course! Why hadn't she remembered that? Because she'd never rated the outward signs of his financial clout, only the man himself. The super-wealthy had the means for getting things done that humble peasants could only dream of, she decided with resignation, as a firm hand in the small of her back propelled her towards two wing chairs at opposite ends of a low, dark oak table.

She sat, was grateful to. She couldn't remember ever feeling this weary and drained in her life before. Dimitri was hovering over her, his hands in the trouser pockets of his superbly tailored pale grey suit, the fabric pulled taut against his pelvis.

Smothering a groan as a hatefully familiar, ultra-responsive frisson lurched through her entire body at his sexy magnetism, Maddie closed her eyes to shut him out. She didn't need that kind of betrayal from her own body—not now, not ever again. All she needed right now was the healing oblivion of sleep.

And if he was waiting for her to ask him to explain himself, to instigate some kind of conversation, then he could wait. This—whatever it was—was his idea, most certainly not hers.

She heard the discreet knock at the door, sensed him move and opened her eyes reluctantly in time to see the night porter place a tray on the table. Something changed hands—a tip, presumably—and Dimitri sat in the chair opposite, surveying her with golden eyes lacking in expression over a lavish platter of sandwiches, a wine bottle and glasses.

Her lungs aching with the effort to hold back a hysterical peal of laughter, Maddie gripped the arms of her chair to keep herself grounded. An outraged husband about to read the Riot Act and explain vile threats to his runaway wife and the first thing he thinks about is his stomach! The situation was farcical!

But there was nothing off-the-wall about his containment as he poured wine into two glasses and slid two sandwiches onto a delicate china plate and put it in front of her. There was even a hint of a smile on that devastatingly handsome mouth as he imparted, 'If, like me, you haven't eaten since breakfast, you'll need this.'

'Not hungry.' Maddie eyed the food with disdain,

her stomach rolling sickly as she experienced total recall of precisely *why* she hadn't been able to face breakfast, or the thought of food since then.

As usual, he had risen first, full of vitality, leaving her to come awake more slowly, stretching luxuriously in the rumpled bed, sated with the passion of the night before. She had pushed away the uncomfortable thought that their time in bed together was the only time she was truly happy. The rest of the time everything conspired to make her feel purposeless, a thing of little use, an unsavoury intruder into a rarefied atmosphere.

She had followed him down, a silk robe covering the naked voluptuous body he always seemed so wild for— gratifyingly belying the snide rumours and wicked lies she'd been fed just lately—expecting to share a pot of coffee with him before he left for his high-tech head office in the city, as she always did. She'd needed her Dimitri fix to carry her through the morning before they enjoyed a long and intimate lunch-break together.

Slipping silently into the sunny room where the first meal of the day was taken, her eyes had gone soppy at the sight of that tall, commanding figure, dressed that morning in pale grey trousers that hugged his narrow hips and skimmed the elegant length of his strongly muscled legs, his white shirt spanning wide shoulders, his suit jacket draped over the back of one of the dining chairs.

His broad back to her, he had been speaking into his cellphone. He hadn't seen her—as the contents of a conversation that was to turn her life upside down soon evidenced.

'Be calm, Irini,' he had soothed. 'We discussed this. It will take time. Please be patient.' A short silence from

him, then, decisively, 'I will be with you in less than five
minutes, and of course I love you. You are—' Another
silence while he had listened to what was being said,
then, his voice full of soft emotion, 'Be calm, sweetheart. Five minutes.'

Heart pounding, blue eyes stunned, she'd watched
him snatch up his suit jacket and stride out through the
open French windows, heading for the woman he *did*
love, leaving the woman who was just a commodity
clutching the doorframe for support, the lies turned into
truth, the rumours into hard, hateful, hurtful fact. The
last straw.

At least he hadn't lied. He had never said he loved
her, had he?

Now, Dimitri helped himself from the platter, golden
eyes assessing beneath the thick dark sweep of his
lashes. She was pale, her skin ashen beneath the light
golden tan, the band of freckles across her nose standing
out starkly. He had always found those freckles endear-
ing—those and the caramel curls now delightfully
tamed by the best hairdresser in Athens. The fierce, rapacious need for her wildly sensuous body, his need to
soften the raging heat of lust into something infinitely
more tender, more fulfilling, made him furious with his
body for responding to his thoughts. Blisteringly angry
with her for what she had seemingly proved herself to
be, he said, with more force than necessary, 'Eat before
you pass out.'

Never one to respond positively to anything
smacking of bossiness or bullying, Maddie flattened
her mouth stubbornly. She crossed her arms over the
breasts he had once said he worshipped, and clipped out

at him, 'I didn't come here to eat with you. I came because you made threats against my parents and I demand to know how you think *you* can threaten them.'

'So, she finally speaks.' Dimitri was lounging back now, holding a wine glass in one beautifully crafted hand. His voice was smooth as silk he told her, 'No one makes demands of me—not even my wife. Understand that and you'll be a wiser woman.'

With an effort he kept his cool. She had never asked for anything—had made *no* demands. Hadn't needed to. He'd given her everything, and gladly. High status, an assured position in Greek society, wealth beyond avarice, jewels—and she'd thrown the lot back in his face.

His heart thumped with the outraged anger of savaged pride. Because she wanted even more. The sort of divorce settlement that would keep her in luxury for the rest of her life without the burden of having a husband. Until she came up with another plausible reason for leaving him, it was the only motive that made any sense.

He was taunting her, Maddie deduced with mounting horror, her skin crawling with the onset of panic. No doubt he would tell her what he'd meant by that threat in his own good time.

But she didn't *have* time, she thought wildly. Draining tiredness, the beginnings of a thumping headache and the awful emotional trauma of the day meant that any minute now she would break down, scream and throw things, or dissolve in floods of helpless tears, betraying how desperately unhappy his betrayal and cynical manipulation of her had made her. She wouldn't be able to prevent it happening if she had to suffer this unwanted confrontation, this not knowing, for much longer.

Dimitri set his glass down with an irate click. The gold of his eyes frosted. Time she learned she couldn't make him look a fool, shame and dishonour him. Time she knew who called the shots.

'You are my wife. There will be no divorce. You will return with me to Greece. If the marriage ends at some time in the future, as seems likely, then *I* will be the one to end it. I demand that much. I will not be made to look a fool in front of my friends and colleagues.'

Because she hadn't given him an heir, Maddie translated, chilled to the bone by his harshly decisive delivery. Hanging on to her rapidly fleeing composure, she managed, 'You can't stop me suing for divorce. Or make me go anywhere I don't want to be.'

Fully expecting a blistering statement of the opposite—because the rich and the powerful had ways of getting everything they wanted—she was speechless when he gave a slight shrug of his magnificent shoulders and uttered blandly, 'True.'

With one hand he loosened his tie and settled back in his seat, graceful in his relaxation. He was more gorgeous than any man had a right to be, she decided in utter misery—then gave herself a sharp mental kick. The days of her overwhelming love for him were over. He was no longer the light of her life, and she no longer felt herself melting inside when she looked at him.

'But?' she all but snapped at him. It wasn't in the nature of the beast to simply cave in. There had to be a 'but'.

There was.

'*But,* if you follow that road be sure that your parents will be homeless by the end of the month. It's in my power to prevent that happening. I will do so—but only if you agree to everything I ask of you. And if you think that you can divorce me, claim a large settlement and help your parents financially, live the high-life, forget it. Any lawyer I employ will make sure you receive absolutely *nothing*.'

CHAPTER THREE

APPALLED by that implied insult, Maddie could only stare at him, feeling her face redden. It showed how little he thought of her! Was proof—if she had needed any after what she'd been told—that outside the bedroom he viewed her with contempt, a necessary evil.

She fisted her hands in her lap—a labourer's hands: short nails, slightly callused palms, as his aunt had commented with acid—and took a long breath. She wasn't interested in his insults. He couldn't hurt her more than he already had done, and she certainly wouldn't lower herself by telling him she'd had no intention of asking him for anything except her freedom because he wouldn't believe her. Why waste her breath when there were more important questions to ask?

The eyes she at last dragged from the cynical gold of his fell on her untouched wine glass. With the distinct feeling that there was worse to come, she reached forward, swept it up and swallowed a long draught. The rush of alcohol into her bloodstream helped her to challenge him, 'I don't believe you. Prove it. Why should my parents lose their home? Why don't we go back right now and ask them?'

'At this hour?' Dimitri drawled, as if hearing words from a total idiot, and leaned forward to remove the half-empty wine glass from fingers that threatened to shatter the delicate stem. He set the glass down on the table and edged the plate of untouched sandwiches further in her direction. 'They are sleeping, happy in the knowledge that we will have kissed and made up after our lovers' tiff and, almost as importantly, that I will help them out of their present difficulties. They have a load off their mind—isn't that how you English would put it?'

Torn between outrage that he should have made light of her precipitate flight back to England and the need to know what the so-called difficulties were, she chose the latter as being far more pertinent.

'What difficulties?' she got out, regretting the urgent note in her voice, but wanting to get it out into the open and get out of here. Away from the man she could no longer stand being near to. 'Tell me!' she pressed, with fuming vehemence, because he seemed to be intent on keeping his mouth shut and his ace up his sleeve, and was looking at her as if she were an object of mild scientific interest.

Dimitri blinked once, then twice. What was that old-hat come-on? *You look magnificent when you're angry!* In this case it was spot-on! However…

Seething with sheer frustration, Maddie watched him tilt his arrogant head, veil his brilliant golden eyes and steeple his fingers as he recited, in a tone so matter-of-fact it made her blood steam in her veins, 'Your father has reached retirement age. The company he works for has terminated his employment, and with it his tenure of the cottage. The accommodation is required by the groundsman who is to take his place, apparently.'

'They told you this?' Maddie asked thinly.

She felt sick. It could be so true. Six years ago old Sir Joseph had sold the Hall and its estate to a business consortium who had turned it into an upmarket conference centre, complete with a golf course, indoor swimming pool and sauna, clay pigeon range and access to excellent trout fishing. Her dad hadn't liked the new regime. Had missed Sir Joseph and the relaxed chats they'd enjoyed over a whisky and a pipe apiece as they discussed estate matters in the cluttered estate office. On one of the last of those occasions the elderly man had confessed that it was time he moved on. He didn't want to, that went without saying. But he couldn't keep up with overheads, he wasn't getting any younger, and he had no family to take over. Miserable situation, but there it was.

But a job was a job, as Dad had said, and the cottage was their family home—and hadn't Sir Joseph promised that it would be theirs for as long as they wanted it?

However, that wouldn't sway the hard-nosed businessmen who ran the estate now. Concessions for loyalty, long service, personal liking and respect wouldn't come into it. None of them would have heard the words 'old retainer', and if they had they would have dismissed them as being laughably archaic. Suddenly the threat of seeing her parents homeless didn't seem empty at all.

'Initially your mother told me,' Dimitri verified. 'When I arrived at your home she was obviously upset. I assumed it was because you'd been in touch and told her you were ending our marriage.' He levelled an incisive look at her, the planes of his darkly handsome face hard and unforgiving. 'But that was not so. When I dealt her that second blow of bad news she broke down and wept.'

Maddie's heart twisted. Anguish leapt to her throat and choked her. Both her parents thought Dimitri Kouvaris was the cat's whiskers. Charming, considerate, super-wealthy, a miracle of perfection—the type of husband they could only have dreamed of for their lovable but unsophisticated tomboy of a daughter. Of course Joan Ryan would have been devastated by his news. But if she'd been able to get her side of the story in first her mother's dismay at the marriage breakdown wouldn't have been so absolute. She would have been disappointed that the dream husband had shown himself to be a cynical, manipulating, cruel brute, but she would have been on her side all the way.

'So you arrived, unasked and unwanted, and put the boot in!' Maddie derided at volume, hating him for causing her mother even more distress. She half heaved herself out of the chair, her only thought to get back to her parents and tell the dark story of why Dimitri had really married a no-account nobody like her. She would do everything she could to help them move, find somewhere else to live, fight the men in suits. Surely there must be a law against that sort of heartless treatment?

'Sit down.' A warning ran like steel through his voice. 'If any *boot*, as you so oddly put it, was used, then it was your foot wearing it. Remember that.'

Subsiding with ill grace, blue eyes simmering with mutiny, Maddie pointed out, 'OK, so you've told me why my folks will be thrown out of their home. But that doesn't change anything. *You* can't do anything about it—'

'True,' he cut across her, smooth as silk. 'I cannot stop them losing the cottage. When the consortium took over your father was required to sign a contract of employment. I saw the document, and I read the small print—which your father failed to do. According to him, he was so pleased to be kept on he signed without reading it. It is watertight. However, if you cast your mind back and think clearly, instead of exploding every two seconds, you will recall that I said I could prevent them being without a home of their own provided you fall in with my wishes.'

She hadn't forgotten—how could she? But, really stupidly, she'd hoped he had. And now she had to sit here and listen—force herself to forget how once she'd loved him and how he'd used that love to blind her to what was in his handsome, cruel head. Difficult to do when faced with all that lean, taut, utterly devastating masculinity, the blisteringly hot memories of how it had once been between them.

She shifted uncomfortably as a responsive quiver arrowed down her spine and lodged heatedly in the most private part of her body. Her face flamed at the uncomfortable knowledge that she still wanted him physically, even as her head and heart hated him.

Mistaking that fiery colour for the precursor of yet another mutinous outburst, Dimitri put in, smooth as polished marble, 'Your parents and brothers have made tentative plans of their own. Not having the wherewithal to buy a property, nor sufficient income as things stand to rent one, Sam and Ben aim to find cheap lodgings. Your parents plan to move into Adam and Anne's spare room while they wait for the council to offer them accommodation—not the most promising situation, I think you'll agree?'

Maddie stayed mute. It was a wretched situation. Her parents had no savings. Any spare cash they'd had had been used to help their children. No matter how her eldest brother and her sister-in-law welcomed them into their small home, things would get tricky. Adam's young family was growing, and space was at a premium and, used to being Queen Bee in her own home, her mother would begin to feel in the way—past her sell-by date. Her parents, bless them, deserved better than that. But she wouldn't give Dimitri the satisfaction of agreeing with him. On anything. Ever again.

Dimitri frowned, slashing dark brows clenching above shimmering golden eyes. Her body language was sheer stubborn mutiny. He would change that. His wife would once again become compliant. It was she who had drawn up the battle lines, and no Greek male could fail to rise to the challenge, meet it and overcome it. Utterly.

Time to deliver his knock-out blow, he decided, harshly ignoring the sharp stab of regret for what they'd once had. Or what he'd *thought* they had, came the cynical reminder.

'When I arrived, your brothers were out, trying to persuade the farmer they rent their piece of land from to agree to rent out the adjoining field and so allow your brothers to produce more and become more profitable.' His tone showed his aggravation as he demanded, 'Are you listening?'

Maddie shrugged, she didn't care if she infuriated him. He deserved it. She was ahead of him in any case. Sam and Ben had often said they needed more land under cultivation. Their organic produce was always in demand. They could sell it twice over easily. But for that they needed more land, another bigger greenhouse, more hours in the day. With Dad out of work it would make sense to expand and let him in as a partner.

Inwardly seething, Dimitri battened down the imperative to shake her until her pretty white teeth rattled—or, more productively, to kiss her senseless until she was clinging, hanging wide-eyed on his every word.

Better yet, and less hurtful to his pride, would be to render the *coup de grace*. Subdue, once and for all the stubborn streak he had never suspected she had.

So his voice bordered on the purr of a jungle cat with its prey within its grasp as he imparted, 'They returned, their plans in ashes. The said farmer had stated that he was selling up. Even renting the piece of land they are currently working might prove to be a problem with a new owner. They could either buy the lot—farmhouse included—or nothing.' He paused a moment to let that further piece of bad news sink in. Then, 'The idea I put to your parents and brothers was this. That *I* buy the farm and they live there and work the land, expand their business.' He allowed himself a small smile. 'To say that they approved the scheme is an understatement. To counter the general non-stop outpourings of gratitude I explained that as they are now part of my family by marriage it is my duty and pleasure to do all I can to help them. Of course,' he completed, in a tone so honey-sweet it set her teeth on edge, 'the whole thing is contingent on your remaining my wife until I, and only I, decide otherwise. Ensuring that I continue to regard your family as my family, my responsibility.'

Her voice faint, Maddie managed, 'That's blackmail! I don't *want* to be married to you. You know I don't!'

'Take it or leave it. Your choice.'

In emotional turmoil Maddie shot to her feet, her fingertips flying to her temples. She couldn't think straight. Her imagination was working overtime as she pictured her family's relief. Even now her mother would be dreaming of furnishing and decorating the farmhouse, of welcoming her menfolk home from the fields with her famous steak and kidney pie!

Her mouth worked with the onset of hysteria, and the edifice of her earlier determination to cut him out of her life crumbled utterly when he rose with languid grace and came to stand in front of her, his voice cool to the point of uninterest as he asked, 'Your choice?' And then, his voice roughening, as if he was uncomfortable with what he had to tell her, he stated, 'And to help you make that choice I'm afraid I have to tell you that less than a week ago your father was taken into hospital with a suspected heart attack.'

He saw her rock on her feet, saw the little colour she had in her face drain away and could have hit himself. Placing his hands lightly on her shoulders, he apologised gently, 'I'm sorry. I could have come at it in a gentler way. The good news is that it was very minor—a warning, and no damage done. Provided he takes his medication and avoids stressful situations all will be well. Your mother told me she was in the process of writing to you to put you in the picture without alarming you unduly.'

This close, she could feel the enervating potency of his lean, hard masculinity, the power of him. That, plus the news of her father's illness, shattered her into honesty, her voice cracking as she cried, 'What choice? I'm between a rock and a hard place!'

'You put yourself there,' he reminded her flatly. 'It's make-your-mind-up time. Return to Greece with me, as my wife, or deny your family the opportunity to make a new life for themselves.' He thrust his hands into his trouser pockets and drawled, 'Tough, isn't it? Turn your back on your hopes of a massive divorce settlement, or—'

'You can be *so* stupid!' she blistered, stung again by his insulting suggestion that she only wanted rid of him because of what she could get out of him. She could put him straight on that score, but the truth would gain her nothing and lose her the only thing she had left. Her pride. And, what option did she really have, especially now that the sneaky wretch had raised her parents' hopes to stratospheric heights? How could she face them with the news that her soon-to-be-ex-husband had withdrawn his generous offer? And heap a bucketload of stress on her father? She couldn't do that to them. Deliberately closing her mind to what she was letting herself in for, she gritted, 'OK—have it your way! And you can keep your obscene fortune intact! Satisfied?'

Not waiting for his response, and hating him for having the upper hand, she turned on her heels, snatched up her bag, headed for the door and said, as coolly as her frustration would allow, 'Take me home. I've got my own key. I can let myself in without disturbing them.'

'You have the regrettable tendency to behave like someone who has had her brain surgically removed— did you know that?' Dimitri enquired silkily, narrowing the distance she had put between them. 'As we have kissed and made up, as far as your parents are concerned, it would look very odd if we did not spend the night together, don't you think?'

Chagrin made her clamp her teeth together. He was right. Give her family one inkling that her husband was blackmailing her and they would close ranks, refuse to accept the lifeline he was offering. And how would *that* affect Dad's health?

It didn't bear thinking about. Her whole system shuddering with reaction, she suffered the indignity of having him remove her jacket, the nerve-racking way those golden eyes drifted over her upper body, where her T-shirt clung to her generous curves, and would have moved smartly away if her legs had had any strength left, and didn't feel and behave as if they were made of wet cotton wool.

'It's been a long day,' he remarked, as casually as if they were an old married couple, perfectly in tune with each other. 'I suggest we turn in. In the morning we will break the good news of our reconciliation to your family, and I will make that farmer an offer he can't refuse.'

He turned away then, a man completely and aggravatingly in control, removing his tie as he reached for his overnight bag, magnanimously offering, 'Use the bathroom first.'

Scooping up her own bag, Maddie scuttled for the *en suite* bathroom and closed the door firmly behind her, regretting the lack of a lock.

It was small, nothing like the luxury she was used to— a huge marbled and mirrored space, an elegant shower room and a spa bath big enough to swim in, surrounded by potted plants with shiny green leaves and glass shelves holding luxurious toiletries—but it was sanctuary.

Her emotions all over the place, she stood for a while, her breathing shallow and fast as she reflected that she'd been right. He'd decided that he might as well get an heir with the wife he did have rather than waste time finding another! And his macho Greek pride came into it, too. Of course it did. *He* would end the marriage when it suited *him*. Anything else would be unthinkable.

Battening down hysteria, she informed herself that she held the trump card. As long as she didn't get pregnant—and she'd make sure he never laid a hand on her again—his hateful plans would take a nosedive. Ignoring her past susceptibility where he was concerned, she felt comforted by the control she had in her hands, and opted for a soothing wallow in the bath rather than the quick shower the lateness of the hour dictated.

She stayed in the water until it began to cool. She had hoped it would soothe her, but it couldn't. The knot of pain inside her intensified until she felt she would die of it. She had loved him so, and now that love had turned to acid, burning her insides. As she heard Dimitri tapping on the door, calling her name, another thought hit her like a falling brick wall, and she jerked upright in sick horror. He had mentioned caring for her family only as long as they were his family through marriage.

Refuse to give him an heir and he would cut his losses and end their marriage.

Give him an heir and still he would divorce her, take her child from her, no doubt using top lawyers and low-down lies to prove to a court that she was an unfit mother.

What price his so-called duty of care then? Her parents and brothers would be out of his property at the speed of light.

She was in a no-win situation. She caught her lower lip between her teeth to stop herself screaming and the door crashed open, to reveal six foot plus of Greek male magnificence, clad only in boxer shorts, and glowering like thunder.

Two paces brought him looming over her as he got out through clenched jaws, 'Why didn't you answer? I thought you might have passed out, hurt yourself! Instead—' Throwing her a look of utter disdain now, he plucked a towel from the heated rail and tossed it to her. 'Cover yourself,' he said, reminding her, to her shame and confusion, that she was stark naked, rivulets of water coursing down her too generous figure. 'If I want what still appears to be on offer, I will take it. But don't hold your breath.'

Humiliated beyond bearing, fingers fumbling, Maddie wrapped herself clumsily in the towel, clambering out of the bath patronisingly aided by one large strong hand around her upper arm.

She shook his supportive hand away as soon as her feet hit the bath mat. He thought she'd planned this. Remembering how in the past she had always responded to her adored and beautiful husband's sexual overtures with greedy, hedonistic delight he *would* think that!

Would think she had decided she might as well enjoy that side of marriage if it would help her towards a large chunk of alimony.

A gold-digger and a harlot!

Smothering a yelp of distress, she darted into the bedroom and stared at the room that had become her prison with wild blue eyes. Impossible to swallow her pride and tell him why she had really left him. Show him the open wounds of the love he had savagely killed, reveal herself to be a victim, still bleeding from his cruel betrayal. Everything in her rebelled against it.

Let him think she wanted a large part of his fortune if he wanted to. But let him think she still wanted him sexually? No way!

In next to no time she had whipped the patchwork quilt off the bed, leaving him with the duvet, snatched one of the pillows and curled herself into a ball on the floor, a bundle of misery as she contemplated a future that looked bleak from every angle. She was fighting tears as she heard him give a low, derisive laugh when he exited the bathroom and encountered her sleeping arrangements, heard the dip of the mattress as he availed himself of the comfortable bed.

And, on a surge of rage, she wanted to go and hit him! Silence.

A thick silence that expanded suffocatingly as the floor beneath grew harder and sleep was impossible to find.

Unable to handle the fact that he should be sleeping the sleep of a man who had got his own way, while his subjugated commodity of a wife lay on the floor like a pet dog, she shot at him, 'Tell me why you would go to so much trouble and expense to keep a wife who only wants rid of you! It doesn't make sense!'

To her it did. Perfect sense from his point of view. But she wanted to force the truth out of him. All she got was a drowsy but blood chilling, 'You are my wife. You will stay my wife until I decide otherwise. There is nothing more to be said on the subject.'

CHAPTER FOUR

As THE chauffeur-driven limo eased to a well-bred halt in front of the magnificent Kouvaris mansion Maddie woke with a start, then momentarily stilled in shock when she discovered that her comfortable pillow was Dimitri's wide, accommodating shoulder, his close proximity teasing her senses with the sensual heat of him, the evocative scent of his maleness.

Extricating herself from the curve of his supporting arm with more haste than dignity, Maddie hurled herself upright. The last thing she remembered was their being met off the Kouvaris jet at the private airstrip by Milo and the limo, then collapsing onto the soft leather upholstery, overcome by black waves of fatigue.

He was still too close. She could sense him watching her in the gathering evening dusk. Gloating now his prey was firmly back in the steel web of his making? His pride demanded that he would end the marriage at his convenience, not at hers. He'd made that very plain.

Fumbling for the door release, she all but fell out onto the wide gravel sweep, her stomach full of butterflies on speed.

'You are now in haste to reclaim your position as

mistress of our home, when yesterday you couldn't wait to leave it, and me?' Dimitri queried in dry amusement, taking only seconds to reach her side and cup a proprietorial hand beneath her elbow.

'That's not funny!' she objected unsteadily, knowing she was too exhausted and feeble to shake his hand off with any hope of success, but standing her corner. 'I just want to go to bed and sleep—alone,' she qualified with pointed emphasis. 'It's been a long day.'

A long, hard, horrible day, she thought with misery. Roused from a scant hour of sleep which had felt more like a heavy coma, she had been unsurprised to find Dimitri already up and dressed, speaking in his own language on his mobile, pacing the room with long, unhurried strides, one dark brow had elevated in her direction as she'd unrolled herself with difficulty from the patchwork bedspread, which seemed to have developed as many tentacles as an octopus during the long uncomfortable night.

Reaching the *en suite* bathroom, she'd clung to the washbasin, feeling queasy and light-headed, meeting the hollow look in her reflected eyes with unaccustomed and demeaning resignation. She hated to admit it, but he had won hands down. Was it any wonder she felt nauseous?

She would get her divorce, but only when it suited him. When she'd given him the heir he so desperately needed. Which wasn't going to happen, because no way would she share a bed with him again. So it would depend on how long that message would take to get through his thick, arrogant skull.

When it finally hit him she would be history. And what price her parents' security then?

Remembering her family's combined and over-whelming gratitude when Dimitri had announced that the sale was going ahead, that everything was in the hands of his English lawyer, who would shortly be in touch with theirs, Maddie felt sick.

Somehow she was going to have to warn them that their days on the farm that was now the property of her husband were numbered. She hadn't had the heart to get her parents on one side and give them that slice of bad news, to advise them to start looking for somewhere affordable to rent and promise she would do all she could to help on the financial front because the generous allowance Dimitri had given her was largely untouched.

It would have to wait until her father was much stronger.

While she'd been helping her mother to make lunch, Joan Ryan had asked, 'Is everything all right? Between you and Dimitri? I was horrified when he told me you'd left him. It was just one blow too many.'

Meeting her anxious eyes, Maddie had mentally crossed her fingers. 'Sorry, Mum. It was just a silly misunderstanding. You know how stubborn I can be! I'm going back with him this afternoon. Don't worry about me. Just concentrate on getting Dad to chill out and take things easily.'

And Dimitri's Oscar-worthy act as one half of a newly reunited happy couple after a silly spat had obviously completely allayed her family's anxieties on that score, but it had made her feel sick with loathing him to see the ease with which he wore his cloak of deceit.

'You will behave as I expect my wife to behave. With dignity.' Dimitri's hand now tightened in warning against her arm. 'As usual, we will dine as a family. You have just over half an hour to shower and change. And then, and only then, will you make your polite excuses and retire.'

He couldn't physically force her to sit at that lavishly laid table beneath the glittering chandelier in the vast dining room. Force her to endure the seemingly endless ritual of many courses, the sideways inquisitive looks of the staff who served them, the disdain and disapproval permanently etched on Aunt Alexandra's haughty features. Of course he couldn't, Maddie consoled herself, and tried to believe it as he ushered her through the brightly lit but echoingly empty hall.

Empty until Irini Zinovieff emerged from the arched doorway that led to Aunt Alexandra's rooms. As impossibly svelte and lovely as ever, her tall, slender body was clad in black that glittered, and her scarlet lips parted in a tremulous smile as her eyes locked with Dimitri's and held fast.

What the hell was *she* doing here? Maddie fumed, taking no comfort whatsoever from Dimitri's evident surprise, the sudden drag of air deep into his lungs, the way his body tensed. He hadn't expected her to be here but no way was he going to keep up his former pretence and treat the woman he really loved as a casual visitor. His hand dropped from Maddie's arm as the Greek woman glided towards him, her long white hands outstretched as if in supplication.

Dimitri took her hands and spoke in his own language, the words rapid, questioning. Irini shook her head, mumbled, managing to look contrite and pitiable. Maddie wanted to slap her! And, as if that thought had penetrated their absorption in each other, the other woman appeared to notice her for the first time.

Hard malicious black eyes belied the sweet tone. 'So you decided to come back? Alexandra told me you'd left and wanted a divorce. I came straightaway—' She swallowed, paused and purred on, 'I came to see if I could be of any help. Perhaps she was mistaken?'

Ignoring Dimitri's sudden look of fury, Maddie countered, 'Then I'm afraid you had a wasted journey.'

Her cheeks streaked with angry colour, she headed for the stairs and took them, her head held high. At least it was coming out in the open now. Her all too brief bid to end their marriage had obviously removed the need for him to show her any consideration at all.

Irini only had to call and he'd drop everything to speed to her side, assure her that he loved her.

Irini only had to hold out her hands to him and she was the focus of all his attention. More ammunition— as if she didn't have enough already—to hurl at him when—*if*—she decided to tell him why she really wanted to get right out of his life!

But when she told him she would have to be feeling far less raw and betrayed than she did now, the severe hurt somehow miraculously soothed into indifference. No way would she let her pain show, give his massive ego the satisfaction of knowing how much she had once loved him.

Entering the magnificent master bedroom, the room she had shared with the man she had loved more than life, she felt her soft mouth wobble. Everything in here had once been touched with magic. Now it seemed unbearably tawdry. The soft words, seductive caresses, the loving—all slimy lies. Instinct told her to gather her belongings and seek one of the many other rooms.

Her mouth firmed. No. No way! She wouldn't scuttle away and hide like something unspeakably vulgar, not fit to be seen in polite society. She wouldn't be banished from the sacrosanct master bedroom. *He* would!

Crossing to a gilded table, she lifted the house phone and briskly instructed the English-speaking housekeeper to remove the master's belongings to another room. She replaced the receiver immediately, unwilling to listen to objections or questions, then walked into the sumptuous marble and gleaming glass bathroom to strip and head for the shower while her orders were being carried out.

She had never ordered any of the staff to do anything for her before—hadn't liked to put herself forward to that extent. Hadn't Alexandra more than hinted that her status in the household came slightly below that of the humblest daily cleaning woman? That this first instruction would cause ripples among the staff went without saying. And it would infuriate Dimitri, prick his inbred Greek pride. He would hate to think that he was the subject of backstairs gossip and whispered speculation.

Spiteful? Perhaps. But comforting. Paying him back for canoodling with that woman right under her nose!

It was an edgy sort of comfort that lasted until, towel-wrapped, she returned to the bedroom to find the housekeeper standing just inside the door.

'Anna. Finished?'

'Kyria Kouvaris.' The middle-aged woman's brows met in a slight frown. 'Had you stayed speaking, I would have told you that your husband had already phoned ahead to ask for his things to be moved from this room. It is done already. Of course, if there is something else I can do for you, I am here.'

'Nothing. Thank you.' How she managed to get the words of dismissal out through her tight-as-a-vice jaw Maddie didn't know. Once again he had wrong-footed her, spoiled her tiny revenge—she wanted to throw things! Instead, she dried her hair on the edge of the towel until it stood on end in unruly spikes.

Seething with scalding emotions, she considered her options. Curl up in bed and refuse to budge when Dimitri, black-tempered, tried to command her to join them for dinner? Or behave with dignity and go down to take her place at that table with all flags flying—show them that the lowly little nobody wasn't going to hide in a corner out of shame at her lower-than-a-cleaning-lady status.

As she had seen, Irini was wearing black, the subtly glittering fabric draping her impossibly slender figure. The way she was dressed had pointed to the fact that she wasn't planning going anywhere soon. Her guess was that the woman would be eating dinner with them. So—

Marching to the enormous hanging cupboard, she plucked out the vivid scarlet dress that Dimitri had said should carry an X certificate.

It was one of the mountain of designer clothes he had picked out—confiding after she'd modelled it for him in that exclusive boutique, that he had never seen anything so sexy in the whole of his life. The husky edge to his thickening drawl had made her flush to the soles of her feet, sending her scuttling to model the remainder of the garments he had picked out with her head in

an impossible spin, and totally vindicating her immediate mental denial of the things Irini had said to her the
night before—the night of the intimidating meet-the-
bride party she had been faced with on her first night in
Athens as Dimitri's brand-new wife.

She had been living in a fool's paradise back then, she
acknowledged with savage self-contempt as she slipped
into the dress, the cool fabric lovingly moulding breasts
that felt slightly fuller than before, strangely tingly.

Nerves. Just nerves, she told herself as she moodily
surveyed her reflection, the way the fine silk clung to
her body, hugging her small waist, the narrow-fitting
long skirt emphasising the lush feminine curve of her
hips, the central slit that denied all demureness display-
ing glimpses of her legs almost to the level of her
creamy thighs.

A wave of cowardice almost had her removing the
dress with all haste and finding something much less revealing—until the recollection of how overawed and
humble she'd been made to feel when first arriving here
as Dimitri's bride stiffened her resolve.

She'd been overawed by the splendour of the
mansion, convinced that the whole of her parents' home
would fit into the immense marbled paved hall with
room to spare.

As if sensing her dismay when faced with a platoon
of servants, Dimitri had tightened his arm around her
waist and bent his dark head to hers as he'd whispered,
'Courage! They don't bite!', then introduced a tall,
imposing woman with greying hair, 'Meet Anna, our
housekeeper. Her English is fluent. Be sure to ask her to
deal with any changes in household routine you require.'

She had known she wouldn't dare! But Maddie had smiled as the rest of the staff had been introduced, the names going in one ear and out of the other, wondering how she would cope with having a horde of servants to feather-bed her life when she was used to getting stuck in and doing things for herself.

But with Dimitri at her side she had been sure she could do anything! She was a married woman; the fact that her husband was a mega-wealthy shipping tycoon needn't intimidate her. Even now her head was still spinning at the speed and cloaked-with-charm determination of his courtship, the way he'd dispelled her doubts, confessed or hidden, the effortless ease with which he'd made her admit she was head over heels in love with him. She had told her mother that, like him, she saw no reason to postpone the wedding he was insisting on before he had to return to Greece, was secretly appalled by the thought that she might lose him if she insisted that they wait.

But she hadn't been able to help feeling overwhelmed when Dimitri had ushered her into a huge salon furnished with what just had to be priceless antiques, murmuring, 'My aunt is waiting to greet you. Remember I told you that she moved here, into the family home, and brought me up after my parents died? She lives here still, but in her own rooms. She can be a touch acerbic, it is her nature, but take no notice. She will soon grow to value you, as I do.'

But doubts on that score had lodged in her brain as a small, rigidly upright elderly woman had turned from a deep window embrasure. She had been exquisitely dressed in black, her expression like perma-frost. 'So you are the Kouvaris bride?'

Maddie had smiled and held out her hand. It had been ignored. Was that a look of contempt, or was it her normal expression? she had thought hysterically as the intimidating elderly woman had raised one carefully plucked eyebrow. 'I missed the wedding, of course. But then I was not invited. I would have liked to have met your family. In our circles family is of the greatest importance.'

To have given them the once-over, Maddie had translated, trying to keep a straight face even as she'd wondered what the impeccable Alexandra Kouvaris would have made of the tiny village church, Mum's best blue coat, Dad's shiny-elbowed suit, her big rawboned brothers, and Anne—obviously pregnant—trying to control her little son, who thought that sitting still and keeping quiet was an overrated pastime.

Instinctively, she had moved closer to Dimitri, but he had given his aunt all his attention, his voice suggesting a rapid loss of patience as he'd pointed out, 'I believe I explained that, having found Maddie, I saw no point in waiting. I had to be back in Athens on business. To have delayed the marriage until I was freed up would have been intolerable to me. Now I suggest you ask Anna to bring refreshments and then—' he'd turned to Maddie, his eyes not smiling, still touched with annoyance '—I will show my wife over her new home.' As his aunt vacated the room, her head at a decidedly regal angle, he'd said stiffly, 'Her greeting was less than warm. I apologise.'

Maddie had reached for his hand. 'You did warn me! And don't be too hard on her. She's probably miffed because she's been deprived of a big splashy do and a splendid new outfit!'

She'd made light of it then, but all her attempts to reach some kind of rapport with the elderly woman since had come to nothing. Oh, she'd always been polite when Dimitri was around, but on all other occasions she'd been at pains to point out that she wasn't fit to clean her husband's boots.

Not wanting to create family discord, Maddie hadn't complained to Dimitri, had done her best to ignore the insults, to discount what Irini said as pure spite, trying to adjust to her new lifestyle. But gradually, like the dripping of water on a stone, her self-confidence had been eroded, and that overheard phone call had been the final confirmation of her painful suspicions.

It was almost laughable, but on that morning she had made her mind up to unburden herself, tell Dimitri what Irini had said and wait for him to dispel those initial doubts about why a man such as he should be so determined to make a very ordinary girl his wife. Doubts that had been systematically fanned by his aunt. But that phone call had forced her to face the truth.

Thrusting unwanted memories aside, Maddie took a deep, calming breath. A final spray of perfume—far more than she usually wore, but who cared?—and she swept out of the room on the highest-heeled strappiest shoes she owned, her face set in a rictus of a smile designed to portray that she was nobody's fool, and not about to be used.

A smile that vanished without a trace as she neared the partly open door of the vast dining room and heard Alexandra's acid tones. 'Do we wait for ever, nephew? I can't imagine why you brought her back here. Why not pay her off and be rid of her? It's what she wanted. Best for all of us.'

Not waiting to listen to Irini's soothing response or Dimitri's harsh interjection, Maddie marched in, swept a bland look at the three of them, and took her place at the exquisitely appointed table, slightly comforted to see a stroke of dull colour outline Dimitri's angular cheekbones.

He was directly opposite her, with Irini on his left— Irini, whose lips curved sweetly as she turned her head to listen or to reply to what he had said, whose black eyes shot contempt when they occasionally turned in Maddie's direction.

As far as Maddie could tell, her wretch of a husband had forgotten she was there. He certainly paid her no attention, addressing his remarks to the others, the flush gone, his startlingly handsome features pale now beneath his habitual tan.

On her right, Alexandra imparted, 'I am spending August in Switzerland this year. No one who is anyone stays in Athens; the heat is unbearable.' There was a rare smile in her voice as she asked Irini, 'And you, my dear, shall you go with your parents to Andros again? Or perhaps I could persuade you to accompany me to the mountains?'

It was the first time Maddie had seen the other woman even slightly discomfited. Colour stained her creamy skin and there was a look of panic in her dark eyes as they turned for reassurance to the smooth brute at her side, the brute—who briefly covered one of the Greek beauty's hands with his own and imparted, 'I believe Irini has plans of her own. Isn't that so?' receiving a subdued nod of assent with a smile of satisfaction.

'Ah—a mystery!' Alexandra smiled archly and Maddie, her mouth tightening with humiliation, guessed that the old lady thought those plans included Dimitri. She was probably right.

It was no secret that the childless, unmarried Alexandra doted on Irini, the only daughter of her oldest friend. She regarded her almost as her own, and had hoped for a marriage between her nephew and the daughter of the highly established Zinovieff family. Greek marries Greek; money marries money—as she'd once scathingly told Maddie.

Just another drip of the poison she'd been careful to keep hidden from her nephew. Barbs Maddie hadn't repeated to Dimitri, not wanting to cause ill-feeling, because Alexandra was the only close family he had and in Maddie's book family was vitally important. Instead, she'd held her tongue and hoped that the older woman would come to accept her. But that hadn't happened.

Silence fell as plates were removed and bowls of plump fresh figs and glowing dark red cherries were brought to the table, followed by the usual *café frappe*. Dimitri at last stopped dredging up innocuous subjects of conversation and raised his eyes to his wife for the first time since she'd entered the room. It sent hot blood flowing to that part of his anatomy he was determined to ignore.

Theos! If she'd worn that dress hoping to drive him wild, she'd succeeded! Throughout the interminable meal it had taken all his self-control to keep his eyes off her. Just looking at her had him aching for her hot, wildly responsive body! A pleasure that he had vowed he would deny himself—and her—for eternity! She would remain as his wife in title only until she came clean about her true reasons for seeking a divorce.

He'd even had the foresight to phone ahead and ask for his things to be moved to another room. He couldn't share her bed and hope to keep his hands off her.

Despising himself now for his lack of control, the way his body was betraying him, his eyes were drawn to the pert roundness of her full breasts, lovingly shaped by the fine scarlet fabric. The smooth, scented skin of her cleavage invited the touch of his hands, his mouth. *Theos!* Not even his blackest suspicions could stop the minx bewitching him!

A sickening pain twisted round his heart. His marriage had been the most important thing in his life. He'd been working flat out to put everything in order, making decisions that would allow him to delegate more with confidence, freeing him to spend far more quality time with his wife and, hopefully, his children, should he be so blessed.

Unconsciously his long mouth twisted. With a few strokes of a pen his wife had turned his life to ashes. So when his aunt asked, with a simper that grated on his nerves, 'And your plans, Dimitri, what are they?' his voice sounded thick to his own ears as he heard himself reply.

'My wife and I will spend the month on the island,' he stated, and told himself that, alone with her there, he would have the best opportunity to get the truth from her. Discover why she regarded their marriage as disposable when it had meant all the world to him.

He pushed back his chair and rose to his feet in one driven movement, his voice imperious as he demanded, 'Come, Irini, I will see you to your room.' And he would discuss with her the plans for the morning, in minute detail, making sure there would be no mistake, that she fully understood this time that she would need to be patient—do exactly what he said, if there were to be any hope of a happy outcome.

Escaping to her own room—denying the old lady the heaven-sent opportunity to drip yet more poison—Maddie scrambled out of the hateful dress. She'd worn it as a statement. To hold her own. But she hadn't, had she? She'd been ignored, like the object they all thought she was. Honour enough to sit at the same table and not have to squat beneath it, begging for crumbs! And what island had he been talking about? She didn't want to go anywhere with him!

Wrenching off her shoes, she hurled them at the wall, then collapsed in a heap of abject misery on the floor, her arms hugging her knees. It was so blatant—at least he was no longer hiding his real feelings. But he didn't know she was aware of his true motives. She would tell him she did—in her own time.

For now there was enough emotional upheaval going on in her head without adding to it, let alone the fact that 'I will see you to your room' had to be an euphemism for *Let's go to bed!*

CHAPTER FIVE

SLEEP proved impossible. Tossing and turning, Maddie did what she'd vowed not to—relived every moment of the evening of that fateful party.

Faced with the bombshell that the great and the good of Greek society had been invited to meet her, as none of his friends or family had attended the simple marriage ceremony back in England, she had dressed with care in a simple cream silk shift—part of the trousseau Dimitri had insisted on providing for her on a two-day spending spree in London.

She'd done her best to circulate, but had felt a bit like a fish out of water amongst all those sophisticated, wealthy socialites. She had endured the endless questions, the minute scrutiny of her appearance, until finally she'd crept away, her head aching from the constant chatter, just wanting a few moments of peace and quiet to gather herself, locate the self-confidence that was gradually slipping away. She'd walked out onto one of the terraces, found a dark corner and perched on the stone balustrading.

But her peace and quiet had been short-lived, because Irini had appeared, looking fabulous in something ultra-sophisticated and gold, her neck and hands dripping with jewels.

Instinctively her own hand had gone up to touch the sapphire pendant Dimitri had given her on their wedding day, saying it reminded him of her eyes—only reminded him, because no jewel could ever compete with the loveliness of her eyes. A pretty compliment that had warmed her heart then and comforted her now. His name and Irini's had been coupled together, she knew that. But he had chosen *her* she reminded herself, on a burst of self-assurance.

Advancing, Irini had said smoothly, 'I believe you English have a saying. You can't make a silk purse out of a sow's ear. Very apt. You'd better make the most of your days of luxurious living. They'll last only as long as it takes you to produce the Kouvaris heir. And with those big hips of yours it shouldn't take you too long!'

She tilted her head on one side, her slight smile chillingly unkind, ignoring Maddie's gasp of outrage. 'You don't believe me? Then let me tell you a story.' Her voice clipped on, dripping with venom. 'Once upon a time a wonderfully handsome Greek tycoon fell deeply in love with a beautiful Greek heiress. They longed to marry, but sadly the heiress had suffered an accident in early life that left her unable to give him a child. And a child was necessary. The handsome tycoon had no sibling to provide an heir. If he died childless then the vast family empire would pass into the careless hands of a distant cousin, a complete wastrel, or one of his fat, lazy sons. Such a sad dilemma!'

'What's this got to do with me?' Maddie hated the way moonlight touched Irini's face, making her look cold and vicious, hated the way her own mind was taking her, how easily this woman could knock her back.

'Work it out for yourself.' Irini moved closer, her voice lower. 'No? Brain not agile enough? Then let me help you. In their desperation to marry, the lovers found a solution. Not ethical—' she shrugged '—but then don't they say all's fair in love and war? He would look for a fertile woman—foreign, of course, not knowing our language or our customs. She would come from a humble background—from the sort of people who wouldn't have the wit or the financial strength to make trouble. Marry her, produce a child and then divorce her. Keep his heir and marry the woman he loved. Simple? And no need to feel pity for the duped first wife. After all, if she couldn't see beyond the end of her own nose, ask herself why a man such as he would want to marry a common, penniless nobody like her, act on it, then end the marriage and return to her peasant family in England, then she deserves all she gets.'

'You're mad!' Maddie got out through lips that felt stiff and cold, shuddering as a goose walked over her grave. Did the ghastly woman really expect her to believe she was talking about herself and Dimitri? Dressing it up as some kind of sick fairy story? She wouldn't let herself believe it.

Seeming to consider the accusation of insanity, Irini tipped her head to one side, then, pulling herself proudly to her slender height, gave her opinion. 'Not mad. Simply unable to give him a child. If he were a bank clerk and I a shop assistant that would not matter. But in the circumstances—I advise you to think about it and consider your position.' She smiled with a sweetness that sent shivers down Maddie's spine and glided away, heading out of the shadows towards the light spilling from the windows of the mansion.

Maddie shot to her feet. She wouldn't believe a word of that rubbish! She would get back to the party. Right now! Grab Dimitri, find Irini, and force the other woman to repeat that story in front of him! And the more people who witnessed her shame and humiliation the better!

She hadn't got further than a handful of snappy paces towards her objective when Amanda appeared, silhouetted against the light from one of the open tall French windows that marched along the length of the terrace.

'So there you are, Mads! I've been looking all over for you.' She pattered forward. 'I haven't had a chance to talk to you. And Cristos is whisking me off on an extended world cruise tomorrow—six months away—so we won't be able to have a good old girlie chat for ages!'

A big hug, then Amanda held her at arm's length. 'What's wrong, pet? Who's rattled your cage?'

Relaxing just slightly from her bristling determination to make Irini repeat what she'd said to Dimitri, Maddie told her. She and Amanda had shared their feelings, hopes and fears since schooldays. When she came to a tight-lipped halt Amanda gave a low whistle of disbelief.

'That woman's a spiteful cow! I never heard such a load of garbage in my life!' she vowed with vehement assurance. 'She's obviously jealous as hell. She's always been potty about Dimitri, and everyone thought they'd marry eventually—until he showed good sense and fell in love with you. You know, I sort of guessed. When you went back to England he couldn't stop asking questions. About you. Your family, where you lived, all that sort of stuff. Cristos thought he was smitten, too!'

Had he asked how many siblings she had? Checking up on the family's fertility record? Guiltily, Maddie thrust that disloyal thought away, but she did confess, 'He's never said it.'

'Said what?' Amanda pleated her brow.

'Told me he loved me.' It had troubled her just a little, but she'd told herself not to be silly. He'd wanted to marry her, hadn't he?

'So?' The other woman shrugged her pretty shoulders. 'Listen, Dimitri lost both his parents in a dreadful sailing accident when he was just three years old. His aunt Alexandra moved in here and brought him up. She's the achetypal cold fish. He was never shown any loving tenderness, according to Cristos, so it stands to reason that he finds it difficult to verbalise his feelings. But he married you, didn't he? Take my advice, pet. Don't go in there and stage a confrontation. He'd hate that kind of scene. And I wouldn't mention any of it, if I were you. You've been married such a short time and you're only just getting to really know each other. He'll assume you didn't trust him—no matter how often you say you didn't believe a word of it! Trust in marriage is vital, especially when you're dealing with a macho Greek male—believe me, I know!' A final hug. 'Tell him, if you still want to, a couple of years down the line, and he can cross her off his Christmas card list! Now, come on, let's go and party—you've been missing for too long.'

'So where exactly are you taking me?'

Lost in unhappy thoughts, it was the first time

Maddie had spoken since boarding the company helicopter twenty minutes ago, sitting stubbornly tight-lipped, refusing even to look at him.

She loathed him for what he had done to her—was doing. Hated him with a passion that shocked her; she who had never hated another living soul in the whole of her life!

A week had passed since her return to Athens, and Dimitri had been away until late last evening. Leaving her to kick her heels and do her best to avoid Aunt Alexandra, who had made it perfectly clear she didn't want her there.

On that first morning the housekeeper had informed her that he and Irini had left at dawn, and that while he was absent Kyria Kouvaris was to think of her parents.

A message Anna plainly hadn't understood but Maddie most definitely had. Do another runner and her parents could kiss goodbye to any hope of moving onto the neighbouring farm at the end of the month.

The warning that their new home, the business they hoped to expand, would be taken from them some time in the not too distant future would have to be given, of course. But not yet. Not until her father was stronger and could deal with the stress. Almost daily phone calls to her mother had confirmed that he was still taking things easily but got easily tired. He was looking forward to moving into the farm—a move her brothers would oversee, down to the last teacup.

She shifted restively in her seat now and Dimitri said, 'We're going to spend a few weeks on my private island.'

The eventual response was tight-lipped, and Maddie didn't comment. She was as unsurprised that a Greek tycoon should own his own island as she'd been to learn that he'd taken off with Irini Zinovieff.

What had they been doing during that week—apart from the obvious? she questioned wretchedly, increasingly wired up inside. Discussing how best to deal with a recalcitrant wife—a wife who should be providing him with an heir but plainly had no intention of doing so?

And had they come up with some plan of action? Bitten the bullet and decided that he must expend his considerable charm and sexual magnetism to get her into bed again and conceive the child that was so necessary to their plans? Was that why he had returned from his idyll with Irini looking so grim and drained?

Well, he could try. And get no place fast, she vowed, bitterly ashamed of the way her heart turned over inside her breast at the very thought of sharing a bed again with her sinfully wilful, drop-dead sexy husband.

A shame that lasted until the pilot put them down on a smooth area of flower-dotted grass a hundred yards from a stone-built villa, when deep apprehension took over, abating just a little as two figures emerged from the side of the building, male and female, stocky, dark, and beaming all over their seamed nut-brown faces.

Coming down to land, she'd seen no sign of a village or a harbour, just a seemingly impenetrable rocky coastline, steep-sided fields, wooded hillsides, and occasional flashes of silver where streams tumbled through ravines down to the silky azure sea.

Fear of being alone with him gripped her, doubly intense because she knew how easily he could, if he wanted to, cleave through her defences as if they were weaker than ill-set jelly, and drive her wild with sexual excitement, with wanting him, needing him, only him.

But the appearance of the approaching couple made

her let out a shaky breath of relief. A least she and Dimitri wouldn't be completely alone here.

Relief, when it concerned Dimitri Kouvaris, had a habit of being short-lived. A lesson rammed home when he imparted coolly, 'Yiannis and Xanthe caretake for me. In return they have their own home and a small farm on the opposite side of the island. I warn you, they don't speak a single word of English. So if you're planning on begging a boat ride with them back to the mainland it's not going to happen.' He proceeded to greet the couple warmly in his own language. His smile was the one she remembered from the days of her happiness, producing a deep ache in her heart for what might have been, had he loved her and not simply used her for his own devious ends.

Yiannis and his stout wife Xanthe obviously thought the sun rose and set with Dimitri Kouvaris, Maddie thought sourly. But she couldn't blame them. Hadn't *she* been completely bowled over by his effortless charm? So who was she to harbour scorn?

Introductions were made, and Maddie submitted to having both her hands clasped with enthusiasm and returning smiles until her face ached, not understanding a word of what was being said to her.

She was sorry to see the friendly couple go, gathering the luggage the pilot had unloaded and carrying it to the villa, where the main door stood open in welcome. She followed them slowly, leaving Dimitri to exchange a few words with the company pilot.

The heat was intense. Her denim jeans and T-shirt were sticking to her body, and her hair felt heavy and damp on her forehead and the nape of her neck. Inside her breast her heart was heavy. She had no firm idea why Dimitri had brought her to this isolated place, just uneasy suspicions, and she knew she wouldn't like it, whatever it was.

'We could both use a shower.' He had caught up with her, shortened his pace to match hers. Pandering to her northern wilting in the face of the fierce Mediterranean heat? Unaffected, he looked as fresh as a daisy, crisp and cool in stone-coloured chinos and a similarly coloured cotton open-necked shirt.

So she was hot, sweaty, bulgy in the hip and bosom department, and couldn't hold a candle to the cool, elegant sophistication of his lover, who had probably never even gently perspired in the whole of her pampered life. But there was no need to rub it in! Too hot and bothered, too incensed by her own interpretation of his remarks she didn't respond, simply questioned sharply, 'So why are we here?'

For a moment there was silence but for the sound of their footfalls on the paved area beyond the flower-jewelled grass. Then, 'It is generally believed that we are enjoying the honeymoon you were denied three months ago.' If he sounded sour, he couldn't help it. He'd been working all hours towards getting a new business regime on track, towards freeing him up to surprise her with a three-month honeymoon—anywhere in the world she fancied, her choice. This—this confrontation over her wish to end their marriage—was the last thing he'd wanted.

The scornful objection she would have lobbed at him died in her throat as she lanced a glare at him. There was a gritty edginess to his unforgettable features, tension in the line of his mouth betraying inner turmoil.

Did he dislike the situation as much as she did? Was his plan to get her pregnant, provide him with the heir he needed, beginning to sicken him, too? To his dynastic way of thinking an heir was all-important. During their short and head-spinning courtship he had often spoken of his desire to have a family—a desire she had matched back then with a retrospectively cringe-making enthusiasm.

Was there yet another side to this need of his? A long entrenched, driving need for a family of his own because from an early age he hadn't had one? Losing both his parents at such an early age and being brought up by his aunt Alexandra wouldn't have been a bed of roses. As far as Maddie could tell, and backed up by what Cristos had said to Amanda, the old lady didn't have an affectionate or compassionate bone in her body.

The odd shift in her mood kept her silent while he escorted her through the house. The cool tiled rooms with vaulted high ceilings contrasted with the heat outside, and the wide white marble staircase with its delicate cast-iron banisters soared up to airy corridors and the room the honeymooning couple would share.

The suitcases had been unpacked, and Xanthe was putting the last of the garments in a vast hanging cupboard, full of smiles, bobs and many words as she made her exit. Not giving the room even a cursory glance, Maddie waited until the door had closed behind the caretaker, then said, 'I know we need to talk—about the divorce.' Her face reddened beneath the chilling impassivity of his gaze but she struggled on, disadvantaged by his seeming indifference to what she was trying to say. It made her feel like a low-grade employee asking for a rise in wages she had done nothing to earn. 'But we could have done it in Athens without putting on this farce.'

'So we could. If there were any question of an immediate divorce.'

He was closing that door. Again. The word *immediate* induced panic. She would get her divorce when it suited him. When she had given him an heir. And if he pulled out all the stops to make it happen, then manufactured evidence to prove she was an unfit mother, a feckless wife, she would lose her child, her sense of self-worth, and in all probability her parents and two of her brothers would lose their home and their livelihood. Because if he were as unprincipled and callous as to hoodwink her into a short-term, no pain no gain marriage he wouldn't think twice about pulling the rug from under her family's feet once the need for blackmail was over.

Her feeling of sympathy for his loveless upbringing, his lack of close family, vanished like a snowflake falling on hot coals. He had strolled over to open the louvres on one of the tall windows that marched down the length of the room. As insouciant as all-get-out, he turned to face her, his hands in the pockets of his chinos, pulling the fabric tight against his hips.

Giving her a glinting look she couldn't read, he drawled, 'Tell me, why do you want a divorce?'

Her face crawling with colour, because that stance shouted animal magnetism and she wanted to be immune but wasn't, she shot back, 'Because I don't want to be married to you! Haven't I made that plain?'

'I think not. I think you don't entirely know what you *do* want.'

He had moved closer now. Golden eyes smouldered, transfixing her like a rabbit in the headlights of an oncoming car.

'I think—' And the thought had only just occurred to him, making him feel as if he'd received a hefty thump in the gut. Had she been in two minds when she'd left him? Half wanting to get her greedy hands on a handsome slice of alimony, the other half regretting the unlimited sex she'd so obviously enjoyed as his wife?

Even now she was giving off provocative vibes. Those emminently kissable lips were parted, her eyes a sultry gleam of sapphire beneath dense dark lashes, the dampened fabric of her T-shirt was clinging to her spectacular breasts—

Theos!

His hard, lean features rigid, Dimitri blanked off that train of thought. The little witch could turn him on without even trying! Pushing his thoughts into less troubled waters, he let his eyes meet hers with controlled intensity. 'You were a virgin when we married. Having sex with me opened up a whole new unguessed-at world of sensation. Sensation you were always eager to indulge in.'

Maddie clasped her hands behind her back to stop herself from hitting him. 'Are you trying to make some sort of point?' she flung at him, loathing him for making her sound like a budding nymphomaniac, and caught her breath in outrage as he gave her another slice of his twisted mind.

'In the process of trying to see inside your pretty head, I am merely stating facts and my suppositions arising from them, since you refuse to tell me why you ran out on our marriage, leaving me trying to make sense of it. You married me. Why? For the life of luxury you knew I could give you? And then, after you experienced it, for the sex?'

Mortified beyond belief, Maddie couldn't speak—couldn't say a word in her own defence. Not only a gold-digger but a nymphomaniac, too!

And there was more. A grim cast to his mouth, he queried flatly, 'Did you make your wedding vows already scheming to sue for divorce after a few months? To secure yourself a slice of alimony that would enable you to lead a life of luxury? And when the time came to carry it out did you realise that you would miss the only other thing you valued in our marriage? The sex.'

'You are so sick!' Maddie spat out in immediate and instinctive repudiation, struggling to understand why he was doing this. Shouldn't he be doing what she had most feared? Sweet-talking her, coaxing her back into the marital bed and trying to convince her that their marriage was viable, instead of accusing her of the most horrible things?

Her throat convulsed, and to her shame she felt hot tears sting the back of her eyes. Was she so inexcusably weak where he was concerned that she actually—in the secret centre of her heart—*wanted* him to try to coax her, convince her?

Her mind in turmoil, Maddie simply stared at him as she grappled with a thought that was far too uncomfortable to be lived with. Of course it wasn't true. Why on earth would she want him to—to coax her?

'And you still want me,' Dimitri countered. His brilliant golden gaze rested explicitly on her mouth, making her bones turn to water and her breasts stir in instinctive response so that she just knew the engorged peaks would be plainly visible beneath the thin, sweat-dampened fabric of her top—a sensation so well remembered and now so unwanted that she scrambled for what was left of her wits and threw back at him, 'If I still wanted to share your bed, as well as enjoy a life of spoiled-rotten luxury, I wouldn't have left you, would I? You're talking rubbish!'

'Am I?' He moved closer, so close that to her extreme distress Maddie felt her own vastly annoying body strain against her will—strain to close that small distance and melt into the hard, dominating maleness of him. 'Correct me if for once in my life I'm wrong,' he asserted, with an arrogance she could have killed him for, 'but I believe that if you weren't in two minds, had truly wanted to end our marriage, you would have made sure you weren't so easy to find. Headed for some place other than the glaringly obvious.' A sardonic fly-away black brow rose. 'I'm right, aren't I?'

Floored by his truly incorrect deduction, Maddie quivered helplessly. She hadn't looked on her flight from their marriage in that light; she simply hadn't taken his Greek pride into account—the pride that would force him to track her down, demand answers.

All she'd wanted was the comfort of the familiar, the people who really loved her, somewhere sympathetic to lick her raw wounds. She'd been ridiculously easy to track down. He'd even arrived at her destination before her! Made sure she returned with him!

'That being so,' he continued, as if she'd humbly agreed with his assessment of the situation, 'I believe that the larger part of you, deep down, prefers your assured lifestyle as my wife because it has the added bonus of great sex on tap, rather than the insecurity of not knowing how great or small a settlement your lawyer could squeeze out of mine, and the bother of finding some other stud to satisfy your sexual needs.'

'No!' Maddie had difficulty finding her voice. She hadn't a clue which accusation she was denying, and wondered what further character assassination he could come up with next to cover his own vile misdemeanours.

'Yes,' he overrode her smoothly. 'You do still want the pleasure I can give you.' An assured smile tugged unforgivably at the corners of his wide sensual mouth. 'Shall I prove it?'

CHAPTER SIX

SHE stared up at him, wide-eyed, dry-mouthed, heart jumping, and pushed out a chokily ambivalent, 'No—' But she shuddered helplessly as he closed the gap between them and enfolded her in his arms.

Blood racing in her veins, Maddie raised her hands to push him away, make him keep his distance. Because distance between them meant she was safe from her own deplorable weakness where this one man was concerned. But without conscious effort she found her small fists unfurling, her palms flat against his broad chest, and the heady warmth of him sent rivers of sensation skittering through her body, paralysing her.

'I think, *yes*,' he corrected her, his eyes a golden shaft of confident male mastery in his leanly handsome features, his clean breath feathering her skin as he lowered his dark head and claimed her mouth with breathtaking expertise, teasing her lips apart with no effort at all, meeting no resistance, until she was kissing him back with an aching hunger she was completely unable to disguise or pretend didn't exist.

Defences shattered out of existence, she gasped

raggedly at the wildly erotic sensation that engulfed her as his strong hands lowered to pull her hips in contact with his hard, demanding arousal, the memories of what had happened since he'd dropped everything to fly to the side of the woman he loved expunged in the wild fever of blind, unthinking sexual excitement.

This was how it had always been. His passionate lovemaking allaying the doubts and insecurities that had grown during those three months at his home in Athens, fuelled by Irini's far-too-frequent presence and Alexandra's poisoned snobbery.

'This is how it should be for us, yes?' Dimitri breathed, his hard thighs pressed against hers as he eased her backwards towards the massive luxurious bed. His mouth invaded hers again with sensual know-how, his voice thick with satisfaction, as if he knew about the burning fire that pooled in the heart of her, that licked the flesh of her inner thighs with liquid, searing heat as he assured her with pure Greek male confidence, 'You know it is.'

The part of her that murmured feebly about self-preservation, the part that told her to deny it, was woefully weak, and even those semi-formed hazy urgings evaporated beneath the heat of what his clever hands were doing. Lulling her into a false sense of security, as they had always done. She tried to fight it. Her breath caught. It was impossible.

Sliding beneath her T-shirt, curving around the engorged, unbearably sensitised globes of her breasts, his long fingers gently teased the tight crests. He knew what this did to her, he *knew* it, and he was using her treacherous body against her.

He was using unfair tactics, playing dirty—and that was her last semi-coherent thought as he eased her back on to the bed, removing her flattie sandals in one fluid movement before turning his smouldering attention to divesting her of her T-shirt. And, fingers clumsy in her complete capitulation, in her unthinking eagerness to aid her own downfall, she helped him, writhing in intolerably aroused abandonment as he dealt with the fastenings at her waistband and slid the denim fabric, the sheer silk of her panties, slowly and tantalisingly down over the swell of her curvy hips, exposing her ripe nakedness to his incandescent golden gaze.

'So beautiful,' he murmured thickly, lowering his head to trail burning kisses from her throat down to the tangle of curls at the apex of her thighs. Helplessly out of control, Maddie gasped wildly, her fingers clinging to the wide span of his shoulders, writhing mindlessly as one of his hands found the melting core of her, cupping her, teasing unbearably, and her voice was a sob of anguished wanting as she cried his name.

'And so willing.'

Distant his voice now, drenching her with icy, scarcely believing shock as he moved away from her, looking down at her splayed nakedness with golden eyes suddenly overlaid with ice.

'You are only with me now for the sex,' he imparted frigidly. 'Sorry, *pethi mou*. But, much as you tempt me, I have to decline the invitation until I know why you left what I believed was a happy marriage and asked for divorce. Until you tell me, you will go unsatisfied. And even then I think I will be strong enough to resist the temptation.'

* * *

The stony track petered out beneath her feet and Maddie stared at the top of a cliff fringed with sparse, thorny vegetation, her heart beating wildly, her mind twisting and turning incoherently.

He had left the room. He had said something about fixing lunch, and something else. She hadn't been listening—hadn't grasped a thing through those shock waves.

The moment the door had closed behind him she'd lurched off the now hateful bed and dragged on her discarded clothing, flying down the curving staircase and out in to the sun. Running.

Running away from him. Running from her shame, from the deep and shameful humiliation he'd so cruelly dealt her. The self-disgust, wave after wave—so much of it she had no idea how to cope with it.

What sort of creature was she to forget his plans for her? Forget he only wanted to use her? To crave the joy of sex with him so much that she would offer it on a plate the moment he touched her?

A silly creature who had loved him once.

Who still loved him?

Her throat closed convulsively as she shook her head in sharp negation. How could she still love a man who, according to his cynical thought processes, had believed that she was only after a fat slice of his wealth in the first place, then, on reassessment, had decided that she might as well have sex thrown into the mix for good measure—a man who would stoop to blackmail to get her back, to get her to resume her brood mare duties?

Frowning, she wiped the sweat from her forehead with shaky fingers. She hated to admit it, but there was something wrong with that line of reasoning. He could have taken her. Just like that. If using her as a walking womb was his only reason for forcing her to return to him, why had he walked away?

A power thing?

To demonstrate that he could have sex with her whenever he liked? To punish her, humiliate her for having had the gross temerity to leave him and say she wanted a divorce? Dimitri Kouvaris was a man who didn't know what it meant to be rejected, who always expected, as of right, to be master of each and every situation.

What else was she to think?

A smothered sob escaped her. The sun was so hot, burning relentlessly down from the piercing blue vault of the sky, that she couldn't think straight.

Below, the blue-green seawater, crinkling onto the shimmering white sand, looked irresistible. The thought of sinking into blissfully cool waters filled her head.

A paved path from the villa led to low cliffs, where shallow stone steps had been cut into the rock for ease of access. She'd ignored it. Too close. She'd needed somewhere to hide, some place where she could get her head straight, escape the awful humiliation of what had happened. Try to forgive herself where her fatal weakness for him was concerned.

During the three short months of their marriage she had lost herself. Lost the independant young woman she'd been before he had swept her off her feet, meeting his passion with her own because only then had her insecurites seemed ridiculous. Now it was time she found herself again.

Heading away, her breath shortening with exertion, she'd cut through a grove of ancient gnarled olive trees and had come out onto parched grassland, scattering a herd of goats. And here, on another clifftop, possibly at least a mile from the villa—and him—she was safe. Safe until she'd pulled herself together and decided to return. To him.

To tell him in exact detail why she'd left him. To grit her teeth and put her pride—the only thing she had left—aside. And end the farce that their marriage had become.

Countless times during those three months it had been on the tip of her tongue to repeat what Irini had said, to ignore Amanda's advice. But something apart from Amanda's sensible advice had always stopped her. The fear that Irini hadn't been lying?

But she had to tell him now. And do her damnedest to hide the hurt that was still so raw it flayed her. Pride at least demanded that much. If she could manage it.

She had to.

In the meantime the cool waters called her. Feeling fresh and clean again would help clear her mind, wash away the still-burning memories that his hands had imprinted on her skin. Unsteadily, she walked closer to the edge of the clifftop. No convenient steps here. Nothing but the rock face, which seemed to shimmer and shift beneath her eyes. But she could do it—climb down, strip off, and walk into the cool, whispering, welcoming sea.

How he'd resisted the temptation of her he would never know. Even as he assembled the makings of a light lunch his body ached for her—for the only woman, the *first* woman, ever to separate his mind from his body, to take him to paradise and far, far beyond. But that way lay madness.

She had left him; she wanted a divorce. Lust he could control. But not the need to know the truth. Until he knew why he would have no peace. Money? The idea sickened him. He'd been the target of too many greedy little gold-diggers in the past to welcome the thought that he'd been well and truly suckered. But, in the absence of any other sensible explanation from her, it was the only viable answer he could think of.

When he'd given her no option but to comply with his demands she'd come back to him decided she would avail herself of the material advantages she could still claim as his wife, plus the thing she had become hooked on, the thing he gave freely. Fantastic sex. He'd just proved it, hadn't he? And he didn't like the feeling.

Carrying the loaded tray, his mouth curling with distaste, Dimitri told himself he'd get a truthful answer if it killed him. Only to discover that she wasn't waiting on the balcony outside the master bedroom, as he'd instructed her to. Leaving the tray on the delicate white-painted cast-iron table, he took in the bathroom. No sign of her having had that shower.

Sulking somewhere because he'd denied her what her eager body had been begging for? With a hiss of impatience he set off to systematically search the empty villa, the grounds behind, the swimming pool and the area around the vine-shaded arbour.

Nothing.

Standing at the head of the steps down to the nearest beach, he scanned the empty sands.

Nothing.

Anxiety made a furrow on his brow. She couldn't go far. The island was a mere five miles by three at its widest point. But the midday sun was ferocious.

His stride, long and swift, took him to higher ground. Beyond the olive grove, Yiannis's goats were scattered. Unused to strangers, something seemed to have spooked them. Or someone.

Moving faster than he had ever moved in his life before, he followed in the direction he was sure she must have taken. Sunstroke or heat exhaustion was a very real danger for someone who wasn't used to the unforgiving midday climate at this latitude.

His features tight, he cursed himself. He'd needed proof that, denied her first choice of a ton of alimony and her freedom, she had settled for the very real perks of being his wife.

But had she wanted to end their marriage, get him completely out of her life, because she no longer loved him? Because unknowingly he'd done something to hurt or disgust her? But, if so, she wouldn't have been so eager to have sex with him. Making love didn't come into it. Much as the idea repelled him, for her it was all about lust. Sex.

Well, he'd had his proof and he didn't much like himself for it. He was tough in business matters, he'd had to be, but never unfair and certainly never cruel.

Yet he'd been cruel to Maddie—driven her to put as much distance between them as she could manage within the confines of the small island. He despised himself for the first time in his life. He had his proof and it left a sour taste in his mouth, because in getting it he had shattered his code of honour.

And then he saw her. His thumping heart picked up a beat. Her bright head bent, she was too near the edge of the clifftop. The sound of his approach brought her head round and she took a step back, thankfully away from the edge. As he quickened his steps to a flat-out run one hand fluttered up to her forehead, and she swayed, then crumpled in a heap on the ground.

Within heart-banging moments he was at her side, kneeling, cradling her head and reaching into his back pocket for his mobile. Her face was deathly pale, and the delicate skin around her eyes looked bruised. Two calls. His instructions, bitten out, concise. Repocketing the slim phone he lifted Maddie in his arms and began the slow journey back to the villa—slow because he didn't want to jolt her. He promised himself that once she'd recovered from this—sunstroke?—they would sit down and talk like the sensible adults they were supposed to be. No more threats, demands, mind-games.

As they entered the shaded area in the olive grove she stirred, her eyes drifting open. 'It is all right,' he assured her softly, his heart lightening as he saw her colour begin to return. 'You collapsed, but we will soon be back at the villa and Dr Papantoniou will be with you within the hour.'

'I don't need a doctor. Put me down. I can walk.' A feeble attempt to struggle to her feet had his arms tightening around her—which was absolutely the last thing she wanted, wasn't it? She wanted distance between them. She didn't want him to think he had to be kind to her just because she'd been stupid enough to pass out. It was demeaning!

'I fainted. No big deal,' she grumbled fiercely. 'I don't

want a doctor! I skipped breakfast, that's all!' Because once again the sight of food had turned her stomach.

'Save your energy.' His golden eyes were dark with concern and something else she couldn't read as he glanced down at her. 'Just forget your middle name is Stubborn and do as you're told for once, yes?'

After that Maddie saw no point in pitting herself against his iron will, and submitted, with gritted teeth, to being carried through the cool interior of the villa and gently deposited on the huge bed that had been the scene of her recent stomach-churning humiliation.

But she drew the line when he attempted to undress her.

'I can do that!' She batted his hands away, squirmed round and planted her feet on the floor, snapping tartly, 'If you've decided it's necessary for me to be in bed in a nightie when the doctor calls, to keep up the pretence of not dragging him out here for no purpose, I won't do it—you can go and wait and make your apologies when he arrives!'

Dimitri stood back, but he didn't leave the room. To her utter chagrin he even looked slightly amused, standing watching her, his arms folded over his chest.

Thinking of the invitingly cool-looking sea water, Maddie headed for the shower in the huge marble and glass bathroom. He followed. She was spikily aware of those unreadable eyes pinned on her, and as the only slightly warm water sluiced over her grateful body her anger with him, with herself, increased in proportion to the ache of wanting that flickered and burned deep within.

Damn him! Damn him for making her feel like this. She didn't want it. It was the last thing she needed, she fumed as she grabbed a towel and stumbled back into the bedroom, pointedly sidestepping when he reached out a hand to help her.

Thankfully, the *whump-whump* of approaching rotors brought an end to the situation that was winding her up to explosion point. Glaring at him, pink-cheeked and furious, she watched him move to the door with the innate grace that was so much a part of him.

'Tell him there's nothing wrong with me,' she flung after him. 'And apologise for wasting his time.'

He turned back briefly. 'You are looking better.' There was an almost-smile on his sensual mouth. It made her want to go and smack it away. 'Nevertheless…'He spread his hands, palms uppermost, and closed the door gently behind him.

Intent on making a fool of her. Again. Paying her back in spades for taking off, not doing as she'd been told. The fleeting, unwelcome thought that he might have been genuinely concerned about her was swiftly knocked on the head. He didn't give a darn for her well-being. The only things that mattered to him were any child she might bear for him and Irini. Of course. Mustn't forget the woman he loved enough to do what he'd set out to do—secure an heir, get rid of an unwanted wife and marry where he truly loved.

Totally unwilling to greet the doctor lying like a wilting Victorian heroine on the bed, when there was not a single thing wrong with her, she grabbed fresh underwear from a drawer and a honey-coloured, gauzy cotton strappy sundress from the closet, dressed at speed, and perched herself in a brocade-covered armchair close by one of the windows, picking up a glossy magazine from a nearby table and pretending to be engrossed.

The doctor had other ideas. A serious-looking beanpole of a man, silver-haired and exquisitely dressed, he indicated the bed and carried out an examination that had her squirming with violent embarrassment—because Dimitri was still looming, taut-featured. Though what *he* had to be uptight about Maddie couldn't begin to guess, and wasn't going to try.

As he removed the blood-pressure cuff Dr Papantoniou stood up, smiling. He swung round to face Dimitri. 'Congratulations. My best estimate is that your wife will give you a child in around seven months.' He turned his smile on Maddie. 'You are fit and well, *kyria*. And pregnant. I forbid any further treks in the heat of the afternoon. Remember, you are carrying a precious life inside you. Take gentle exercise in the cool of the day, rest and eat well, and be sure of a happy pregnancy.'

Turning to a shell-shocked Dimitri, he advised, 'I will visit again when you return to the mainland, to arrange tests and make a referral to a top gynaecologist. I foresee no difficulties, but you will naturally demand the very best for your wife and child.'

CHAPTER SEVEN

IF DIMITRI had looked positively shell-shocked at the doctor's announcement, then Maddie couldn't have described what *she* felt. The news that there was a tiny baby growing inside her had made her feel light-headed with something she could only define as fierce protectiveness, all mingled up with the razor-sharp, icy edge of fear.

Because this was the news that Dimitri and Irini had been waiting for. The safe conception of a rightful heir, then—bingo!—get rid of the unwanted wife and marry the so beautiful, so suitably wealthy, so upper-crust love of his life!

How could she have not known? Or at least suspected? But she'd put the extremely scanty nature of her last two periods down to the stress she'd been under, and her early-morning queasiness hadn't occurred often enough to ring alarm bells. If she'd suspected she might be pregnant he could have threatened all he liked but she would *never* have agreed to come back to Greece, she thought wildly.

She would fight him to the last breath in her body before she let him take her baby from her, she vowed staunchly. Then, choking as tears clogged her throat, she buried her head in the pillow. She only realised Dimitri had re-entered the room when his hand touched her shoulder.

Her heart gave a sickening lurch as she twisted round on the massive bed, sitting with her hands tightly wrapped around her updrawn knees to hold herself together, and trying to gather the coherent yet cutting words that would tell him in no uncertain terms she was aware of his sick plans, and that no way would she allow him to bring them to fruition. Even if she did come from a humble background—fit, as his ultra-snobbish aunt would have it, only to scrub his floors— it didn't mean she didn't know how to fight her corner, or that she wouldn't!

But before she could formulate a single phrase, let alone anything approaching a sensible sentence from the mayhem going on inside her head, he took her hands, gently unknotting her savagely clenched fingers, and spoke with a warmth that momentarily drove every-thing out of her mind and left her gaping.

'Between us we have created a precious new life. There will now be no question of a divorce. And, whatever your reasons for wanting one, I do not wish to hear them. I *will* not hear them,' he stressed with fierce insistence. 'As of the moment your pregnancy was confirmed past differences are forgotten. By both of us,' he stressed again, this time with a blithe arrogance that literally took her breath away.

Just like that! Maddie exploded internally, her gaze narrowing to needle-points of glittering bright blue as she tried to read the golden eyes partially obscured by the thick dark sweep of his ebony lashes. She was as sure as she could be that *divorce* would be the first word to trip smartly off his tongue the moment his son or daughter was born!

Removing her hands from his gentle grasp, she sat on them, speedwell-blue eyes daring him to take them back. He didn't, simply brushed the tumbling silk of caramel curls from her forehead with tender fingers and smiled that slow, devastating smile of his that always before had had the power to send delicious tingles up and down her spine. Now it just made her hate him!

'Today we start our married life afresh, *chrysi mou*. For the sake of our child. And it will be good, I promise. You will want for nothing. Whatever you desire, you will have,' he claimed with extravagant emphasis. 'And now—' he got to his feet '—I will make that belated lunch. You must eat for two now, and I am ravenous! But the food I prepared before will be unfit to eat. I left it on the balcony in my panic to find you.'

The light kiss he dropped on her cheek made her heart leap like a landed fish, and there was anger sparking in her eyes as she watched him walk to the door, turning, giving her that bone-melting smile as he invited, 'Come down and join me.'

The silence that followed his exit was thick with her rage and pain as she vowed she would not be taken for a sucker. Not again!

He had got what he wanted.

Her pregnancy.

Of course he would sweet-talk her—he was very good at it! Brush aside her request for a divorce as the utterings of a retard. Use soft-soap by the bucketful to keep her with him until the child was born. He'd want to keep a close eye on her to make sure she didn't take up sky-diving, get drunk every night, or in any way put his heir at risk!

Swinging her feet off the bed, she stood slowly, straightened her skirt and headed for the bathroom, sluicing her burning cheeks with cold water and dragging a brush through her tangled hair. Staring sightlessly at her reflection, she took several deep, calming breaths.

Dimitri thought he'd got her right where he wanted her. But she would prove otherwise. Always up front— what you saw was what you got—she would change the habits of a lifetime and learn to be as devious as he. She'd had a top-flight tutor in that regard, hadn't she?

Useless to confront him now with what she knew. It was far too late. Pointless to repeat what Irini herself had told her, his aunt's sly hints, or to remind him forcefully of the evidence of her own eyes and ears. The way when Irini was around, he'd always give her the undivided attention she routinely demanded—the way he'd dropped everything on that last morning, not hanging around even to share morning coffee with his wife as he always did. His avowal of love to the other woman would continually haunt her nightmares.

And other things—things that hadn't troubled her one iota before—had fallen into place when she'd been forced to face the truth on that dreadful morning.

Their low-key wedding in the tiny village church, with only her immediate family invited to witness the event, for instance. As if he was ashamed of marrying so far beneath him and regarded the ceremony as a necessary evil, the tedious preliminary to a hopefully short-lived marriage that would provide him with what he really wanted.

Greeks made a great celebration of marriage, and in the normal course of events a man such as Dimitri Kouvaris would have wanted an almighty splash—with his aunt there, of course, and all the distant relatives Irini had spoken of, his large circle of friends and business colleagues, the press, all in admiring awestruck attendance.

Useless to confront him with what she knew— because with the heir he wanted so badly now on the horizon he would deny everything until his face turned blue. There was too much at stake for him to do anything else.

So for the next few weeks she would play it his way. Grit her teeth and fall in with the charade of starting their marriage afresh. There was too much at stake for her to do anything other. Oh, how she wished she'd come straight out with it on the night of that party— insisted that Irini repeated what she'd said in front of Dimitri. On the face of it Amanda's advice had seemed sensible after all, she was married to a well-heeled Greek herself and would know how their minds ticked. But, oh, how she wished she hadn't taken it!

She would have to find a way to warn her parents that their comfortable new lifestyle would soon be a thing of the past, give them time to make contingency plans. And plan her own bid for freedom—because no way was he going to take her baby from her.

If she couldn't bear the thought of giving up the tiny life inside her now, she couldn't begin to contemplate how very much worse it would be after the birth.

When they were back on the mainland she would be able to work on what she had to do. Transfer some of what she had always considered to be the over-the-top personal allowance he'd made her from Greece into her still open but paltry account back in England for starters.

Not that she wanted anything from him for herself. She definitely didn't, and the thought of actually doing it turned her stomach, but for her baby's sake she had to have some funds behind her. Enough to live frugally until the birth, until she could rebuild her career and work to keep them both.

And back in England she wouldn't make the unthinking mistake she'd made before. She wouldn't go near her family, but hide somewhere he'd never find her.

In the meantime she would bide her time, let him think she was willing to make a fresh start. It was the only way she could ensure that he didn't suspect what she was planning. Besides, pulling the wool over his eyes while playing him at his own game was one way of paying him back for what he had done. Taken her heart and broken it.

She left the room and went down to find him, her head high, the welcome upsurge of renewed self-confidence momentarily smothering the pain of what was happening. It lasted until she tracked him down, hearing his voice, the tone low and warmly intimate, issuing from what turned out to be the huge airy kitchen. That upsurge of self-confidence drained away as he abruptly ended a call as soon as she entered the room, closing down his mobile and slipping it into his back pocket.

'Maddie—'

'Dimitri—' How she kept her voice cool, her smile pleasant, she would never know. He looked—what? Guilty? Glittering golden eyes, a faint band of colour across those sculpted cheekbones.

'You look so much better. Pregnancy suits you!'

'Does it? That's nice.' She wandered further into the room. He'd been working at the huge central table, but the much smaller one beneath one of the open windows had been laid. Plates, a bowl of crisp salad, rolls, cold chicken and a ham.

The way he'd ended what had obviously been a highly personal conversation, judging by his intimate tone, the spattering of endearments she'd recognised in his native tongue, the call ending so abruptly at her approach, made the hairs on the back of her neck stand up on end.

'Who were you talking to?' She was making like a suspicious wife—but who could blame her in the dire circumstances she found herself in? 'Irini, was it? Couldn't wait to tell her the good news?'

She watched his features harden, the softness in his eyes replaced by an unhidden glint of cold anger. Noted that he didn't answer her specific question directly. 'I'll never understand what you've got against her,' he stated in a cool challenge. 'Whenever she's around you show all your prickles, close down, and when she tries to speak to you you answer in monosyllables. It upsets her. She would like to be your friend. And believe me, Maddie, she needs friends.'

So protective of the woman he loved. Her cheeks burning, she could have ripped her tongue out. She would have to watch what she said in future, especially when it concerned that woman!

She could tell him exactly what she held against Irini. Starting with that hateful conversation at that first party, when she'd told her her days as Dimitri's wife were numbered, and why. But doing so now would put him on his guard, put her plans to leave him in jeopardy. Unfortunately, the time for coming out into the open was past.

So she simply shrugged, essayed a smile, and told him, 'Sorry, I'll try harder. She's just not my cup of tea, and we've nothing in common. But, I don't think we should quarrel about it, do you?'

Dimitri expelled a slow breath. He felt something warm enfold his heart, banish irritation. Did she know how adorable she looked? How the band of freckles across her pretty nose moved him to an unbearable tenderness? An almost painful hunger gripped him in a vice as he met those clear blue fathomless eyes, his heart turning over and swelling within him. Maddie, his wife, was carrying his child. Nothing would put that child at risk.

Nothing! For the sake of his child, for his child's future happiness and security, with two parents in apparent harmony with each other, he would wipe her rejection of him from his mind. Forget it. Try to make their marriage work. And to do that, to forget what she had done and why, it must never be spoken of. That he was determined on.

He extended his hand towards her. 'Come and eat.' He waited, his shoulders relaxing when, after a tension-filled moment, she gave him her hand. A ghost of a frown darkened his brow as, slightly ahead of her, he led her towards the small table beneath the window. It seemed as though she was falling in with his earlier stated wishes. Making a fresh start, burying the past, wiping the word *divorce* from her vocabulary.

Why? Should it matter? He knew his reasons, knew they were sound. Was the news of her pregnancy her reason? Had it settled her, made her earlier behaviour appear as the nonsense it was? Or had his promise that she would want for nothing, that whatever her heart desired would be hers, been the deciding factor?

The former, he devoutly hoped. Until she'd left him for no good reason that he'd been able to come up with apart from a fat divorce settlement, he would have said she didn't possess an avaricious bone in her body. And yet how could he know what went on inside that lovely head of hers?

The time was past when he could have done what he'd brought her here to do—insist that she reveal her true motivations behind her desire for a divorce. Such an insistence would be counter-productive in the new regime he'd set up. No arguments about that!

No looking back.

Slate wiped clean.

Fresh start.

Seeing her seated, he helped her to a little of everything on the table, slid the plate in front of her and sat opposite, his own appetite—roused and ravaging after the news that he was to be a father—completely gone. Was it pride that kept him from acknowledging that he wanted her to stay with him, make their marriage work, because he was important to her?

He refused to dwell on that possibility. She had wronged him, shamed him, but he was now prepared to overlook that. And whatever her reasons for her seeming compliance to his wishes it was a step in the right direction—a step towards what he must have: a stable relationship for the sake of their unborn child.

He had endured a cold and loveless childhood following the deaths of his parents when he'd been too young to properly remember them, so he was determined that his child would be surrounded by the permanence of parental love.

And no way would a child of his suffer the trauma of a broken home, a marriage gone wrong, with all the attendant recriminations and back-biting, the divided loyalties that would torment any child shunted between two bitter parents.

Watching her eat a little of the food and push the remainder around her plate, he wondered how far her compliance with his wishes would take her.

As far as the marriage bed?

And did he really want that?

The answer, he knew, to his annoyance, was yes. Despite her past behaviour, the shaming of his honour, he wanted her. Even more than when he'd first encountered her in Cristos's courtyard.

And that was saying something!

CHAPTER EIGHT

DIMITRI rose from the table as if propelled by a rocket, pushed back his chair and, sounding almost painfully polite, said, 'You must rest this afternoon, Maddie. I insist. It has been a traumatic morning.' One dark brow elevated as she stubbornly remained seated. His mouth flattened. 'Come, I will see you to your room.'

Leaving her barely touched meal, Maddie got to her feet with extreme reluctance. An hour or two of solitude, the opportunity to at least try to relax and consider her situation calmly, had its glaringly obvious advantages. But, perversely, she didn't want to give him the satisfaction of seeing her meekly fall in with all his orders. He had managed to demean her until she felt lower than the ground she walked on. Was she to have no pride left whatsoever?

Suddenly her legs felt horribly unsteady. He was spot-on about this morning's trauma. And every bit of it was his fault!

It had started with his humiliation of her and come to a dramatic crescendo with the news of her pregnancy. So a short rest, the brief and blessed oblivion of sleep, seemed like the best idea she'd heard in a long while.

And if he smugly assumed she was falling in with his wishes it couldn't be helped.

'I'm sure I will be all right on my own,' she was forced to point out, not wanting him anywhere near her, because he was no longer her dearest love, he was her enemy. Her pregnancy had rammed that reality home as nothing else could have done. Muttering vociferously, he ignored her statement of independence, swept her up into his arms and headed for the staircase.

'Put me down! I'm not an invalid! I can manage!'

'I'm sure you can. But while I am with you, you don't have to.'

He knew he sounded cold. Could do nothing about it. He could barely trust himself to speak. Watching her across that table, he'd been hit by the usual upsurge of savage hunger that always afflicted him in her presence—had done ever since he'd first set eyes on her for the first time. The wanting was strong enough to cause actual physical hurt, leading inevitably to the thought of the marriage bed.

But he knew that resuming those mind-shattering pleasures was out of the question until things were calmer between them and he could begin to forgive himself for the earlier humiliation he'd dealt her, which now severely appalled him.

Whatever her reasons for wanting out of their marriage—and he no longer wished to know them because the future was all that mattered—she didn't deserve that type of treatment.

He hoisted her body closer to the hard strength of his and effortlessly mounted the stairs, while Maddie desperately tried to stop the tears that stung the back of her eyes from falling. Held this close to him, to the man she had adored with everything in her, was torture. Worse than torture. Because her body was letting her down again, responding wholeheartedly to him even as what little was left of her brain told her all she wanted to do was punch him!

Wicked, treacherous heat flared deep inside her as he shouldered through the door to the master bedroom and slid her to her feet at the side of the massive bed. He was still so close, too close. He was so magnificent, so unfairly sexy, full of careless masculinity. It was as if his body was a silent call to her—a call which drew an immediate response from her soul, from a loving heart her logical mind was unable to control.

Maddie turned swiftly, caught between the edge of the bed and his superbly powerful frame. A smothered sob snagged her throat as blistering heat gathered deep inside her and made her heart flip over.

She despised herself for her body's unmanageable response to him. She knew what he was. Cruel enough to make her love him and then toss that love back in her face as if it were something of no value whatsoever. So why did she crave him like a forbidden drug? She would never have described herself as weak, lacking will power, but she obviously was, and the knowledge flayed her.

As if sensing her distress, he stepped away from her, his strong jaw set, golden eyes uncompromisingly grim as he told her, 'Rest now. I shall be working in the study at the far end of the old wing should you need me. And, Maddie—' His voice faltered momentarily, then incised on. 'Please accept my apologies for my earlier despicable behaviour. Such a thing will never happen again,

I promise on my life. I quite understand why you felt the need to run from the house. From me.'

Turning with his inherent grace, he left the room. Stunned, Maddie plopped down on the bed and just sat there. Shaking.

The arrogant, domineering Greek male had actually apologised! The moon must have turned blue and she hadn't noticed!

Unused to putting a foot wrong in his world-spanning business dealings, or in his relationships with friends and colleagues, he had actually admitted being in the wrong. Why? Unaccustomed humility? Or an integral part of his cynical kiss-and-make-up scenario?

But there wouldn't be any kissing, would there?

She was safely pregnant. There was no longer any need for him to grit his teeth, take her to bed and think of Irini!

Curling up on the tumbled sheets, she buried her face in a pillow and eventually fell into an uneasy sleep, wondering why that obvious conclusion didn't bring her the deep relief it should.

It was cooler when she woke. The searing midday heat had been replaced by a soft, balmy warmth that drifted through the open windows, fluttering the delicate muslin drapes. Her eyes felt gritty, her mouth parched, her brain fuzzy. She would have to freshen up, she decided vaguely. Get out of the dress she'd fallen asleep in, move herself. Then the hateful reality of her situation hit her like a sledgehammer and enfolded her.

Staunchly telling herself that she was going to have to get used to it or lose her sanity, she firmed her soft mouth and swung her feet to the floor, her eyes lighting on the jug of orange juice and the single tall crystal glass on the bedside table.

Dimitri? Had to be. Schooling the sudden and unwelcome mush out of her heart and replacing it with cold reality was easy. He hadn't provided the freshly squeezed juice because he cared about *her*. He cared about the welfare of the coming baby. He would cosset her, wrap her in cotton wool until her child was born. Then get rid of her.

She would take his plans and reduce them to ashes. Even if it did mean having to grit her teeth and play him at his own devious game for a few more weeks.

She hated him! Nevertheless, she poured and drank gratefully, noting that the ice cubes hadn't begun to melt. So he must have come to the room in the past few minutes. Was that what had woken her? Was she that aware of him, attuned to him, even in sleep?

It was a shattering thought. She didn't want it to be like that. She had to learn to be indifferent to him. Had to.

Starting with doing her own thing.

Hoping he'd gone back to his study and intended to stay there, she stripped off the now crumpled and wilted sundress she'd put on for the doctor's arrival and got into a sleek white one-piece swimsuit, bemoaning the fact that, sleek as it might be, it did nothing to disguise the curve of her breasts and well-rounded hips.

Not for the first time she wondered how he could have brought himself to make love to her, preferring, as he obviously did, the ultra-sophisticated stick-insect type such as his beloved Irini.

Dimitri had mentioned a swimming pool, so she was going to find it and enjoy the cool waters and continue the long haul of not only acting but actually *being* indifferent to him. To knock firmly on the head the sneaky wish that her husband truly loved her, only her, and that their time here in romantic seclusion really was a belated honeymoon.

In a hollow beyond a sweeping stone terrace lay the immense oval pool, surrounded by slender cypress trees, blue water lazy, limpid, inviting.

The gentle breeze caressed her exposed skin, carrying the scents of sea, dried grasses and aromatic herbs. Dropping the fluffy jade-green towel she'd brought with her onto the cool marble surround, Maddie took a deep breath and dived in at the deep end, determined to forget her situation and the shameful fact that she'd been too stupid to smell a rat when the super-eligible Dimitri Kouvaris, charismatic and absolutely gorgeous, and a millionaire many times over, had proposed marriage to an insignificant grubber-around-in-the-soil-nobody like her, after such a remarkably short acquaintance.

She would relax, do a few gentle lengths, empty her mind to everything but the perfection of the early evening, the soft caress of the water, and find tranquility—because bad thoughts and a brain that was in knots couldn't be good for the baby inside her.

And she was doing just fine in that respect when a splash at the opposite end of the pool, the deep end, had her feet finding the bottom in a flurry, her eyes widening, sparking blue fire, as Dimitri scythed through the water towards her in a powerful crawl.

Did he have to spoil everything? Even her relaxing half hour in the swimming pool—not to mention her whole life!

With water lapping her waist she was too stricken to move until he got close. Then, galvanised, she hauled herself out of the pool in a shower of water droplets and headed like a bullet to where she'd left the towel.

But he was there before her, blocking her way. Thankfully, she was able to keep her instinctive groan internal as his honeyed drawl sent shivers right down to her toes. She wanted to drag her eyes from him but couldn't as he said, 'Slow down! Honeymoons on secluded Greek islands are meant to be slow and lazy. Relaxed. I will help you to learn that much.'

Her toes curled in reaction to his nearness, to the bronzed body glistening with moisture, tempting her to touch and go on touching, to slide her hands over the muscular strength of his chest, the skin like oiled silk and just as sensuous. Her fingers would glide lower, over the washboard-flat stomach, to the top of the black briefs that did nothing at all to modestly disguise his manhood—

Smartly clasping her hands behind her back to stop them straying of their own volition, she countered on a rasp of breath, and with no pretence of the rapprochement he'd earlier suggested, 'I was perfectly relaxed until you showed up!'

She bent to retrieve the towel and cover herself up, because he was no one's fool and would have no trouble working out why her wretched breasts were pushing at the clinging fabric of her swimsuit as if hedonistically eager for the touch of his hands, his mouth.

But he stayed her before she could reach her objective, strong, finely made hands on her shoulders as he brought her upright, moving in closer as he reminded her grittily, 'I am not your enemy. I am your husband. And I want you so much it hurts.'

Shaken by that admission, she allowed her eyes to meet his. His hands on her naked shoulders sent electrifying shivers down her spine. His eyes were hot gold, burning into her where they touched—her shamefully peaking breasts, the quivering curve of her tummy, and lower, making her shift her feet, part her thighs with blatant invitation and no conscious thought whatsoever.

She jerked in a ragged breath as his hands slid slowly down from her shoulders to fasten around her slender waist and pull her with aching deliberation against him. He hadn't been lying, was her almost incoherent thought. The state of his arousal left her in no doubt as to the truth of his gritty statement.

Unable to decide what she was thinking, she felt terrifyingly vulnerable, torn between the conflicting need to distance herself from him in every way there was and wanting her charismatic, once-adored husband just as much as she ever had.

The deed was done. She was pregnant. So why should he still want her sexually? She had expected a spurious kindness—not for her sake, but for his child's. But this? 'We are not enemies. What we once had was beautiful. We can and will reclaim it,' Dimitri reiterated rawly. 'Between us we have made a baby, have created a new life. The future can be golden, *chrysi mou*, if you will let it be. You still want me—as I need you—I am ready and willing to forget the immediate past, and I hope you are, too.'

A gentle hand slid up behind her head, long fingers slipping through her bright hair, lifting her face, her

mouth, to the seductive invasion of a kiss that proved
his point—because she could not resist the hunger of his
lips, the tongue that dipped, teased and tormented until
she was writhing against him, heart hammering, veins
running with liquid fire.

Everything inside her quivered as with one fluid
movement he lifted her in his arms and carried her to
the bedroom, his mouth unceasing in its ravishment of
hers until he laid her on the bed and came down beside
her, divesting them both of damp garments in the time
it took to draw breath.

She had expected immediate consummation, indeed
her body craved it, but he whispered, 'Slowly, my sweet,
slowly,' which she translated as *Gently, for our baby's
sake.* But then she didn't care, because the wicked expertise of his sensual mouth, his knowing hands, as he
brought every inch of her restlessly writhing body to a
wild crescendo of excitement drove everything else out
of her mind until at last, responding to her moans of
'Please—Dimitri, please!' he sank between her thighs
and with one long thrust instigated an unstoppable storm
of white-hot passion that spiralled until control splintered and was lost in the primitive rhythm that swept her
up and beyond the very pinnacle of ecstasy.

Held in his arms, his fantastic body melded to the
yielding softness of hers, Maddie floated gently back to
earth, loving the way he dropped tiny kisses on her
damp forehead, the tip of her small nose, the corner of
her mouth, revelling in sweet satiation until, at the unmistakable hardening of his body, he released her with
a shaky laugh, a reluctant, 'I am too greedy for you! I
hadn't meant this to happen.

But you, alone among women, are too much temptation for me!'

He sprang off the bed, telling her after a rapid glance at the watch that adorned his flat wrist, 'Xanthe will arrive at any moment with the evening meal she has prepared.' Slanting her a smile he promised, his stunning eyes filled with dancing golden lights, 'I will be patient until after we have eaten,' and strode to the bathroom where, above the sound of the shower, she could hear him singing in the tuneful baritone she had once delighted to hear.

Pleased with himself, she thought sourly, as bleak despair again settled around her, a too-regular visitor, and as demeaning as it was unwelcome. So he had a highly over-active libido. He could have sex with her while loving another woman. No problem when his eager wife was so obviously more than willing to participate.

And as for her—well, she was deeply ashamed of herself. Telling herself that sexual desire—lust, if you like—had the habit of taking over, crippling the mind, filling the body and heating the blood to boiling point, did nothing to excuse what she had done.

Her body aching from his intimate possession, she waited, scrambling a sheet around her nakedness. At one time nothing would have prevented her from joining him in the shower, delighting in the welcome she knew he would give her as they teased each other with soap-slicked, deliciously tormenting hands, laughter dissolving into the ecstasy of out-of-this-world passion.

Now, nothing would make her join him in there. And so she waited, subduing the sob of self-loathing that was burning her lungs, compressing her lips to stop her soft, kiss-swollen mouth from trembling, until he emerged from the *en suite* bathroom, towel-drying his thick dark hair, his smile something else as he imparted, 'I heard the quad bike arriving.' His smile widened to a grin. 'Yiannis will have nothing to do with it, but Xanthe uses it at every opportunity—flat out!'

Unable to respond for her swamping awareness of that naked, lithely lean and powerful physique, Maddie willed her pulses to stop racing, waiting until he had rapidly clothed himself in narrow white jeans topped by a silky black shirt, open-necked, sleeves rolled up to display tanned, muscular forearms, before getting out, 'I would like to phone my parents.'

She marvelled at his duplicity as he reached his mobile from the top of a dressing chest, found the number, and passed the instrument to her, saying, 'Of course—you'll want to tell them our good news. I know they'll be delighted to hear they can look forward to being grandparents again. Be sure to give them my regards.' A swift kiss landed on her brow. 'Don't be too long. I'd speak to them myself, but I must see to Xanthe. We'll eat on the terrace and count the stars as they come out to celebrate our new beginning.'

And he was gone, leaving her listening to the ringing tone and fuming. Give them his regards—oh, the low-life! How could he? When all the time he was doubt-lessly planning on throwing them off his property when he no longer had need of his disposable wife!

She had to warn them of that strong possibility.

But how to do it gently, without creating panic and outraged anxiety, when her mother's bubbly conversa-tion was filled with enthusiasm for the farmhouse they had recently moved into, her redecorating plans, the imminent arrival of the new glasshouse, and the hard work her menfolk were putting in? 'No, not your father,' she said soothingly. 'He is being sensible. He takes gentle exercise each day and contents himself with keeping the accounts.'

Eventually Maddie slid in a question—when her mother drew breath after happily imparting the fact that the old fellow hadn't farmed intensively for a decade, merely keeping a flock of sheep and a few free-range hens and pigs, so the land wasn't contaminated with nasty chemicals—'Did Dad go over the small print of the lease for the farmhouse and land?' And fingers crossed, but without too much hope, 'There *is* a properly drawn-up lease?'

Ringing silence greeted the question that had stopped the flow of excited information in its tracks. Maddie felt truly dreadful.

Was poor old Mum belatedly recalling that Dad had failed to check the details of his contract of employment when the men in suits had taken over the estate? Maddie hated having to do this to her family, and her heart plummeted even further when Joan Ryan asked with some bewilderment, 'What lease?'

So nothing had been put in writing concerning her family's security of tenure. Even though Maddie had known what would happen, having the fact thrust under her nose reminded her much too forcefully of Dimitri's threats, and made her feel dreadfully nauseous.

Until her mother questioned, 'Didn't Dimitri tell you? No, I suppose he wouldn't. He's too big-hearted to boast about his generosity! He bought the property, but it's in my and your father's name. We *own* it,

Maddie. We did feel a bit awkward about it—poor but proud, as your Dad always says! He tried to persuade your Dimitri to make it a capital loan, but he was having none of it. We were family, he said, and the cash outlay was peanuts to him. You married a man in a million!' This was followed by a slightly anxious, 'Everything's still all right between you? We were worried. On the face of it, Dimitri's everything a parent could want for a daughter. But—'

Her head reeling from what she'd heard, Maddie put in, 'We're fine, Mum.' And, because they had to know, 'I'm pregnant.'

No need to worry them now. It would be a few more weeks before she had to tell them the truth. She was more than happy to listen to her mother's overjoyed exclamations as her mind spun, trying to make sense of this new information.

CHAPTER NINE

AFTER the call ended Maddie stood immobile under the shower, her brow furrowed, as she grappled with Joan Ryan's revelations, and what they meant.

Thanks to Dimitri's generosity her parents' home and livelihood were safe. There was, of course, huge relief because from the start he had led her to believe that her family would be out of their new home and business like a shot if she didn't toe the line and stick with their marriage—but the question remained.

Why? Why had he done that?

To force her to resume her marital duties? Share his bed until the child he needed was conceived.

Obvious.

And yet…

That kind of thoughtful generosity didn't gel with the kind of guy she had categorised him as being—a heart-less blackmailer who would use any means to get what he wanted and suffer not one pang of conscience when he made her family face real hardship when he'd got it, because they were unimportant, mere peasants. He didn't fit that box now.

It looked as if he were the kind of guy who would

spend vast amounts of money setting her parents up in their own home and business, generously sorting out the difficulties they were facing and were financially and emotionally unable to cope with.

In the situation that had faced her parents any other needle-sharp, super-wealthy businessman with a phil-anthropic streak a mile wide might have done what he had done, she conceded, but he would have kept the deeds in his name, as an investment, one among many.

But Dimitri had gone one huge stride further. His generosity shook her, made her acknowledge that he wasn't all as bad as she had named him. Far from it.

Could she have misjudged him in other aspects of their relationship?

Irini?

The attention he lavished on the other woman when she was around—which had always been far too often for Maddie's liking—could be explained away by the fact that his aunt had counted her as one of the family from the time of her birth. And the relationship had rubbed off because for Dimtri family was all important.

Having lost both his parents at an early age, he was determined to create a family of his own. She could understand that because he would lavish care on anyone he considered part of his family, as witness how he had helped his parents-by-marriage.

But she couldn't explain away that overheard tele-phone conversation when he had confirmed his love for the beautiful Greek woman, dropped everything and shot off to be with her. Nothing could. Or the way the two of them had vanished together during the week before he'd brought her here to this island. And, although he hadn't confirmed it—or denied it either, come to that—the intimate-sounding phone call she'd interrupted had to have been to Irini, breaking the news of the pregnancy they had both waited so anxiously for.

And Irini's spiteful warning on the night of that party, spelling out exactly why the man who was probably the most eligible bachelor in the whole of Greece had chosen to marry an insignificant nobody like her, was solid, irrefutable fact.

Her mind preoccupied, Maddie dressed and went down to find him, uselessly wishing yet again that she had never taken Amanda's advice and kept quiet about Irini's warning, sticking her head in the sand and putting it down to the malicious spite of a jealous woman.

Her pride had stopped her flinging what she knew and what she strongly suspected at him after he had flown to England to find her and force her to return to him. And now, it seemed, it was too late.

He had categorically stated that he no longer wished to know why she had left him. He wouldn't listen and, knowing him, his masculine pride, she could understand why. In leaving him, demanding a divorce, she had rejected him and all that he was. His ego wouldn't let him listen to why she had done it. Not if he wanted them to start over, wipe the slate clean. Make the marriage work.

Until the safe delivery of their child?

'We'll stop here. You mustn't overtire yourself.' A couple of days ago she had accused him of wrapping her in cotton wool. True, he conceded with a wry twist of his mouth. He simply couldn't help himself. He took this pregnancy seriously, and his part in it was to cherish her.

Dimitri slid the strap of the picnic bag off one broad shoulder as they reached one of his favourite spots on the island. A gentle green hollow beside an abundant freshwater spring, shaded from the burning sun by a grove of ancient, long-neglected olive trees.

Golden eyes soft and slightly narrowed between thick black lashes, he watched her wander over the lush green grass, down to where the water bubbled into a natural stone basin. The gauzy cotton skirt she was wearing, in shades of primrose, pale blue and cream moved against the lovely legs that had acquired a healthy tan over the week they had spent here. He adored looking at her. He only had to look at her to want her.

Their time here together during this past week had been perfect. Their marriage was back on track.

Or almost.

Swimming in the pool or in the gentle waters of one of the small bays, exploring the island and the dozens of tiny beaches, lazy afternoons and languid evenings, hot sex—everything was pointing to her willingness to put the recent past behind them, to make a fresh start, as he had wanted, for the sake of the coming child.

Except…

He missed her once-ready, infectious laughter. Had caught the wistful look in those clear blue eyes, quickly extinguished when his eyes connected with hers. But it was there, all the same, in his memory.

It troubled him. But no way was he prepared to question her.

Because he wouldn't like the answer?

The thought came unbidden. She'd wanted a divorce. Since the news of her pregnancy there was no chance of that. And even if he strongly suspected her reasons, he would have to live with those suspicions and do his damnedest to disregard them. If she'd wanted her freedom with the financial cushion of a hefty slice of alimony he didn't want to hear her confess it, not now!

He'd said they were to make a fresh start, wipe the slate clean. Every child had a right to a close, loving family, the care of both parents, and he had a duty to provide it.

And that was how it was going to be. His decision. End of story. Their future and that of the coming child was all that mattered—unsullied by a knowledge he didn't want to have.

Thrusting the unwelcome and rare bout of introspection out of his head, he strode towards her. She was kneeling by the spring, her hands gliding slowly back and forth in the cool clear water. As he reached her she glanced up at him from beneath the wide brim of the straw hat he insisted she wear and smiled. Her smile touched his heart, turned it over. It always did.

'It's lovely! So cool!'

His heart twisted, the breath in his lungs tightening. The band of freckles across her neat little nose was more pronounced, and perspiration dewed her short upper lip. The blue of her eyes between those thick fringing lashes was clear and perfect. She was the loveliest thing he had ever seen.

Leaning forward, she cupped her hands in the water and sluiced it over her face in one graceful movement, then rose to her feet, gasping just a little as her hat tumbled off her head.

Her skin glistened. Droplets trickled onto the soft,

tempting skin between firm breasts that were partly exposed by the buttons she'd undone at the front of the sleeveless, cream-coloured fine cotton cropped top she was wearing. With him she was so uninhibited, her sexuality so natural. It blew his mind.

Instinctively, his hands went to her upper arms to steady her. He heard the tiny huff of expelled breath as her soft lips parted at his touch, felt the inevitable answering excitement tighten his body.

Those soft, full lips promised passion—the spectacular passion that neither of them could deny. He bent his head and touched them with his own, revelled in her immediate response. Driven as he always was with her, he parted his mouth from hers, going lower, to capture the crystal droplets that sparkled between her breasts. His hands followed. Hands and mouth.

His hunger for her was as intense as ever, but, mindful of the tiny life inside her, he was now more than ordinarily gentle as he lowered her to the cool green earth. Ignoring the way her body arched impatiently into his, he slowly removed her clothing, the fever grew in her beautiful eyes as fine tremors of tension rippled over her gorgeous nakedness when his hands, a whisper of motion, moved over her engorged, divine breasts, down over the slight curve of her tummy to rest, trembling now, on the springy nest of curls between her parted thighs.

He heard her near-desperate sigh of need just as he felt control slip away from him, and he breathed her name, thrusting with as much tenderness as he could find deep inside her as she wrapped her legs around his narrow hips in eager welcome.

* * *

Later—how much later Maddie neither knew nor cared—Dimitri moved in her arms, his own arms releasing her, the smile he gave her soft and satisfied. Precisely mirroring her own, she guessed.

It was always like this for them. They only had to touch each other and hot passion, driven need took over, Maddie dreamily acknowledged as he got to his feet, locating his stone-coloured chinos and getting into them with the economy of movement that was so much a part of him.

'We forgot the picnic. Xanthe will be irredeemably upset if we take it back untouched.' Humour warmed his fantastic amber eyes as they caressed her flushed features. 'Get dressed, *chrysi mou*, while I sort it out.'

Hoisting herself up on one elbow, the lush grass cool beneath her naked body, the slight breeze from the sea caressing her skin, she watched him move away to the lip of the green hollow where he had left the picnic bag Xanthe had filled for them this morning, missing his physical closeness already.

A too-familiar ache took possession of the region around her heart. His absence from her side, short-lived though it was, still felt like a pain.

When she was with him, close, talking, swimming, lazily exploring the island, touching, hands clasped, fingers entwined she could forget—lose herself in the wonder of him, even convince herself that he wanted a happy, stable marriage as much as she did, that she came first with him and always would.

And their frequent lovemaking had nothing to do with primal animal lust. At least to her it always seemed so. There was passion, yes, but tenderness too, a feeling of closeness, of a bond of deep love that couldn't be broken.

And yet…

Separated from him, even for a short while, at such a small physical distance, as she was now, she felt the doubts return, chilling her, eating into her. And the searing near-unbearable sorrow.

At the start of this week she had made up her mind to go along with his fresh-start dictate, because that would put him off guard, make it much easier for her to bring her plans to fruition, to make her bid for freedom when they returned to Athens and put herself and her coming baby right out of his and Irini's reach.

And now she knew that whatever she did her family's home and livelihood were safe, there was not a single thing to stop her.

But every hour that passed had made her hate that decision, despise herself for reaching it. It had been made with her head, but her heart had swiftly overruled her brain, leading her to fall ever more deeply in love with him, wanting, needing to be with him always.

The thought of leaving him broke her heart.

Aware that Dimitri had almost finished laying out the food he'd taken from the cooler-bag on the vivid scarlet cloth Xanthe had provided, Maddie pulled herself together and hurried into her discarded clothing.

And made her mind up.

Despite his firmly stated order that they were to forget she'd ever wanted to end their marriage and were never to speak of it, she was going to have to. Would tell him exactly what Irini had told her. He would, in any case, staunchly deny it, in view of her pregnancy. That was more than a strong possibility. But at least he would know the truth of what had lain behind her headlong flight from him and their marriage. She owed herself that much.

'Come, slowcoach! Remember our baby is hungry, even if you are not!'

That slow, magical smile of his made her poor heart flip over. He had straightened, was standing tall and proud now, hands on his narrow hips, bare feet planted firmly, a little apart, on the sun-warmed sparse grass at the top of the bank. He was shirtless, his magnificent upper body exposed, his skin sleek, tanned olive by the Greek sun. Much too touchable.

As usual his sexuality disorientated her, but her eyes shadowed as she walked towards him, and she knew she had to be strong and tell him the truth. But feed it in gradually, at the right opportunity. That way maybe she'd get the truth from him.

Blurting it out like a bolshie teenager might release the knot of tension that coiled painfully inside her whenever she thought of what Irini had told her, of his aunt's unpleasant comments about her gross un-suitability as a bride for her high-status nephew, re-membered the tone of his voice as he'd assured the other woman that he loved her.

Yes, getting it off her chest, where it festered, out into the open, might release that tension. But hurl the accusation at him and he'd instinctively and immedi-ately deny it.

She had to be more subtle than that.

That look was back in her eyes again, Dimitri noted, his own brows lowering in response as she sank onto the ground beside the lavish spread. Perhaps time and patience on his part would remove it. The thing to do, he assured himself firmly, was to concentrate on the positive side of their marriage. Forget everything else.

'How long can we stay here?' Even to her own ears her voice sounded overly-bright, she decided helplessly as she obeyed his hand gesture and helped herself to one of Xanthe's delicious stuffed vine leaves.

'Bored already?' Lightly said, but the thread of anxiety was there. He deplored it.

'Not at all. Just interested. It's so lovely here.' The morsel eaten, she reached for a tiny cheese pastry, not looking at him until he told her, 'Another two weeks, *pethi mou*, and then back to Athens to get the refurbishment of the nursery wing in hand, and get you to a top-notch gynaecologist. Sound good?'

Glancing at him then, she ached with love for him, felt an onslaught of longing that was frightening in its intensity. He was so compelling, so beautiful. The hard, tanned planes of his sculpted features, the soft sable hair, the sensual line of the mouth that promised and delivered heaven, the warm golden eyes.

The ache intensified. Two more weeks of ecstatic self-delusion and then…

Reaching forward, he opened a flask and filled two glasses, telling her, 'There are lemon trees here. Yiannis tends them and sells the ripe fruit on the mainland. And Xanthe makes the best lemonade you will ever have tasted.' He handed a glass to her and tipped his own against it. 'A toast. To our baby—may he or she live long and happy and much loved!'

Her eyes misting as the delicious chilled liquid slid down her parched throat, Maddie thought, He *does* want our child, more than anything. The only contentious issue was why.

He confirmed it when he told her smokily, 'I am filled with delight at the thought of the child you will give me, my Maddie.' Almost reverently he laid a hand on her tummy, surprising her with his words. 'Before our marriage we spoke of our desire for children, do you remember?'

Maddie dipped her head in silent acknowledgement. Not answering vocally because her throat had tightened too much to allow her to speak. Not looking at him, although she could feel his eyes on her.

Of course she remembered! He had been at pains to make sure she wanted his baby before the actual low-key ceremony because that had been the whole point of the exercise, hadn't it? And, gullible sucker that she'd been then, her head spinning at the way he'd romanced her, swept her off her usually firmly-grounded feet, she'd given him the answer he'd been looking for. Of course she wanted children—his children. The more the merrier!

If she'd turned round and told him that, no, she didn't want motherhood for at least ten years—if then, if ever—the wedding would never have taken place. He would have disappeared in a puff of smoke! Would it have happened that way? Dear God, she hoped not! But how could she know?

Then further confounded her when he said, with a sincerity she could not doubt, 'I confess I would like more than one child, but it's not a burning issue. Growing up, I missed my parents, wished they were still alive, wished I had brothers and sisters, a close family.'

Naked, powerful, sun-kissed shoulders lifted in a wry shrug. 'I guess that explains why I would like a whole gang of them!' His eyes held hers—soft eyes, soft mouth, soft smile. 'But I promise you, *chrysi mou*, there is no pressure. I might desire to give you at least three babies, but it will be for you and you alone to decide. If you decide that one pregnancy is enough for you, then he or she will be enough for me, too. This I promise.'

CHAPTER TEN

For several moments Maddie was silent. Her brain had gone numb. She couldn't think of a single thing to say. At least nothing that would verbalise her muddled feelings in any way that made some sort of sense.

Then, deep blue eyes wide and uncomprehending, she got out, 'Do you really mean that?'

If he did, it altered everything. In her favour? She was unsure of that. A puzzled frown appeared between her eyes. On the one hand her whole body tingled with the electric sting of unsquashable hope, while on the other suspicion of his motives made her heart shrivel.

'Of course I mean it!' Lean bronzed fingers brushed her tumbling fringe aside, gently caressing away the tiny frown line. 'Every word. It is for you to decide how large our family grows or how small it stays. What you wish is my wish too, my Maddie.'

The way he said her name made her heart turn over. As if it were spoken with devotion.

Devotion?

She might be a self-confessed hopeless sucker when he turned on the charm, but she really couldn't let herself believe that!

Once she had believed it with all her heart and soul. True, he had never actually said he loved her but she had truly believed he did. But everything was different now. Painfully, horribly different. And she would be a fool to forget it, to let herself be carried away by the prospect of paradise—the true and loving marriage he appeared to be offering.

But those brilliant dark-lashed eyes were mesmerising her. For the life of her she couldn't look away, even though she knew that every look, every soft word, might be hiding the harsh and ugly truth.

Unconsciously, she shook her head. 'And if I said I wanted you to give me at least six babies…' Her voice tailed off on an intake of breath at the enormity of her weak and instinctive compliance in his—his what?— Manipulation?

He smiled that slow, melting smile of his. 'Then I would rejoice in your maternal if excessive desire! But I would, I think, gently persuade you to consider three a happy number. I could not stand by and see you exhaust yourself by producing the beginnings of a football team! You are far too precious to me.'

The tips of his fingers trailed lightly from her cheekbones down to the side of her jaw. Maddie closed her eyes, lost in his touch. So gentle, so caring, so achingly seductive.

The trouble with loving someone as much as she loved Dimitri was the way you wanted to believe everything he said—clung onto it because it gave you hope, conveniently forgetting everything else, she thought to herself, appalled by the weak stupidity she seemed incapable of kicking into touch.

Her mouth dry, her heart thumping heavily, she steeled herself to broach the subject of his mistress. She couldn't afford to be confrontational, she knew that. An open attack on his motives—his downright wickedness—would only serve to elicit an immediate and vehement denial.

Aiming for a light, only vaguely interested tone, she made herself relax back against the arm he held around her waist, leaning into him, and ventured, 'I believe Irini is unable to have children?' She waited, feeling downright nauseous, for the telltale and instinctive tightening of his body that would tell her that her words had put him on his guard.

It didn't come as he bent his head to rest it against hers and confirmed, sounding completely relaxed and unfazed about it, 'No. An accident when she was a child.' She felt his minimal shrug. 'But it's not the tragedy it would be for most women, believe me. Irini has a positive aversion to children; she can't stand to be around them. There's not one maternal bone in her body, so her infertility is for the best in my opinion. Children need love more than anything else.'

His deep, exotically accented voice carried total conviction, Maddie recognized. A long-held conviction springing from his own childhood when he'd had precious little love and affection after the deaths of his parents when he was little more than a baby.

Her mouth ran dry as her heart picked up speed. He was genuinely as pleased as punch at the prospect of fatherhood. Surely he wouldn't contemplate giving any child of his into the care of a woman who plain didn't like children and wouldn't give the child the love he claimed was more important than anything?

Her head spinning with what her heart was telling her, she found herself looking up into his riveting, fantastic golden eyes as he shifted slightly and cupped her face in large, gentle hands.

For better or for worse. Logically, that was what she was accepting. Give him the children they both wanted and their marriage would remain important to him, *she* would be important to him.

And Irini? Well, as sure as night followed day Maddie couldn't see her hanging around while she, Maddie, produced gorgeous babies in the image of their charismatic father.

He loved the other woman—she herself had actually heard him express that emotion, so no way could she pretend it wasn't the case—and according to Amanda their names had been coupled, eventual marriage between them the general expectation, long before she, Maddie, had come on the scene.

Could she live with him, bear his children, knowing he still wanted the Greek woman, still loved her?

She could if she tried with everything in her to earn his love for herself. As the mother of his children she could make him forget the other woman, she answered herself, with the kind of elated determination she hadn't experienced for ages.

Feeling hypnotised by the warmth of those glinting, tawny lights, she felt her own eyes widen as her breathing fractured, the familiar tightening, the pooling of heat that surged to electrifying excitement swamping her as he murmured, 'Do we make tracks? Or do we spoil ourselves and make love again?'

'What do you think?' Her smile was luminous. Slim

arms reached for him as unstoppable response rocked through her. She simply couldn't stop loving him, wanting him, needing him. She might be stupid, walking into a trap with her eyes wide open, but this last week had taught her that she just couldn't help herself and that the trap, if there was one, could be rendered harmless by the strength of her love for him.

Even in the gathering twilight those thickly fringed eyes gleamed with molten gold as Dimitri offered, 'I forgot to ask—was your mother half as delighted as I was when you told her our news?'

Gathering her thoughts, Maddie forked up a morsel of the tender lamb in a delicious herby sauce Xanthe had prepared for the evening meal. The stone-paved terrace was lit with lanterns, and between them a candle in an amber glass bowl cast a warm glow over the delicate cast-iron table, set with dishes of salads and tiny almond cakes.

Reaching for her glass of iced water, Maddie let her eyes drift over his impressive frame. He was wearing a white shirt in the softest of cottons, tucked into a pair of narrow-fitting beat-up denim jeans, his dark hair just slightly rumpled, the evidence of emerging dark stubble shadowing his tough jawline.

In Athens he was never less than perfectly groomed, dressed in beautifully tailored dove-grey or light tan suits over pristine, exquisite shirts, and he could look intimidating. But here, like this, though still just as shatteringly handsome, he seemed warmer, wonderfully approachable.

Easy to talk to. 'I did get round to mentioning it—although I almost didn't,' she confessed, laying down her fork with a small sigh of repletion, listening to the soothing sound of the whisper of the sea as it caressed the shore far below, feeling more relaxed and at peace than she had felt in ages. 'I was too busy listening to her telling me how you bought the farm and put the deeds in their names. Why didn't you tell me?' she probed gently.

His own fork abandoned, Dimitri leant back, his features shadowed now. 'I thought you already knew—that your parents would have told you.'

Then, rough-edged, showing the first sign of discomfiture Maddie had ever seen in him, he leant forward again, fisting his hands on the top of the table, the gleam from the candle picking blue lights from his rumpled raven hair, and admitted, 'That's not true. I allowed you to believe that your parents' security depended solely on your agreement to come back to me, stay with me. When the truth is that I would have helped them regardless, because I like them and saw the injustice of what cold, big-business brains could do to small, good people with no possible means of self-defence.'

Helplessly in love with him, Maddie felt her heart twist behind her breast. Behind the tough business tycoon façade beat the generous heart of a truly good guy—a guy who would always put his family first and, in time, learn to stop loving Irini and begin to love her instead. At least that was what she was now determined on. It might take some time, but it would be worth waiting for.

Her heart melted further, until she thought that poor organ must resemble a pool of hot treacle, when he castigated, 'What I did was dishonourable! I threatened you, let that threat lie between us as the only way I could think of to make you come back to me! It was a despicable thing to do. So—'

Steeling himself, doing his best to appear to be relaxed over what in all honour had to be said, Dimitri leaned back in his seat again. For the first time in his adult life he was losing control, giving control over his happiness to another. Knowing it was what honour demanded didn't make it any easier.

'So the threat no longer exists,' he intoned heavily. 'It never did. You are free to make your own decisions about our marriage. You wanted to divorce me,' he reminded her with a studied calm that almost killed him in its achievement. 'If your reasons for wanting to end our marriage still exist—' a sudden, involuntary downward slash of one strongly crafted hand betrayed the inner tension he was trying to hide '—and whatever they are or were, I do not want to hear them, then you are free to do as you think fit.' He breathed in deeply, then stipulated forcefully, 'However, I would demand that you remain in Greece, that I have full visiting rights where our child is concerned.'

Silence hung, thick and spiky with expectation. Maddie's eyes were liquid sapphire, drenched with understanding. And awe.

This gorgeous man must have wanted her to return and take her place as his wife really badly for him to have done what he had himself named despicable and dishonourable. And it would have taken guts for him to come straight out and admit that the threats had never been real, to let it be known that the tough exterior hid a marshmallow centre.

It hadn't been about forcing her back to get her

pregnant and then rob her of her child. She knew that now. She was expecting their first baby, and already he was talking about having more children. With her. All this talk of freeing her to sue for divorce if she still wanted to was just his way of satisfying what he saw as his honour!

Happiness bubbled up inside her like a hot spring. Their future could be good. *Would* be good, she mentally emphasized. Because, on the evidence, maybe he'd already started to forget Irini and begun to fall a little in love with her before she'd left him and asked for a divorce. And he had to have been desperate for that not to happen, otherwise he wouldn't have compromised his so-valued honour and lied—in an oblique sort of way—about her parents being homeless if she dug her heels in and went for that divorce.

'Well?'

His voice was flat, but Maddie, attuned to every single thing about him, detected the underlying tension. She had kept the poor darling in suspense for far too long. Patience, as she well knew, wasn't a virtue that came easily to him.

She reached for his hand, felt his immediate response as he tightened his fingers around hers.

'Like you, I think children need both parents around on a regular basis,' she told him, with only the slightest emotional wobble in her voice she was pleased to note. 'So we stay married.'

She would be making a crucial mistake if she were to follow the impetuous need to fling herself at him and tell him she loved him to death, and that it would take a bulldozer to prise her away from him.

It was too early in their new relationship to load that onto him. He was still having to deal with his strong feelings for Irini, and if, as everything she had seen with her own eyes and heard with her own ears pointed to, they had been in love, and lovers, for ages, then at the moment that was enough for him to contend with.

He was having to face the fact that his love for the other woman was doomed. That his unsuitable wife was already pregnant. That because of his sense of what was right he could no longer contemplate handing over a large part of the coming child's care into the hands of a woman he had admitted possessed not a single maternal bone in her svelte and sexy body.

Maddie, fiddling with the stem of her glass, could only suppose that his passion for the other woman had so clouded his judgement that he had agreed to the cruel plan in the first place as being the only way out of the impasse.

And that his deep passion for another woman was something she was going to have to deal with in private if their marriage had any hope of succeeding. It was something that savaged her every time she thought about it and had to acknowledge that she was a very poor second best in his estimation.

Suddenly conscious of his silence, the quality of his concern-filled golden eyes, the tension stamped on his taut bone structure, she knew he was waiting for something more—some further assurance that she had changed her mind about leaving him and was now content to settle for being the mother of his children. She knew she had to lighten the atmosphere.

So, finding a teasing tone, she released the hand that still lay in his, ran the tips of her fingers across the slash of his rigid cheekbones and down to the corner of his sensual mouth, and told him, 'And, apart from the good parents bit, the sex is out of this world!' Inwardly she quailed at the lightness and sheer shallowness of that remark when she loved him so much it actually hurt, but she forced a smile, managed a tiny shrug. 'Why would I deprive myself of it?'

CHAPTER ELEVEN

ATHENS still sweltered in the late summer heat. It was
pointless wishing he and Maddie were still on the island,
safe and secluded. It smacked of cowardice, a head-in-
sand syndrome, and that went against all he was!

But he couldn't rid himself of the feeling that there
was tension in the air, because he could sense it—an unwelcome and unprecedented feeling that something cat-
astrophic was about to happen.

Dimitri closed the door to his aunt's quarters behind
him, and fought to control both his unease and his anger.

His father's sister had been back home for three days,
and each of those days had been peppered with increasingly petulant demands to know where Irini was.

'I haven't heard from her in weeks. I expected her to
come and welcome me home!' had been her latest com-
plaint. 'She's not answering her mobile phone, and
that's most unlike her,' she'd fretted. 'If her parents
know where she is, they're not saying. I can't imagine
what the big secret is! If anyone knows, you do! I know
just how close the two of you are and always will be,
despite your marrying a girl who's little better than a
peasant, with her eyes on your fortune!'

A man would have felt the full force of his fist at that, and known what it felt like to be flattened against the nearest wall!

As it was, his bitten out, 'If I ever hear you say one word against my wife again, or learn that you've spoken unpleasantly to her, then I shall forget the duty I owe you and ask you to leave my home,' had had to suffice.

Now he made a conscious effort to relax his rigid shoulders, unclench his teeth, calm down, and stride through the relative coolness of the house looking for Maddie. Not finding her, he bellowed to his house-keeper for information on where his wife was hiding.

He wouldn't have admitted it to a living soul, but leaving her, even for an hour or two, left him feeling wired-up, unable to forget that day—such an ordinary day, or so he'd thought—when he'd returned and dis-covered she'd left him.

Today, a crucial early-morning business meeting had necessitated his absence, and Alexandra had waylaid him on his return. And infuriated him!

He wasn't a fool. He could put two and two together as well as the next man. Since his aunt's return from Switzerland a subtle change had come over Maddie. She was strangely subdued, even with him, and that worried him. And in his aunt's presence, especially at shared mealtimes, she seemed to shrink into herself, as if trying to make herself invisible.

Couple that with the way she had seemed similarly subdued and withdrawn during the few weeks prior to the time when she'd shocked him rigid by demanding a divorce, and it didn't take a genius to work out that his aunt had been throwing a few poisoned darts in her direction!

Time to sort it out!

No one would get away with upsetting his wife while he had breath in his body!

On the arrival of the stout personage of his long-time housekeeper, he learned that Kyria Kouvaris was in the garden. He huffed out a long sigh of relief, mentally chiding himself for doubting her, for fearing that she might have broken her promise to stay with him, make their marriage work.

He who had feared nothing in the whole of his life, believing whole-heartedly that he could bend any circumstance to his will, overcome anything that life threw at him, had discovered his Achilles' heel!

She was reclining on a lounger beneath the shade of the vine arbour, a pristine folder held loosely in her hands, her eyes closed.

For a moment he allowed himself the sheer luxury of feasting his eyes on her. She wore a filmy sundress in a cool cream colour that drew attention to the honey-gold tan she had acquired on the island, the tiny shoe-string straps revealing the smooth perfection of her arms and shoulders, the soft fabric of the dress moulding those beautifully formed breasts, skimming her waist and flowing around her lovely legs.

You had to look very hard to detect the swelling of her tummy—something he allowed himself to do at leisure each time he stripped her willing body.

Abruptly he pulled himself together, his long mouth twisting wryly. He only had to see her to want her, and now was not the time!

He moved towards her. She felt his presence, turned

her head and smiled radiantly for him. 'You're back. Good! Come and see what we've got!'

Shifting into a sitting position, she moved her legs to one side, making room for him to perch on the end of the soft lounger.

Her eyes gleaming with pleasure, Maddie opened the classily presented folder. 'Look. It was delivered by hand this morning.' Spreading the enclosed papers around them, she revealed detailed sketches of the nursery Dimitri had commissioned from the team of top-flight designers he'd chosen with such care. 'It looks perfect. I love the colour scheme—pale lemon-yellow, off-white, and touches of that misty green—perfect for a baby boy or girl. And will you just look at that rocking horse? Should we give them the go-ahead to start work?'

'Of course.' Her delight was infectious. So easy to let himself get caught up in it, in the more than welcome return of the sunny smiles and easy chatter that had been markedly absent for the last few days.

But.

He collected the sketches and replaced them in the folder, then took her hands in his, his eyes serious, holding hers. 'Maddie, we'll look at them together later. Right now, I want you to tell me the truth. Has Aunt Alexandra said or done anything to upset you? Something's taken the spring out of your step since she returned. I know from experience that she has a vicious tongue when she feels like using it. And I promise you, if she has upset you and continues to do so, she will be asked to live elsewhere.'

Maddie's body clenched to stillness and her eyes smartly evaded his.

The truth? How could she?

Her joy in the morning fled. Gone was the snatched tranquillity out here, away from his aunt and the hurtful remarks the old lady had made on finding her breakfasting alone. The relaxation of the soft lounger in the welcome shade, the excitement over the plans for the nursery that had helped push the latest insult to the back of her mind faded.

'So you've got yourself pregnant? No doubt you're pleased with yourself for cementing your position as the wife of one of the wealthiest men in Greece! Well, don't make too many plans for a long-term future—I know my nephew better than you do. It won't last. He'll see through you and you'll be history!'

How could she tell him that his aunt hated her and lost no opportunity of letting her know it? The old lady had brought him up—probably done the best her intrinsically cold nature had let her, and looked on him as if he were her own son.

She couldn't in all conscience cause a family rift. And how would the old lady feel about being thrown out of the home that had been hers for so many years?

Much as she would prefer Aunt Alexandra's absence to her presence, she couldn't do it!

Conscious of his watchful silence, the increased pressure of his hands, she lifted her eyes to his and told him, trying to smile, 'There's no question of your aunt losing her home here with you. She'd be dreadfully hurt, so you mustn't even think of it! I'm a bit of a disappointment to her, that's all.' She shrugged, aiming to portray the subject's lack of importance. 'And it's understandable if you think about it, because, reading between the lines, I guess she secretly had her heart set on you marrying Irini. She's bound to be miffed because that didn't happen. Give her time and she'll get over it.'

That was as far as she could go. And if it caused him pain with the reminder that he had loved Irini for years but felt unable to marry her because of her infertility, she regretted it.

That rang true, Dimitri conceded heavily. Alexandra had doted on Irini since the day she was born, and *had* wanted to see her in Maddie's place. She probably did look on his poor darling as a usurper. But, 'There's more? Has she actually come out and said she finds you unwelcome?'

'No.'

It was horrible to lie to him. But the truth would hurt both him and his aunt. And for what? The relief of ridding herself of the old lady's insults and snide remarks? Seeing her banished would hang heavily on her conscience. Too great a cost.

It was time, more than time, that she stood her ground and refused to let Alexandra Kouvaris make her feel worse than worthless.

She found a reassuring tone. 'I guess your aunt doesn't make friends easily, but she'll come round after our baby's born—you'll see!' And if she didn't she would learn to live with it, ignore it.

'You're sure?'

Her eyes slid from his again, he noted. Her affirmative nod was ready. Too ready?

Releasing her hands, Dimitri stood. His shoulders tensed beneath the fine fabric of his smoothly tailored business suit. One of the first things that had drawn him to Maddie was her transparency. Hiding her emotions didn't come easily to her.

She was hiding something now. Something wild horses wouldn't drag from her.

But loving patience might?

Right now patience was a virtue he was struggling to achieve. He said, as evenly as he could, 'It's time for lunch. Bring the folder. We'll look at the plans in detail together.'

Misery engulfing her, Maddie swung her sandalled feet to the ground, gathering the folder of sketches and colour swatches that had earlier so delighted her.

He had sounded so flat. He was going away from her, distancing himself. Deep in the stark reminder of his lost true love?

Telling herself that she was going to have to live with the knowledge that she was second best, pretend she didn't know that savagely cutting fact for the sake of their long-term future, waiting for the gift she so longed for—the precious gift of his eventual love—she walked to where he was waiting for her.

Maddie jolted awake, naked beneath the thin cotton sheet. The house was silent as evening approached. Dimitri was no doubt still in his study, concentrating on the raft of paperwork that needed his attention—a fact he'd imparted when after lunch she'd pleaded a sudden and very real weariness and come up to their room to rest.

She had slept the whole afternoon away. Was sleep an escape mechanism? she pondered wryly, remembering how she been itching to get away from the lunch table. Away from the atmosphere.

Dimitri had been distant, as if he were lost in thought, and his aunt censorious when she, Maddie, had made the first approach of conciliation after their run-in

earlier, determined not to act like a wimp and let herself
be walked all over.

Passing the folder over to the old lady, she'd found
a smile. 'These are the designs for the new nursery.
What do you think? We'd value your opinion.'

Ignoring the folder—and the tentative peace
offering—Alexandra had replied repressively, 'One
doesn't read at meal-times. Besides, my opinion is unnecessary. My nephew wouldn't dream of using a
designer who did not cater to his impeccable taste.'

Another put-down.

Maddie had left the room, left them to it, the atmosphere brittle.

Swinging her feet to the floor now, she noted that her
slight headache had been joined by a dull ache in the
small of her back. She ignored both and headed for the
en suite bathroom and a quick shower. She would
freshen up, find something pretty to wear from the lavish
wardrobe Dimitri had provided after that party of unfond
memory when she'd first come to Athens as his bride.

She would find Dimitri and sparkle. Coax him out of
that distant mood—if he was still in it! She had recently
discovered that he liked her chatter. That, according to
him, she could charm the birds from the trees with it!

Did Irini babble on about this, that and everything
else? Or were their private conversations more serious,
more intense, centring on their love for each other? The
possibility of their marrying was now never to happen,
because Dimitri had gritted his teeth and settled for
second best for the sake of the family he was creating,
his belated sense of honour making him discard their
original plans.

And because the sex was good. More than good. Though he wouldn't confide *that* slice of information to Irini!

Furious with herself for her unacceptable bout of morbid introspection, she dragged the door of the hanging cupboard open and pulled out the first garment her hand encountered. A silk shift, the colour of cornflowers. Dimitri had said it matched the colour of her eyes.

Surely he was beginning to love her just a little? Or at the least feel fondness?

It wasn't too much to hope for, was it? Because it certainly felt that way. As if he meant to play a full and dedicated part in their marriage's fresh start.

As if he was now putting her needs and happiness first, relegating Irini and his love for her to the past. So, okay, he had gone all quiet and distant on her when what she'd said had forcibly reminded him of the love he had put away from him. That was to be expected. It was early days yet, and he was to be excused because he had done the right thing, decided to make their marriage work for the sake of their coming child. Talked of their having more children in the years to come.

Promising herself that she had to believe that, she brushed her hair until it fell in soft, silky curls and tendrils around her face, applied the minimum of make-up, and set out to run him to earth.

But he seemed to be missing. The house was silent, the atmosphere heavy, as if a storm were about to break. Maddie felt perspiration on her upper lip, between her breasts. The aggravating dull ache in the small of her back seemed to be getting more intense. She must have slept in a awkward position. Strained a muscle.

When Dimitri turned up she would suggest they eat out tonight—anything to get away, to be alone with him, out of reach of the woman who always made her feel so worthless.

Yet…

Running away from a problem wasn't her style. Or it had never used to be. Only since coming here as Dimitri's bride. Irini's poisonous revelations, the way his aunt lost no opportunity to drum the fact of her nephew's enormous wealth and high social standing down her throat, contrasting it with her own lowly status, the fact that she wasn't fit to touch the ground he walked on, had turned her into a cringing wimp!

Time to sort it out! Ignoring a sudden gripping sensation in her pelvis, she headed over the main hall, making for the door that led to Alexandra's quarters. She was determined to tell the old lady that the put-downs had to stop, to suggest they try to be friends. And if she couldn't manage that, then politeness and respect would do.

Her legs felt unaccountably heavy, slowing her progress, but through the open main door she glimpsed Dimitri, jeans and T-shirt-clad, approaching along the wide driveway. He must have been for one of the long walks he was so fond of.

About to put a spurt on, let herself into his aunt's quarters before he reached the house, because for the sake of family peace the conversation she was intent on having had to be completely private, she frowned in annoyance as the telephone on a rosewood hall table shrilled out imperatively.

She couldn't simply ignore it, she decided frustratedly. But there would be other opportunities to confront the old lady, she told herself as she lifted the receiver and gave her name.

'Oh—it's you! I need to speak to Dimitri. *Now!* Fetch him!'

Irini!

She sounded hysterical. Maddie's heart went into overdrive, constricting her breathing.

'I can give him a message,' she managed, more or less evenly. Had Dimitri broken the news that he was going to stick with his marriage? Was that why the other woman sounded so manic?

A series of what sounded like curses in her own language almost split Maddie's eardrum, then, on a wild crow of spite, 'I phoned Alexandra this afternoon. She tells me you're pregnant. So don't come the high and mighty with me! The moment you've given birth you'll be yesterday's wife—I warned you, remember?'

Speechless, Maddie felt the colour drain from her face. Was he *still* putting his love for Irini first? It couldn't be true. She wouldn't let it be true!

Aware for the first time of Dimitri's presence at her side, his questioning frown, she handed him the receiver and sagged back against the wall, fighting a tide of nausea as she heard him say tersely, 'Where are you calling from? Here in Athens?' He fell silent, listening intently to what the other woman was saying, those wide shoulders tensing. Then, 'I'll be with you in fifteen minutes. Do nothing. Promise me? Let me hear you say it!'

Her breathing shallow and fast, her skin turning clammy, Maddie struggled to come to terms with what she had heard. Irini had called, and as ever he would drop everything to go to her, be with her. The undeniable fact dealt her a body-blow, left her in mind-numbing shock.

The pain around her pelvis stabbed wickedly, and white-hot horror engulfed her at that precise moment. Was she about to lose her precious baby? It mustn't happen! She wouldn't let it!

Opening her mouth to alert him to the alarming possibility, she closed it again as he turned to her, his voice sounding as if it were in an echo chamber. 'I'm sorry, but I have to go. Don't wait dinner for me.'

He mustn't! She needed him! But he was already turning towards the open doorway again. Maddie blurted the first thing to come into her head. 'Don't go—I need you!' Panic accelerated her heartbeat. He must put her first, he *must*!

But he turned back to face her, and she was sure he wasn't actually seeing her. He couldn't wait to leave. 'I have to. Irini needs me. She's threatening—' He caught the words back between his teeth. 'One day I'll tell you why, I promise. But not now. I don't have time for this. I'm sorry.'

That did it. Cleared her brain. When Irini called he had no time for his wife. Ice-cold now, her mind crystal-clear, she stated, 'Leave now and I'll take the other option you mentioned. I'll leave this marriage.' And she meant it, even though she felt her knees might buckle beneath her at any moment.

While there had been hope that they had a chance of finding happiness together she had been willing to do everything in her power to make it happen. But she would *not* be second best to that hateful woman for the rest of her days!

Dimitri went still. 'I don't accept ultimatums. Know that about me. I made a promise. I'm not about to break it.'

The ice in his tone chilled her to the depths of her being, and then he lobbed over his shoulder, already walking away from her, 'If you can make such childish threats then our marriage can't count for much, can it? Think about it. We'll talk later.'

Her brain buzzed and fizzed with dizziness, and blackness claimed her just after she watched him walk out through the door.

CHAPTER TWELVE

DIMITRI left Maddie's gynaecologist with a terse word of thanks and strode out of his office, where he'd been given a reassuring update on her condition, and along the length of the wide hospital corridor to the private room where Maddie had been for the last two days.

Hating him? Lying there, frightened for their baby, fuming because he hadn't been at her side?

Or planning to carry out her threat to walk away from their marriage as soon as she was back on her feet?

He would never understand what went on inside her head! Until that ultimatum she'd thrown at him—in an inexplicable fit of pique, or so he had supposed at the time—everything had been more than fine between them as far as he knew.

As far as he knew!

His jaw clenched. The hidden thing! Her untold initial reason for asking for a divorce.

He had categorically refused to hear her tell him those reasons. Stubbornly not wanting to know, and just as stubbornly believing that he had no need to know something that might be a constant source of distaste and sorrow in the new start he had determined they embark upon.

Something on the lines of a greedy plan to gain her freedom and take him to the cleaners at the same time? A scenario his aunt had immediately hit on, and one that he, albeit reluctantly, had almost accepted, unable to see any other.

He hadn't wanted to know, had hated the thought of having to accept that the woman he adored saw him as little more than a gold-plated meal ticket.

Head in sand, or what?

His fault!

And now that she was again threatening to end their marriage, *it,* whatever it was, had to be forced out into the open.

At least she hadn't lost the baby. And, according to her doctor, provided she took things easily for the next two or three weeks, the remainder of her pregnancy should proceed without a hitch.

And come hell or high water he'd be around to make sure she and the baby were fine.

His lean, strong features grim, he paused as he approached the room she had been given, ran his fingers through his already rumpled hair, over his stubble-roughened chin, and mentally cursed Irini and her problems. Problems she'd landed on *him*, gaining his reluctant promise to tell no one else, hysterically vowing that the only way she'd agree to taking the professional help she so obviously needed was on hearing his promise that no one else should hear about it.

It had been young Eleni who had found Maddie crumpled on the floor two days ago, who'd rushed to alert the housekeeper, who had then had the presence of mind to phone for an ambulance.

Two days. Forty-eight long hours while his Maddie had suffered. Waiting, alone, in a fever of anxiety through a whole slew of tests to discover if the tiny life inside her was safe.

Two unforgivable days since his aunt had seen fit to stir herself, lift a phone to reach his mobile and tell him of the emergency!

Two days while he'd been pandering to the needy Irini, convincing her that life *was* worth living, that her threatened overdose was foolish talk, eventually persuading her that at long last her parents must be told of the drug problem she had vowed was sorted.

Had he had the slightest idea that his Maddie was in danger of losing their baby he would not have answered Irini's hysterical call for the help she'd always insisted he alone could give her.

His teeth clenched until his jaw ached.

Had he known what he knew now the wretched woman would have been left to sort her own problems out. But at the time—to his own deep shame—he had put what he had mentally named Maddie's tantrum down to her mysterious jealousy of the other woman.

Cursing himself to hell and back, he dragged in a deep breath, expelled it slowly, relaxed his tautly held shoulders and opened the door.

Propped up against the pillows, Maddie had another stab at concentrating on the magazine one of the nurses had given her to look at. But she still felt a little drowsy from the mild sedative she'd been given yesterday, to help her relax, and the magazine—Greek language, but glamorous fashion shots—couldn't hold her interest.

Besides, she couldn't imagine herself ever trying to shoehorn herself and what she'd always considered to be her over-generous curves into any of the skinny garments so enticingly displayed. They all seemed to be designed to be worn by the models pictured—walking skeletons! Women like Irini!

Despite her earlier good intentions, tears scalded her eyes. Dimitri hadn't even bothered to phone her and see how she was doing, let alone visit. Too bound up with that dreadful woman to give a single thought to his second best wife. Had it come down to this? That Irini was even more important to him than the fate of their baby? It certainly looked like it!

A lump the size of a house brick formed in her throat. She swallowed it angrily and scrubbed at her eyes with a corner of the cotton sheet.

Enough!

What had she promised herself?

That he wasn't worth a single tear and Irini wasn't worth so much as a glancing thought. That she would think about only really positive things. Her hand moved to rest gently on her tummy. Her baby was safe. Nothing else mattered.

Certainly not a low-life like her husband, with his sordid obsession with a stick insect!

As soon as she felt able she would take the second option he'd offered back on the island. Leave him. But she would return to England, pass the waiting time at her parents' new home, where her mother would pamper her and love her. And understand.

No way would she agree to his stipulation that she stay in Greece to enable him to have frequent and ongoing access to his child. Seeing him often would keep raw wounds open and bleeding. She wouldn't do it. It would have to be a clean and total break.

By flying to Irini's side when she, his wife, had pleaded with him to stay with her, he had forfeited any rights.

And if he decided to take her to court to challenge her right to custody she'd fight him down to the last breath in her body!

Oh, for pity's sake, calm down! she told herself. Getting in a state over an unworthy slimeball would do nothing but harm. Sinking back against the pillows, she closed her eyes and tried to visualise peaceful things, like gentle waves lapping on a soft shoreline, or tranquil woodland carpeted with bluebells that swayed in an early May breeze.

But all she could see was his face!

When she heard the door open she opened her eyes, expecting to encounter a nurse, come to take her blood pressure. Again. And opened them wider when she saw the real thing, not the image that seemed indelibly printed on her retina.

Had she had a missile heavier than a mere magazine she would have thrown it at his head! As it was, she had to be content with muttering fiercely, 'Go away!'

Dimitri had to summon all his reserves of self-control to stop himself striding over to her and enfolding her in arms that ached to do just that. Hold her close and never let her go.

She had every right to be angry. But she was over-wrought, and it was imperative that she stay calm. There were dark smudges beneath the blue brilliance of her eyes, and a new fragility marked her delicate skin. His throat tightened as his hands made fists at his sides.

'You have every right to be angry,' he verbalised, his voice steady, much against his expectations. 'I only learned of what had happened half an hour or so ago, when Aunt Alexandra decided she could be bothered to contact me. I have informed her that she has to make other living arrangements before the end of the month, if not sooner. Like today!'

Maddie's fingers clutched at the edges of the sheet. She met the golden glitter of his eyes with icy determination. 'That won't be necessary,' she said flatly. 'Since there's no need to pussyfoot around now, I can tell you the truth. Your aunt's hated and despised me since she first met me. But I won't be around for her to be less than kind to, will I? Our marriage is over—remember?'

Not while he had breath in his body! Dimitri bit back that slice of information. For the next two or three weeks Maddie had to be soothed, not rendered over-emotional through arguments and recriminations.

Schooling his hard features into a mask that verged on indifference, he reminded her, 'Nevertheless, I insist you return with me—home—where you can be guaranteed peace and quiet for the baby's sake. Just until you regain your strength and we know there will be no further problems.'

And while that was happening, while he saw she was wrapped in cotton wool, was pampered, treated as if she were made of the most delicate spun glass, he would get to the bottom of the unholy mess they seemed to have created between them.

'I have spoken to your doctor and he is sure everything will be fine now—provided you take things easily for the next few weeks. That I can guarantee. You are to be discharged this evening into my care. I will collect you at six,' he added, with measured cool.

He turned then, congratulating himself that he had handled that without even a hint of an emotion that might have set her off into a frenzy of telling him that she would go nowhere with him because their marriage was dead as a dodo.

But there was little joy in that achievement, and not even the sternest self-lecture could stop him turning back at the door, his voice riven with painful regret as he announced, 'Had I had the slightest idea that a miscarriage threatened I would have told Irini in no uncertain terms to sort her own problems out. I would not have left your side for one moment!'

She had done the right thing for her unborn child, Maddie assured herself for the umpteenth time. Not for her own sake, because seeing him, being around him, nearly tore her in two.

But haring back to England the moment she was discharged from hospital would have been an irresponsible thing to do the way things were. Hadn't she been told by the best gynaecologist money could buy that she needed regular check-ups, but most of all, rest and tranquillity?

She was getting rest in spades. But tranquillity?

For the last two weeks she'd been doing her best to achieve that enviable state.

Dimitri, too, seemed to be doing his best in that regard, she acknowledged, with a dismaying lack of satisfaction.

On her return from hospital he had flatly relayed the news that his aunt was now living with Irini's parents while she looked for a suitable apartment in town and engaged a companion. Other than that there had been nothing personal, nothing that touched on their past or their future.

She saw very little of him. He appeared briefly each morning while she breakfasted, to politely ask how she was feeling. Then again at the evening meal, which they shared, imparting snippets of general information—innocuous stuff, mostly, about his friends and business colleagues, which went in one ear and out of the other because, inevitably, she itched to discuss the future, to get her life sorted, fix the date of her departure for England.

But he had made sure that didn't happen, and she knew why. He was anxious for their baby. And all that talk of making their marriage work, the future children they might have together, had to have been a con trick to make her feel secure enough to stay with him until the birth, when he would have put his cruel plan into action.

The coming child and Irini came first with him, and always would. She was simply a disposable and distant second. He had said he wouldn't have dropped everything to be with that wretched woman, had he had the benefit of hindsight, but she wasn't about to believe that. When Irini called he would go, no matter what! Otherwise he would do anything, say anything, to make sure Maddie didn't get in a state of agitation and thereby, in his mind, threaten the wellbeing of their baby.

As if she could help it!

Because although she saw so little of him, was stuck

in an uncomfortable limbo, his hand was everywhere—and it churned her up!

There in the parcel of English novels by her favourite authors which had appeared as if by magic, in the gorgeous bouquets of flowers that graced the suite they had once shared, the bowls of fresh fruit and posies of blossoms that found their way to wherever in the house or gardens she opted to settle.

This morning, restless, she had walked the perimeter of the huge grounds. The weather was pleasantly cooler now, and the emphatic expert opinion, after her latest check-up the day before, was that everything was going along just fine, absolutely as it should. She was to get on with her life as normal. That made her unaccountably edgy. Almost as if she didn't want to leave him. When she knew darn well she did!

What had been totally unexpected had been Dimitri's reaction to the welcome news. He had stared at the doctor as if hearing something deeply unpalatable, his features assuming a chilling distance, and he had barely exchanged a word with her on the drive home, engrossed in private thoughts. And last night he hadn't dined with her as usual. The housekeeper had imparted the information that he had been unavoidably detained and that she wasn't to wait for him.

So what? She shrugged slim shoulders in an effort to put him right out of her mind as she came full circle, back to the terrace. She had the all-clear. There was now nothing to stop her leaving, making flight arrangements to take her back to England and away from him, making a new life for herself and her baby, leaving him to his obsessive passion for the stick insect!

Opting to rest on one of the loungers instead of going inside the house, she closed her eyes and waited for the inevitable.

Eleni with her tray! No doubt the staff had instructions to keep an eye on her. One of the gardeners would have relayed the information that she was back at base! Dimitri's orders, naturally. He wouldn't want her doing a disappearing act with her precious cargo.

Hearing footfalls, Maddie let her mouth curve in a smile. She had grown fond of the young Greek girl, and they had tentatively begun teaching each other their own languages. It could be hilarious, and provided a more than welcome respite from her tangled emotions where Dimitri was concerned.

Turning her head in the young girl's direction, Maddie opened her eyes—and her heart bumped to a standstill, then thundered on.

Him!

She never laid eyes on him between breakfast and the evening meal. And not always then. And now, as ever, his stupendous sexiness set off a totally unwanted leap of sensation deep in her pelvis, almost pulverising her with longing.

Hoisting herself up on her elbows, all thoughts of relaxation flying, she watched as he put a tray on a small glass-topped table within easy reach.

Coffee, for two, a plate of the little sweet cakes that were so delicious she was developing a needing-to-be-watched passion for them, the never absent small posy of flowers, and a bowl of fresh fruit.

She tensed. Speechless. Now was the perfect opportunity to put him in the picture regarding her set-in-stone decision to end their marriage. But the words wouldn't come. Her mind was in chaos.

When he sat on the end of the lounger she moved her legs sideways at the speed of light. Physical contact would make the chaos worse!

Turning to her, the force of his steely will holding her unwilling sapphire eyes, he stated flatly, 'Our child is no longer in any danger. That being the case, we have to talk. And I want the truth—the whole truth. I've been too blinkered to want to hear it. But now it's time.'

CHAPTER THIRTEEN

MADDIE'S heart leapt like a landed fish. Her hand lifted automatically to her breast, where she could feel it bumping through the fine white organza of her sleeveless top.

Why now, when everything was over between them? When she could walk away with some dignity, without laying her broken heart before him, suffering his scorn or—heaven forbid—his pity?

Yet—her brow furrowed with indecision—maybe telling him what she knew, had known for ages, would be a catharsis, a cleansing. Keeping it locked inside her, where it would fester for the rest of her life, would do her no good at all, deny her any kind of closure.

'Maddie?' he prompted. His voice was gentle. 'Tell me what made you demand a divorce all those weeks ago.'

A muscle in her throat jerked and her eyes slid away from his.

Dimitri knew he couldn't take it if she refused to give him any explanation, or told him that his suspicions had been right all along.

Whatever—he had to know why she was determined to end their marriage. 'When we agreed to make a fresh start, after we discovered you were carrying my child, I wouldn't let you tell me why you'd left me. I was wrong to insist that the slate had to be wiped clean. It was a form of cowardice and I'm not proud of that. I was desperate to keep you, to make you happy. I just wanted to start over.'

A sigh was wrenched from him before he stated, 'But the slate isn't clean, is it? Again you threaten to leave me, so the stain must still be there. So tell me. Is it money? I need to know.'

He enclosed her hand in his lean, bronzed one and his touch was fire in her veins. Maddie swung her feet to the ground and shot upright, dragging her hand from his.

She didn't need this! This instinctive reaction to his touch!

And she didn't want a pay-off. How could he think that? His wealth had never interested her. And now this demeaning physical reminder of the way he could make her feel, the agony of loving, wanting and needing him that she couldn't shake off—no matter how often and how staunchly she informed herself that she hated and despised him!

The trouble was, she knew herself too well. With him she had always found it so easy, so imperative, to give of herself, to respond. But she was not going to let herself fall into the abyss of blind love and yearning again!

She turned back to face him. He was standing now, and his tall, powerful physique gave her the feeling of being overwhelmed. Wrapping her arms self-protectively around her midriff, she met his eyes, determination in the sparkling blue.

But her mouth shook a little when she got out, 'We'd

been married for just a few days when Irini told me exactly why you'd picked me.'

'And?' His hands came down on her rigid shoulders.

He looked bemused. His strongly marked brows drawn together in a slight frown of incomprehension. Her spine stiffened until she thought it might splinter.

'Big hips, humble background. No-account,' she supplied, on a hiss of breath. 'The sort of dumb-cluck who wouldn't know how to fight you when you did what you meant to do.'

'*Pethi mou*—'

'Don't!' She wrenched away from him. Empty endearments she could do without! Fat tears scalded her face. With one swift movement he captured her waist and drew her back to him.

'Irini made these insults?'

His eyes challenged her, as if he believed she was lying. Or perhaps as if he couldn't believe his lover's stupidity in showing her hand so early in the game?

'Who else?' Maddie ground out, frustrated at his pretence of not knowing what she was on about. 'And for good measure she told me the rest of it! You're madly in love with each other but can't marry because she can't give you the heir you need!'

She was almost yelling now, incensed by the hurt she'd been dealt. 'So *bingo!* You'd get yourself a no-account wife, get her pregnant, and as soon as the child was born you'd take it and dump her. Goodbye, and thanks a bunch! And, hey! Know what? You'd be able to take the wife you *really* loved and wanted! So it's no good you trying to pretend you want me for anything other than the baby!'

Suddenly the fight drained out of her. She felt limp and utterly wretched.

Her head drooped. His hands tightened about her waist as he moved her back to the lounger. 'Sit. Before you fall down.'

Those strong, lean features might have been carved out of granite, Maddie registered as she did as she'd been told—sat, because she felt weak and empty and keeping upright suddenly seemed beyond her.

'So when did this—conversation—take place?' He sank down beside her. Much too close. She was far too aware of his body heat, the signature scent of him, all male, and faintly, cleanly lemony. It was sheer torture.

What did that matter now? Numbly, she considered his question. He was obviously intent on prising every last detail from her, and she really didn't want to talk about it any more. Why didn't he just face the fact that he'd been found out? Admit it and start negotiations— involving money, of course—to try and persuade her to hand her child over willingly?

Drained, Maddie passed a hand over her forehead. The skin felt tight. He was waiting, watching her intently. 'The meet-the-bride party you threw for your friends, remember?' She answered at last with listless resignation. Even thinking about that encounter turned her stomach, and talking about it with the man who was the co-instigator of all her humiliation and misery was a thousand times worse.

'Maddie—' Lean fingers cupped her chin, forcing her to meet his eyes. Shamefully, hers misted with tears. 'Why didn't you tell me?'

He wasn't denying it, she registered with helpless

misery. Had she wanted him to? Wanted him to force her to believe him so that she could go on living in a fool's paradise for just a little longer?

Appalled by her weakness, she twisted away from him, hauled herself together and admitted tersely, 'I wish I had! I'd been out on the terrace, hiding from those of the guests who looked at me as if I were some kind of strange peasant who'd wandered into a royal gala occasion by mistake! I was on my way back in, all fired-up. I was going to ask you if it was true. But I bumped into Amanda and she told me to cool it. She said Irini was a spiteful, malicious bitch and jealous. We'd only just got married, and she said if I went in there and caused a scene it would embarrass you in front of your classy guests and make you think I didn't trust you.'

Her fingers were pleating the white organza of her floaty skirt and, her head lowered, she muttered, 'I took her advice. And then it was too late.'

'Why?' Feeling shell-shocked Dimitri knew that Maddie's well-being, the reassurance he must give her, was the only thing stopping him marching out of there, dragging Irini back by the scruff of her neck and forcing her to get down on her knees and beg his darling's forgiveness for such monstrous lies.

'None of this rubbish is true,' he hastened to tell her, desperately trying to smother the fear that it might, as she'd said, be too late, that the damage done was irreparable. Those telling words *too late* echoed hollowly in his brain, and he took her restless hands in his.

'Isn't it?' She answered his repudiation flatly, almost without interest, as if his denials were worthless, not worth listening to.

Her hands lay limply within his. She hadn't the energy to drag them away, simply told him, 'Your aunt lost no opportunity to remind me that I wasn't fit to touch the ground you walked on. And between that and the way Irini took all your attention when she was around, and the way you'd insisted on a dead quiet wedding, as if you were ashamed of me, I lost all my self-confidence. It all seemed to add up—and that was really awful. So I couldn't tell you what I knew, what Irini had said to me, because I wouldn't be able to hide how very much you'd hurt me. I might not have your breeding, your social clout or your hefty bank balance. But I do have some pride!'

She gave a monumentally inelegant sniff, gathered herself and reminded him shakily, 'That last morning I came down and you were speaking to Irini on the phone. You said you loved her. That you'd be with her in minutes. I knew the worst then. It wasn't just a nasty niggle at the back of my mind. So I left. And how could I tell you why?' she blurted, her eyes brimming. 'Tell you how much I was hurting because I loved you to pieces and to you I was just a means to an end?'

By that admission she'd gone and betrayed herself, she recognised agonisingly. To make up for that too-telling slice of information, she blurted, 'Then you forced me to come back to you with a lie! And went on about how many children we'd have. So, sucker-like, I swallowed it. I decided you'd put what you felt for Irini behind you and settled for me because I could give you the family you wanted, and perhaps you were even getting just a bit fond of me.'

'Just a bit—' Dimitri began, astounded, hurt by her hurt.

She snapped his words off with an anguished, 'Shut up! I knew just what a fool I'd been because you went to her when I'd pleaded with you to stay with me. You point-blank refused. You went to her. And stayed with her. For two whole days. When I needed you!'

With a heartfelt groan Dimitri ground out, 'I will never forgive myself for that, *chrysi mou!* I can only plead ignorance of the facts!' Sweeping aside any objection she might make, he lifted her in his arms and strode through the vast house as if burdened with no more than a feather, bellowing for the housekeeper, issuing to that startled personage instructions for chilled fruit juice to be brought to their suite.

'I have much to explain—my case to plead,' he imparted briskly as he closed the door to the master bedroom with an Italian-crafted-leather-shod foot. 'And you, my sweetest delight, are overwrought when you must be calm,' he stated firmly, as he tenderly laid her stunned-into-compliance form on the bed, arranged pillows behind her head and removed her shoes.

Watching the assured movements of that perfectly honed body as he strode back to the door, flung it open and just stood there, waiting, clicking his fingers with an impatience which boded no good at all for any tardiness, Maddie decided she might as well stay just where she was. She was too emotionally wrung out to dredge up the strength to do anything else.

Taking the tray, dismissing the breathless housekeeper, Dimitri carried it to the bed-table, set it down, and poured chilled fruit juice into a tall glass.

His heart clenched with the pain of all that bitch had put Maddie through. The reason he'd misguidedly attributed to her desire to leave their marriage was contemptibly way off the mark.

She was lying where he'd left her, her soft mouth still mutinous. But her huge eyes were lost, haunted and hollow, the tissue-thin skin stretched tightly over her cheekbones, strain showing in her pallor.

He swallowed around the tightness in his throat. 'Drink this.' She was slow to react, but eventually she took the glass, took a mouthful, her teeth chattering against the glass, and handed it back. Sitting beside her, he fought the instinct to take her in his arms. Too soon. He needed all the patience at his command.

'Let me explain about Irini. You overheard me say I loved her. I do. Or did. After what you've told me I think I despise her.' Briefly, his long mouth compressed. 'As a child, after the deaths of my parents, Irini was the only playmate I was allowed to have. I came to look on her as a sister. Loved her as a sister. Nothing more. As she grew into her teens she seemed to rely on me more and more. I became the recipient of all her troubles—which were, as I told her, either of her own making or in her imagination.'

His brows drew down. 'With hindsight, I should have seen the growing problem. But I didn't. Her neediness brought out a half-exasperated protectiveness in me. I looked on her as the little sister I'd never had, remember?' He sighed, touched her hand just briefly with his. 'And now I will break a promise for the first time in my life, because you, your happiness, are far more important.'

Expression flickered in the blue depths of her eyes for the first time since he'd carried her up here. The beginnings of belief in him? He hoped so.

He captured both her unresistant hands. 'Irini has a drugs and drink problem. When I discovered this, I was appalled. I made her face up to the damage she was doing to herself, persuaded her to seek professional help. I booked her into a clinic here in Greece. In return she made me swear I would tell no one. Not her parents, and certainly not Aunt Alexandra, who has always doted on her and from whom she expects to inherit a large fortune,' he added drily. 'The phone call you overheard—well, that was a shock to me. She'd walked out of the clinic, was back in Athens and threatening to take an overdose. She was weeping, asking me if I loved her. I said I did—but as an exasperating and worrying little sister. I had no option but to try to reassure her, to go to her, persuade her to return to the clinic. I saw her into a taxi, then called into the office. I came home and you'd gone.'

'She was here when you brought me back from England. All over you like a second skin,' Maddie reminded him thinly.

Heartened by the first tangible sign that she'd been listening to a word he'd been saying, Dimitri agreed. 'So she was. And no one could have been more annoyed than I! But because of the state I knew she was in I had to treat her with kid gloves. Apparently she'd instructed the driver to bring her straight back to Athens, had arrived here and obviously heard from Aunt that you'd left me. It was what she wanted—though I had not the slightest inkling of that then. I knew something had to be settled. With her adamant hysterical refusal to let her parents know what was happening, the responsibility fell on me—even though it was the last thing I wanted or needed at that time. All I wanted, needed, was to put our marriage back on track.'

'Why?' Maddie hoisted herself up on her elbows. She felt stronger now, more alive, determined to get to the bottom of this unholy mess. His talk about Irini's problems, his brotherly love, did ring true. Yet… 'For the children I could give you?'

'Chrysi mou!' A ferocious little frown had gathered between her crystal-clear eyes. 'That you will give me children, God willing, is a blessing. But I will still love you until the day I die if that never happens,' he assured her emotionally, leaning forward to kiss the frown away, murmuring, 'You will get wrinkles!'

'And?' she got out chokily.

'I will love them. As I will always love everything about you.'

'You've never said the love word.' Maddie could hardly speak for the fluttering of unbearable hope that coursed through her. But could she trust it?

Cupping her face between his lean hands, he had the grace to look discomfited as he confessed, 'I never got the hang of it. I don't remember if my parents told me they loved me, but I know they must have done. After that, my life was a series of chilly rules and regulations.' He shrugged. Then beamed. 'But I'm telling you now! I fell fathoms deep that first day, remember? In the courtyard. You were wearing tatty old shorts, had smears of dirt on your lovely face. And freckles! I knew I was in love for the first time in my life, and vowed I would make you my wife!'

Somehow he was on the bed beside her, holding her, but Maddie wasn't going to let herself melt into him.

Instead, she said firmly, 'Do you promise on our child's life that all that stuff Irini told me wasn't true?'

Golden eyes widened. He looked as if she had asked him to swear the earth wasn't flat. He hoisted himself up on one elbow, his mouth quirking. 'My Maddie, sometimes I think you don't possess even one streak of logic in your beautiful head!' A gentle finger made an exploratory journey over the fullness of her lower lip.

'Think about it. If she and I had indeed made such absurdly Machiavellian plans, would she have alerted you to them right at the beginning of our marriage, when it would have ruined everything? Of course not!' He answered his own question with that well-remembered supreme self-assurance. 'She would have held her tongue, done and said nothing to make you suspicious, kept her fingers crossed, and hoped you remained in ignorance!'

'Oh!' Feeling monumentally stupid for not having worked that out for herself, she felt colour wash over her face.

Contrite at having pointed out her lack in the logic department, he amended, 'I can see why you fell for it, though. You implied you were feeling out of your depth at the time. And Aunt's spitefulness would have further dented your feelings of self-worth. For which she will go unforgiven. And as for Irini—well, my only guess is she saw you as a threat to what I can now see as her possessive feelings towards me. She wanted you out of my life and used the most far-fetched and ridiculous pack of lies I have ever heard! Amanda was quite right in insisting that Irini was just a spiteful, malicious woman. But wrong in advising you not to tell me.'

'Don't I know it?' Maddie mourned with real regret. And then forgot any further explanations as he kissed her.

He lifted his handsome head long minutes later to state thickly, 'Now everything is right between us? No more misgivings, doubts, *chrysi mou?*'

Everything inside her yearned to say *Yes, of course!* But there was still that raw spot, so recent it was capable of hurt. 'So what was so important that you had to go to her a couple of weeks ago, when I asked you to stay with me?'

He stilled. She thought he wasn't going to answer. Then he shrugged, his golden eyes rueful. 'I'm sorry. I don't like to be reminded of the worst failure of my life.' He took a long breath. 'I was absent for the week before we went to the island, remember?'

Maddie nodded speechlessly. How could she forget? She'd been convinced he and Irini were together.

'I was at the end of my tether,' he confessed impatiently, as if that state of affairs was anathema to him. 'You'd told me you wanted a divorce. I was determined to make you change your mind. On top of that, in refusing necessary treatment Irini had become a constant albatross around my neck. I needed all my energy to convince you to stay with me. So I decided to get her sorted out once and for all—get her off my back. I booked her into a clinic in California and personally escorted her there, thinking she'd be in good hands and far enough away to ensure she would think twice about just walking out.'

Anger darkened his eyes. 'But that is what the wretched woman did! She was back in Athens and again threatening to kill herself. I couldn't take the risk that she didn't mean it. I wouldn't have my worst enemy's death on my conscience, never mind the woman I'd always looked on as a needy little sister. It took me two days to convince her that her problems weren't over, as she claimed, and that her suicide threats were simply a cry for help. That I could no longer provide that help and her parents had to be told.' He sighed heavily. 'Apparently Aunt Alexandra was the first person she contacted when she got back to Athens. She learned that you were expecting our baby, and I guess that tipped her over the edge.'

He cupped her face in his hands and Maddie noticed the strain etched on his tight features, the set of his sensual mouth. 'I will never be able to get within two miles of that woman without wanting to throttle her!' His voice was roughened, the sexy accent more pronounced than she had ever heard it. 'She did you great harm. Can you ever forgive me for failing you when you most needed me?'

For answer Maddie leaned into him and wound her slender arms around his neck. 'I already have!' Her smile was radiant. He loved her, and she loved him to pieces! And the feared Irini was just an irritating thorn in his side! 'You didn't know what was happening to me. It had only just dawned on me—that I might be about to miscarry, I mean.' His fantastic eyes were beginning to lose that self-condemning harshness, so she pressed on, 'You were doing the honourable thing—looking out for someone in distress. I know you'd never understood why I disliked Irini—how could you? And when I threw that panicky ultimatum at you, naturally you decided I was throwing a jealous tantrum.'

He closed both arms tightly around her and she laid

her bright head against his shoulder and murmured, 'Try not to think too harshly of Irini. Her head must have been really messed up. After our marriage she could see her prop—you—being taken away so she lashed out at me.'

That fairy story had probably been wishful thinking. Irini had been in love with Dimitri for years, hanging on to his protective concern for her for grim life, because that was all he'd ever offered, privately hoping for his love. But Maddie wouldn't offer that piece of logic. Why burden him with it when in the past he had been unable to see what was right under his nose?

'You are too generous, *chrysi mou*. Every day, every hour, I love you more and more, until I think I will explode with it!'

She could feel his heart thumping against hers. Her breathing quickened. She could afford to be generous when she had the blessing of his love. When she knew he would avoid the other woman like the plague in future. She lifted her face to his, her eyes drenched with emotion. 'I love you more than I can ever tell you,' she confessed.

His beautiful eyes were intense. 'Then our marriage is safe?'

'As the Bank of England! Please kiss me!'

So he did. He took her lips with an aching tenderness that brought tears of joy to her eyes and she wriggled closer to him and felt his body leap at the contact. The kiss deepened until she quivered with longing and just had to lie back against the pillows, making sure he came with her. In no time at all he was reverently sliding the fabric of her top away from her shoulders, until something stilled his hands and made his voice emerge on a determined tone.

'Did you really mind about having a quiet wedding? If I deprived you, then I will arrange a blessing—a fabulous designer gown, bridesmaids, flowers and bells, a zillion guests in fancy hats! Just say the word!'

Giggling at his extravagance, Maddie ran her fingers through his rumpled hair. 'I *loved* our wedding! I don't go a bundle on splashy displays. And I promise I only threw that at you because your aunt tried to use it to make me feel inferior!'

Pushing her tumbling fringe out of her eyes, he kissed her again, briefly, then held her eyes with his and said ruefully, 'If I'm honest, then I have to tell you that had I had my way we would have had a wedding to rival royalty! I wanted to show you off to the whole world! But…' His lips compressed. 'Your father is the most stubborn of men.' His sudden smile dazzled her. 'I think you inherited the pride gene from him! Imagine my dilemma when, as father of the bride, he insisted that he should pay for the wedding—every last penny. I guessed he didn't have money to throw around, so what could I do but settle for the most low-key celebration known to man and announce that that was what we wanted—much though it went against the grain?'

'Not just gorgeous, but sensitive and caring! Oh, Dimitri, I do love you!' She tipped her head to drop kisses along his tough jawline. 'Now, shut up, do! Stop tormenting me—and carry on where you left off!'

So he did. To her complete satisfaction. And his.

Maddie walked up through the gardens. Sweltering. Her knees were grubby where she'd been kneeling in the earth. Her face would be smeared with perspiration and dirt, too. But she couldn't be happier. Her work on the neglected hollow of land at the far end of the grounds had afforded her great satisfaction, and Dimitri had looked on with interest and pride as she'd transformed it into an oasis of perfumed lilies, jasmine and lavender. The loveliest of places to sit in the cool of the evening, talking, laughing and relaxing together over a shared bottle of wine.

She couldn't be happier if she tried, she reflected as, reaching the terrace, she saw her darling little Nik wriggle down from Eleni's arms and scamper towards her on his sturdy little legs.

Lifting him up, she cuddled him closely. At sixteen months old he showed definite promise of becoming the spitting image of his handsome father.

Dismissing the smiling Eleni in the Greek she had been at pains to acquire, she dropped a kiss on the end of Nik's little nose and reverted to English, 'Time for your afternoon nap, sweetheart. And Daddy will be back to play with you after tea.'

Dimitri had proved to be a very hands-on father, and her heart wriggled inside her as she thought about the news she had to give him. But telling him he was about to be a father again would wait until they were on their special island tomorrow. And this year they would be taking Nik, which would be wonderful.

Alerted, as she always was, she looked up to see Dimitri emerging into the sunlight from the cool interior of the house. Wearing an immaculate dove-grey business suit, he was handsome as all-get-out. And when he gave her that slow, sexy smile of his and remarked, 'Tatty old shorts, dirty face. And freckles,' her heart just turned to treacle.

He loved her to bits, no matter how dishevelled she looked. And tonight she would be in a completely different guise. Wearing a sleek and beautiful designer gown, jewels at her throat, her hair tamed and piled on top of her head, she would be ready to mingle with the great and the good at the glittering charity gala that marked the end of the social season before everyone who was anyone fled Athens for cooler climes.

Because Dimitri treated her like a princess her self-confidence had returned in spades, and she was comfortable in any company.

Their eyes held as he took his excited little son into his arms and told her, 'I'll settle him for his nap while you get ready to take a shower. Then I'll join you. I've got the feeling that some pretty extensive work with a soapy hand is called for.'

Meeting the devilment in those fabulous gold eyes turned her grubby knees to water, and, in a fever of excitement, it was all she could do to get up to their room, where she stripped off and felt her breasts tighten in anticipation. The liquid, wanton heat pooling between her thighs was sizzling, the sizzling intensifying a thousandfold as he walked in to join her.

His tie had been discarded, and he'd left his suit jacket somewhere, and his lean hands were already dealing with the buttons of his pristine shirt as his eyes drifted over her with possessive intent and he said, 'Serious soapy attention, indeed...'

THE GREEK TYCOON'S
INNOCENT MISTRESS

BY
KATHRYN ROSS

Kathryn Ross was born in Zambia, where her parents happened to live at that time. Educated in Ireland and England, she now lives in a village near Blackpool, Lancashire. Kathryn is a professional beauty therapist but writing is her first love. As a child she wrote adventure stories, and at thirteen was editor of her school magazine. Happily, ten writing years later, DESIGNED WITH LOVE was accepted by Mills & Boon. A romantic Sagittarian, she loves travelling to exotic locations.

CHAPTER ONE

NICHOLAS ZENTENAS found his quarry as soon as he stepped into the room. Although the wedding reception was in full swing, the ballroom crowded, he spotted her without difficulty. She was standing slightly apart from the mass of people between the bar area and the dance floor and there was something about her isolation amidst the crowds that drew him.

For a moment he was content to stand just inside the open French windows and observe her. The bright disco lights swirled around the darkness of the room, playing over her long blonde hair and highlighting her in a myriad of different colours that washed over her shapely figure in the long green dress.

She turned slightly and suddenly their eyes connected. He was momentarily taken aback by how beautiful she was. The snapshots taken by his private detective hadn't done her justice.

Their eyes held for what seemed like a long time but was probably only seconds. He felt a sudden fierce buzz of adrenalin. The fact that she was desirable was going to make his task all the more pleasurable.

Cat dropped her eyes from his as her friends returned to her side. She was used to men looking at her but there was something about this man's dark steady gaze that was different. It wasn't just the fact that he was simply gorgeous; it was the way he had looked at her—like a hunter weighing up his prey. She had felt suddenly vulnerable and breathless all at the same time. It was a sensation she had never experienced before and it had left her strangely shaken. Even now, surrounded by the friendly chatter of her colleagues, she could still feel the heavy sensation of her pulse-beat as if it were in tune with the bass of the music pumping around her.

She took a long drink of her water and tried to dismiss the feeling. Maybe she was just hot. London was sweltering in a heatwave and, even though it was nearing midnight and all the doors and windows of the room were open, the temperature had to be around thirty degrees.

Maybe she was also a little too wary of men at the moment, she acknowledged to herself wryly. Recently she had found herself carefully judging every man who spoke to her, wondering if they had been sent by her father or half brother. Crazy really, but the closer she got to her twenty-first birthday the worse these feelings of distrust and anxiety became. Her birthday was now a little under three months away and she couldn't wait for it to pass, she just wanted to get it over with and forget it.

She shouldn't feel like this, she thought sadly. A twenty-first should be something to look forward to, a time of happy family celebrations. If her mother had been alive she felt sure things would be different. But the problem was that the only family she had left was her father and half-brother Michael, and both of them had their minds solely on the money she could inherit if she fulfilled the terms of her grandfather's will and got married before the date of this birthday. She was just a pawn as far as they were concerned. They wanted to move her one step forward towards marriage and then *checkmate*, all the money would come pouring in. Well, she wasn't going to marry for money; she would go to hell before she went along with their plans and she had told them so quite implacably, not that they had paid her any attention.

Why couldn't her father's main concern have been for her happiness—surely it wasn't too much to ask?

The question stirred up the shadows of the past. She felt them inside her now…felt the acute loneliness that had stalked her since childhood. It was amazing how that feeling was never far away, even in a room filled with people. It was the curse of the McKenzie money.

'Hey, Cat, do you fancy dancing?' Some friends caught hold of her on their way towards the dance floor.

Thankful for the interruption to her thoughts, she put her glass down and allowed herself to be drawn along with them out on to the packed floor.

For a while Cat forgot everything and became absorbed by the music. She was here with the rest of the workforce from the advertising company where she had worked for the last three months to celebrate their colleagues Claire and Martin's wedding. The couple had got married in the Caribbean last week and now they were partying in style at this top Knightsbridge hotel. Cat could see them on the centre of the floor, entwined in each other's arms, dancing slowly even though the beat was fast.

That was how love should be, she thought wistfully. Maybe one day she would meet someone who made her feel like that. Someone who loved her, someone she could trust. She had thought that she had met that person last year. Ryan Malone had been handsome and charming and little by little she had found herself falling under his spell, had started to think that this was the real thing. Then she had discovered that Ryan was in fact a business associate of her brother's and that all he was interested in was wedding her for her inheritance. That discovery still hurt. It had made her more wary than ever about trusting men.

As she turned something made her look distractedly back towards the doors, searching for the man who had been watching her earlier. She had the distinct feeling that his eyes were still on her. He wasn't there and she couldn't see him in the room. She was obviously imagining things. She tried to dismiss the feeling and concentrate on the music but she couldn't get the memory of that dark, broodingly intense gaze out of her mind.

Nicholas watched Cat from his vantage point. She was a good dancer, her movements were lissom and she had a natural rhythm that was very sexy. He had heard it said somewhere that if you were good at dancing you were good at sex. Maybe later he would test that theory; he was looking forward to feeling her move sensuously beneath him. Possessing that curvaceous body was going to be a real pleasure.

However he was deliberately not making a move on her too soon. Instead he was carefully monitoring the situation to see who approached her. He wanted to know if her father or brother had any spies in the camp. He knew they would want to protect their golden heiress. He wouldn't even have put it past them to line up a suitor for her. They had three months to secure the inheritance. He knew that Cat was just as hungry for money as the rest of her family and no doubt the three of them would be determinedly working towards getting their hands on the cash.

Well, Nicholas had different ideas. While he had breath left in his body he wasn't going to allow them to get their hands on that money. He knew it would only be used to wreak more destruction in people's lives.

The very name McKenzie made anger and distaste shoot through his blood like venom from a snake bite. Carter

McKenzie was a snake, he thought acidly, a sly conniving, dishonest reptile. Eight years ago Nicholas had made the mistake of trusting the man with a land deal. Carter had lied to him and dishonestly duped him. As a consequence Nicholas had lost a lot of money trying to put things right, but what really infuriated him was the fact that he had almost lost something far more precious than money. Carter had tried to rob him of his reputation...and had almost succeeded.

It had been a lesson hard learnt. Since then Nicholas had built his own empire and was wealthy beyond his wildest expectations, but he hadn't forgotten his old enemy. He had bided his time, watched and waited from afar. During that time he had noted that Carter McKenzie's son and daughter were exactly the same as their father. Michael McKenzie certainly hadn't broken the mould, he was no more than a con artist, and Catherine... Well, she had financed them through one shady deal after another, was complicit in their greed.

According to his sources, there wasn't a lot of money left in the trust fund that she had been using up until now, and without the rest of the McKenzie inheritance she wouldn't be able to fund them for much longer.

Roll on that day, Nicholas thought now with determination. Because he intended to step in, sweep Catherine McKenzie off her feet and take what was theirs. Carter was going to rue the day he had ever crossed him. Revenge was going to be very sweet.

Cat left the dance floor and with quiet resolution he moved after her, surprised to see that she was heading for the main exit with speed. It was as if she was suddenly running away from something. He lengthened his stride and followed her.

A few minutes later Cat was standing outside in the heat of the night. The London street was strangely deserted; even the doorman who had been on duty at the hotel earlier was gone.

She felt better being away from the crowds. The panic that had gripped her on the dance floor seemed absurd now. Of course there had been no one watching her. Even so, all she wanted to do now was get back to the quiet safety of her flat.

There was a taxi rank across the road and she had thought she would just be able to jump into a cab straight away, but the rank was deserted. A gentle breeze rustled through the trees in the park opposite but apart from that there was an eerie silence. Cat delved into her handbag and took out her phone to call for a taxi. Then she turned to go back into the hotel to wait.

It was as she turned around that she bumped into a youth wearing jeans and a T-shirt. For a moment she thought it was her mistake and was almost about to apologise to him, tell him she hadn't seen him. But then he pushed her hard against the wrought iron railings and grabbed for her handbag and phone. Shock rushed through her as she realized she was being robbed.

Her phone was torn easily from her grasp, but instinctively she held on to the straps of her bag and for a moment a struggle ensued. She had a fleeting glimpse of his face; then the bag was wrenched away and he turned to run. He didn't get very far, a second later he had fallen heavily on the pavement. She heard the thud of his body and then the sound of her phone and the contents of her bag clattering across the concrete.

It was only when a dark shape detached itself from the shadows that she realized someone had tripped him up.

'I wouldn't push my luck if I were you.' A foot landed on the man's wrist as he attempted to pick up her purse. 'The police are on their way.'

The youth didn't need telling twice, he was up on his feet in a second and running away, his footsteps echoing down the empty street.

'Are you all right?' Her rescuer bent to pick up her belongings. Cat noticed distractedly that he sounded calm and that there was a hint of a foreign accent in his deep tone. As he straightened and looked over at her she saw his face clearly in the street light. Dark intense eyes met hers. It was the man who had been watching her earlier.

She guessed that he would be about thirty-two. His hair was raven-dark, thick and straight. He was very handsome but not in a conventional sense, more in a dangerous, hard way. Everything about him, from the molten dark eyes to the sensual curve of his lips, spoke of power and control.

Aware that he was waiting for her to answer him, she hastily pulled herself together. 'Yes, I think so. Thank you for helping me.'

'You shouldn't have fought him for your bag. You could have been hurt,' he told her bluntly. 'Your life is more important than mere possessions.'

He was right. The realization of how much worse this could have been was just starting to sink in. As she reached to take the bag he held out to her, her hand trembled slightly.

'Come on, let's get you inside.' The hard edge in his tone softened slightly, but the arm he placed at her back was firm.

Cat didn't try to pull away; instead she allowed him to guide her back into the light and security of the hotel. There was a strength about him that was almost overwhelming and she was aware of his hand against her skin in a way that stirred up a fierce shiver of tension inside her. It was a feeling she couldn't quite comprehend. After all, she was safe now…wasn't she?

'Mr Zentenas, is everything all right?' A receptionist looked over at them as they stepped into the foyer.

Cat noticed that she knew his name; she also noticed that as he spoke people jumped to attention. The manager of the hotel appeared, the police were phoned and then abruptly she was being swept away from everyone towards the lifts.

'You can wait for the police upstairs in my private suite.'

It wasn't an invitation; it was more of an order. The doors closed and suddenly they were alone in a very confined space.

She glanced across and met his gaze and once more her senses prickled with awareness. It was hard to identify the feelings he stirred inside her. He was generating something deeper than just the usual feeling of wariness she experienced around men.

She couldn't understand why a total stranger should have such a profound effect on her senses. Maybe it was just the fact that he was exceptionally handsome in a dark Mediterranean kind of way. Perhaps it was the way he looked at her as if he were trying to read the secrets of her soul.

He pressed the button for the top floor and there was silence between them as the lift started its ascent.

Nicholas watched as she leaned her head back against the mirrored interior. She looked pale and fragile and young. Her eyes were an almost impossible shade of jade-green as she looked up at him.

She wasn't what he had been expecting, and that threw him. He certainly hadn't imagined for one minute that he would have protective feelings for her. They had struck from nowhere when he had handed back her possessions, and he had been annoyed by the momentary weakness, had shrugged it off with determination. This was Carter McKenzie's daughter, he reminded himself fiercely, and she was well able for anything… He knew for a fact that she was as conniving and sharp as her family. He had read the reports on her and he wouldn't allow himself to be swayed from his mission of revenge by her deceptive air of vulnerability.

Cat took a deep breath and tried to pull herself together. 'This is…er…very kind of you…' She sought to break the silence and the tension.

'It's my pleasure.' The words were silky smooth.

Was it her imagination or was there a cynical edge to his expression, a harsh coldness?

'I saw you at the wedding reception earlier.' Her eyes narrowed as she looked at him now. 'Do you know Martin and Claire?'

'No.'

The nonchalant admission rang alarm bells. Had her first instincts been correct; was he someone her brother had sent to approach her?

'Why were you at the reception?'

'Because, as the owner of this hotel, I can go where I please.'

'Oh! Oh, I see.' Now that she thought about it, the air of authority that surrounded him was blatantly apparent. She felt foolish in the extreme for imagining her brother had sent him. If he owned this hotel he was obviously a very rich and powerful man, not the kind of person to do anyone's bidding.

'I'm Nicholas Zentenas.' He introduced himself smoothly and then searched her face for any sign that the name was familiar to her. Eight years ago he had been her father's business partner and, although he had never met Catherine McKenzie, she could have known his name.

If she did, she didn't betray the fact even by the flicker of an eyelash.

'Cat McKenzie.' She extended her hand towards him.

He hesitated before taking it, but when he did the firm touch of his skin against hers made little shivers of electricity run through her.

Her eyes locked with the coffee darkness of his and she wondered if he could feel the fierce sensual chemistry that swirled between them, or whether it was just in her mind.

Shakily she pulled away from him, glad that the lift doors opened, freeing her from the intensity of the situation.

Nicholas smiled to himself as he followed her out into his suite. So far the evening was going well for him.

Obviously she had no idea who he was.

He'd intended to track her down next week, as he knew her father would be out of the country then and therefore the risk of discovery was smaller. But as soon as his private detective had told him that Cat would be attending a wedding reception at one of his hotels he had brought his plans forward and had flown in from Athens this afternoon.

He was glad he had taken the risk now. Time was of the essence anyway.

The thief striking outside had been most fortuitous. The fact that Cat was so gorgeous he ached to bed her, even more so.

Revenge was going to be so easy.

His fish was hooked; all he had to do now was reel her in.

CHAPTER TWO

HIS hotel suite was more like a penthouse apartment. Ultra modern in design, it had black terrazzo floors with circular white sofas positioned to take full advantage of the glittering view out across London.

'This is a fabulous place.' Cat walked across towards the window to look out, her gaze taking in the floodlit rooftop garden and the swimming pool.

'Yes, not bad,' Nicholas agreed. But, as he moved to stand next to her, his eyes were on her rather than the view. The green silk material of her dress moulded to the slender curves of her body. She had a very desirable shape—a waist he could probably span with his hands and breasts that were ripe and ready for a man's mouth to explore. The mere thought of having that pleasure made him harden. 'I keep a suite like this at all of my hotels; it serves well for business purposes, although, as I travel so much they are only used on the rarest of occasions.'

'So where do you call home?' She looked up at him curiously.

The name Cat suited her, he thought, she had the intense gold-green eyes of a cat, almond shaped, somehow bewitching. 'I have a house on the island of Crete.'

'You're Greek.' It was an observation rather than a question and he just inclined his head.

'Crete is very beautiful,' Cat reflected softly.

'You've been there?'

'Yes, my grandfather owned a villa just outside Xania and I spent a few family holidays there when I was young.' For a moment she remembered the sparkling beauty of that white mansion overlooking the sea. She had loved her summers there with her grandfather, had felt surrounded by love and happiness. Then the accident had happened and her mother had died. She had been only ten years old but from the day that her father's car had spun out of control on that coast road everything in her life had spun around too. Crete had stopped being a place of happy memories.

Nicholas watched as her face clouded with some dark emotion and for some reason he found himself wanting to reach out to her and soothe the shadows away. 'Have you been back there recently?' he asked softly.

Cat didn't even want to think about her visit there last year. Her father had prevailed upon her to bail her brother out of a business deal that had gone wrong. When she had got there she had discovered that, far from something going wrong, Michael had deliberately set up a very shady deal. It had been an unpleasant episode and a shock to learn how low Michael could stoop. She had spent the week tracing the people he had conned and giving them their money back.

What was that old saying? You can choose your friends but you can't choose your family? She ran a hand distractedly through her hair.

Nicholas saw her brief hesitation, and then she seemed to gather herself together. 'I've no time for holidays these days.'

She hadn't lied, Nicholas noted, she had just skipped over the truth. His sources had told him she had been back to Crete last year to financially back her brother in one of his deals. His private detective had taken photographs of her coolly visiting the victims of the scam to lend her brother more credibility. A little later, with Cat safely back in London, they had cleaned up on an even bigger con. He really needed to remember that, despite her air of delicate vulnerability, she was a true McKenzie, he told himself firmly. They all seemed to have a knack for lying by omission. The reminder strengthened his resolve.

Cat was surprised to notice a harsh glitter in the dark eyes that raked over her now. It made a shiver run through her, as if someone had just walked over her grave.

'You should go back when you get a chance,' he said, turning away.

The lightness of his tone belied that fiercely intense look, making Cat wonder if she had imagined it.

'I'm going to have a whisky. Can I get you a drink?' he asked nonchalantly. 'A brandy, perhaps; they say it's good for shock.'

Of course she had imagined it, she thought, relaxing. 'No, I'm OK, thank you.'

'You're feeling better now, I take it.'

'I feel more embarrassed than anything else.'

'Embarrassed?' One dark eyebrow rose wryly.

'For having caused so much of a fuss. I should have just gone home. Nothing has been stolen from me and the police aren't going to achieve much; the man is long gone.'

'That's not the point. They might catch him and that would save someone else going through a similar ordeal.'

'I suppose so.'

Her eyes followed him contemplatively as he poured himself his drink and then walked back towards her. The dark suit he wore looked expensive; it sat well on his broad-shouldered frame. She couldn't help but notice that he had a very impressive physique; lean and well honed, he gave the impression of someone who could handle himself in any situation.

There was no denying the fact that she found him extremely attractive. But he wasn't her type, she told herself firmly. Too much money and power was a turn-off for her. She had grown up around wealth and she hadn't liked it, hadn't liked the traits it brought out in people. He was probably arrogant—went after what he wanted and always got it. And there was an air of danger about him that made her feel intensely unsure of him.

But he was overwhelmingly handsome; her senses pressed the point as he reached her side. She couldn't ever remember feeling an instant magnetism like this before.

He seemed to be looking at her very intently. Although he wasn't physically touching her, she suddenly felt aware of an intimacy about the situation. She could almost feel his eyes moving over her face, lingering on her lips. Subconsciously she moistened them, her heart starting to thud erratically against her chest.

As his eyes moved lower she felt her breasts tighten against the satin of her dress. It was the weirdest sensation. No matter how sensibly she tried to tell herself that he wasn't her type, her body seemed to be paying no attention whatsoever. The heat of sexual desire was curling inside her with fierce intensity. She wanted him to touch her…kiss her. In fact, more than that, he made her long for an intimacy she had never known before.

She swallowed hard and wrenched her eyes away from him. This was craziness. 'I seem to be taking up a lot of your time.' She hoped she didn't sound as breathless as she felt. 'I wonder how long it will be before the police arrive?'

'It's Friday night and the call wasn't an emergency.' He shrugged.

'Maybe I should just go.' She tried to think sensibly, but she knew it was panic that was driving her. Nicholas Zentenas was having the strangest effect on her and if she stayed around him she might do something she would regret. She opened her bag to take out her mobile phone and, as she did, she noticed that her keys were missing.

'Something wrong?' Nicholas watched impassively as she scrabbled frantically through the contents of her bag.

'My keys aren't here!'

'I picked everything up from the street,' Nicholas said calmly.

'But I'm locked out now! And I don't have a spare key anywhere.'

'Well…let's see… You can get your locks changed first thing tomorrow and in the meantime you can stay here.' He made the offer in a nonchalant, offhand way.

She watched as he took a sip of his drink and put it down on the table beside him. 'That's very kind of you! But I know the hotel is full. Some of my work colleagues tried to book a room here for tonight and there was nothing available.'

He met her eyes directly. 'I meant you could stay here in my suite.'

The quiet invitation sent her senses into overdrive.

There was a long silence and she could almost feel the crackle of electricity that flowed between them. She noticed the way his eyes moved again towards the softness of her lips and her heart thudded unsteadily. What would it feel like to share a bed with this man? To be kissed all over, have his hands touching her intimately? The question made her feel hot inside, it also made her senses do a weird flip with the intense desire to find out the answer.

Hastily she tried to rein in those feelings. Cat was a virgin. She would have liked to say that she had chosen to remain so because she was waiting for the right person to come along, but that wasn't the real reason—the truth was far more complex than that. The truth was that no man had turned her on to the point that she'd wanted to give herself totally to him.

And the one man who had, had turned out to be after her money—thankfully she had discovered this before giving herself to him, but it had been a close call. Now she found it hard to trust anyone.

And yet here she was, in a hotel suite at one in the morning with a total stranger, feeling more aroused by just the way he looked at her than any other man had managed with numerous kisses and caresses. What the hell was she thinking? The question seared through her. She didn't know this man—and, although she didn't think he was in any way connected with her father or Michael, for all she knew he could be married with four children.

'Are you…propositioning me?' She cautiously sought to clarify the situation and he gave her a smile that was slightly mocking.

'I have to admit that from the moment I saw you downstairs in the ballroom I wanted you in my bed.'

The admission made her remember the way he had looked at her across that crowded room. Yes, there had been purpose in his eyes; he had watched her like a predatory male marking his quarry. She had known it at the time, had known it and been turned on by it. The realization suddenly flooded through her consciousness. Those feelings were part of the reason she had felt so afraid, part of the reason she had left the party and the hotel as if pursued by the devil himself.

He reached out a hand and touched her face. It was the most gentle of caresses, his fingers soft as they moved over the creamy smoothness of her skin. Then his hand moved lower to the sensitive cords along the side of her neck as he tipped her chin up.

His eyes raked over her face with an almost hungry posses-siveness and she felt an answering pang of desire deep inside. For the first time in her life she felt like throwing caution to the wind, felt like leaning closer inviting his lips and his hands to take this feeling all the way to its ultimate conclusion. She couldn't understand her reaction. There had been no shortage of boyfriends in her life but she had never felt anything like this before. Even with Ryan she'd had no difficulty in pulling back from making love. Deep down she had sometimes wondered if there might be something wrong with her because she could think so rationally about passion. Now this man—a man she knew nothing about—was stirring all kinds of wild feelings inside her. It was bizarre. It was also deeply worrying. She felt as if she were out of her depth.

With a strict effort of will she forced herself to break the contact with his hand and take a step back from him.

'I don't sleep with strangers.' She held his gaze with difficulty, fighting the demons that were drumming against her heart, insisting she was making a big mistake here.

'Well, then, maybe we should get to know each other…and fast.' There was a dark teasing light in his eyes.

Most women melted when he looked at them; in fact he couldn't remember the last time a woman had given him the brush-off. By contrast Cat held his gaze with an almost fiery determination.

He had to admit he liked that spark in her eyes and he found himself respecting her blunt rebuff.

She raised her chin a little and met his eyes firmly. 'Are you married?'

The sudden question amused him. 'No…not yet.'

'You do have a partner, then?'

He shook his head, a half smile tugging at his lips. 'Why? Are you interested in applying for the position?' He crossed his arms and leaned back against the window frame behind him, watching her with that hooded look of amusement still in his eyes.

'Don't flatter yourself!' She felt a flare of annoyance. She had been right in her first assessment of him. He was arrogantly confident—a man who always got what he wanted when he wanted it. 'I just have a feeling that back home you have a woman in your life who would be deeply unhappy if she knew you were propositioning me tonight.'

'What makes you think that?'

'You are a wealthy…not unattractive businessman who has jetted into the country on business. It doesn't take rocket science to work out that you probably already have a partner and are just looking for a bit of recreational activity to fill a momentary gap.'

'You are very suspicious,' he said quietly. 'And, if you don't mind my saying so, you don't seem to have a very high opinion of wealthy not-unattractive businessmen, do you?' Although the question was asked in a mocking tone, there was enough of a cool serious edge about it to strike a chord inside her.

He was right—she was suspicious. She didn't trust any man easily, which begged the question—why was it taking so much strength to turn him down? Why did she want so badly to feel his lips burn against hers? The question pounded inside her.

'Maybe you are right.' She shrugged and forced herself not to think about that. 'And maybe I was naïve, accompanying you up here to your suite, but I did assume that because you had helped me earlier that your offer was made with chivalrous intentions.' She raised her chin higher.

He smiled. 'Well, just for the record, there is no woman waiting for me in my bed at home.'

She was aware that she was more pleased than she should have been to hear that. She shouldn't have cared, because she wasn't going to sleep with him. When she did choose to divest herself of her virginity it would not be on a one-night stand with a stranger.

'And unfortunately I do have a chivalrous side.' His lips

twisted wryly. 'It's over there.' He nodded towards a door at the far end of the room. 'And it's called the spare bedroom.'

'Oh!' Against her will she found herself liking that lazy, teasing note in his voice.

'So if you would like to avail yourself of it—the offer is still open.'

'Thanks.' She smiled suddenly and it was as if her warmth lit the room.

She had probably practised that look in a mirror, Nicholas reminded himself sharply.

'If I thought the worst of you I'm sorry,' she added softly.

'You mean thinking I was married and looking for some fun on the side?' He shook his head. 'Don't worry about it. I'm not.'

She cringed. 'I really am very grateful for your help tonight.'

The contrition was probably as false as that feigned look of innocence. But she acted the part very well. He could almost believe that she was softness and morality personified and not a money-grabbing witch who had stumped up several thousand pounds to fund a con trick for her brother.

A witch had no right to be this beautiful, he thought distractedly.

The ring of an intercom on a bureau at one side of the room interrupted them. Nicholas walked across to answer it.

'Mr Zentenas, the police are here,' the receptionist informed him.

'Send them up.' He flicked the switch off and glanced over at her.

Something about the bold sensual glitter in his eyes made a shiver run through her, but she wasn't sure if it was a shiver of apprehension or desire. Feeling as she did, she should have been out of here in double-quick time.

Yet the feeling was exciting, a double-edged sword. She would just have to be careful not to sway too close to the blade.

CHAPTER THREE

NICHOLAS listened as she gave her statement to the police and Cat could feel his eyes resting on her and it made the hairs on the back of her neck stand up.

Why did she feel as if he were weighing her up? Why did she feel this constant tug of almost hostile sensuality between them every time their eyes connected?

There was one point when an officer asked her a question and she couldn't even think straight about the incident outside; it seemed to have paled into insignificance next to Nicholas's powerful presence.

He helped her out at that juncture. She noticed that he spoke with the quiet authority of someone who was used to being in command, and the officers treated him with the utmost deference.

'That was probably a complete waste of time,' she reflected a little later as Nicholas came back into the room after showing them out.

'Not necessarily; you gave a good description of your assailant.' He glanced across at her. 'Would you like a nightcap or do you want to turn in?'

The direct question made her heart thump uncomfortably against her ribs.

She wondered if she had made a fool of herself tonight, asking him outright if he were married! She cringed at the memory, and his arrogant rejoinder—*Are you interested in applying for the position?* Very funny, she thought dryly. Although if her father had heard the conversation he would have rubbed his hands together in glee. The thought flicked through her mind with brief amusement that threatened to turn to aching sadness—her father would probably marry her off to the lowest bidder if it meant he and Michael got what they wanted.

'I think I'll just turn in. I'm quite tired.'

He nodded and led her towards the door he had indicated earlier.

The room he showed her into was extremely stylish, dominated by a huge king-sized bed. 'There is a bathroom through to your left.' He indicated the *en suite* bathroom at the other side. 'Make yourself at home.'

'Thank you.' She turned and looked at him. As their eyes met she felt again the fierce tug of attraction rise deep inside her. 'Well, goodnight, then,' she added firmly.

He smiled. 'Goodnight, Cat.'

As Nicholas closed the door behind him he was aware that the evening hadn't gone quite as smoothly as he'd thought, and it wasn't just that she hadn't capitulated and slept with him; it was more than that. It was a bit like hooking what you thought was a small fish on a line only to discover it could pull you off your feet.

He crossed to where he had left his drink and, picking it up, downed the contents in a single gulp. Then he stared sightlessly out at the glittering lights of the city.

For a second he remembered the softness of Cat's skin beneath his fingertips, the way she had looked up at him with sweet fiery warmth. He'd wanted her with an urgency he couldn't remember feeling in a long time, an urgency that hadn't gone away despite the interruptions and her hasty departure to a separate bedroom.

With a frown he put his glass down and reminded himself whom he was dealing with. That episode in Crete last year had been particularly unpleasant. If she got her hands on that inheritance, God alone knew what strokes she and the McKenzie men would pull.

She was very sexy though, he acknowledged with a frown. Dangerously so, with the figure of a siren and those come-to-bed eyes.

But sex wasn't his ultimate goal, he reminded himself firmly. What he wanted was total possession of her and, through her, total revenge on Carter McKenzie. Their inheritance would be sent to some worthy cause—he had one all lined up, an orphanage in Greece. Quite fitting, he thought with a smile.

So he would bide his time about bedding her, he told himself as he switched off the lights and headed for his own room. His intuition told him that if he tried to rush things with Cat she would pull away from his grasp. Nevertheless he was confident that before very long he would have this all wrapped up. She would soon be his for the taking—along with the McKenzie inheritance—and it would be a most satisfactory arrangement.

Cat lay in the large bed and stared up at the ceiling. She could hear Nicholas moving about, switching off lights. Although she felt exhausted, she couldn't sleep; images from the evening were flicking through her mind.

Something wasn't right.

She saw again the man who had tried to steal her handbag, then Nicholas Zentenas making his timely intervention. What had he been doing outside the hotel? she wondered suddenly.

She turned over and pummelled the pillow beneath her head, willing sleep to claim her. Did it matter why he'd been outside? He'd helped her and that was the main thing.

Cat closed her eyes again but this time she could see Nicholas's face clearly. The dark glittering eyes, the sensual curve of his lips. He was very handsome but she couldn't work out what it was about him that gave him that dangerous edge. Maybe it was just that she was scared of the attraction she felt for him. He wasn't the type of man that she wanted.

When she fell for someone, she wanted him to be a nice uncomplicated kind of man. She wanted an ordinary life where she and her partner worked together to achieve their goals. That was her dream. She didn't want wild excesses of money or to get involved with some power-hungry person who lived for his next deal. She had seen that kind of life up close with her father and she didn't want it.

It was a strange coincidence that this man who had helped her and who she was so attracted to was from Crete, a place that held the key to so many emotions inside her.

You should go back, he had suggested lightly. She had returned to Crete to help Michael last year only because she had felt obliged to. It was a familiar scenario. Her father played the guilt card and she found herself dishing out money to Michael— money that had ostensibly been left for her education.

Her half-brother was trouble, Cat thought darkly. But still her father couldn't see it. He adored his only son, blamed any problems he had on the terms of her grandfather's will—on her—on anything except Michael. And, who knew, maybe it was the will that had caused Michael to stray into troubled waters. He had certainly been hurt by it and so had their father. Cat still felt guilty about the way her grandfather had left things, even though logically she knew it was not her fault.

Cat had been ten when she had discovered that she had a

brother. Four months after her mother's funeral, her father had announced he was getting married again to a woman called Julia. He had then coolly introduced Julia's son Michael as his son. Cat had found she had a half-brother only six months younger than she was.

The revelations had shocked her. Julia had been her father's mistress for eleven years, and yet she had never suspected that all had not been well in her parents' marriage.

Her grandfather had been furious and had made it clear to his son that he disapproved of him marrying again so soon.

'She's a gold-digger.' He had practically spat the words out in front of everyone and a heated argument had ensued. 'She's only hung on to you for all these years because you have wrapped her in the luxury of the McKenzie money and now she wants more. But if you marry her she won't get anything more, I'll make sure of that. I'll change my will.'

The words had certainly stirred up a lot of unpleasant feeling. But her father had taken them as an empty threat; after all, he was an only child, how could his father not leave him his inheritance? His marriage to Julia had gone ahead.

In the intervening four years before her grandfather had died, her father had worked very hard to get back into favour with him. So hard in fact that Cat had rarely seen him. He had thrown himself into the family real estate business, making deals and money that he'd thought would impress his father. Some of those deals had slithered close to the edge of what was acceptable. They hadn't been illegal but they hadn't been moral either. At least that was what her grandfather had told her.

Her grandfather had been less than impressed. He had blamed his son's ruthless dealings on Julia. But in fact Julia had been too busy spending money to be interested in how it was made. She hadn't been a particularly bad woman; Cat would certainly never have classified her as the clichéd cruel stepmother. She was just not the maternal type; she wasn't particularly interested in Michael, let alone Cat.

So Cat had grown up in a household where money was plentiful and love non-existent. She had tried to befriend Michael but he had been a sullen and withdrawn child. They had been lonely years. Cat had thought that things couldn't get any worse until, when she'd been fourteen, her grandfather had died.

She remembered the day the will had been read quite clearly. Remembered the extraordinary fury it had unleashed.

Her grandfather had been a very wealthy man. He had left his property in Crete and in London to his son. Then he'd stipulated that the businesses were to be sold and that the money, along with the bulk of the McKenzie fortune was to be placed into trust for Cat. The rest of the money, which had been a small proportion, had been put into accounts for her education. There had been nothing for her half-brother.

At the time it had seemed harsh. Cat remembered naïvely looking over at her brother and saying softly, 'Don't worry, Michael, I'll give you a share of the money when I get it.'

She would never forget the look he had given her; it had been one of pure hatred.

Her father had sold the house in Crete and used the money to try and get the will overturned in a court of law, but he had not been successful. Gerald McKenzie had been deemed sound of mind and she would inherit the McKenzie fortune on her twenty-first birthday but only if she was married. If she were still single on reaching that birthday, the money would stay in trust for her until she was thirty.

Cat's lips twisted as she thought about it. She didn't know why her grandfather had placed such a stipulation in the will. Perhaps he had wanted to further frustrate his son and grandson by protecting Cat and his fortune from their greedy mitts for a bit longer. Whatever the thinking behind it, Cat didn't want the money. In her eyes it was cursed and had already done enough damage. Soon after the last court hearing, her stepmother had walked out on her father. It had been the final lesson on how money could tear people apart; as far as Cat was concerned, it could rot in the bank.

Her father and Michael, however, had other ideas. They had continually harped on about how wrong it was that she should be left everything. And she saw their point—her grandfather should never have left his will like that. It was that guilt which had driven her to open up the accounts supposedly for her education to give the money to Michael. She didn't want it anyway. She had taken a student loan and, with the help of two jobs, had supported herself through university.

Michael, meanwhile, was into property development and had tried his hand at a number of get rich quick schemes. She hadn't realized what kind of schemes they were until last year when she'd had to go to Crete to bail him out. She had been sickened to find out just how he had been using her money.

When she had told him how disgusted she was, a terrible argument had risen up, fueled by Michael's bitterness. He had let it slip that he knew Ryan and that even Ryan thought she was impossible. After that it hadn't taken her long to discover that her romance had been a set-up. The discovery had hurt her deeply and she had immediately ended the relationship.

She hadn't spoken to her brother for months afterwards. But then at Christmas Michael had turned up on the doorstep of her flat, filled with remorse for the things he had said and done.

For her father's sake she had accepted his apology. She'd been glad that the last of the money for her education had been used; at least he couldn't ask for any more.

But now it was three months until her birthday and Michael was starting to call around at her flat again; the air of friendly politeness was slipping and he was starting to mention the money again, getting increasingly desperate, increasingly angry.

Her father had rung her a few weeks ago. *'You did promise Michael half of that inheritance,'* he had reminded her tersely. *'Things haven't been easy for your brother.'*

She had wanted to say, Things haven't been easy for me either, but I've got myself an honest job and I haven't been deceiving people. But she had held her tongue. Criticizing Michael upset her father and led to arguments. It was best to gloss over things and keep them both at a distance. But she had told him categorically that she would not be getting married in the near future so the problem of the inheritance money would be in abeyance for another nine years.

There had been an ominous silence.

She hadn't heard from either of them since. But she had a horrible suspicion that they were up to something. The truth was that Michael had always been able to twist their father around his little finger. And her father probably wanted his share of the inheritance as well.

She tossed and turned in the bed. Her father was as cold and calculating as her half-brother. It was something she kept pushed to the back of her mind, too painful to dwell on and acknowledge.

After her birthday things would calm down again, she told herself soothingly. All she had to do was hold her nerve for another few months and steer clear of any romantic involvements.

But, as she closed her eyes again, a different problem plagued her—the problem of her powerful attraction to Nicholas Zentenas.

She needed to keep her distance from that man, she told herself fiercely. She needed to leave here first thing in the morning and not look back.

* * *

As soon as Cat stepped out of her bedroom the following morning she could hear Nicholas Zentenas's deep tones. He was speaking in rapid Greek and for a moment Cat was transported back to Crete, to the sizzling heat and the days of childhood. She followed the sound through to the lounge and then round a corner, where she found him outside on the terrace.

He was sitting at a table laid for breakfast. A crisp white linen cloth and silverware sparkled in the early morning sun. However, there was no food on the table; instead he had paperwork spread out in front of him and he was talking on his mobile phone. Cat couldn't help thinking that he looked the epitome of a successful businessman in his dark suit, a blue shirt open at the neck.

Behind him, the rooftop view out over the city was even more spectacular by day. She could see the green swathe of St James's Park and the blue curve of the River Thames.

Nicholas glanced up and their eyes locked. Although she tried not to acknowledge it, she could feel the instant attraction and desire firing her body with a wave of heat. She noticed that his eyes drifted almost lazily to linger on her lips, making her feel even hotter inside.

He smiled and indicated that she should take a seat in the chair opposite his. Cat, however, did not move from the doorway. She intended to wait until he had finished his call, thank him politely for his hospitality and then make a swift exit. She needed to get out of here. The warning bells that had been ringing through her consciousness all night were clamouring insistently now.

As he talked his eyes moved from her face and hair, down over her body as if he were undressing her. She felt a lick of heat deep inside.

Hastily she looked away and tried to pretend that she was

studying the swimming pool and the terrace, but she was aware that his eyes were still on her.

She felt out of place in her silk evening dress, as if she had been summoned like a lady of the night for his pleasure.

Abruptly he ended his phone call. Cat understood enough Greek to know he had promised to ring whoever it was back.

'Forgive my manners, Cat. That was an important business call.' He switched to speaking English with fluent ease. 'How did you sleep last night?'

The polite tone contradicted the way he had been looking at her, making her wonder if she had imagined that raw sensuality.

'Very well, thank you,' she lied with a smile. In truth her troubled thoughts had kept her awake until the early hours.

He indicated the seat opposite his again. 'Join me and have some breakfast.'

'Actually I won't, if you don't mind,' she said firmly. 'I have to organize a locksmith so I can get back into my flat, so I thought I'd head straight off.'

'Pity—I wanted to ask you a little about Goldstein Advertising. You work for them, don't you?'

'Yes.' She frowned. 'How do you know that?'

'It wasn't such a hard deduction; most of the people at the wedding party last night work there.'

'I suppose they do.' She was nonplussed at this sudden turn in the conversation. 'Why are you interested in Goldstein Advertising?'

'Why is any businessman interested in advertising?' He fixed her with a wry look. She was very suspicious and the barriers he had sensed around her last night seemed to be raised even higher. Why was that? Maybe she had been involved in so many dishonest deals with her brother and father that she naturally assumed everyone was as crooked as she was?

'A company called Mondellio handled my last campaign,'

he continued nonchalantly. 'Maybe you saw it; it featured some of my hotels in the Caribbean—the tag line was "Relax in style".

Was that his chain of hotels? Cat's eyes widened. She was impressed; everyone in the advertising world knew that campaign. It had been huge and the envy of all its competitors. 'Yes, I saw the ads; they were good. Mondellio are very well thought of in the business.'

'It was successful,' Nicholas continued smoothly. 'But I think it's run its course. I've been considering changing tack this year, switching accounts.'

Cat found her business mind clicking on like an illuminated sign. If she could bring in a large account like the one Nicholas was talking about, it would be a major boost for her career.

A waitress appeared and placed a pot of coffee on the table.

'But if you have to rush off…' Nicholas concluded with a shrug. 'Goldstein was only a passing thought, anyway—'

'No, I have a few minutes.' Cat found herself walking over towards the table, pulling out a chair.

Work-wise, this could be a lucky break. Things hadn't been going too well for her at the office so far. The money wasn't bad but a lot of the pay was structured around bonuses and she had felt frustrated by the fact that accounts were given to favourites—people in the know who networked. She knew that she was the new girl on the block, but she had student loans to pay off and living in London was expensive. She needed an opportunity to show her bosses just what she was capable of and this might just be it.

Nicholas tidied away some of the papers whilst the waitress poured them both coffee. That had been almost too easy, he thought with a smile. The lure of a lucrative deal was something a McKenzie never could resist.

The waitress handed Cat a menu before discreetly withdrawing.

She glanced down at the choice of food but didn't feel like ordering. She couldn't eat anything—not with Nicholas watching her so closely from across the table. Her burst of enthusiasm for work had suddenly been overshadowed by her awareness of him again. Maybe she should have followed her instincts and left. She could have asked him to come into the office on Monday to discuss business.

But then maybe he wouldn't have come, she told herself sensibly. And an opportunity that she badly needed would have been missed.

She frowned and put the menu down. 'So in what way exactly were you thinking of changing tack with your advertising?'

Nicholas noted that instead of trying the hard sell she was making an effort to find out what he wanted. Obviously she had a shrewd business mind. 'Do you want to order some breakfast?' He deliberately ignored her question and glanced down at the menu.

'Actually, Nicholas, I don't eat much in the morning but the coffee is most welcome, thank you.'

He looked over at her in amusement. 'You know the first rule of making a good deal is never to negotiate on an empty stomach.'

'Well, as we are just chatting and I'm not looking to make a business deal, that's all right then.'

The laid-back approach was also impressive.

He glanced over at her with a quizzical light in his dark eyes. 'How long have you worked at Goldstein?'

'Three months.'

'First job since leaving university?' He pretended to hazard a guess.

'First full-time job. I've worked evenings and holidays all the way through university.'

Why had she done that, he wondered, when her grandfather

had set aside more than enough money to fund her education? He took a sip of his coffee. Maybe she had just preferred to speculate with that money on her brother's dirty schemes.

'If you are thinking that I am not capable of handling an account of your company's size then you're wrong,' she said quietly.

'Really.' His lips twitched. Not so blasé now, he thought sardonically.

She sat back in her seat and as their eyes met she found herself having to be honest. 'Actually, the truth is they are confining me to quite small accounts at the moment but I've got lots of fresh new ideas and I could do so much more.' Her eyes sparkled earnestly. 'The fact that I've got so much to prove and you are looking for something different could work in both our favour.'

She had just hooked him back in with a gold star; those big green eyes were very enticing and so was her zesty attitude.

He had to hand it to her; she was a witch of the highest class. Nicholas hesitated and then reached into the pile of papers next to him and passed her a file that Mondellio had sent him. They had set out a few proposals for amendments to the original ad. 'See what you think,' he invited lazily.

Nicholas watched as she leafed through the pages and read selected areas carefully.

Silence stretched between them. He noticed little things about her—the long sooty darkness of her eyelashes and the natural blush of colour along her high cheekbones. She bit down against the softness of her lips with pearly white teeth as she concentrated.

'Well, it's perfectly obvious that this isn't the way to go,' she said at last as she put the file down.

He had expected her to say that, but what he hadn't expected was for her to continue swiftly and identify exactly what the problem was. He was surprised by how insightful she was, but he was stunned when she started to come up with some very novel ideas of her own.

'If you go with this deal it will be modestly successful, but that's all. What you really need is to grab the public's attention all over again.' She flicked the folder closed. 'Obviously I could come up with some ideas if I was given time to work out the details.'

She glanced over at him when he made no reply.

'I may be fresh in at Goldstein but they are an excellent company. With their experience and my new approach you could have a very exciting and successful promotion. Think about it.'

Goldstein was lucky to have her—the grudging light of respect lingered inside him for a moment. She was intelligent, sharp and creative. Pity she was also insincere and corrupt like the rest of her family, he reminded himself quickly.

'But don't think about it too long,' she added with a smile.

He was aware that she had turned the tables on him slightly. When he had set out to get her attention with business this morning, he'd had no real intention of switching accounts. That had just been a piece of bait to cast out before he went back to Mondellio to ask for changes.

Now—well, now he was undecided. He really didn't like Mondellio's proposals. Maybe he would think about Cat's ideas. She was right—Goldstein did have a first-rate reputation and business had to come first after all. Also it had occurred to him that this might be just the excuse he needed to break through those barriers of hers and draw her closer into the net and into his bed.

'You have made some interesting suggestions,' he said. 'Maybe I will want to delve deeper, hear more.'

She tried to draw her eyes away from his, but somehow she couldn't; he held her locked into that powerful gaze. And suddenly her mind was veering away from business towards altogether more risky terrain. Delving deeper had a tantalizing ring about it.

From nowhere she found herself remembering a snatch of their conversation from last night.

I don't sleep with strangers.

Then maybe we should get to know each other...and fast.

She was very glad when the waitress returned to the table. She didn't know why she was thinking again about that conversation; it was embarrassing.

'Can I get you anything else, sir?' the woman interrupted quietly.

Nicholas glanced enquiringly over at Cat and she smiled politely and shook her head.

'No, that will be all, thank you.'

The waitress withdrew and then stood at a discreet distance, waiting and watching in case Nicholas should summon her. His every whim was catered for, Cat thought as she took another sip of her coffee. His days were probably filled with staff dancing attendance and women fawning over his every word. Well, she was glad she hadn't given in to her desires last night, she told herself firmly. She'd just have been another notch on his belt. Sex would mean nothing to him; it would have been merely a passing recreational moment.

You could never trust a man like Nicholas Zentenas. He would look on a woman as no more than a plaything in the bedroom.

But doing business with him—well, that was another thing entirely. She had not missed the gleam of respect in his gaze as she'd told him her ideas and she had got quite a buzz out of it. Business was everything to a man like him. Making money was probably more of a turn-on for him than sex and, as for love… Well, the only thing a man like him would love would be a successful deal.

She had learnt a thing or two about relationships from watching her father.

'If you want to drop into my office some time next week we can talk about my ideas in greater detail,' she invited coolly.

'I'll see how I'm fixed. I've got a pretty hectic schedule lined up.'

Cat allowed the subject to drop. Despite his offhand response, she was quietly confident. She had made her pitch and it had been good; she was content to sit back and wait.

'You certainly started work early.' Her glance moved towards the stack of paperwork he had placed on the empty chair between them.

'I'm in the midst of negotiations to buy another hotel and I'd like to get things wrapped up as soon as possible. Time is money.'

'Well, I'm sure the deal will fly through. You strike me as a man who always gets what he wants,' she said flippantly.

'Not always.' He looked at her and for a moment there was a gleam in his dark eyes. 'But I enjoy a challenge.'

Something about the way he said those words made her tingle inside.

The ring of his mobile cut the silence between them and with a sense of relief Cat pulled her gaze away from his and reached to finish her coffee.

She listened as he answered his phone. It was another business call in his native Greek language. Something was displeasing him; his voice was crisp and authoritative, his look intently serious.

Although Cat couldn't speak Greek fluently, she had picked enough of the language up when she was younger to be able to make a competent stab at it. And she understood it pretty well. Nicholas seemed to be checking on the progress of some building work for an orphanage—no, she must have got that wrong, she decided quickly. He must have said building work for offices; he spoke so quickly that she couldn't catch the details.

After a while Cat found herself tuning out as her eyes moved contemplatively over his features. He just oozed sensuality. Her eyes drifted down towards his lips. What would it feel like to be kissed by him? He would be very experienced, would probably be an incredibly masterful lover… Her heart gave a weird little flip.

He hung up and glanced across at her and with a jolt she realized the errant direction her thoughts had taken.

Gathering her scattered wits together, she pushed her chair back from the table. 'I really should be going,' she said quickly.

'Yes, me too.' He glanced at his watch. 'I'll drop you off,' he offered.

'No, it's OK—'

She supposed it was churlish to refuse but she really did just want to get away from him. She didn't like the effect he had on her one little bit.

'I insist. If you are ready, we'll go. My driver should be outside by now.'

Nicholas led the way through the apartment towards the lift. As soon as he pressed the button, the doors swished open.

'I think the waitress got the wrong impression about us this morning,' Cat remarked as they stepped inside and the doors closed.

'In what way?'

Cat tried not to look embarrassed. 'Because I'm still wearing my clothes from last night, I think she assumed that something was going on between us.'

'Does it bother you what people think?' The deep velvet tone seemed laced with amusement.

'No, not at all!' She held his gaze steadily.

He smiled. 'It's just unfortunate that I have a crystal-clear conscience about last night.'

Something about that smile and that teasing light in his dark eyes made her feel that he was right and it was very unfortunate that last night hadn't gone further.

Hurriedly she looked away from him and told herself to snap out of this. 'It would have been a mistake!' She hadn't meant to say the words aloud; they escaped impulsively and quite vehemently before she realized it.

'Maybe… Maybe not.'

Cat made the error of looking over at him. He really was far too attractive for any woman's peace of mind. 'Well, we will never know now,' she said softly.

'Won't we?'

He countered the question in a tone almost as provocative as the glint in his eyes. That raw sexuality made her want to lean closer, beg him to take her here and now.

He was toying with her, she told herself sensibly, teasing her to gauge her reaction and see how far he could go with her. In reality he wasn't interested in her. And certainly if she had slept with him last night he would be checking his watch and running through his business plans now as if she didn't exist.

Yet, for all those sensible thoughts she ached for him to come closer.

For a moment Nicholas considered reaching out to halt the lift. He could see heat in her eyes and, as his gaze moved over the curves of her figure he found himself imagining how easily her breasts could be freed, her skirt hitched.

The only thing that stopped him was the undercurrent of tension. He sensed that, beneath those sultry smouldering eyes, Cat's defences were still on high alert. The time wasn't right for her surrender to him…but it soon would be.

His lips curved in a mocking smile. 'Maybe we'll test that out some other time when I haven't got such a busy schedule.'

He really was arrogant! The words caused her head to snap up and her eyes to blaze. 'I don't think so.'

He laughed at that.

The lift doors opened into the lobby and she marched out ahead of him.

The normality of the reception area seemed almost unreal after her tumultuous thoughts. He really was the worst kind of man—full of his own importance and far too confident. And he had the worst kind of effect on her. She hated herself for the weakness that invaded her as soon as he was too close.

There was a doorman on duty this morning and he swung the heavy glass doors open for them so they could step out into the brightness of the morning.

The air was buzzing with the sound of the London traffic and there were a few people strolling past, but it was the white Rolls Royce waiting by the kerb that drew Cat's attention. As they walked down the red-carpeted steps, a uniformed chauffeur sprang from the driver's seat and came around to open the back passenger door for them.

'Actually, Nicholas, I won't take a lift with you.' Cat stopped a few paces from the vehicle, the thought of being in a confined space with him for even a few moments longer making her very nervous. 'I've just remembered I have to stop off somewhere.'

'I see.' There was a gleam in his dark eyes as he looked over at her.

Did he see? Did he know that she was running scared? She hated the fact that he might, just as she hated the swirling conflicting emotions he could create inside her.

'There are plenty of taxis at the rank across the road, so I may as well take one.'

'As you wish.'

He sounded vaguely amused now. She tipped her chin a little higher. 'Anyway, thank you for all your help and if you need to discuss those business ideas we talked about earlier, do give me a ring—'

She forced herself to hold her ground a moment longer and opened her purse to take out her business card.

His hand brushed against hers as he took it and she immediately felt a flare of arousal. She found it incomprehensible how just the smallest touch could have that kind of effect on her. Business was the only thing that mattered, she told herself firmly. 'My office number and my mobile number are on there. I'm in from about eight-thirty until six most weekdays.'

Nicholas smiled. 'I'll give that some thought.'

She watched as he coolly tucked the card into his jacket pocket.

She would probably never see him again. The thought was disappointing—but only because it would be a business opportunity lost, she told herself quickly.

'See you some time, then.' With a cool smile, she turned away.

CHAPTER FOUR

THE office was crowded and airless and Cat was not having a good day. In fact it had not been a good week. Her immediate boss had overlooked her again and handed out two lucrative contracts elsewhere.

'Sorry about that, Cat; you did come a close second,' Victoria said smoothly as she brought the meeting to a close. 'But I feel I've got to play safe. This is an old and valued client and it's experience that counts at the end of the day.'

'Well, it's your decision to make,' Cat said as she started to fold away her presentation. What else could she say? Anything else would sound like sour grapes. But inside she was fizzing. Especially as the contract had been given to a man Victoria was rumoured to be having an affair with—a man whose pitch had been the least exciting of the afternoon. Cat hated gossip and paid no heed to it usually but she really was starting to wonder if there was something in the stories now.

One of the receptionists put her head around the door, interrupting the general feeling of unrest in the room. 'Cat, there is someone downstairs to see you.'

Cat's heart sank even further. She assumed it was her brother; he'd phoned three times this week and she had avoided him on each occasion. It would be typical of him to barge into the office and try to create a scene. Her nerves stretched; she really could do without that! No one here knew about the situation with her family because it wasn't something she liked to discuss. In fact, when anyone questioned her about her background she always pretended everything was fine in her life and that she was close to her father and brother. The truth was too sad to acknowledge and too embarrassing. For one thing, she would have men mockingly asking her to marry them if they knew about the inheritance!

'It's not my brother, is it?' she asked cautiously. 'Because I'm too busy for personal matters, you'll have to tell him—'

'No. This is business.' Judy cut across her swiftly. 'His name is Nicholas Zentenas—owner of the Zentenas chain of hotels.'

Cat's wasn't the only head that swivelled around towards the door. Judy had everyone's attention now.

'He was Mondellio's client,' someone remarked quickly. 'Isn't he that Greek tycoon? Remember that huge campaign— *Relax in style*?'

There was an excited buzz around the room.

'So what is he doing here?' Victoria cut across the noise sharply, her eyes boring into Cat. 'And why is he asking to speak to you?'

'I ran a few ideas by him last week.' Cat tried to keep her voice nonchalant but inside her heart was starting to speed up. A full week had passed since she had given Nicholas her card. She had hoped every day that he would phone her—*only for business purposes, of course*—but hope had faded midweek. Now it was Friday afternoon and he had casually just dropped in!

'You've run ideas by Nicholas Zentenas?' Her boss sounded as if she was having difficulty with her English. 'Ideas for a new campaign?'

'It was just a few off-the-cuff suggestions.' Cat rose to her feet. 'I told him to come in if he wanted to hear more.'

Victoria's face had turned a strange shade of puce. 'Well… I'm sorry, Cat, but as senior management I will have to handle this.'

'He specifically asked for Cat,' Judy interrupted casually. 'He was most precise on that point. I got the impression that if she wasn't free he would leave.'

The puce shade was turning to purple.

'Don't worry, I'll deal with it, Victoria.' Cat swiftly headed for the door.

'I enjoyed that!' Judy said with a grin as she followed Cat along the corridor towards the lift. 'That woman is getting very irritating.'

Cat couldn't have agreed more, but she was too wound up about the fact that Nicholas was in the building to be able to concentrate on anything else. She brushed a nervous hand over her black pinstripe trousers and then buttoned up the matching waistcoat as she tried to focus her mind on the business aspects of this visit—yet she was aware that her heart was racing with a peculiar emphasis not normally associated with work-related problems.

She wondered if she had time to refresh her lipstick, comb her hair? Maybe not—Nicholas wasn't a man to be kept waiting. The thought had just entered her mind when the lift doors opened and he stepped out.

'Ah, there you are, Cat. I was starting to think you'd got lost.'

He was every bit as commanding as she remembered. Commanding and handsome. A lightweight beige suit fitted the broad-shouldered physique perfectly, hinting at the muscled torso beneath. His dark hair was swept back from his face with a careless indifference that was downright sexy and his dark eyes followed her progress along the corridor with an intensity that made her footsteps falter.

'Sorry to keep you waiting, Mr Zentenas,' Judy called out.

Cat noticed that the indomitable receptionist sounded flustered. It wasn't just her, then—Nicholas probably had this effect on the entire female population. The knowledge helped her to gather herself. She wasn't going to crumble like everyone else.

'Nicholas, this is a pleasant surprise.' Her voice was brisk and businesslike. 'If you had rung, I'd have made an appointment for you so you wouldn't have had to wait.' As she reached his side, she held out her hand.

That was almost her undoing. The firm touch of his skin against hers made her hot and breathless and the amused glint in his eyes told her he knew she wasn't quite as composed as she pretended.

'I found I had a spare half hour and thought I would take a chance that you were free.'

In other words, appointments were for mere mortals; he was above such things and had known she would see him no matter what.

And of course, business-wise, he was right. He was the most impressive and important client to step over her threshold since she had been here.

'Come through to my office.' Cat led him down to the room that had been assigned for her to use when meeting clients. It was effectively the size of a broom cupboard and she left the door open behind them so as to minimise the intimacy of the situation.

'Please sit down.' She waved him towards the leather chair opposite her desk. 'So how has your week been?' She tried to maintain a friendly yet impersonal attitude. 'Have you acquired your new hotel?'

He leaned back in the chair and regarded her laconically. 'The deal is going well.'

'Good.'

Nicholas watched as she manoeuvred herself behind her desk without touching him. The suit looked great on her; the tailored lines of the waistcoat scooped low over her breasts, giving subtle emphasis to her curves. She sat down and reached to open a drawer and he noticed the way her blonde hair spilled silkily over her shoulders and the way her white blouse was unbuttoned, giving a glimpse of a lacy bra and firm rounded flesh. A business outfit had never looked so sexy. He was aware that his mind had moved away from practicalities. It was probably just the thrill of the chase, but Catherine McKenzie was the most attractive woman he had come across in a long time....

'I take it you've had a chance to think about some of the ideas I mentioned last week?' she asked.

He smiled at that.

'Obviously they were just sketchy outlines,' she continued swiftly. Despite the brisk confidence of her tone, there was a sudden vulnerability in her demeanour, her skin flared with heat and the green eyes were shadowed with uncertainty as she slanted a glance towards him.

He knew there was nothing remotely vulnerable about her, but she played the part well, the illusion was tantalizing.

'Anyway, I took the liberty of filling out some of the details for you in case you would be interested.'

He watched as she opened up a file and brought out sheets of paper.

'Now, what I thought was…' She turned the pages around and slid them towards him so that he could see. 'If we started focusing on one hotel and then developed the idea…' She turned over more of the pages. 'We could make a fantastic impact.'

'You have been busy.' Nicholas leaned forward and studied the pages intently.

Busy was an understatement. Cat had worked all last

weekend to finish this for Monday in case he came in. When he hadn't, she had taken it home in the evenings and had honed it some more. It had occupied her every spare minute of the week.

She watched restlessly as he read it and then re-read it. 'Not bad,' he said at last as he sat back.

Not bad! Cat fought down the annoyance that flared at those words. 'I think it will be a massive success,' she said instead with quiet confidence.

'Maybe.' He regarded her for a long moment. Despite his non-committal tone, he was impressed. He just didn't want to tell her that. He intended to make her work a little harder for him first. 'So you recommend concentrating on one hotel—'

'Just to start the ball rolling, because it will give the whole campaign a more personal slant and it will stress the individuality of your hotels.'

Nicholas didn't say anything for a while. Cat could feel the nervous tension knotting inside her but she refrained from pushing her point. She didn't want to sound desperate.

'You might have something with this,' he said finally.

'I know I do.'

'However, selecting the right hotel might be tricky.'

'I don't see why.' Cat picked up the pencil that she had been using earlier and tapped it against the papers. 'You have a lot to choose from. All your hotels are sumptuously upmarket yet unique. But you should select the one with the most character, the most romantic… Yes, that's it. Go for the most romantic.'

He shrugged. 'They say Paris is the most romantic city in the world and I have a superb hotel there overlooking the River Seine, but—'

'A little obvious,' she said quickly.

'Just what I was thinking.'

She smiled at him but it was clear that her mind was racing ahead as she gave the question some thought.

She tapped the pencil against her lips for a second, then ran it softly over the inside of her lower lip.

He knew her mind was firmly on business but Nicholas found the action provocative. She was all brisk professionalism on the outside and wanton sex goddess within. He wanted her…wanted her with even more urgency than before.

'Maybe somewhere closer to home would be better,' she said softly. She remembered the hotel from last weekend with its beautiful restaurant and terraces. 'Isn't there a rumour that Casanova attended a masked ball at your hotel here in London?'

Nicholas laughed at that. 'Yes—there's a commemorative inscription in the ballroom. But—'

'It might be a good hook.'

It wasn't the kind of hook Nicholas was interested in right now. What he wanted was a place far enough away that there would be no distractions…*somewhere he could undress her and have his fill of her at leisure*. 'Actually…you might be on to something there…' he said slowly as an idea occurred to him.

'So does that mean you like the idea enough to go ahead with the campaign?' She fixed him with a direct look, anticipation in the green depths of her eyes.

'No, it means I'm thinking about it.'

She frowned.

'I'll have to look at the hotel with your plans in mind, try and picture your ideas and get back to you.'

'Oh, come on, Nicholas!' She dropped the pencil and the pretence of being laid-back. If he walked out of here now she could be stewing for days about whether he was going to come back or not!

One dark eyebrow lifted wryly as he looked across at her.

'The offer on the table is a good one and you like it—you know you do,' she insisted.

He smiled. Yes, he did like it; it was a definite bonus—but he would like it better if she were on the table alongside. And yes, he knew he had three whole months to work on getting what he wanted. But he was getting a little tired of telling himself to be patient—patience had never been his strong point.

'I tell you what—you come and have dinner with me tonight at the hotel in question and give me your take on exactly how we could use the place for the advert. And then I'll give you a yes or no before the end of the day.'

The offer made a wave of heat sweep through her—heat that had nothing to do with the excitement of business; this was an altogether more dangerous anticipation. And that was why she swiftly turned the invitation down.

'I'm sorry. Unfortunately, I'm busy tonight.' It was a lie; she had nothing at all lined up. But how could she spend an evening with him in romantic surroundings when he made her pulses race like this? Even with a business desk between them it was hard to ignore the attraction she felt for him.

She didn't want to feel like this, she wanted to concentrate on work. She needed this contract!

'Pity.' He stood up. 'This is the only evening that I can spare.'

Cat was suddenly filled with the horrible certainty that she was making a huge mistake! He was going to walk out and she would be left to field her boss's questions without any precise idea on where she stood. And, what was more, if Victoria found out she had turned down a business dinner with Nicholas Zentenas she would be apoplectic!

'Well, maybe I can do some reshuffling,' she said hastily as she also rose to her feet.

'That would be good.' He didn't sound surprised by her

sudden change of heart. Obviously he was used to calling the tune like this. It annoyed her to have to meekly submit but what could she do? It *was* business, she reminded herself firmly. And if he agreed to her ideas she would have to take another look at the hotel anyway, to plan what they could use.

He glanced at his watch. 'What time do you finish here?'

'Another couple of hours.' She frowned. 'Why?'

'I need to make reservations.'

'Well, I could probably be ready for seven-thirty.'

He shook his head. 'You'll have to be ready earlier than that otherwise we won't be eating until after ten.'

'Why so late?'

'It's about a two hour flight to Venice.'

'Venice?' She looked over at him in consternation. 'I thought we'd decided that your hotel here in London would be the best location for the first advert.'

'Who decided that?'

'I thought it was what we agreed!' Her voice rose slightly. She was totally panic-stricken now. She couldn't go to Venice with him! It was bad enough thinking about having dinner with him here in London, let alone flying hundreds of miles away with him!

'I haven't agreed to anything—yet,' he reminded her coolly.

She refused to be intimidated by that. 'Yes, but the hotel here in London would be perfect! It has a great hook because of that masked ball.'

'And the hotel in Venice has a better hook, because Venice is the home of the masked ball.'

She couldn't argue with that.

'So I'll pick you up in about an hour.'

'That's not giving me very much time to get ready! How long is this trip going to take?'

'You don't have to pack anything, if that's what you mean,'

he said laconically. 'I'll have the company jet on standby. You'll be back before midnight. Unless, of course, you would rather stay overnight?'

Their eyes collided across the table.

'No! I've got a busy day lined up tomorrow,' she told him quickly.

He smiled. 'Well, you just need to bring yourself, then.' He tapped the folder on the table. 'Oh, and a copy of this. We mustn't forget why we are there, must we?' he said teasingly.

'There's no chance of that, Nicholas.' She didn't know why she felt the need to say that, but she did.

He seemed to find the words amusing.

For a moment their eyes held and she could feel her heart thudding uncomfortably against her ribs.

She suspected that he knew she was drawn to him against her will. And he was enjoying the fact that he had power over her senses.

Why? Was it just the fact that he was an arrogant male who saw her as some kind of a challenge?

Probably. If she had to put money on it, that was where she would place her bet. She didn't trust him. But then she didn't trust any man, she thought wryly, she knew the deceitful games they could play and Nicholas epitomised everything she most detested in a man—he was arrogant, powerful and interested in only one thing. Money.

But he *was* interested in her business proposal, she reminded herself swiftly. There was no denying that look in his eye when he had leafed through her work.

That was all that mattered. If she secured him as a client, her troubles at Goldstein would be a thing of the past. She would have proved herself without doubt and the contracts would roll in after that. Her student debt would be paid off in no time.

With that in mind she could cope with everything else, including the demons within who lured her into thinking how wonderful it would be to be wrapped in Nicholas's arms.

CHAPTER FIVE

WHEN Cat arrived back at her flat it was after five. Getting away from the office early had not been as easy as she had imagined. For one thing it had taken time to have a few contracts drafted ready for Nicholas to sign. Although she had given her boss a copy of her proposals for the Zentenas campaign and had brought her up to speed with the situation, Victoria had kept her hanging around. She had wanted to go through every detail again, her manner agonizingly slow.

In the end Cat had looked at her watch and had told her bluntly that if she didn't leave now, the deal would probably be in the bin by tomorrow as Nicholas wasn't a man to be kept waiting.

Victoria had shaken her head. 'Well, you'd better go, then,' she had said as she'd closed the files and contracts and slid them back to her. 'Just don't mess this up, Cat. I'll expect a signed contract before you return to the office on Monday.'

The cheek of the woman, Cat thought crossly now as she took the stairs up to her flat two at a time rather than wait for the lift. She had used her own initiative to tempt one of the biggest clients Goldstein had seen in a while and the woman hadn't even said well done!

As she rounded the corner on to her landing she saw her

brother lounging against the wall beside her front door. He brightened as he saw her approach, but Cat's heart sank; she really wasn't in the mood for this right now.

'Hi, sis!' Michael was dark-haired and rangy, not bad-looking in a sullen kind of a way. He always dressed in designer gear; today was no exception, she noted.

Although his tone was friendly, Cat wasn't fooled for one moment; she knew he hadn't come to exchange pleasantries with her.

'Hi, Michael.' Her tone was clipped. 'Sorry I haven't got time to talk. I'm in a rush; I've got a business dinner tonight.'

There was a wounded look in his eyes. 'Cat, I've rung you several times this week and you haven't returned one of my calls. When will you have time to talk to me?'

'Maybe after my twenty-first birthday.' She gave him a pointed look. 'When we can drop the subject of the inheritance money.'

'I can't believe you are being so unreasonable!' His good looks screwed into a frown. 'This is important. I need that money, Cat! Business is slow. I'm really stretched.'

Michael always told her that business was slow. But he was living in an apartment at Canary Wharf and she guessed if she glanced out of the window she would see his red sports car parked by the kerb. She wasn't sure if her brother was just living beyond his means…or lying to her completely. Only one thing was sure—no matter how much money he had, it was never enough.

'I'm sorry to hear that,' she said, getting her front door key out. 'But I just haven't got time for this.'

'So you're not going to do anything about claiming our inheritance?' he asked abruptly as she turned away.

He always referred to the money as *our* inheritance…and

Cat never argued the point. 'If you mean am I planning my wedding …then the answer is no, Michael, I am not.'

'For goodness' sake, Cat,' he grated. 'You could do with some of that money yourself! Your life isn't that great; you are living in a shoebox, working all hours and you don't make great money.'

'I'm doing all right,' she said curtly. 'And I'm happy.'

'You are used to better things, Cat. You were brought up in luxury.'

'I'm sorry, Michael, but I'm not marrying just to get that money.'

He raked a hand through his hair. 'Dad and I have been talking—'

'Good for you.' Cat put the key into the lock and opened the door. She didn't want to hear any more. 'Please go, Michael.'

'Just give me one minute.' Michael reached into his pocket, took something out and shoved it towards her.

'What's this?' Startled, Cat took the piece of paper and, glancing down, found she was looking at a photograph of a dark-haired man in his twenties.

'He's called Peter and he's a friend of mine. I've told him about our problem and he's willing to meet you at the register office and tie the knot… You never need to see him again.'

Cat felt a wave of fury. 'It never ceases to amaze me how low you will stoop.' She tried to push the photograph back towards him but he wouldn't take it.

'Look, I'm being upfront with you this time—I know I shouldn't have deceived you and set you up with Ryan. And this is just a means to an end,' he insisted. 'I've had a word with a lawyer friend and we can draw up a prenuptial agreement so that the money is secured. And Peter would be very happy with the arrangement. So you see everyone will win from this situation.'

'You can forget it, Michael. I'm not doing it!' she said flatly.

Michael stared at her calmly. 'That money should never have been left to you, Cat. By rights it belongs to Dad. You know that.'

'I'm not responsible for the way the will was left!' Cat glared at him. 'Is Dad happy with this? Does he really want me to marry a total stranger?'

'He thinks it's a great idea!'

A sharp stab of pain twisted inside her. Hurriedly she turned away and, before her brother could stop her, she went into her flat and slammed the door.

'Just think about it!' Michael's voice was muffled from outside.

She squeezed her eyes tightly closed; it didn't come as any real surprise that her father cared so little about her. They hadn't been close in a long time and deep down she had known something like this would be suggested. But it still hurt because he was her father and because she remembered a time before her mother had died when she had idolised him. Pulling herself together, she threw the photograph to one side.

She had discovered a long time ago that her idol had feet of clay. Feeling sad didn't solve anything; she just had to get on with her life. And that meant throwing herself into work and forgetting about relationships.

Nicholas pulled up outside Cat's flat at a little after six. He felt a gleam of satisfaction at the way things were playing out; it was reminiscent of the way he felt when he was about to close a major business deal. In fact, if anything the thrust of adrenalin was perhaps greater. The scent of revenge was close and sweetly exhilarating.

He stepped out of the limousine into the warmth of the evening and strolled towards the entrance of the old Victorian building. Cat lived in a decent area; the road was tree-lined and had an air of prosperity about it. But Nicholas knew it was a million miles away from how she had lived when she was growing up.

He wondered not for the first time what she was planning to do to get her inheritance. She was a beautiful woman and could have bagged herself a husband without too much of a problem but, according to his sources, she had no boyfriend. Apparently there had been someone in her life last year but it hadn't worked out—now she just had casual dates every now and then. She seemed to be content playing the field with her friends, living her life like any normal twenty-year-old.

Maybe she was wary of marriage as a partner could walk away with a chunk of the inheritance. She might have decided to keep her options open; the money would be hers in nine years anyhow, with or without marriage. But of course waiting wouldn't please her father or brother. They, no doubt, had plans and schemes for that money.

As Cat had gone along with their schemes in the past, maybe she was content to do so again. In that case they would be organizing some kind of arranged marriage—some deal that would prevent a new husband having a legal claim on what was theirs. The thought made a twist of distaste stir inside him.

Whatever they were planning, they were going to be very disappointed. He smiled to himself as he stepped out of the lift and rang her doorbell. He would really like to see the look on their faces the morning they woke up and realized that someone had got to the pot of gold first.

The door swung open. Cat was wearing a plain black dress that hugged her slender figure. She looked businesslike, but so sexy and breathtakingly beautiful that he almost forgot why he was here.

'Hello, I'm nearly ready.' She stepped back from the door, her manner brisk. 'Come in for a moment.'

Nicholas wrenched his eyes away from her as he stepped inside and focused his attention on the surroundings.

The flat wasn't at all what he had been expecting. He had assumed because it was in an old Victorian building that the rooms would be huge, but the place was small. She had decorated with style, however; it had a homely, welcoming feel. Bright canvases adorned the white walls and the old sofas were draped with throws and scatter cushions in a rich gold and tangerine. One alcove was filled with books and there were fresh flowers in a crystal vase on the mantelpiece.

'Sorry to keep you waiting,' she said coolly.

His glance moved back to her. She was perched on the arm of the sofa, slipping on a pair of high-heeled court shoes.

She had lovely legs, he noticed. They were very long and very shapely. In fact everything about her was enticing. His eyes travelled upwards over the silk stockings and the knee-length dress, noting that she wore no jewellery to adorn the square neckline. Her hair was secured in a casual twist with an amber comb. The style drew attention to the long length of her neck

Cat looked over at him. She was well aware of his scrutiny and she was trying very hard not to let it unnerve her. 'I had…' As their eyes connected she almost forgot what she was saying. There was something almost primal in the way he was looking at her, as if he were touching her, possessing her with his gaze. It made her senses flood with wild heat and she hated that! With difficulty she maintained her poise. 'I had difficulty getting away from the office. It's been a very busy day.'

'It will be a busy day on the roads too; Friday always is.' He glanced at his watch. 'The road to the airport will be jammed if we don't leave soon.'

His tone was businesslike, totally at odds with the way he had just looked at her. She didn't know if that made her feel better or not—she couldn't work out the undercurrent between them at all. 'I just need my passport. Won't be a second.'

It was a relief to escape into the bedroom and, although her passport was sitting on top of her dressing table, she didn't immediately pick it up; instead, she took a few moments to compose herself.

This feeling of desire that attacked her senses every time she looked at him was going to have to stop. For one thing, she couldn't allow anything to mess up the opportunity of this business contract—that was all that mattered. For another Nicholas Zentenas had danger written all over him.

If she lowered her defences around him he would take what he wanted and then walk away to get on with the business of making money. She would mean less than nothing, and she wasn't going to allow any man to treat her like that. Snatching up her passport, she returned to the lounge.

She was taken aback to find him studying the photograph that she had flung down on the sofa earlier. 'Who's this?' he asked casually.

'Nobody.' Cat flinched as he turned it over. She knew the words *Looking forward to meeting you* were scrawled on the back, along with a telephone number. 'It's just some friend of my brother,' she found herself adding hurriedly.

'Trying to fix you up on a date, is he?'

The sardonic observation hit a nerve. 'How do you know I'm not already seeing someone?'

'As you attended a wedding party on your own last week, I assume you are unattached. Am I wrong?'

She would have liked to lie but somehow she just couldn't so she found herself shaking her head.

The ring of his mobile phone halted the conversation and Cat was extremely glad of the interruption. How dared he ask about that photograph and her social life? It was none of his business.

As he spoke on the phone Nicholas put the photograph down on the table and she took her chance and went across to pick it up and toss it out of sight into a drawer. She didn't want to talk about it; she didn't even want to think about it or Michael or her father, because when she did it felt as if someone had taken a sledgehammer straight to her heart.

Nicholas watched her through narrowed eyes.

'That was our pilot,' he told her as he hung up. 'Our departure is scheduled for less than an hour.'

'Well, I'm ready.' She slammed the drawer closed with her hip.

There was something determined about the action. 'Got a drawer full of potential beaus in there, have you?'

'Well, you know what brothers are like. They only want the best for their sisters.' She matched his flippant tone but inside the lie hurt. She wished so much that was true.

Nicholas watched as she picked up her briefcase and her bag. She was one cool customer, he thought. Obviously his suspicions were correct and once more she was planning to go along with her family's shady ideas. Daddy had probably sewn up some poor guy and got him to agree to the union for a pittance. He felt a twist of pure distaste. The words *as thick as thieves* sprang to mind.

Yet there was something about the way she held herself, the proud tilt of her head, the sparkle of her green eyes, that made another emotion flood through him—determination. No matter how far Carter or Michael McKenzie were prepared to go he was prepared to go, further. He was the one who would claim Cat and the inheritance.

Nicholas's limousine waited at the kerb and a chauffeur jumped out and opened the doors for them.

It was luxuriously fitted out inside and extremely comfortable. If it hadn't been for the situation, Cat might have enjoyed the drive. But she was intensely aware of Nicholas in every way—his cologne, the light touch of his arm against hers, even the silence seemed loaded with tension.

She kept her gaze averted from him and searched for something to say—something that would break this feeling.

Clearing her throat, she made an attempt at business. 'Have you thought any more about what we discussed this afternoon?'

He glanced over at her. 'All in good time, Cat.'

He was infuriating, she thought. 'Don't forget that you did promise to give me an answer before the end of the evening,' she felt compelled to remind him. She didn't want him stringing her along. Men were good at that and she wasn't going to be walked over.

'Oh, I haven't forgotten anything,' Nicholas assured her. 'But, until we actually get to the hotel, there is little new of value that we can discuss—businesswise, that is.'

Their eyes met.

'So I suggest that we relax,' he continued smoothly. 'The flight will take about two hours so we may as well use the time to relax, get to know each other a little better...hmm?'

His words and the way he was looking at her held a provocative power that made her temperature sizzle.

With difficulty she tried to dismiss the feeling. 'Actually, there is a lot we didn't cover this afternoon,' she said firmly. 'I thought we could go over some of the ideas for the follow-up adverts.'

'I think we need to walk before we can run,' he contradicted silkily.

He really was maddening but she couldn't think of a suitable reply because the way he looked at her made all her thoughts run riot. She fell silent and for a moment their eyes held.

Hurriedly she glanced away from him and out of the

window. They were on an airfield now and she could see a private jet ready and waiting with the steps down.

It wasn't too late to turn tail and run, a little voice told her insistently.

And how would that look in the office on Monday morning? she asked herself sternly. She was being ridiculous.

They pulled to a standstill within a few feet of the aircraft and their driver came around to open the passenger doors for them. The noise from the aircraft filled her eardrums as they stepped out into the warmth of the sunlight.

'Good evening, Mr Zentenas.' The man waiting for them had to practically shout to make himself heard. 'Everything is ready for you, sir, exactly as stipulated.'

What had Nicholas stipulated? Cat wondered. But there was no time for further conversation; Nicholas waved her to go ahead of him up the steps into the aeroplane.

She was amazed when she stepped inside to find that it was unlike any other aircraft she had ever travelled in. Deep leather seats faced each other across a desk. There was a state-of-the-art office to one side, and through a door at the back she could see a double bed.

Had Nicholas been thinking about that bed when he had suggested using the flight time to get to know each other? The thought filtered through her and with it a deep burning swirl of pure desire.

Fiercely she tried to maintain a sense of perspective. Yes, Nicholas probably wouldn't mind amusing himself with her to pass a few spare hours, but did she really want to be used as some millionaire's plaything for a few fleeting hours of short-lived pleasure? This was an important business trip. She wanted him to treat her seriously—not as some sex kitten.

Nicholas joined her in the cabin and immediately the door

of the plane was closed behind him with a heavy clunk that almost matched the slam of her heart.

'Everything OK?' He smiled over at her.

'Yes, thank you.' She put her briefcase in an overhead compartment and then selected a seat so that her back was towards the bedroom. She really didn't want to be reminded of that for the entire journey.

Nicholas took off his suit jacket and put it away in another compartment. The white shirt he wore was open at the neck; she noticed the wide muscular width of his shoulders, the lithe hips, the very taut line of his buttocks—before quickly looking away again.

He took his place in the seat opposite and a few moments later the engine noise increased and the safety belt sign was illuminated.

'The pilot doesn't believe in hanging around,' she said lightly, trying to stem the rising feelings of apprehension.

'We've got a clearance slot from air traffic control for take-off and if we don't take it immediately we could be hanging around on the tarmac for another hour.'

Cat looked out of the porthole as the plane taxied on to the runway, then stopped. There were a few moments while they just sat and waited. Her eyes met Nicholas's and the feeling of tension inside her escalated wildly.

'Do you like flying?' he asked nonchalantly.

'I don't dislike it.' The feelings inside her were nothing to do with flying and everything to do with him. 'It gets you places quickly… It's a means to an end, isn't it?'

He smiled at that. 'It is indeed.'

Was it her imagination or was his reply loaded with some other meaning?

The engine noise suddenly whooshed into powerful life as the jet thundered down the runway at a speed that made Cat's stomach feel as if it had been left behind. Outside the window Cat could see that London was already looking like toy-town, the grid pattern of the roads and the parks getting smaller as they climbed higher. Then they straightened out and a few moments later the seat belt sign went out.

Nicholas unfastened his belt and stood up. 'Would you like a drink?' He moved towards a fridge at the far side of the cabin and looked around at her enquiringly.

'Just water, please,' she said briskly. 'I want to keep a clear head.'

He smiled at that.

'Have I said something amusing?'

'No. I just wondered if you ever did anything other than keep a clear head and think about business.'

She tried to ignore the remark, but it rankled. 'That's rich, coming from you!'

'How's that?'

'Well, you must never think of anything other than making money! How else would you achieve all this?' She spread her hands, indicating the luxurious aircraft.

'I work hard when necessary and I'm focused. But I also play hard.'

'I'll bet.' Cat couldn't resist the retort. 'Money mogul by day and playboy by night.'

Nicholas laughed at that.

He had a nice laugh, she thought. It was warm and provocative and infinitely sexy. Their eyes met as he passed her the glass of water.

'Is that how you see me?'

She shrugged and looked away from him, feeling most uncomfortable now. What on earth had possessed her to say such a thing? 'How you live your life is none of my business.'

'No, it's not,' he agreed smoothly. 'But you've obviously

made some sweeping assessments anyway. I noticed this about you when we first met.' He sat down again in the seat opposite.

'Noticed what, exactly?'

'I suppose you would call it an inbuilt wariness.' He took a sip of his drink and watched her skin tinge with colour.

'I don't know what you mean,' she said stiffly.

'No?' The amusement was still there in the darkness of his eyes. 'My mistake, then.'

It rankled that she amused him. 'Well, you are obviously a playboy,' she muttered in annoyance. 'You are—what—thirty and unmarried?'

'Thirty-three and divorced,' he cut across her wryly.

She was surprised by the disclosure. She hadn't realized he was divorced.

'You see, you don't know me at all. And before you hazard a guess, it was my wife who was—now, how is it you English put it?—playing away.'

She frowned; he was right that she had made a lot of assumptions about him.

'On the first night we met you accused me of wanting to cheat on my partner,' he reminded her with a grin. 'You assumed, in fact, that it was a mode of behaviour that I would regularly put into practice.'

'I did apologise for saying that.' She shifted uncomfortably.

'Do you know what I think?' He looked over at her with a bold light in his dark eyes. 'I think you're so attracted to me that you have to keep telling yourself these things so that you can fight the feelings.'

The fact that he wasn't far wide of the mark was very disconcerting. 'And do you know what I think?' she retorted quickly. 'I think that you are one of the most arrogant men I have ever met.'

'There you go again…another excuse.' His eyes glinted

mockingly. 'You've got a better defence system than London has with the Thames Barrier.'

'And you've got an even bigger ego.'

He laughed and relaxed back in his chair. 'You know, I enjoy our little sparring sessions; they are like an exhilarating form of foreplay…don't you think?'

'No, I don't.' She glared at him.

'If the real thing is anything as fiery, I think we would need flame-proof bedding,' he continued.

'Why don't you just drink your whisky and we'll get down to business?' she said. He really was going too far with this.

'Actually, I'm drinking iced tea.' He smiled at her. 'And I've never been propositioned quite so bluntly before.'

'You know exactly what I mean.'

He laughed. It was strange, but he did enjoy sparring with her. Most people deferred to him. Women especially tended to submit eagerly and immediately to his ideas and needs. But Cat's eyes glinted and blazed with feeling. She was like a wild kitten that needed taming—he just needed to keep in mind that she may look beautiful but she was a kitten hiding extremely treacherous claws.

'Shall we forget this nonsensical conversation and look at the plans I have drawn up for the campaign?' she continued crisply. Her green eyes held with his but beneath the cool, competent veneer there was a flame that excited him beyond reason.

Oh, yes, he was very much looking forward to breaking her will until she was purring and submissive to his every desire.

He smiled and pretended to relent. 'Go ahead, take your papers out.' But in truth he had no intention of looking at her business plans just yet. They could wait until later.

Nicholas watched as she unfastened her seat belt and stood up. He was treated to a pleasurable view of her figure as she stretched to open the overhead compartment.

Desire escalated inside him and he allowed her to struggle with the catch for a few moments more before offering assistance. He knew full well that she couldn't get into the compartment because he'd locked it with a flick of a button just before take off.

'Need some help?' he asked laconically.

'Yes—it seems to be stuck.' As she stepped back from it, he surreptitiously pressed the button on the arm of his chair releasing the lock and then stood up to help.

She watched with a sense of frustration as Nicholas opened the compartment with ease and took out her briefcase. He put it down on the desk beside them but didn't immediately return to his seat.

'Thanks.'

'You're welcome.' He returned some files that had been sitting in a rack by the door into the locker. 'I'll just tidy these away.'

The confines of the aisle meant she couldn't get back to her seat without moving nearer to him and, as she was too close for comfort as it was, she stood and waited.

'You've got a great office in here,' she remarked, trying to take her mind off the way his muscles flexed under the fine silk material of his shirt.

'Yes it comes in useful when I'm on business trips. Means I can utilise my time efficiently—'

Cat's gaze moved towards the sliding door through to the bedroom. He caught the glance and smiled. 'And I like my creature comforts.'

'So I noticed—' Her words were abruptly halted as the plane hit some turbulence and gave an unexpectedly violent judder.

'Are you all right?' He reached and caught hold of her arm and then the plane lurched again and she lost her balance completely and found herself slammed against his chest. His arm went around her, steadying her, holding her close.

The shock of the contact was immense; it flooded through her system, disorientating her like a shot of some mind-altering drug. And in that second wrapped in his arms she was achingly aware that this was a place she wanted to be. Here loneliness was relegated to the furthest corners of her heart, chased away by the hard, powerful body crushed against hers.

'Cat?'

She was vaguely aware that the plane had stopped shuddering and that he was waiting for her to answer him.

With difficulty she lifted her head from his chest and looked up at him. Something happened as their eyes met, something that sent wild spirals of heat pulsating through her.

'Sorry…I lost my balance.'

'You don't need to apologise,' he said with a smile.

Danger signals escalated and she tried to make herself move away from him but her limbs wouldn't cooperate.

His gaze moved towards the sensual curve of her lips and her heart skipped violently against her chest.

'So…what are we going to do about this?' he asked softly.

'Do about what?' Her voice was no more than a husky whisper.

'This…' He reached out a hand to stroke it down along the long line of her neck. The caress made the heat of sexual need increase; she could feel it curling inside her now as if it were a living entity.

She swallowed hard, terrified by the feeling and desperate to dismiss it.

'I don't know what you mean.'

He laughed; it was a low, very sensual growl of a laugh that made her tingle. 'I think you do.'

There was a purposeful gleam in the darkness of his eyes that made her pulses race. Then suddenly he lowered his head towards hers and fear was replaced by a wild excitement. For a moment it didn't matter that she was probably playing with fire. All that mattered was that he was going to kiss her.

As his lips captured hers the world seemed to tip and spin on its axis and this time it had nothing to do with the turbulence outside the aircraft. This time the turbulence was in her heart and in her senses, pounding through her with a relentless searing force.

Cat felt so light-headed that she had to reach up and put her hands on his shoulders to steady herself. And at the touch of her hands his kiss changed from gently persuasive to powerfully fervent, crushing against hers with an almost ruthless intensity.

She kissed him back with equal passion, meeting his demands with a hunger she had never realized lay within her.

In that moment Cat wanted him with every thread of her soul. Desire pumped through her as if someone had broken open a door to a reservoir of need…a reservoir that was so secret that even she hadn't known of its existence until this very moment.

Nicholas was the one to pull back from her, leaving her shaky and bewildered by what had happened.

'That was some kiss,' he murmured.

'Was it?' She tried very hard to sound casually indifferent but, to her distress, her voice was breathless and shaken. She was furious with herself for responding to him like that. 'I didn't notice anything…special…'

Although she tilted her chin defiantly, Nicholas could see a chink in her armour, a receptive light in her eyes.

He smiled. 'A sexual heat exists between us, Catherine. We've both known about it very forcefully since the first moment our eyes met.'

Even the way he spoke her name sounded dangerously provocative. She started to shake her head, but his hands were around her waist now, pulling her back into his arms.

'This is inevitable,' he murmured, 'because the truth is that you want me as much as I want you; I can see that in your eyes, taste it on your lips.'

'It was just a kiss, a reckless spur of the moment kind of wildness…'

She was desperate to justify her response, to herself as much as to him.

'It was more than that.' As he spoke his hands moved upwards, boldly stroking over the firm curves of her breast. He found her nipples through the soft material of her dress and brushed his thumbs over them in a rough caress. It was a blatant demonstration of the power he wielded over her senses because, to her shame, they hardened even more beneath his touch until they were throbbing with need.

Cat closed her eyes and desperately tried to fight against the erotic sensation that flooded through her, but her body was crying out for more. She wanted him so badly, wanted him to tear away her dress and her underwear and just assuage this unbearable aching need.

'You do want me, Catherine.'

The arrogant words should have made her pull away but she couldn't; she was so aroused by the way he was touching her that she was powerless to fight against it.

CHAPTER SIX

HIS lips trailed up along the sides of her neck in a heated blaze before capturing her mouth again. And at the same time she felt his hands moving over her possessively, pulling up her dress, finding the lace tops of her stockings and then stroking higher over her naked flesh to the flimsy lace briefs. Cat found herself pressed back against the wall that led through to the connecting room, her arms wound around his shoulders, her fingers raking through the dark thickness of his hair.

'Tell me you want me,' he demanded and, as he spoke, his hand moved to pull at her flimsy underwear, tearing the briefs so that they fell easily away to leave him unconstrained access. When his fingers found the warm wet centre of her she gasped in ecstasy and shock.

In the past she had always been coolly in control of her desires, had always been able to pull away without difficulty. The feelings inside her now were totally different. She was shocked that Nicholas could touch her in a way that made her lose her mind to pleasure, made her writhe instinctively against him.

'Tell me,' he demanded again, his voice fiercely insistent.

'You know I do.' She whispered the words incoherently and saw a smile of satisfaction curve the sensual line of his lips.

His fingers continued to tease her softly while his other hand unfastened the hook at the back of her dress and, with a practised ease, pulled it down to reveal the black lace of her bra and the creamy swell of her breasts.

'You are very beautiful, Catherine…provocatively bewitching and ready for me, is that not so?' He switched to speaking in Greek almost without realizing it. Holding on to his control by a thread, all he wanted now was to plunge himself into her soft warmth, to take her here and now against the wall and watch as she shuddered and convulsed against him. The mere thought almost made him burst with crazy feverish anticipation but he forced himself to control it…forced his mind to think instead of the revenge he wanted—the control he needed.

She wanted him, she would do anything now for release, and he could taste her need as his mouth covered hers, his tongue moving against hers. One hand moved to push away the restraint of her bra and his mouth travelled downwards so that he could take one rosy erect nipple into his mouth.

Her body was gorgeous, her curves lusciously full. His tongue licked against her, noting how her breasts tilted upwards in response to him, inviting his mouth.

She arched her back in ecstasy and drew in her breath in a shuddering sigh as he took her inside the warmth of his mouth, nuzzling her, softly sucking one moment and then taunting her with the tip of his tongue the next.

'Nicholas…please…please.' Cat didn't know what she was saying any more; she was almost delirious with need. In fact, if someone had asked her name right now she wouldn't have known it.

'Please what?' he mocked her softly, his hand moving to cup her pert derrière and press her against him. 'Is it this that you want…?'

She could feel his arousal straining against the material of his suit, large and tauntingly hidden from reach.

'Yes…' As she gave the answer she felt her heart miss a beat almost as violently as the way the aircraft had shuddered earlier. 'Yes, Nicholas, I want you… now.' She closed her eyes and capitulated to the weakness that screamed insistently inside her. Maybe if she sated this desire now she would be able to forget about it and he would no longer wield this power over her senses? She urgently wanted to be back in control—almost as much as she wanted him.

When he made no move to comply with her words—just continued to hold her back against the wall—her eyes flicked open and met his.

The shimmering green eyes were hauntingly beautiful. She was his for the taking. His hand toyed with the triangle of hair between her legs, feeling her wetness and enjoying the low moan that escaped from her throat.

'Nicholas…? Please…'

The whispered plea echoed inside him. He had her completely within his power. Right now she would do anything for him. He wanted to take her, absorb himself completely into her womanly core. But he was aware that, once he sated her, his power would momentarily diminish.

Nicholas leaned closer and kissed the side of her neck and, breathing in her perfume, he forced himself to focus. This wasn't simply about sex, he reminded himself forcefully. If his plan for revenge was to succeed, he needed to draw her closer than that and, to keep the reins of control, he needed to keep her hungry. Therefore pulling back now would be the right decision; it would facilitate his plans for the rest of the evening and make it much easier to manipulate his way under her defence mechanism.

'Maybe now isn't the right moment for this.' It took every

shred of willpower that he possessed to draw away and coolly say those words.

'What do you mean?' Her voice trembled slightly and he saw the incomprehension in her beautiful eyes.

'I mean that in about half an hour we will be landing.' His gaze raked over the breasts that were still swollen with arousal from the warmth of his mouth and his erection throbbed viciously.

Why the hell hadn't he just taken her and alleviated his desire here and now? The question held a kick like an angry mule.

With determination he shut the thought out and forced himself to concentrate. 'A quick release isn't going to put out this fire.'

She shot him a hurt look.

'That was blunt.' He held up his hands. 'I'm sorry.'

'Well, I'm not!' She was hurriedly reaching to cover her nakedness from him now, pulling up her bra and her dress with hands that were shaking. 'I'm glad you've put it in context—it's helped bring me to my senses. I don't know what I was thinking.'

For some reason the huskiness of her tone disconcerted him. 'Catherine.' He reached and caught hold of her, stilling her hands.

There was a mutinous expression in her eyes as she looked up at him but behind that fierce gleam there was something else—a rawness that caught him completely off guard.

Cat looked away from him, scared in case he saw how hurt she was. He was the first man she had ever wanted to give herself to and he had rejected her. But it wasn't just the rejection that hurt—it was the way he had spoken to her as if she were…less than nothing. And yet his caresses had been so tenderly provocative, his kisses had tasted as if they meant something. How could she have been so stupid as to imagine he might actually have feelings for her?

'What I meant to say in a very clumsy way was that the

passion between us is so intense that it would be almost a sin not to savour it at leisure.'

She tried to close her emotions, shut out the power his gently coaxing tone had over her senses. 'The only sin would be if I allowed you to touch me again!'

Nicholas smiled to himself—ah, now, this emotion was one he understood. 'I've hurt your pride.'

'You have not!' She glared at him. 'I just can't believe that I allowed this to go as far as it did. We are supposed to be discussing business plans, not…not having a…a quick…' She couldn't bring herself to refer to it the way he had. 'Anyway, you know what I mean.'

He smiled. 'Yes, I know what you mean. And we will discuss our business over dinner and then I will take you to bed.'

'You will not!'

He laughed. 'But it is inevitable, Catherine.' As he spoke, he straightened her dress, allowing his hand to run lightly over the top of her breast, feeling her instant response to him. 'You see? We'll stay overnight at the hotel.' His voice was cool. It wasn't a request—it was a demand.

Before she could say anything else, he leaned closer and captured her lips in a slow-burning, sensual kiss that made her whole body turn over with longing—the feeling blew her mind. She still wanted him; in fact, if anything, the hunger she felt inside was sharpened.

She couldn't look at him as he pulled away; all her life she'd had no problem in exercising restraint and now, when she needed it most, the ability seemed to have completely vanished.

The aircraft gave a jolt as it hit some more turbulence.

'We'll be landing soon. We should return to our seats,' Nicholas said coolly. He watched as she ran a smoothing hand down over her dress and then reached to pick up the flimsy lacy briefs that were on the floor.

They were ripped and beyond use and, with embarrassment, she was forced to step out of them.

Nicholas watched as she reached to pick them up. 'You won't need those, anyway.' He calmly took them from her and tossed them in the wastepaper bin beside the desk. 'I don't want you to wear underwear tonight. I want to know I can touch you—whenever I might please.'

'You really are the most arrogant and…' she searched desperately for adjectives to describe him '…egotistical man I have ever met!'

He laughed. 'But you still want me.' The gleam of self-assurance in his tone made her bite down on her lip so hard that she could taste blood.

'No, I don't! I don't want you to touch me ever again!'

He touched her face lightly and even the soft caress brought forcibly home the fact that she was lying. He was right—she did still want him. Flinching away from him, she returned to her seat, aware that Nicholas was calmly returning her briefcase into the locker.

A limousine met them at the airport. Cat sat as far away as possible from Nicholas as it swept them away down a narrow country road. She stared out at the dark landscape and tried to get the turmoil inside her under some control. Winning the account for Goldstein was what mattered, she told herself furiously. Nothing should be allowed to interfere with that. What had happened—or nearly happened—between them on the journey here meant nothing.

She bit down on her lip and tried not to think about how she had felt when she was in his arms, how she had begged him to make love to her. What worried her most was that bizarre sense of how right it had felt to be held by him—and the feeling of hurt when he had pulled away so cavalierly. Cat had always sworn that a man would never use her the way her father had used her mother.

Early on in her teenage years she remembered that she had questioned her father about his affair with Julia. Had asked him bluntly if her mother had known about it.

'Of course she did.' He had shrugged. 'She put up with it because she wanted to—because she wanted me.'

The words had stayed with her. Her mother's situation was a salutary lesson on how important it was to stay in control, never let your guard down.

'Cat?' Nicholas's voice brought her out of her reverie and she realized the car had pulled to a halt down by the edge of a ferry terminal. 'We have to take a boat from here.'

'Fine.' Gathering her briefcase up, she stepped out into the warmth of the evening air.

Nicholas watched as she walked ahead of him down on to a wooden jetty. She seemed coolly composed and he knew she was making a determined effort to erect her barriers and retreat from him. He had to admit he was impressed by how quickly she had been able to do that. In all honesty he still felt as if he needed to take a very cold shower.

He couldn't remember the last time he had wanted a woman so desperately and it amazed him that he could feel this level of attraction for a woman who was a McKenzie— cunning and fraudulent.

They stood in silence on the pontoon. It was a clear night and a full moon shimmered down over the water, casting it with a silvery glow. Nicholas noticed how it also held Cat as if in a spotlight, highlighting the luscious curves of her figure and turning her hair to the colour of spun gold, her skin to porcelain. As if sensing his gaze she glanced over at him, her eyes jewel-bright, seeming too large, too intense for the delicate face. He sensed anger first in the blaze of her look—but then something else—a poignancy that hit him like a blazing arrow. She didn't look like someone who was cunning and fraudulent; she looked—pure—like a girl afraid to trust, afraid of her emotions.

Then, with a sweep of long dark eyelashes, the look was gone. A trick of the light, he told himself sharply. But the protective feelings the illusion had roused were slow to recede and that made him angry with himself. He couldn't allow himself to get sidetracked and deceived by her beauty and by the fact that he wanted her. What she looked like on the outside and who she really was were two entirely different things.

She put up barriers to assert a rigid control over her emotions. He couldn't quite work out why she did that or what drove her. Maybe just a natural need to be focused on business—maybe just a determination to be as tough and ruthless as the rest of her family. Yes, probably the latter.

Nicholas had learnt a thing or two about women since his divorce. He had learnt that they could be naturally duplicitous; they could draw you in with a soft smile and a delicate femininity that hid a tough calculating mind.

He remembered the look on Cat's face earlier as she had tossed the photograph of the man her father had lined up for her into the drawer. It had been a look of resolve. His first assessment of her had been correct. Catherine McKenzie was nothing but a siren—and she certainly didn't need anyone's protection.

'Here's our water taxi now,' he said briskly as the distant chug of a boat cut the silence.

Considering they were at the gateway to a large city, the place was strangely deserted, the only sound the taxi as it pulled in beside them, then, as it cut its engine, just the swish of the sea against the platform.

Cat felt as if she had reached more than a gateway to a

city—she felt as if she had reached a threshold and, once she stepped over it, there would be no going back. Hastily she told herself that she was being fanciful. She would conduct herself in a businesslike manner, get Nicholas to agree to the ad campaign and then she would insist he take her back to the airport and home. Despite the firm assurances, she could feel her heart thumping against her chest in slow painful beats.

Nicholas jumped down into the boat and then held a hand out to assist her. She pointedly ignored it and stepped down unaided. The boat rocked slightly but she managed to keep her balance and her dignity and move past him to sit down at the back. A few moments later he sat beside her. He was too close for comfort; she could feel the warmth of his thigh pressed against her, smell the provocative scent of his cologne. She wanted to move away but there was nowhere to go.

The engine flared into life and the boat backed out into the dark silky waters before turning and skipping across the waves with speed. The night air was hot against her skin, the spray from the boat misting in the air, white against the stark darkness. Then the boat rounded a corner and she could see the city shimmering in golden light. The domes of the cathedrals and churches, the bridges and the dark shapes of the gondolas moored alongside were like something from a film set. It looked so beautiful that she drew in her breath in pleasure.

'First time in Venice?' Nicholas's voice close against her ear made her senses quiver in response.

She nodded, aware that if she turned her head a fraction towards him their lips would meet. Instantly the feeling of need that had overwhelmed her earlier started to surface again.

'Tomorrow, if we can get out of bed, I will take you out and show you the sights if you'd like.'

The self-assured words seared against her consciousness. 'Tomorrow I will be back in London,' she stated firmly.

He laughed but said nothing. For the time being he was content to allow her to pull her barriers up. For the next hour or two he wanted to concentrate on the ad campaign. Business was important and her ideas merited a deep consideration. But once work was out of the way, he would bring her back to where he wanted her. He was confident after the way he had left things earlier that he wouldn't have too much difficulty with that. Once he held her in his arms again she would realize the futility of pretending and she would be his—totally his to take again and again as he pleased.

After that her defences would be trampled to dust, paving the way for his ultimate goal—revenge.

CHAPTER SEVEN

THE Hotel Zentenas was a magnificently restored palace that had been designed in the late fourteenth century to meet the requirements of Europe's travelling nobility. Its impressive exterior was lit up by golden lights that reflected softly over a small terrace at one side with ornamental box hedges and yew trees and shimmered over the waters of the canal.

The water taxi left them directly at the private pontoon leading up to the front door. And this time as Cat left the vessel she was forced to take Nicholas's hand as the boat bobbed unsteadily beneath her and the water swished against the building.

'Are you OK?' he asked solicitously, keeping hold of her as she found her balance.

'Yes, thank you.' She pulled away from the warmth of his grasp and tried to ignore the heat that even the most casual of contact seemed to stir up inside her. Instead she turned her attention to the hotel.

The heavy front door lay open and as they stepped inside Cat was completely overawed by the majesty of her surroundings. Enormous Murano glass chandeliers lit the medieval entrance hall, sparkling over Persian rugs and marble floors. Candlelight flickered in the deep recesses by the mullioned windows; antique gilded furniture and sumptuously comfortable sofas were positioned there for privacy and relaxation. And further back at one side there was a reception desk in polished rosewood, at the other an imposing staircase.

It was a lesson on how a place could be luxuriously refurbished without losing its authenticity and character. And Cat was completely enchanted by it.

'I thought your hotel in London was fabulous, but this is something really special,' she said softly.

'Yes, I have to admit this place is a particular favourite of mine,' Nicholas said with a smile. 'It has a unique character.'

Before Cat had time to answer, the hotel manager hurried over to welcome them.

'Nicholas, it is good to see you again,' he said as they shook hands.

'You too, Antonio,' Nicholas smiled and then smoothly introduced him to Cat.

Antonio Belgravi was a tall handsome Italian in his late thirties. His dark sensual eyes flared with undisguised interest as they fell on her. 'Ms McKenzie, it is indeed a pleasure to meet you,' he said as he took her hand and, to Cat's surprise raised it to his lips.

'Call me Cat, please, everyone does.' She tried to sound nonchalant but, in honesty, she was a little embarrassed by the warmth of his welcome.

Nicholas watched as a faint tinge of colour lit the pallor of her skin and felt a twist of impatience. 'Shall we get on?' he said abruptly. 'We have rather a lot of business to get through and then we will dine, Antonio. You did make the necessary arrangements for that?'

'Yes, of course.' The manager smiled at Cat. 'Please come through to my office.'

As Cat followed behind the men she noticed that, although

Antonio was tall, Nicholas still had the advantage of a few inches and he was also more powerfully built, his shoulders wide, tapering down to narrow hips. She liked Nicholas's body—liked the way it felt to be held by him. Realizing the direction of her thoughts, she frowned and hurriedly looked away. She really was going to have to stop thinking like this.

Once off the main hall, there were a few small boutiques selling jewellery and designer clothes. She glanced in the windows as she passed but there was no time to linger. The men stepped back, allowing her to enter the office ahead of them. And for the next hour there was no time to think about anything except her proposals for the campaign.

She was impressive in business, Nicholas thought as a little later they went through to the ballroom to assess the strategic elements of how the advert could work. He watched as she stood in the centre of the dance floor and looked around the baroque interior with undisguised excitement.

'This is fabulous,' she breathed. 'It will be perfect for what we were discussing. You can almost sense history in here.' She glanced up at the high ceilings and the walls, decorated with gold leaf and elaborate frescoes. 'Do you still host masked balls in here?' she asked Antonio.

'Oh, yes, in Carnival time, which is just before Lent, we have many evenings of masquerade balls. You should come, the historical costumes are magnificent and you—if I may be so bold—would look ravishing in one, don't you think, Nicholas?'

Cat caught the sardonic glitter in Nicholas's eyes at the comment and blushed. 'Well, thank you, Antonio,' she hurried on, returning the focus of conversation firmly back to business before he could reply. 'I was thinking that we could film a few people in costume at strategic places around the hotel—' She wished Nicholas wouldn't watch her so closely. He made her nervous—he also made her intensely aware of the fact that she wasn't wearing any underwear. 'Em…linking in with what we were er…discussing in the office.' She glanced down at her notes and tried to gather her senses. 'We should take a look at one of the master suites next. I think if we—'

'We will go up there now, Catherine, as I think we have detained Antonio long enough.' Nicholas had been leaning almost indolently against one of the pillars in the room but he detached himself from it now to walk forward. 'I've requested my private suite to be prepared for us. We will take dinner there and conclude this conversation.'

Cat felt her heart thump with nervous anticipation. She was desperate not to be left alone with Nicholas, but Antonio was already taking his leave, assuring them of his utmost assistance for the plans they had been discussing. 'Let me know when you have finalized your decision on this, Nicholas. And meanwhile may I wish you both a pleasant evening.'

'Alone at last,' Nicholas said mockingly as the hotel manager strolled away. 'I think you made yourself a conquest there.'

She ignored the observation. Antonio probably treated every woman with the same level of charm. 'You shouldn't have been so quick to dismiss him,' she said instead.

'You think so?' Nicholas's eyes blazed with heat for a moment. 'Well, you will have to contain your disappointment, Catherine.'

The derisive words made her blush wildly. She glanced down at the notes in her hand. 'I meant that we still have rather a lot to get through,' she blustered. 'We could have used Antonio's input—for instance, these outdoor shots—'

'Right now my mind is focused on indoor pursuits.' His eyes met hers boldly as she looked up.

She hoped he was referring to taking dinner but somehow, just by the way he was looking at her, she doubted it. And, to her horror, she was aware that, along with the feeling of apprehension inside her, the heat of sexual excitement blazed fiercely.

Angrily she fought the sensation down. For the sake of her self-respect as well as her work she couldn't afford to let herself become used as just another conquest. 'Well, if you don't want to discuss the finer details of the advert any further, we should finalize the deal right now.' She raised her chin and met his gaze firmly.

An enigmatic smile curved the corners of Nicholas's mouth. 'Let's go upstairs, Catherine.'

The words were dangerously quiet. Go upstairs for what? she wondered frantically. To sign the deal—to have sex?

He stepped back, indicating with a rather imperious sweep of his hand that she should accompany him out. Cat hesitated, then, taking a deep breath, she walked ahead of him towards the door.

There was a lift directly outside the ballroom and the doors were open as if waiting for them. As they stepped inside, Cat was reminded forcefully of the first night they had met.

She watched as he pressed the button for the top floor and snippets of conversations played mockingly through her mind.

A sexual heat exists between us, Catherine. We've both known about it very forcefully since the first moment our eyes met.

Her eyes collided with his for a second and she could almost hear his voice.

This is inevitable, because the truth is that you want me as much as I want you.

Hurriedly she wrenched her gaze away from him. This wasn't inevitable, she told herself fiercely—she would remain aloof and she *would* concentrate on business.

The lift opened and Nicholas led the way down a richly carpeted corridor to open a door at the end. Then he stepped back to allow her to precede him inside.

The room that Cat entered was exquisite. Whereas the suite at Nicholas's London hotel had been ultra-modern in design, this one was completely in keeping with the character of the hotel, baroque yet lavishly elegant. They were in a lounge area and the Venetian glass chandeliers sparkled over gold-leaf antique furniture and heavily brocaded sofas. Outside on a terrace overlooking the floodlit beauty of the city, a candlelit table was laid for two.

Cat put her briefcase down on one of the side tables and tried not to look through the door that led towards an enormous four-poster bed draped in white muslin and rose-patterned chintz.

They were the most romantic surroundings she had ever seen, and the perfect setting for seduction.

But she wasn't going to allow herself to be seduced, she reminded herself firmly. 'I took the liberty of bringing along a contract for you to sign. It's for the first three adverts.'

'Did you indeed?' Nicholas sounded amused.

The fact that her attempt to be businesslike somehow amused him galled her deeply, and somehow that anger helped to suppress the weak feelings of inevitability as she turned to look at him.

'Don't patronize me, Nicholas,' she said quietly. 'I've come here to discuss business with you. And you promised me an answer before the end of the day, as I recall.'

'Yes, I did, and I am a man of my word.' His dark eyes held hers steadily. 'But the day isn't over yet.'

Her hands curled into tight fists at her sides. 'Why are you—playing with me like this?'

He smiled at that.

'So what's the score, Nicholas?' she whispered huskily. 'I give myself to you and in return I get the contract for the commercial? Is that how you do business?'

As soon as the words left her lips she regretted them. They conjured a scornful anger in his eyes that lashed against her raw senses.

'Sorry to disappoint you, Cat, but no, that is not how I do business.' There was harsh derision in those words. 'If you remember, I was the one to insist we got business out of the way before we enjoy ourselves, but maybe that kind of strategy is more your style?'

He watched her skin flare with furious heat. 'How dare you suggest that?'

He had to admit that he liked her tenacity, liked the way her head tilted upwards and her eyes flared with almost regal pride. Was she capable of using all of her charms including her considerable beauty, to get what she wanted? Probably, he conceded grimly. She *was* considering marriage purely to get her hands on her inheritance, he reminded himself—she was a McKenzie. She was a woman.

'A word of warning,' he said smoothly. 'Don't dish out what you can't take.'

Cat's eyes blazed with fury and for a moment she just wanted to turn around and leave the room. She took a deep breath and forced herself to calm down. Running away wasn't going to get her the contract—and she supposed she had hurled the first insult. 'Are you going to sign this contract?'

'No, I'm not.'

The cool words hit her like a blow to her solar plexus. Deep down she had been so sure that he liked her ideas—in fact this evening she had almost taken it as a foregone conclusion that they would be going ahead. 'Why not?'

'Because the contract you have with you is for a series of three different commercials and, as I stated specifically from the beginning, I want to walk with this idea before I run.'

'Oh!' She felt her body relax and relief pound through

her. He wasn't telling her he didn't want the campaign, just that he didn't want to make such a big commitment to it—yet. 'Well, I did bring a contract solely for the first advert—just in case.'

'Very wise.' He shook his head and came closer to her and she could see a grudging respect for her in his eyes. 'You make a worthy adversary, Catherine McKenzie.' As he spoke he reached out and touched her face.

A worthy adversary—she didn't think he was referring to business now, but to the fact that she was probably the first woman in a long time to try to resist him. He viewed her as an opponent to be conquered and, judging by the gleam in his eye, he also now assumed because of her weakness earlier this evening that the battle was over.

'Well, I would advise that you don't underestimate me,' she breathed softly.

'Oh, I can assure you that I have no intention of doing that.' Something about the way he was touching her and the huskily soft words struck a chord inside her. His eyes locked with hers before moving hungrily towards her mouth. And suddenly unwelcome thoughts were plundering through her mind. She didn't want to be his adversary… She wanted to be as close to him as she could get… *She wanted him so badly it hurt—*

Swiftly she closed the torture of her needs away. She wasn't going to be driven by sexual desire into surrendering her control. No man—and certainly not one as arrogantly confident as Nicholas Zentenas—was going to exert that power over her.

Hastily she pulled away from him. 'We need to get this wrapped up.' She turned to search blindly through her briefcase. 'I have the relevant contract somewhere in here,' she mumbled.

Nicholas noticed that her hands weren't at all steady and he smiled to himself.

'Ah, yes—here it is.' She pulled out a file like a conjurer. 'Do you want to read it?'

He laughed at that. 'Of course I want to read it.'

'It is all in order.' She watched as he calmly took it from her and scanned the details.

Silence descended and she found herself holding her breath. This was what was important to her, she told herself fiercely. This would be her first major deal and so, hopefully, the beginning of a more settled phase in her life—a flourishing career away from her family, her debts little by little repaid and, most of all, complete independence.

'Have you got a pen?' He asked quietly after a moment.

Their eyes met and she smiled. Then hastily she turned to scrabble in her bag to find one.

He signed the contract with a flourish and then a copy for his records. 'Good, now our business is successfully completed.'

'Well, the first part of our business,' she corrected him hastily. She still needed the rest of the campaign.

Amusement gleamed in his dark eyes. 'I'm glad you reminded me about that.'

There was suggestive warmth in his voice that wasn't lost on her, but she tried to pretend that it was. 'And now we can head straight back to the airport,' she continued hastily and turned to lock the paperwork safely away.

'We could, but I don't think we will,' he said softly. 'As you said yourself, we have unfinished business.'

'Nicholas, I—'

Whatever she had been about to say—and really she wasn't even sure—was cut off by the fact that he moved closer in behind her and put his hands firmly on her waist. The feeling was provocative and firmly proprietorial. 'Why are you trying to pretend that this afternoon didn't happen, Catherine?'

The whispered question against her ear made her senses pound.

'You wanted me,' he reminded her teasingly. 'In fact you begged for me.'

The reminder made her flush with heat.

'Do you know what I think?' His tongue licked at the sensitive cords along her neck. 'I think you are frightened by the way I make you—feel.'

'I'm not frightened of anything,' she lied fiercely, but the remark was so accurate that it was scary.

'You like to be in control and, when you're with me, that doesn't happen.' The lick of his tongue became a gentle butterfly kiss and at the same time his hands stroked firmly up over her hips in a way that pulled up her skirt.

She closed her eyes, fighting desperately against the sudden violent desire his caress unleashed. 'Please—don't, Nicholas!' To her disquiet the whispered words held more emphasis on the word *please*, making it sound more like an invitation than rejection.

He picked up on the weakness immediately. 'You mean please don't…stop.'

'Nicholas…' Her voice was a low groan of need now as his hand stroked up underneath her dress, finding the tops of her stockings and then smoothing upwards over the naked flesh of her hips and across the flat lines of her stomach before softly skimming downwards between her legs with ruthless concentration.

As his fingers lightly brushed against the moist heat of her sensitive core, her eyes flew open and connected with his in the ornate Venetian mirror directly facing her.

'I think we were about here this afternoon…weren't we?' His voice rasped against her ear, husky with sensual pleasure.

When she didn't answer him immediately, his fingers toyed

with her, making her quiver with a sharp, achingly sweet
need. He watched the way she gasped and then caught the
softness of her lower lip with her teeth to stifle the sound.

'You want me as much as I want you—don't you?' His
voice was as tormenting as the fingers that invaded her wet
softness. 'Surrender to me now, Catherine.'

'No!' The fact that he was watching her every reaction in
the mirror made her feel overwhelmingly helpless. His touch
lightened as if he might pull away from her and she gave an
involuntary sob of need. 'Yes…don't stop!'

'Not quite clear enough. Tell me how much you want me.'

Her dress was now completely hitched up around her waist
and, as he held her back against him, she could feel his erection
through the linen of his trousers, pressing against her bottom.

She fought against saying those words and, to her mortifi-
cation, he lightened his caresses even more until her whole
body screamed out in need for him to continue. 'All right, you
win.' She turned her head away from her reflection; she
couldn't bear to witness how weak she was. 'You know that…
I want you.'

She heard her dress rip as it was forcibly tugged down and
then his other hand found her breasts, jerking down the lace
of her bra so that they were pushed upwards, nakedly inviting
his eyes to rake over their throbbing peaks.

'You are so beautiful.'

There was a momentary splinter in the harsh tone, a note
that she caught and held on to because with it came a measure
of empowerment. OK—he'd won, she acknowledged. She
had been lying to herself when she had told herself she wasn't
going to give in to this. The fact was she was desperate for
him and her surrender was now unconditional. *But she wasn't
the only one who had lost control.*

Her eyes flew to his in the mirror and she saw the fierce

blaze of need in the dark depths and smiled. Sensuously she moved her hips and rubbed herself against him, feeling him strain against the tight constraints of his clothes.

'Why, Nicholas, the steely control is slipping.' She almost purred the words, her satisfaction intense as she saw the dark eyes narrow. *She liked this power!*

She lifted her arms and wound them back around his neck, stroking her fingers through the dark thickness of his hair. The movement lifted her breasts even further and she heard his sharp intake of breath. 'Maybe you should be the one surrendering to me,' she suggested playfully.

'I knew you were a witch, Catherine McKenzie.' He growled the words out in a ragged tone as she turned to face him. Coolly she stood before him and unzipped her dress so that she could step out of it properly. Then she took her bra off and dropped that on the floor. All she was wearing now were the silk hold-up stockings and her high heels. For a moment she stood quite still, inviting his gaze.

His eyes ravished her body with hungry intensity. She had the most incredible figure, her breasts full and firm and her waist tiny before flaring out to the womanly curves of her hips. His gaze lingered on the triangle of gold hair between her legs before drifting down over their shapely length.

'You like what you see…don't you?' Calmly she reached out, allowing her fingers to stroke over his erection and unfasten the zip of his trousers.

The size and strength of his arousal made her heart start to race with anticipation. 'Maybe you should be the one saying please to me,' she whispered tremulously as she knelt down in front of him and touched the tip of her tongue against him.

'Why don't you try it—please—Cat?' With each word she took him into the warmth of her mouth.

Nicholas felt a piercing thrust of need; he closed his eyes

against it but it was violent and insistent and the force of the intensity shook him.

She looked up at him, a secretive smile curving her lips. 'I'm waiting for you to tell me how much you want me.' She whispered the words and allowed her breasts to brush against him playfully.

Suddenly a red mist of need seemed to possess him. 'I've got a better idea.' He took a deep shuddering breath as he strove to take back his control. 'Let me show you instead.'

Before she realized his intention, he caught hold of her and, scooping her up into his arms, strode through to the bedroom.

For a moment panic gripped her as her control over events vanished.

'Nicholas, I…'

He wasn't listening; he was undressing and then snatching back the covers of the bed to fling her down against silken sheets.

'Nicholas!' She stared up at him, wide-eyed, and for a moment excitement gave way to fear. Maybe she shouldn't have teased him…maybe she should tell him that she had never done this before…maybe…maybe…

But it was too late for talking. He straddled her with a fierce determination and parted her legs with his knees.

She was pinned down and helpless. A smile curved his lips now as his hand trailed down over her, his thumbs grazing against her swollen nipples. 'That's better.'

Their eyes met and held. 'Now, Catherine, I will teach you how to submit properly to me…' He spoke in Greek and as he did so he rubbed his erection over the wet softness between her legs. His hands moved to pin her wrists to the bed and then suddenly he bent and kissed her. She expected the pressure of his lips to be fiercely demanding but by contrast it was a gently provocative kiss, almost tender in its assault on her senses. She kissed him back hungrily, opening her mouth for his tongue. He let her hands go and her arms moved to twine around his neck, so that she could pull him closer and hold him.

His hands stroked down over her body and as he pulled back to look at her she smiled at him. This felt so *right*.

He moved her legs further apart with his knee and then suddenly he was inside her.

It hurt and she cried out involuntarily. She closed her eyes against the pain as he started to move and his name was just a gasp on the softness of her lips.

'Catherine—are you all right?' Instinctively he eased back for a moment. And, as their eyes met, she realized that despite the pain she didn't want him to stop. She wanted the full force of him—wanted him beyond reason.

'Yes…'

He stroked his hands over her body and she squirmed with pleasure. 'Oh, Nicholas…yes.'

Then he drove deeper into her, taking her shuddering gasps with his mouth, plundering her lips and the inner core of her mouth with brutal passion. She wanted to cry as pain turned magically to pleasure.

His hips moved against her and she writhed sensually beneath him. She wanted this feeling, this need, to go on and on for ever but it was rising insistently to a crescendo, ebbing up and up like an underground spring about to transform into a waterfall.

She sobbed his name as the release came flowing through her, sending her body into spasm after spasm of pure ecstasy.

He jerked against her as finally he allowed himself to follow. And for a while they clung together, swept away by the feeling. Cat's head was buried against his shoulder, her arms wrapped around him, holding him tight.

He pulled away slightly to look down at her.

Cat didn't want him to say anything; she didn't even want to think too deeply—she just wanted to luxuriate in the afterglow.

She reached up and stroked her hands through his hair, her eyes moving over the handsome contours of his face, lingering on the sensual curve of his lips. As if reading her mind, he leaned closer against her and kissed her deeply. It was a kiss unlike anything that had come before; it was so sweetly passionate that it made her want to cry.

Nicholas held her tenderly for a moment, his hand stroking down over the long length of her spine. He'd taken a lot of women to bed over the years but this had been the most incredible experience. He'd never wanted someone so intensely before; she had driven him into almost a state of delirium. Even now, holding her close, breathing in the scent of her perfume, feeling the warmth of her sensational body, he was aware that he wanted her again.

He frowned. This wasn't supposed to happen. He was supposed to leave her wanting more, not the other way around. Nicholas pulled away from her abruptly and reached for his clothes. He'd forgotten to use contraception, he realized suddenly—that had never happened to him before. It wasn't even as if he had been unprepared—he had condoms in his trouser pocket. How could he have been so stupid?

She stretched languorously and the sensual movement made him remember exactly why he had got so carried away. 'You've got a beautiful body,' he murmured.

The coolness of his tone flayed her sensitive nerves and Cat was suddenly acutely aware of the fact that she was naked except for her stockings.

She watched as he raked a smoothing hand through his hair and stood up. His eyes flicked over her nakedness and instantly she felt herself burn with desire. She still wanted him! The shame of that fact was like a punch striking into her. She had hoped that once she had surrendered to him she would be free of this need—that she could shake his control over her senses. But if anything her reaction to him now felt worse! She knew the pleasure he could give her and it was like some mind-altering drug that she desperately needed.

'You'll find a dressing gown in the *en suite*,' he told her nonchalantly. 'Put it on and come through to the terrace. I'll ring down for room service and we'll have dinner.'

She didn't want to eat! In fact she didn't think she *could* eat! All she wanted to do was run away and hide. Unfortunately she wanted to hide from herself and her own feelings as much as from him, and that wasn't so easy.

Cat was glad that he didn't wait around for an answer. She watched as he strode through to the other room and then she fled for the sanctuary of the bathroom.

Ripping off her stockings, she turned on the shower and stood under its forceful jet, trying to scrub away the weak feelings that had invaded her.

Cat had always prided herself on being strong. Although the sham of her romance with Ryan had hurt her greatly, she had made herself face the reality and had brushed him away with stoicism. She had told herself that no man would ever get under her skin again—she was too sensible, too wary of the pitfalls for that. She had known that she was nothing like her father, but she had also convinced herself that she was nothing like her mother either.

The episodes from the past that in adulthood had taken on a horrible clarity had been alien to her.

Her mother crying alone in her room when her father had rung yet again to say he wouldn't be home that evening.

'It's just because I miss him,' she had told Cat brokenly when she had tried to comfort her. 'I love him so very much.'

And when he did come home her mother had been so

happy. She would spend ages getting ready for him, making herself beautiful.

Cat had never understood that. Why would an intelligent woman waste herself on a man who didn't love her? In a way it had made her angry. It had driven her forward with her fierce determination to be independent. It was why she had always held herself back from emotional and physical commitment. It was why she'd had no difficulty finishing with Ryan and not looking back.

But now, as she wrestled with these feelings for Nicholas, she understood for the first time how her mother had felt and realized that maybe she wasn't so different from her as she liked to pretend. And that scared her more than anything!

Cat squeezed her eyes tightly closed as tears threatened to fall. She couldn't allow herself to be weak—she just couldn't.

CHAPTER EIGHT

NICHOLAS paced up and down the terrace. Below him the majesty of Venice glittered in all its beauty, but he was blind to it. All he could think about was Cat and the way she had felt in his arms, the shuddering beauty of her body, the way she had looked at him with those mysterious and beautiful eyes.

His heart twisted. He had to stop thinking like this he told himself fiercely. Cat meant nothing—she was a McKenzie! Leaning against the stone balustrade of the building, he forced himself to remember exactly why he was doing this.

Nicholas's parents had died when he was three and he had been brought up in an orphanage on mainland Greece. The regime of the institution had been strict; there had been no love, no maternal influence, just the rigour of schoolwork and the ethic that to get anything in this life you had to earn it. By the time he had reached the age of ten he had given up on ever having a family life. Nobody really wanted to adopt a ten-year-old.

Then Stella and John Zentenas had walked into his life. From the moment they had first met, something magical had happened; straight away it was as if he really did belong some-where. The day they had adopted him and brought him back to their home in Crete had been the proudest day of his life.

Although Stella and John had no children of their own, they both had large extended families who all lived in the same village. Suddenly, from having no relatives, Nicholas had cousins by the score, aunts and uncles and grandparents. And they had all shown him remarkable kindness and love, had embraced him and absorbed him into the community.

He had vowed to himself back then that he would never let them down—that he would repay their kindness, make them proud.

When Nicholas was nineteen his father had become ill and he had taken over the reins of his publishing business—a business that up until then had been struggling. Nicholas had always had a natural aptitude for figures—he had a shrewd brain and the Midas touch. Within a year profits had doubled, enabling him to buy his parents a new home with every convenience for his father's disabilities. Within two years the business had been worth a small fortune. He had advised his father it was time to sell and John had gone along with him. It had meant a very comfortable retirement for his parents whilst Nicholas had reinvested in other businesses—namely hotels—and the money had just kept pouring in.

In his mid-twenties Nicholas had taken a calculated risk to expand his small chain of hotels. For a while finances had been tightly stretched and it was at that time that the ancient olive groves that surrounded his village had been under threat from developers.

His uncle had come to him, asking him to help. The person who owned the land needed to sell and a developer had already approached him with a substantial offer, but he had plans for a housing estate that would rip the heart out of the countryside. There was land at the far side of the groves that would be ideal for a small hotel—could Nicholas step in and develop the area with sensitivity, giving the owner the money he needed whilst safeguarding their idyllic surroundings for the heritage of the village?

If the request had come even three months down the line, Nicholas could have bought the land outright and gifted it to the village without any development, but bankers had tied his hands. To finance the purchase he'd needed a partner, and a business partner obviously wanted profit. Developing a small hotel as his uncle had suggested seemed the only option as it meant the surrounding area could be preserved.

A banking associate had introduced him to Carter McKenzie and a partnership had been drafted.

Their business deal had been supposedly straightforward. Nicholas had made it clear that certain large sections of the ground were not to be developed and Carter had agreed to this without reservation. In fact he had heartily concurred that it would be almost sacrilege to destroy an area of such outstanding beauty. They had drawn up plans for a new hotel—plans that fitted the requirements. Then Nicholas had left Carter to oversee the project as he had business interests in the Far East that had needed urgent attention.

When he had returned a mere seven weeks later he had found the plans had been altered; the hotel hadn't even been started, but the ground that he had expressly promised to keep as greenbelt had been bulldozed and ripped out, ready for contractors to lay the foundations of a new housing estate.

Nicholas hadn't been able to believe what his eyes had told him and he would never forget returning home. The village where once his friends and family had welcomed him had been turned into a place filled with hostile stares and words of reproach. They had blamed him and he had blamed himself—but mostly he had blamed Carter McKenzie for lying to him and for trying to steal the two things that mattered to him most—his honour and his family.

Even when angrily confronted, Carter had just shrugged his shoulders. 'I've done you a favour. We will make much more money out of the deal now.'

'Money wasn't the main issue,' Nicholas had ground out furiously. 'You stood to make a hefty profit on the deal that we agreed. But instead you've decimated land, burnt ancient olive and lemon groves that went back generations and were important for a whole community.'

'Money is always the main issue,' Carter had sneered. 'I did what you didn't have the guts to do. You should be thanking me.'

'I gave my word to the community that this wouldn't happen,' Nicholas had said quietly. 'You know that.'

Carter had merely laughed.

Remembering that laughter strengthened Nicholas's resolve now. At the time the only thing he could do to put things right was to buy Carter out and luckily he'd been able to afford to do that as his Far Eastern hotels came on line.

But of course that had been Carter's plan all along. Their mutual acquaintance in banking had informed him that if Nicholas's gamble in the Far East paid off he would be a millionaire. Carter had then taken a calculated risk that Nicholas would be successful and deliberately he had started to destroy the land. Then he had sat back and waited, knowing that in order to reclaim the land Nicholas would have to buy him out. It had almost amounted to legalized blackmail and it had galled Nicholas to pay, but to reclaim the land before the builders moved in there had been no alternative.

However Nicholas had always sworn that one day he would make Carter McKenzie pay. He had watched from afar as he'd continued to go through life walking over people—extorting money. The man was without morals or principle. His son Michael was the same and so was his daughter.

He ran a hand through his hair and forced himself to look at the facts and forget the heat of their lovemaking, the warmth of her embrace. She was as guilty as her father, tainted by association, complicit in a major swindle only last year. He couldn't forget that—couldn't allow himself to be swayed from what he had to do.

There was a knock at the door. It was room service and he let them in and then watched as they laid out a selection of dinner dishes under the covered hotplates out on the terrace.

'Thanks.' He tipped them, closed the door behind them, then went to see what was keeping Cat.

The bedroom was deserted and he could hear the shower running in the bathroom.

He began thinking again about how pleasurable their lovemaking had been. And then he found himself thinking back to earlier in the evening, remembering the way she had looked at him when they had stood side by side on the jetty waiting for the water taxi. He had imagined she looked pure—like a girl afraid to trust, afraid of her emotions.

But that had just been a trick of the moonlight—hadn't it?

For a moment he thought back to the earlier events in this suite, analysing—dissecting.

Surely Cat hadn't been a virgin?

No! He shook his head as he remembered how she had saucily turned the tables to torment him—kneeling before him, kissing him, her eyes flashing with provocative fire.

Then later, as he had carried her through to the bedroom, she had been sensationally wild, there had been nothing timorous or even mildly restrained about her responses. Except when he had first entered her—she had cried out. The memory crystallized in his brain like a snapshot of time. Now that he thought about it, she had tensed enough for him to pull back slightly. Had he hurt her?

He sat down on the edge of the bed and felt shaken by the idea. Cat McKenzie couldn't have been a virgin—could she? Confusion muddied his clear views of what she was.

His assessment of her as a conniving siren sat awkwardly alongside the fact that she might have been a virgin. With determination he stood up from the bed and headed for the bathroom.

'Cat, can I come in?' He knocked loudly on the door.

'I'm in the shower. I'll be out in a minute.' Cat turned her head up to the water, allowing it to wash the tearstains from her face. She had to take charge of her emotions—she was stronger than this!

It was a shock when the door of the shower was wrenched open. Her vision was blurred from her tears and for a moment Nicholas was just a dark silhouette against the brightness of the room.

'What on earth are you doing? I'd like some privacy, please. I told you I would be out in a moment.'

'I have something to ask you.'

She frowned, trying to work out what it was about his tone of voice that was different. He sounded brusque yet…off balance, somehow.

'Nicholas, go away!' She pushed her wet hair back off her face with an unsteady hand and rubbed at her eyes and then, as the watery blur started to focus, she was aware that his gaze was raking over her naked body with unrelenting, almost punishing appraisal.

Self-consciously she brushed a hand over the soapsuds that glittered against her skin. 'Whatever it is, it can wait,' she said tensely. 'I'll only be a minute.'

Nicholas ignored the request and instead he reached out and turned the water off.

His hand brushed against her breast as he pulled back and suddenly she was frighteningly aware that her heart was thumping now with a different emotion. She wanted him again.

Fury pounded through her senses, mingling with red-hot desire. She had to get rid of this feeling—get rid of Nicholas. She met his eyes defiantly.

'Are you a virgin?'

He ground the question out in such a way that she took an instinctive step back. Shocked, she stared at him, and for a few seconds there was a tense, unnatural kind of silence. Then she laughed—she didn't know if she was laughing because she was so nervous and appalled by the question or if she truly found it funny. 'Why are you asking me that?'

He held her eyes with a stubborn determination. 'Are you, Catherine?'

'How can you ask me that after what we've just done?'

'You know what I mean.' He wasn't amused. His dark eyes seemed to slice into her very soul.

'Pass me a towel, please.' Any pretence at amusement was now dead. She tried to avoid the question along with his eyes.

'Not until you answer me.' He sounded dangerously angry now.

'How dare you? It's none of your business what I am,' she flared.

He reached out and touched her face, tipping her chin upwards, forcing her to make the connection with his eyes. 'Answer me now,' he ordered softly.

'You've got a flaming nerve, Nicholas Zentenas. Just because we've had sex, it doesn't give you the right to barge in here, disturbing my privacy, asking personal questions.'

He didn't release her; in fact his grip was like iron, forcing her to maintain contact with his gaze.

She bit down on her lip. He was so arrogant and she wanted

desperately to tell him she had slept with hundreds of men. But she couldn't.

'I was a virgin.' She admitted the truth huskily. 'But it doesn't mean anything!' Her eyes flashed fire.

'Of course it means something!' His grip relaxed and then his thumb brushed over her lips, making her tingle with need.

She hated the fact that he could do that to her. Hated it with almost as much intensity as she loved it.

'You should have told me, Catherine—I'd have been more gentle.' There was a strange huskiness to his tone that she hadn't heard before. 'Did I hurt you?'

'No!' Her heart thumped uneasily against her chest. But he could hurt her... Oh, so easily he could emotionally destroy her... She acknowledged the truth to herself quietly. She needed to take back some control; she needed to drive him away.

'Why didn't you tell me?'

She took a deep breath. 'Because you might have thought it made you special. And it doesn't. It was just sex.'

The coldness of her response made Nicholas shake his head. The kitten had very sharp claws indeed. She was well able to look out for herself. 'I'm sorry to disappoint you, but I think it does make what just happened between us pretty special.'

'Don't be so sure of yourself, Nicholas.' Her voice trembled alarmingly. 'I got carried away...' She struggled to find an excuse for her actions and failed.

'You'd just signed your first major business contract and it was a powerful aphrodisiac, is that it?' He supplied the reason dryly as some of the certainties about her character slipped back into place. He'd been taken in by a beautiful woman once before—and it had led to the divorce court. He wasn't going to be duped a second time.

The suggestion stung but it was better than looking weak,

so she forced herself to hold his gaze mutinously and just shrugged. 'I suppose so.'

In a way he was relieved—it absolved any guilt that had momentarily assailed him.

'That's fine because I wasn't expecting anything deeper.' As Nicholas grated the words he was surprised to feel a flare of anger inside himself that he didn't fully understand. 'But one thing I'm certain of. No matter what has sparked it, there is a powerful chemistry between us. I'm the one who has awakened your sexual appetite. I'm the one who is going to teach you all there is about making love.'

'It was sex, not love-making, and it's not going to happen again.' She angled her chin up with fierce determination.

He laughed at that but it held a raw edge. 'It's going to happen whenever I want it to happen.' As if to illustrate the fact, he ran his hand down from her chin, over the glittering suds on her body, smoothing over the satin wetness of her breast, feeling how she instantly tightened beneath his fingers, her nipples hardening to throbbing peaks. 'You see!' He felt a flare of triumph mixed with arousal.

With difficulty she forced herself to flinch from the touch but the desire he had stirred up inside her was still vehemently insistent. 'That doesn't prove anything. Go away, Nicholas!'

He smiled and for a moment she thought he was going to comply as he reached and flicked on the water again. Then he started to unbutton his shirt, a look of deliberation in his dark eyes.

'What are you doing?' Her voice raised in alarm.

'What does it look like?' he drawled sardonically. 'I'm going to join you.'

'Nicholas, don't!' Her heart thudded fiercely as he dropped his shirt on the bathroom floor and then reached to take a condom from the back pocket of his trousers before unzipping them.

He had the most magnificent body—a bronzed, strongly muscled, smooth torso that tapered down to narrow hips and an absolutely flat abdomen. His erection was enormous and she averted her eyes from it hastily, her skin tingling with searing heat.

'This isn't a good idea,' she breathed huskily as he stepped into the cubicle beside her, but her voice lacked conviction now.

'Whether you like it or not, you want me, Catherine. So your body belongs to me right now; you may as well stop fighting the fact.'

There was determination on his handsome face as he moved forward and she backed against the tiled wall.

Water pounded down over them as he bent his head and captured her lips with his. The kiss was sweetly searing and it made her stomach turn over with longing. He could kiss so well, she thought hazily.

Almost of their own volition, her arms went up and around his shoulders. His hands smoothed over her, drawing her closer, then holding her bottom he pressed himself against her.

She groaned with need, kissing him urgently now.

'I thought you said this wasn't a good idea?' he teased her softly as he pulled back a little, his eyes gleaming with hunger.

'Well, I was wrong.'

Smiling, he reached to open the condom packet. 'This time I'd better be a little more responsible…hmm?'

She shuddered with desire as he lifted her off her feet and, holding her back against the shower wall, peppered her face and her neck with kisses whilst his hands stroked over her body with sensuous caresses. He was right, she thought dazedly. The chemistry between them was too intense. She didn't understand why he made her feel like this; all she knew was that she couldn't fight it. Even when he entered her, it was as if she still couldn't get close enough to him.

Despite the strength and the force of his passion, he was infinitely gentle and she wound her legs around him and gave herself up to the bliss of the feelings he could conjure up.

His hands cupped her bottom squeezing her against him, gently rocking her. She raked her fingers through his wet hair and tried to stop herself from crying out with ecstasy.

'I want you so much.' The words burst out of her uncontrollably with the feeling.

'Do you want to come?' He whispered the words huskily, his tongue licking against her earlobe, then lower down her neck.

'Yes…yes.'

He thrust into her with a passion that made her senses spin and her body convulse with delicious waves of sensuous pleasure.

She hadn't thought it possible for the feelings to be more intense than they had been the first time around, but they were. It was so earth-shattering that she wanted to cry tears of sheer joy.

He waited for her pleasure to spiral out of control before joining her, thrusting into her deeply, alleviating his desire with a forceful intent that turned her on all over again.

Breathless and spent, she clung to him under the jet of water. She wanted to be held like this for ever, with his heart thudding against her breast and his lips nuzzling against her neck.

Nicholas frowned to himself as he realized that once again he had completely lost control.

'Every time you touch me I seem to lose all perspective.' She whispered the words almost to herself.

He smiled. 'You can't fight chemistry. We may as well just let the sexual heat play out between us.'

The deeply taunting voice hit the rawness of need inside her.

'Are you hungry?' he asked suddenly.

'Not really.' She didn't want him to let her go but he was already pulling away from her.

'Well, I have to tell you I'm starving.' He lifted his head to the stream of water and let it wash over him. For a second her eyes raked over the perfect symmetry of his features, drinking him in whilst his eyes were closed. She wanted to stand on tiptoe and kiss his eyelids, kiss his lips; she itched to reach out and touch him again. Instead she balled her hands into fists and forced herself not to move.

He stepped away from her, out of the cubicle, and wrapped a towel around his waist before holding a bath sheet out for her.

'Just leave it over the heated rail,' she said as she raised her face towards the jet of the shower again. 'I'll be out in a moment.'

'Don't be long.' He did as she'd asked and then padded through to the bedroom, closing the door behind him.

Well, she had done it again—so much for being strong, she mocked herself fiercely. So much for keeping him at arm's length!

Switching off the water, she stepped out of the shower and wrapped herself in the warm towel. She should really get dressed and demand to be taken home right now.

Except that she didn't really want to go home now! Cat closed her eyes as memories of the way he had taken her seared through her mind. He'd started something inside her, had stoked a flame of desire that was now raging out of control. And, worse than that, he knew it.

She'd done the one thing that she said she would never do—she had given a man the power to control her.

Of course she couldn't leave things like this. She needed to take that power back from him before she lost every scrap of her dignity. The only problem was that, right at this moment, she didn't have a clue how she was going to do that. Was Nicholas right? Was she just going to have to give up and stop fighting against this, let him make love to her whenever he wanted until the feelings—whatever they were—had burnt out?

As the steam cleared from the mirrors in the bathroom, she had a clear view of herself within the gilded frame. Her lips were swollen from his kisses, her eyes were over-bright with emotion. And she was filled with anger at allowing herself to be so stupid.

First thing she had to do was get dressed; at least that would be some measure of armour in her defence. Hurriedly she went through to the bedroom to find her dress. It was lying on the floor just outside the bedroom door and as soon as she picked it up she realized that she would never be able to wear it again. It was ripped along one side, prompting memories from earlier. How his impatience had excited her—how she had eagerly welcomed the forceful way he had torn it from her.

She bit down on her lip as she tried to close her mind to that and the fact that exactly the same had happened to her underwear earlier! The single item of clothing she had left was a bra! Her only option was to put on the white towelling robe that was hanging behind the bathroom door.

As armour went, it was lamentably poor. She could hardly march out of the hotel wearing nothing but a bra and a bathrobe!

It seemed that Nicholas held all the cards in this game. And it was just a game—she had no doubt about that. He was toying with her, enjoying the fact that in the end she had been powerless to resist him.

She hated him for that—but she hated herself even more.

CHAPTER NINE

NICHOLAS was uncorking a bottle of champagne when Cat walked out on to the terrace.

The first thing she noticed was that he had changed into a pair of faded denim jeans and a white shirt. She had never seen him dressed so casually. The attire suited him, made him look relaxed and impossibly handsome. She felt her pulses quicken in response and then quickly tried to quash the emotion.

'Where did you get the clothes?' she asked with a frown.

'I keep a spare wardrobe at all of my hotels. It saves time having to pack.'

'Very convenient,' she said dryly. 'I don't suppose you keep a spare set of clothing for—' she hesitated, not wanting to say the word *mistresses* '—your guests,' she finished lamely.

'Sorry, no.' His lips twisted in an amused grin. 'But you look good in the robe.' His eyes swept over her. It was a size too big for her and seemed to dwarf her slender frame. Yet on her it looked incredibly sexy. He noticed how her hair was drying in soft curls around her face and her skin was glowing from the heat of the shower—or was it from their lovemaking?

He found himself wanting to walk across to untie the belt of that gown and allow his hands to run over her naked body. He couldn't seem to get enough of her!

'Unfortunately my dress is torn so I wasn't able to put it on.' Her eyes were bright with emerald sparks of fire as she caught the sensuality of his appraisal.

There was a spark of anger in her voice and he noticed how she also raised her chin defensively. He smiled to himself. Even though he had proved to her that she was his for the taking, she was still trying to assert her control over the situation and against him. He had to admit that he admired her tenacity. She also excited him beyond reason.

'Well, don't worry about that.' He lowered his voice huskily. 'Because you don't need any clothes right now and I'll buy you some new things tomorrow.'

He watched as her skin flared with heat. 'I don't want you to buy me anything!' she blazed. 'I can buy my own things.'

'Whatever you say!' He raised his hands in surrender.

'And I want you to take me home,' she said, pushing her advantage, and was taken aback when he laughed.

'Do you?'

The sardonic question made her blush wildly. 'I just said so, didn't I?'

'Well, if you want to go home tonight I will, of course, arrange it,' he agreed smoothly. 'But first I think we should have something to eat.'

Cat was about to say that she didn't want anything but as he took the covers off the silver tureens the delicious aroma of pasta floated in the air and she realized suddenly that she hadn't eaten since early this morning.

'Let's see, what have we got?' Nicholas read the menu that had been left for them. 'To begin with, Seafood Linguine, spaghetti with artichokes and herbs or Penne Arrabbiata?'

'That does smell good,' she conceded as she came closer towards the table.

He pulled out a chair for her. 'Come, sit down and I'll get you something. What would you like?'

She hesitated for just a second and then complied. What was the point in starving herself? She couldn't go anywhere until she had sorted out the problem of her clothes. And Nicholas was obviously not going to arrange for her to get back to the airport until after he'd eaten. 'Some linguine would be nice, thanks.'

As he pushed in her chair he leaned down close to her. 'By the way, I meant it when I said you look great in that robe— very sexy.' His breath was close to her ear and she could smell the clean male scent of him and her senses leapt uncontrollably.

'Well, as I'm sure you say that to all your guests, I won't take it personally.' She was proud of how cool she sounded but when he kissed her neck she found herself turning to jelly.

'Not *all*,' he drawled teasingly. 'You are in a class of your own, Cat.'

As he turned away to get their food he was aware that there was an element of truth in that statement. Catherine was different from any of the other women he had dated in his life. For one thing, she turned him on so completely that when they made love he forgot everything—even the fact that this was all about revenge.

He frowned, angry with himself for even conceding the thought. It was true that she turned him on with an incredible force; just a smile or a certain look in her eyes was all it seemed to take to make him want her like crazy. But he had to remember she was naturally duplicitous and this was just sex. Once he'd taken her to bed a few times the novelty would wear off, he assured himself forcefully. Certainly by the time he had got around to taking the McKenzie inheritance she would be well on her way to being history.

He put their plates down on the table and sat opposite her.

'Would you like a glass of champagne?' Without waiting for her to answer, he leaned across and filled her glass.

'Thank you.'

Their gazes collided across the table. She saw the fierce intensity in his eyes and it made her shiver. What was he thinking? she wondered. That he had enjoyed his *release*? Deliberately she reminded herself of the insensitivity of his remark on the plane. She thought it would help her to detach herself emotionally from the effects of those sensually gorgeous dark eyes. But strangely the memory just hurt.

Swiftly she looked away from him, out towards the glittering beauty of the city. They had a fabulous bird's eye view whilst being completely private. 'It's lovely out here, isn't it?'

'Yes.' Nicholas's eyes were still on her face. How was she able to switch on that vulnerable look with such unerring precision? She wasn't vulnerable, he reminded himself fiercely. It was an act.

She was a true McKenzie—driven by business deals and money, nothing more. Yet, despite the assurances, he couldn't help but wonder about that look in her eyes and the fact that she had been a virgin.

'You know you should have told me that you hadn't slept with someone before.' He hadn't intended to bring up that subject again but somehow he couldn't leave it.

She looked back at him coolly. 'I thought I made it clear that I didn't think it was any of your business.'

'Pardon me for being old-fashioned, but when two people have been as intimate as we've just been, I think it was very much my business.'

'You are not old-fashioned.'

He couldn't help but smile at the assertion. 'Maybe you're right, but strangely, the fact that you chose to give your virginity to me intrigues me.'

'Because you view it as an ego boost.'

'No, because I view it as something special.'

There was an honesty about the way he said those words that tore at her.

'Don't, Nicholas.' It was as if he had found an open wound and pulled at it.

'Don't what?'

'Pretend.' For a second her eyes were almost pleading with him. It took him aback and he fell silent. 'Perhaps you are a bit flattered by the fact that I was a virgin—but you and I both know that nothing out of the ordinary is taking place here. You probably do this kind of thing every week with a different woman.'

He laughed at that. 'I can assure you I don't.'

She looked over at him, her eyes mocking him now.

'I'm not trying to tell you that I haven't been out with lots of women. Of course I have—but not a different one every week!' He smiled and shook his head. 'I've got to leave myself with enough stamina to get some work done, you know.'

The throwaway remark made her laugh.

She had a very attractive laugh, he thought distractedly; it seemed to light her eyes with warmth. If it were true that the eyes were the windows of the soul, then he had seriously miscalculated in his assessment of her.

The thought was not welcome. Why the hell did he keep thinking things like that?

'So tell me a bit about yourself,' he invited suddenly.

Instantly her wary expression returned. 'Why?'

He laughed. 'Why not? That's what two people do when they have dinner together for the first time—isn't it?'

'We don't have that kind of relationship,' she said quickly. She didn't want him pretending to be interested in her in any deep, meaningful way. Maybe she couldn't control the intensity of her responses when it came to making love with him, but she could guard her innermost self—at least that way she could keep her heart safe from him, keep some pride intact.

'Don't we?'

She shook her head. 'Any conversations we have should be centred around business.'

'We dispensed with business earlier.' His voice was dry.

'Not entirely,' she disagreed. 'We didn't actually get around to discussing the outdoor shots and whether or not the rest of the campaign should follow the—'

'Cat, the rest of the campaign hasn't been agreed on yet. And there is no point in discussing it until we've completed the first ad.' He bit the words out tersely. 'I've already made that quite clear. So stop trying to hide behind work.'

'I'm not trying to hide behind anything,' she said quickly. 'I'm simply saying that we need to at least keep future adverts in mind when we are making this first one.'

'Just leave it, OK.'

'If that's what you want.'

'It is.' He frowned and watched as she toyed with her food. 'What I want to talk about now is you.'

'There's not much to say on that subject.'

'I don't believe that.'

'Well, it's true.' She shrugged. 'I graduated from university earlier this year, found a job in advertising. That's it.'

'And you're—what—twenty?' He pretended to hazard a guess and she nodded. 'That's young to have graduated.'

'Is it?' Cat shrugged. She had always been focused. She had wanted to leave home as soon as possible, and in her mind qualifications had equalled independence so she had pursued them with alacrity.

'When are you twenty-one?'

'Just over three months.' She reached for her glass and took a sip of the champagne. Why was he asking these questions?

She didn't want him analysing her life—her reactions. And she certainly didn't want to discuss her birthday!

'Are you planning anything special?'

'No.'

'I suppose your family will be throwing you some kind of celebratory event?'

She shrugged and her eyes met his with a kind of stony indifference.

What had he expected? he thought angrily. She was hardly going to admit to the fact that she was considering a marriage of convenience to get her hands on her inheritance. But she could say something!

'But you do have a family?' he pressed. 'Didn't you tell me something earlier about having a brother who dotes on you?'

She took another few sips of champagne and felt the alcohol hitting her system. 'He's my half-brother. My mother died when I was young and my father married again.'

He already knew all of that, but at least she was giving him a piece of personal information at last rather than monosyllables.

'And what about your father—are you close?'

She swept a hand through the length of her hair. 'He's my father—what do you think?'

He frowned. 'Well, fathers usually adore their daughters, don't they? So I presume you're Daddy's girl. Spoilt rotten and his adoring number one fan.'

'Absolutely.' She took refuge behind the illusion and smiled at him.

The candlelight flickered and danced as a warm breeze suddenly disturbed it, but not before he had witnessed the intense glitter in the beauty of her eyes.

She was obviously very defensive about her father; maybe people had openly criticized him in the past and she had built up a natural antipathy to anyone delving too deep.

It stood to reason. If she didn't adore her father and her brother she wouldn't go along with their crooked schemes. He didn't know why he kept feeling these momentary pangs that he was wrong about her. He'd had her checked out thoroughly by his private investigator. He knew what she was like.

'What about you?' She switched the subject hurriedly before he could ask anything else. 'Have you got any family?'

'Yes, like you, family is very important to me.' His eyes held hers steadily. 'My father died some years ago, but my mother and extended family all live in the same small village in Crete where I grew up.'

The sudden insight made her look at him with renewed interest. Because he was so wealthy and powerful, she had assumed that he would be too busy making money to have much time for family affinity.

'And what about children; did you have a family with your ex-wife?'

'For a woman who only wanted to talk about business you've suddenly changed your tune.'

The mocking tone made her withdraw instantly. 'I was just curious.' She shrugged.

'Well, in answer to your question—no, we had no children. Probably just as well, seeing as the marriage only lasted six months.'

'I'm sorry.'

The gentleness of her tone made his lips twist derisively. He didn't want a McKenzie's sympathy. 'Don't be. Sylvia was no great loss.'

There was an edge of rawness about the statement that made Cat frown. Had his ex-wife managed to cut through that haughty exterior? Had she dented his pride and hurt him? For a second she wanted to believe that because it made her understand why he seemed so remote sometimes. She knew what it was like to feel rejected—she'd felt like an outsider in her own home for nearly all of her childhood. She knew what it was like to have your feelings trampled into dust, how wary it made you of people and how much it hurt, and it made her want to reach out to him.

Then, as she met the harsh, almost ruthless expression in his eyes, she quickly blocked out the thought. Reaching out emotionally to Nicholas Zentenas would be as stupid as reaching out to a man-eating tiger.

This was the problem when you slept with someone, she told herself furiously. It was all too easy to start trying to attach real feelings to the situation, to start reinventing your lover's persona, distort reality.

Well, she wasn't going to be that stupid!

He watched as she put her cutlery down. She hadn't eaten much. 'Shall we move on to the main course?' he suggested. 'I think there's—'

'Actually, I couldn't eat another thing,' she cut across him quickly. 'I'd prefer it if you would just arrange for me to head back to the airport.'

He sat back in his chair and regarded her steadily. 'I take it you don't mind travelling back dressed as you are?'

'Don't be ridiculous.' She glared at him. 'I thought we could phone one of the boutiques downstairs. I'll have to buy something new.'

He glanced at his gold wristwatch. 'Cat, it's late. The shops are closed.'

She felt a rising sense of panic. 'Yes, but you could get them opened if you wanted.'

'I don't think so. The staff will have gone home.' He got up and cleared the dishes from the table, then placed a bowl of strawberries down between them.

She watched him through narrowed eyes as he sat back in

his chair. 'You never had any intention of getting me back to London tonight, did you?'

He shook his head. 'But I'm a man of my word. If you really want to leave, I'll arrange for my jet to be on standby and a water taxi to come and pick you up.'

'In a dressing gown!'

'Well, as I already said, there's nothing I can do about that.' He nonchalantly reached out and picked up one of the strawberries. 'You should try these; they are lovely with the champagne.'

'I don't want anything, Nicholas.'

She had no doubt that if he wanted to get the boutiques downstairs reopened he could make one phone call and it would be magically arranged. She had a good mind to call his bluff and tell him to go ahead and make the travel arrangements for her.

'Shall I tell you what I want?' he asked quietly.

When she made no reply he smiled.

'I want to spend the whole night making love to you.' He said the words softly as he met the shimmering intensity of her eyes. 'I want to kiss you all over, hold you in my arms and take you over and over again.'

Something about the way he said that made her heart turn over with longing. He watched the heat rise in the creaminess of her skin and laughed. 'And I think that is what you want too.'

'You are an extremely arrogant man, Nicholas,' she murmured angrily.

He smiled and reached out to touch her hand. 'But you want me as much as I want you—why do you keep fighting against this truth?'

'I'm not fighting against anything,' she lied breathlessly. His fingers ran softly over her hand, stroking against the inside of her wrist and stoking her senses almost absently.

How was it that he could turn her on so effortlessly? She closed her eyes for a moment and strove to find some sense within the torrent of emotion. It was just sex, she told herself fiercely. As long as she recognised that, he couldn't reach her on an emotional level and therefore she would be safe. 'But I guess I'm stuck here, aren't I, seeing as you ripped my dress.' She tried to make her voice indifferent as her eyes snapped open.

He smiled and she tried to ignore the gleam in his eyes that told her he was not fooled.

'But tomorrow we should discuss business again,' she continued hurriedly. 'Sort out the outside shots and how we can carry the theme through to—'

'Cat!'

She broke off disconcertedly as he squeezed her hand. 'Yes?'

'Come over here.'

'Don't talk to me like that!'

He looked at her mockingly. 'You asked me not to pretend. But you are the one who is putting up the pretence. We moved on from the subject of work—remember?'

She shrugged, at a loss for what to say. Her eyes travelled from the searing power of his gaze to the way his hand held hers. The gentle touch of his skin against hers made her shiver with need.

'Are you cold?'

She laughed; the summer night was intensely hot, to say nothing of the way he made her feel. 'No, I'm not cold.'

'You're shivering.' He pulled her hand. 'Come over here.'

It was hard to ignore the order a second time because there was a gentler note hidden in the deep tone. He pushed his chair back and drew her around the table until she stood before him.

'That's better—you were too far away over there.' There was satisfaction in his voice as he caught her other hand and then pulled her down to sit facing him on his knee her legs either side of him. 'You're too tense, you need to learn how to relax.' He stroked a hand through her hair, brushing it back from her face so that he could see her more clearly. 'And I think I might just have the answer.'

'What would that be?' she asked huskily.

Their eyes locked.

'Maybe a few strawberries with champagne.' He murmured the words playfully as he slipped her dressing gown down and kissed her naked shoulder. 'And a little bit of this…'

The touch of his lips against her skin was wildly provocative. She closed her eyes as he worked his way higher, kissing the vulnerable curve of her neck.

'And a little bit of this…' He cupped her face and held her while his lips captured hers.

The feeling inside her was like a flame melting sweet chocolate. 'You are really bad for me, do you know that?' She whispered the words unsteadily as he released her.

'On the contrary—relaxation is very good for you.' His hands moved to the belt of her robe. 'It lowers the blood pressure.'

She laughed breathlessly as he untied the belt. 'That's definitely debatable.'

Why did everything feel right when she was in his arms? she wondered hazily.

This was a dangerous madness but she just couldn't resist him.

The dressing gown slithered to the floor and she looked up at the star-studded sky as his hands moved possessively over her.

It was easier to give in and infinitely more enjoyable than fighting him.

CHAPTER TEN

WHEN Cat woke up she was alone in the double bed. For a few moments she stretched out a hand towards the empty pillow next to her as she remembered the night of wild passion.

A strange ache seemed to curl in the pit of her stomach as she remembered the strong arms that had held her so tenderly, the whispered words of arousal and the possessive warmth of his kisses.

'Wake up, sleepyhead.' Nicholas came into the room and pulled back the curtains. Sunlight filtered across the room with a dazzling intensity.

'What time is it?' she murmured, putting a shielding arm across her face.

'Almost eleven.'

'Eleven!' Instantly she struggled to sit up, holding the sheet across her naked body with a measure of shyness that was absurd considering the fact that he had explored every inch of her with fervent concentration last night. 'I can't believe that I've slept so late!'

'Well, we were rather busy last night,' he murmured. 'Room service have sent up some tea.' He put a cup down on the dressing table beside her and she noticed that he was fully dressed in chinos and a white shirt. He looked suave and refreshed and by contrast she was suddenly aware of her dishevelled hair and sleep-smudged face.

'Thanks. You should have woken me earlier! How long have you been up?'

'I had a business call that I had to take at about nine. So unfortunately, I had to drag myself away—otherwise…' his eyes lingered on her creamy skin and the luxuriant mass of blonde waves on the pillow '…I would have definitely woken you up.' He smiled as he watched the rise of heat under her skin and the way she bit down on the rose-coloured softness of her lips—lips that were still slightly swollen from his mouth.

He felt a sudden urge to pull the sheet away from her and take her again. The impulse was stronger than he wanted it to be and, impatient with himself, he turned away. 'Drink your tea and then get dressed,' he murmured. 'I've had some clothes sent up to the suite for you. They are hanging on a rail outside in the lounge. Take your pick of what you want when you are ready.'

'Thanks.' His businesslike manner disconcerted her after the intensity of their passion last night. She didn't know how to deal with the situation. 'What time are we heading back to London?' she asked cautiously.

'I've spoken to the pilot this morning and he informs me that the first available air-space is six-thirty this evening.' He slanted a wry glance over at her. 'I know it is later than we had hoped, but unfortunately air traffic control has the last word on these matters, so it is out of my hands.'

'It will have to suffice, then,' she said quietly. But perversely she wished that there had been no available air space until the middle of next week. She also wished that Nicholas had sounded a little more enthusiastic about spending the day with her. The feeling was most unwelcome. What on earth was the matter with her? she wondered crossly. Last night she had at least attempted to think sensibly—now she wanted to stay here in a kind of limbo, luxuriating in his lovemaking, blocking out all logical, sane thoughts.

Get a grip, Cat, she told herself fiercely. They had enjoyed a pleasurable interlude last night—but it was unreal, it meant nothing to either of them and it certainly couldn't last.

The ring of the phone in the other room made him turn away. 'I'd better get that.'

'Yes, it might be important.' As the door closed behind him, she hurriedly gathered herself and got out of bed. She needed to shower and clear her head and then she needed to change the focus of her thoughts back towards work, she told herself firmly. As they were stuck here for a while, it was an ideal opportunity to consider some more ideas for the forth-coming campaign.

A little while later, showered with her hair dried into straight silken submission she looked around for the dressing gown she had worn last night—then remembered it was still out on the patio. For a second her mind stole back to the way he had made love to her out there under the bright starlit sky, candles flickering in the warm air as he'd slipped himself into her. Although she had been sitting on top of him, he had been the one in control, dominating her senses, making her writhe with need.

Hastily she snapped the memory closed as she felt the heat of desire flare up inside her all over again. It was over, she told herself fiercely. Time to move on.

Wrapping herself in one of the bath sheets, she cautiously stepped out into the lounge to look for the clothes Nicholas had left for her.

There was a rail just by the front door and, to her relief, Nicholas was out on the terrace talking on the phone, so she was able to flick through the clothes in privacy.

After she had got just halfway through the selection it

became clear that they were all designer labels and, although she couldn't find a price tag on anything, she was sure they would all be exorbitantly expensive and well out of her price bracket. They were gorgeous, though…and with each outfit there was a hanger with coordinated underwear, all in the correct size.

One summer dress in particular caught her eye; it was pure silk and the colour of the Caribbean sea on a summer morning.

She pulled it out and held it up to the light, admiring its iridescent sheen as the sun hit it.

'Strange you should select that dress.' Nicholas's voice from behind made her whirl around in surprise. 'It was the one that caught my eye too. I thought it would be stunning on you.'

'It's certainly very beautiful.' As he walked closer she tightly held the edges of the towel wrapped around her.

'You should try it on,' he suggested firmly.

'Actually, Nicholas, I don't usually buy designer clothes.' She put it back on the rail. 'They are beyond my budget.'

'They only sell designer labels here.' He reached behind her and pulled out the dress again, to hold it out towards her. 'Don't worry, I'll pick up the tab.'

When she still didn't take it from him, he shrugged. 'It's either that or go home as you are.'

Slowly she reached out a hand and took the garment from him. 'Well, I suppose I have no choice, then—but I will pay you back.'

For a moment he found himself captivated by the way she looked up at him. He had to hand it to her; she was a very good actress. There was a husky integrity about her tone, a light of clear principle in her green eyes. He'd have sworn that she really was uncomfortable accepting the gift and that she really wanted to pay him back. But then, to be successful at conning people you had to be a good liar—her father had been pretty plausible as well when he had agreed that it would be a felony to rip out the heart of a community.

'Don't worry about it,' he said dryly. 'I'll settle for seeing you in the dress—oh, and in these.' He picked up some blatantly seductive underwear and hooked it over the hanger of the dress. 'That will be payment enough.'

He noticed how her eyes shadowed as if he had struck her and against his will he wanted to reach out and gather her into his arms.

'I said I'd pay you back and I will,' she said tightly. 'And I won't be needing these…' She put the basque and the silk stockings back where he had taken them from and then, with her head held high, she marched back into the bedroom and shut the door firmly behind her.

Cat was shaking as she flung the dress down on the bed. She couldn't describe it but there had been something in the cool glint of his eyes that had struck her like a whip against raw flesh. He'd just treated her as if she were nothing more than a concubine—someone to be used like a plaything.

How could he look at her like that when he had made love to her so tenderly last night?

Idiot! Cat berated herself fiercely as she struggled with unfamiliar emotions. She couldn't understand why she was allowing him to get to her like this. Of course last night wasn't anything serious. But, that aside, she wasn't going to let him treat her like some kind of kept woman whom he could buy with a few trinkets and treat any way he damned well pleased. She had some self-respect left!

Strengthened by determination, she turned to pick up the dress. She had stepped into it and was just struggling to reach the zip when the bedroom door opened and Nicholas followed her in.

He cast his eyes over the long length of her back. It was

strange but he had never found a woman's back so incredibly erotic before. Something about the light golden tan of her skin made him want to run his fingers over her.

'Need some help?' he asked as he noted her struggle to reach the zip.

Blonde hair swished as she glared at him over her shoulder, her eyes like bright emerald splinters. 'No, thank you.'

Ignoring her words, he walked across towards her and took hold of her, one hand firmly at her waist whilst the other found the zip.

'What's wrong?' He whispered the words huskily against her ear as he ran the zip lightly up.

She closed her eyes, fighting the treacherous weakness that his close proximity always induced. 'You mean apart from the fact that you've just made me feel cheap?' she muttered sardonically.

'That wasn't my intention.' His hands lingered at the curve of her waist before sliding the zip all the way up, his fingers brushing provocatively against her skin. 'I ripped your dress last night, now I've replaced it. What's wrong with that?' He swept her hair away from her neck and kissed it softly.

Immediately she felt the rekindling of fire inside her. What was wrong with her? she wondered hazily. As soon as he held her and kissed her, everything was magically OK again! It was crazy.

'I'll tell you what's wrong with it.' She pulled away and turned to face him. 'You think because you've got money that you can buy anything you want—*anyone* you want. Well, I'm not for sale, Nicholas. I'm my own woman and I always will be.'

He smiled at that but it was a smile singularly lacking in humour. 'Actually, Catherine McKenzie, right at this moment you are *my* woman.'

She shook her head but her heart leapt as he took a step forward, his gaze hard and determined. 'And I can assure you I don't want to buy you.' She felt breathless as he reached out and touched her face, tipping it upwards so that his eyes could run over her with fierce intensity. 'I just want to possess you.'

The words sizzled through her consciousness with searing force. But before she could even formulate some kind of a reply he lowered his head and kissed her.

It was a hard, punishing kiss, yet it was so provocative and intense that she found herself melting and responding, returning it with a fierce need that tore through her very soul.

'I'm glad you didn't accept the underwear.' He growled the words against her ear as he pulled her skirt upwards, his hands possessively caressing her naked curves. 'I much prefer you without.'

Why did she let him do this to her? she wondered as she closed her eyes in sweet blissful submission. Why did she want him so much that nothing else mattered?

It was later in the afternoon before they finally ventured out of the hotel to go and have some lunch. The sun was sizzling down out of a clear blue sky and the waters of the canal looked an almost surreal turquoise against the backdrop of beautiful buildings.

Nicholas insisted that instead of waiting for a water taxi they took a ride in a gondola. 'You can't come to Venice and not take a trip in a gondola,' he said firmly.

'You are not going to turn all romantic on me, are you, Nicholas?' she quipped lightly.

He laughed and made no reply to that and immediately she wished she hadn't made the joke. What on earth had possessed her? Probably the same kind of madness that made her surrender to him every time he so much as brushed his fingers against her skin. Nicholas didn't want to have a romance with her—just sex.

She glanced away from him, stunned by how much it hurt when she reminded herself of these things. A gondola pulled alongside the jetty for the hotel and the gondolier held the boat steady, while Nicholas stepped down and reached to help her in. The boat rocked alarmingly until they sat down in the red velvet cushioned seat. Then the gondolier pushed them away from the platform and they glided smoothly out.

There was a good view of the hotel as they pulled back from it and Cat tried to concentrate on that rather than on the fact that, due to the close confines of the boat, she was pressed against Nicholas and his arm was draped across her shoulder, his fingers stroking absently along the bare skin at the top of her arm.

'The hotel looks fabulous from here,' she murmured. 'Maybe the outside shots for the advert should be taken from this angle.'

'Maybe.' Nicholas frowned and listened as she launched into a discussion on the merits of shooting the whole commercial with a soft focus lens. Cat was still an enigma to him. Sexually he had total control of her now; she was his for the taking and the passion between them was incredible. Yet as soon as he broke her barriers down, she deliberately started to rebuild them again. Why was that?

She should be ripe for reeling in now and yet she was still trying to twist away from him. He really hadn't foreseen this kind of problem. Usually when he took a woman to bed she wanted to curl up against him and turn the relationship into something deeper. Yet Cat seemed to deliberately seek a businesslike retreat.

It was a bit of a role reversal and it was very irritating. He was going to have to pull the strings a little harder, he thought decisively. He would get Catherine, hook, line and sinker, body and soul, if it was the last thing he ever did!

'Do you know what, Catherine? I really couldn't care less how we shoot the advert right now,' he cut across her firmly as she paused to draw breath, and his fingers ran upwards to stroke through her hair. 'All I can think about at the moment is how much I've enjoyed our time together here. In fact, you are having a very unusual effect on me.'

'Am I?' She slanted a curious look at him.

'Yes…' His eyes moved to her lips. 'The thing is, I can't seem to get enough of you.'

As he said the words Nicholas realized that they were true. Sexually speaking, she was driving him out of his mind.

'Don't say things like that to me, Nicholas,' she murmured huskily.

'Why not, when it's true?'

'I just… I don't want you to say things like that to me.' Her heart was thudding erratically against her chest as she met his eyes.

'What are you so frightened of?' He asked the question almost to himself.

She made no reply, but he could see the shadows of consternation in the beauty of her eyes. He frowned and ran a hand gently along her jaw, tipping her face upwards so that he could kiss her.

It was a tender kiss, unlike anything that had gone before, and it seemed to melt Cat's senses until she felt dizzy with need for him.

The gondola smoothly swished along the narrow maze of canals, under bridges, past houses and hotels. But for a while Cat was oblivious to everything except the pleasure of just being held and kissed. As the boat turned a corner out into the Grand Canal a breeze swept up and the waves were choppy. Some spray swished over the boat and they laughingly pulled apart. Then, without saying a word, she curled in against him again.

It was probably crazy but she couldn't remember ever being this happy before.

'You can see the Bridge of Sighs from here.' Nicholas pointed down one of the waterways. 'There it is.'

'It's beautiful, isn't it?' she said dreamily. 'Everything about this city is so perfect—it's like a romantic film set.'

'Yes, but appearances are deceptive. It's the bridge leading to the prison and it's called the Bridge of Sighs because the window was the last view a condemned man had of the city before incarceration.'

'I guess it's what you call reality—which is rarely romantic.'

'You are much too young and beautiful to be so cynical,' he said, laughing. 'Let me tell you, lots of romances have flourished in this city. For instance, it is rumoured that Casanova escaped from the prison to meet his one true love.'

'Casanova didn't have one true love,' she said with a laugh.

'How do you know that?' he teased. 'He just got really bad press. To coin a cliché, you should never judge a book by its cover.'

'You should never ignore the facts either—otherwise you could end up making a serious error of judgement.' She leaned her head back against his shoulder and tried to disregard the fact that she wanted to ignore the reality about Nicholas and believe that this was the start of something serious.

For a moment silence fell between them.

Was she starting to fall in love with him? As soon as the question entered her consciousness, she cast it away. She was enjoying his company—enjoying the intimacy of making love with him. *Nothing more.*

The boat glided smoothly in towards the shore.

'I hope you enjoyed that,' Nicholas said as he climbed out and reached to help her step on to dry land.

'Yes, it was great.' Cat avoided eye contact with him. Like

pebbles thrown in a pond, her thoughts had sent out disturbing waves that couldn't be ignored. She wasn't in love with him because she wasn't that stupid—for one thing, Nicholas would never return those feelings. She would never have the kind of life that she craved with someone like him; it could never be settled and ordinary. Women were just playthings to him.

So this wasn't love, but perhaps she was developing feelings for him and, if so, that was very dangerous territory. If she spent more time with him, those feelings could grow. Before she knew it, she could wake up one morning and be in love with him! Then her life really would be a mess.

She was going to have to finish this and the sooner the better.

They wandered along by the side of the water and she tried to think about the beauty of her surroundings and not what she had to do.

They turned a corner and walked into St Mark's Square; pigeons scurried and fluttered into the air against the impressive background of the basilica. A string quartet was playing classical music outside one of the pavement cafés.

Nicholas led her over to a table and summoned a waiter.

'You are very quiet, are you OK?' He looked across at her with that dark-eyed stare that seemed to cut straight through her.

'Yes, fine.' She tried to summon a smile.

He ordered champagne and then passed her a menu.

When they got back home he probably wouldn't even want to see her again. So she should reassert her independence. Finish this now, before he did.

She looked across at him and he smiled and suddenly she was backtracking. She couldn't do it now, she told herself violently. As soon as the plane touched down in London and they were back to reality—that would be the right time—that was when she would do it.

CHAPTER ELEVEN

CAT put some order forms down on her boss's desk and returned to the main office. It was raining outside; heavy slanting sheets of water were hitting the windows with a drumming sound. The heatwave had broken, summer was officially over and Cat's mood was as dark as the weather.

'There is a call for you on line two,' one of the secretaries informed her as she sat down at her desk.

'Who is it?'

'I don't know—they didn't say.'

Cat pushed a hand through her hair and tried to compose herself. Then, with a deep breath, she reached and lifted the receiver.

'Cat McKenzie here, how may I help you?'

'Oh, I can think of a number of ways you can help me, Catherine.' Nicholas's warm, teasing tone instantly made her blood run to fire.

Memories flicked through her mind—memories of how they had made love on his plane on the return journey from Venice. Memories of how, in the intervening weeks since that trip, she had been powerless to resist him. It seemed he just had to snap his fingers for her and she was there. She kept telling herself that she was going to finish things, but each time she spoke to him or saw him she put it off. She couldn't do it.

Then he'd informed her that he had to go away to Switzerland on business and she had convinced herself that he probably wouldn't return to London and that the affair was over. He'd been away for five days now, and as he hadn't phoned once, that certainty had grown. She'd tried to tell herself that she didn't care but just hearing his voice now made her realize what a lie that was.

'Hello, Nicholas, where are you?' Somehow she managed to make her voice sound coolly polite.

'I'm in London, at the hotel.'

'Was it a successful trip?'

'So-so. My work schedule has been a bit hectic. How about you? Have you missed me?'

The arrogance of the man still had the power to incense her. 'Well, like you, I've been a bit busy for that.'

'Sounds like we are both in need of some relaxation. Why don't I send the car over for you this evening and we'll have dinner at the hotel?'

He really thought that he could just pick her up and drop her at whim! Admittedly, over the past weeks, she'd agreed to see him many times—and had very much enjoyed the time they'd spent together. But she couldn't help thinking he'd had things far too much his own way for too long.

'Actually, tonight isn't good for me. I've got to work until seven; I have a few meetings and it's going to be pretty intense. I'll be fit for nothing except an early night when I get home.' It was true; she really did have to work late. The only pretence was the fact that she really would have given anything to see him afterwards.

'An early night sounds good to me,' he replied huskily. 'My driver can pick you up from your office.'

'And how is that going to look?' She lowered her tone and glanced around the open-plan office to make sure no one could hear what she was saying. 'I thought we'd agreed to keep our private life secret?'

'We did,' he agreed nonchalantly.

'Well, then, it's hardly going to be a secret if there is a great big white stretch limo outside the front door of the office waiting for me, is it?'

He laughed at that. 'Make something up. Tell anyone who asks that I wanted to see you to discuss the campaign.'

'And then my boss will want to know exactly what was said—and if, for instance, you've made up your mind about the follow-up adverts.'

'Tell her I'm thinking about it.'

'And are you?'

There was a slight pause. 'Not right now—no, I told you, I want to see how the first run of advertisements work out before going any further.'

'Well, that's fair enough, but I don't feel like drawing attention to the fact that you are thinking about it so hard. Let's just leave it tonight. I don't feel a hundred per cent well, anyway.'

'Why, what's the matter with you?'

'I'm just tired, I guess.' Cat glanced up as one of her colleagues approached her desk. 'Look, I've got to go; it's very busy in here. Ring me next week if you get time.'

She put the phone down.

'Cat, can you process these figures for me?' Claire put a stack of papers down in front of her.

'Yes—sure; when do you need them?' Cat was only half interested; her mind was going back over her conversation with Nicholas. Perversely she wished she hadn't put the phone down on him and that she had agreed to see him tonight. She really missed him. But that was pathetic—and she wasn't going to be like that, she told herself. Anyway it was true; people at the office would get suspicious if they saw Nicholas's car picking her up.

She had asked that they keep the affair secret because she had been concerned that it would reflect badly on her work—mixing business and pleasure wasn't encouraged—plus it might undermine the accomplishment of bringing in such a good client.

Nicholas had agreed without hesitation; in fact, he had added a few provisos of his own and suggested they keep the affair secret not only from her office but from friends and family too. 'It's best that way,' he had told her smoothly. 'Once the news is out that I'm seeing someone, the gossip columnists start getting involved and, before you know it, they will be printing stories about us, delving into your family background. Any privacy you had will be lost and sometimes it's not pleasant.'

It probably wasn't pleasant and she had agreed readily. She was an intensely private person anyway, and she certainly didn't want any scandal about her family and her inheritance circulating. But it was also very convenient for Nicholas. It meant he didn't have to introduce her socially; it meant that she was officially just a mistress.

She looked down at the papers in front of her and tried to concentrate. She felt a bit sick, but then that was nothing unusual—she'd been having bouts of nausea all week. There was obviously a bug going around the office. Claire had been off work all last week with it.

'Sorry, Claire, when did you say you wanted this?'

'You couldn't do it before our meeting tonight?'

Cat looked up at her drolly. 'That's not giving me much time!'

'I know.' Claire pulled a face. 'I'm sorry. I've had things on my mind.'

'Well, I suppose it's understandable. You haven't been well,' Cat conceded. 'Don't worry; leave it with me.'

'Thanks.' Her colleague smiled. 'Actually, Cat, you're looking a bit peaky yourself. Are you OK?'

'Yes, fine—although I think I'm coming down with a mild version of what you had last week.'

Claire blushed. 'I don't think there is a mild version of what I had last week.' She lowered her voice to a whisper. 'Unless there is such a thing as being a little bit pregnant.'

Cat looked up at her in surprise. 'You're not…are you?'

Claire nodded and put her finger to her lips. 'Don't say anything to anyone yet. I don't want it to be common knowledge around the office because it's early days.'

'Gosh! Congratulations. Claire.'

'Thanks. I have to admit it was a bit of a shock. I must have conceived on honeymoon. Like you, I thought I'd just got a bug. I was so tired and I kept being sick. Anyway, I bought one of those tests from the chemist and it's positive. Martin is so excited.'

'I'm really pleased for you,' Cat said sincerely.

Claire smiled. 'So is there something you want to tell me?'

'Sorry?' It took a moment for Cat to realize what she meant. 'Oh! No, I've just got a bug.' But even as she said the words, her eyes were flying towards the calendar on her desk. And she felt her heart start to thump against her chest with sudden and unequivocal panic as she realized that the joke might not be too far from the mark—her period was late.

It was still raining when Cat finished work. She stood in the Goldstein foyer and watched the water bouncing off the pavements. It was only a fifteen-minute walk to the underground station but she was going to get soaked. She debated going back to the reception desk to ring for a taxi, but on a Friday evening with the weather like this she could be waiting a long time. Plus she wanted to stop at the pharmacy down the road, which would involve leaving the driver with the meter running.

Pulling up the collar on her raincoat, Cat took a deep breath and hurried outside. It was dark and cold and the rain lashed against her skin with stinging force. Within a few moments her hair was plastered to her head.

She crossed over at the lights and hadn't gone very far when she realized that there was a vehicle drawing level with her. Glancing around, she saw it was Nicholas's limousine. An electric window wound down.

'Mr Zentenas has sent me to give you a lift, Ms McKenzie. Would that be acceptable to you?'

The situation and the chauffeur's polite offer seemed somehow bizarre in the middle of the ordinary street. She wanted to say no, it wasn't acceptable, that she had already told Nicholas she was unavailable, but the driver was so courteous that she refrained. 'That's very kind of you, but I won't if you don't mind. I have shopping I need to do now.'

'I can take you shopping. Mr Zentenas said I was to take you anywhere you wanted to go.'

'Before dropping me back at his hotel?'

'That was the general idea.' The driver shrugged. 'But I'm at your disposal, Ms McKenzie, and, if I may say so, you are getting very wet out there. Why don't you climb in and make yourself comfortable?'

She hesitated for just a second before nodding. 'OK, thank you.' What the heck? she thought as she opened the door and slid into the deep comfortable warmth of the heated leather seats. The driver was here now so she may as well take the lift.

Nicholas was sitting at his desk in the hotel suite. He had a mountain of correspondence still to get through, but Cat would be here soon and he wanted to check in with his private investigator before she arrived, so he put everything to one side and lifted the phone.

'Keith, it's Nicholas Zentenas.' He didn't waste time on preliminary small talk. 'Is there anything I need to know?'

'No, Mr Zentenas. Nothing. I've followed Ms McKenzie, as you asked. I've watched who comes and goes at the office and the flat and I've nothing to report.'

'So she hasn't met up with her father or her brother?'

'Her father is still in Germany on business. He is due back tomorrow. Her brother seems to be keeping a low profile.'

'What about that man from the photograph?'

'No one answering to that description has spoken to her. She did some shopping on Monday night but, apart from that, all she's done is work. But then I've told you all that. She leaves the house each day at seven and returns each evening at seven. She has made no stops, she's had no visitors.'

'Right.' Nicholas drummed his fingers against the desk.

'Oh, except tonight—she asked your chauffeur to drop her off at a chemist shop.'

'That's hardly earth-shattering, is it?' Nicholas murmured dryly. 'OK, thanks, Keith.' Putting down the phone, he reached into a drawer and took out the ring box.

It was now just over a month until Cat's birthday. The business trip to Switzerland couldn't have come at a worse time. He hadn't wanted to leave her; in fact, he'd thought about taking her with him but he'd known what her answer would be. She kept insisting that her work was her priority in life! And getting her to come away with him and sit around while he dealt with his business wouldn't have been a smart move right now. The closer he tried to reel her in, the more she pulled away. That was when he had decided that maybe reverse psychology was needed. If he left her alone for a week, maybe it would give her time to reflect on their relationship. The passion between them was red-hot. She was bound to miss him!

It had been a risky strategy so close to her birthday so he'd given his PI rigid instructions to monitor her every move and contact him if anything unusual happened.

Even so, two days into his business trip he'd woken in a cold sweat in the middle of the night. He'd dreamed of Cat walking down the aisle of a church. She'd been wearing a long white dress and she had looked so breathtakingly beautiful that he had been filled with desire. She'd looked up and smiled—it was that special smile that she gave him sometimes when he reached to take her hand—but the smile hadn't been for him; it had been for the man in the photograph, the man her brother had set her up with! He'd woken in a complete state of shock!

That was when he'd decided that now was a bad time to be so far away from her. Important trip or not, he must have been an idiot going to Switzerland when he had so much more to lose in London. Cancelling the rest of his schedule, he'd flown back immediately. He'd felt a bit better, knowing that he was just a short drive away from her. So he'd held his nerve and kept his distance for a few days longer, phoning the PI for constant updates. But today he'd had enough. Five days was enough breathing space. He needed to wrap this up. He would propose tonight.

The ring was a spectacular solitaire; he was sure she would take one look at it and say yes. After all, marriage to him would solve all her financial problems. Not only would she claim her inheritance, but also she would bag a wealthy husband. In true McKenzie style, she wouldn't be able to resist. He wouldn't mention the fact that he wanted her to sign a prenuptial contract until just before the big day—by which time she wouldn't want to back down because she wouldn't want to lose her inheritance. It would all work out fine.

He heard the lift doors opening in the lounge area and put the ring in his jacket pocket before walking out to greet her.

But, to his surprise, his chauffeur was alone in the room.

'Where is she?' Nicholas glanced into the lift as if Cat might be hiding somewhere.

'Sorry, Mr Zentenas, but Ms McKenzie wanted me to drop her home. She said to tell you thank you for the lift and that she would phone you tomorrow.'

For a moment Nicholas was completely nonplussed. Even though Cat had told him on the phone that she didn't want to see him tonight, he hadn't really taken her seriously. 'What's she playing at?' He spoke more to himself than the driver.

'I don't think she is playing at anything, sir. She was wet through from the rain and—'

'I need to go over there and sort this out,' Nicholas murmured, a look of determination on his face.

Cat had just had a shower and put on a T-shirt and a pair of shorts that she wore for bed when her front doorbell rang. She frowned and looked at the clock. It was almost ten.

Putting the door on the catch, she swung it open a few inches and peered around the edge. She was surprised to see Nicholas standing outside. He looked very attractive in a dark suit and a pale blue shirt open at the neck.

'Hi!' she murmured distractedly. How did he manage to look both businesslike and overwhelmingly sexy? she wondered as her heart did a strange leap of pleasure.

'Hello.' He smiled. 'Are you going to let me in?'

'Oh! Yes.' She closed the door and then looked down at her clothing; if she had thought for one moment he might come over, she would have put something more glamorous on. But it was too late to do anything about it now, so she unfastened the chain before swinging the door open again. 'What are you doing here, Nicholas?'

'I wanted to see you. I thought I made that clear when I sent my driver over.'

'But I thought I made it clear that I wasn't up to seeing you tonight.' Her pleasure at seeing him turned to annoyance. He had no right to come over here laying down ultimatums. He didn't own her!

He closed the door. 'Catherine, it's been five days and I think that is quite long enough for you to be rested and ready for me.'

'I beg your pardon?' She put one hand on her hip and her eyes flashed fire at him. 'I think maybe you'd better just go.'

He smiled. 'I'd almost forgotten how much that temper of yours excites me.'

'And I had almost—but not quite—forgotten how arrogant you are.'

He smiled and his eyes took in the heat of annoyance on her high cheekbones and the soft curve of her lips, before moving lower to see the way her T-shirt clung to her curves and the white shorts revealed long, shapely golden brown legs. She was achingly gorgeous.

He reached out and took hold of her hand to pull her a little closer to him.

'Nicholas, I—'

The pressure of his lips against hers cut off her words. But it was a surprisingly tender kiss and it instantly made all her reservations start to crash down around her. Before she could help herself, she was kissing him back with equal tenderness and then suddenly the kiss changed from gently provocative to hungrily possessive.

She wanted him so much, had missed him so much. She lifted her hand up to stroke against his face. She loved the taut feel of his skin, the slightly rough bristle of his jaw line, the silky softness of his thick dark hair.

'You are so beautiful.' He breathed the words against her ear as his hands moved under her T-shirt to caress the warm silk of her naked skin. 'I've missed this…' His lips trailed down over her neck, his hands stroking over the firm curve of her breast, his fingers finding the hard aching peaks of her nipples.

'Missed *me*—don't you mean?' Even through the delirium of need that he stirred up inside her, she was aware that the sentence wasn't enough. She pulled back and looked up at him questioningly.

A man could drown in those sensual green eyes, he thought hazily. 'Missed *you* like crazy,' he murmured softly.

She smiled at him then. 'Well, that's OK, then.'

'Yes, I think it is.' Pulling the T-shirt up over her head, he tossed it on the floor.

He smiled and then, before she realized his intention, he lifted her up over his shoulder and carried her through towards her bedroom.

It was the first time she had made love with him in her own bed and it seemed strange somehow, seeing him surrounded by the familiarity of her own things. The scatter cushions on her bed were well and truly scattered; the old teddy bear that was of sentimental value because it had been a last Christmas gift from her mother was similarly dispatched.

She arched her back against the cool sheets and invited his touch, his lips, his body.

'I don't know what you do to me.' He growled the words as he ripped off his jacket and started to unbutton his shirt.

She smiled at the words. Yes, Nicholas held control of her but she had a certain power over him as well. The knowledge was delicious; it made her feel as if everything was going to be OK, that the untamed seducer could be won over.

They were foolish thoughts but when they were together like this she allowed them full rein.

Naked, he joined her in the deep comfort of the double bed. He kissed her all over, luxuriating in the warmth of her responses. Because it was five days since he had made love to her, his pleasure seemed heightened and he had difficulty holding back. Every sinuous movement of her hips brought him closer to climax. It took all his self-control to tease her a little—torment her with his tongue, make her gasp his name.

Only when she begged him for release did he allow himself to let go. But even then, after taking her and pleasuring her and feeling the thrill of completion, when he pulled her close he wanted her all over again.

He could feel her heart beating against his chest as if she had been running a race, could smell the fresh scent of shampoo in her hair as he nuzzled against the silky blonde tresses.

'That was incredible,' he breathed softly against her ear and kissed the side of her face. She smiled a sleepy happy smile.

'Tell me about Switzerland,' she murmured, cuddling closer.

'Switzerland? Why do you want to know about that?'

'I'm just interested in how your days have been filled since I saw you last.'

There was something ingenuous about the statement and he felt a wash of shame that he had lied to her about staying away so long. 'There is not much to tell. It was just business.' He stared up at the ceiling and wondered what the hell was the matter with him.

'There must be something to tell. Was it snowing? Were the women very beautiful?'

'No, it wasn't snowing. The women, well…' He shrugged. 'I didn't have much time to look at the women, to be honest.'

She closed her eyes. All week she had been imagining him with incredibly sophisticated and gorgeous women, having dinner with them—making love to them. It had almost driven her out of her mind. She hated herself for being foolish enough to care.

But she did care. She cared about everything where he was concerned. 'Well, if there's not much to tell about Switzerland—tell me about Crete,' she invited softly.

'You know what Crete is like—you've been there.' She certainly had been there, he reminded himself staunchly. Between them, the McKenzie clan had pulled quite a scam.

'No, I mean what is it like where you live? What is your house like?'

'Why do you want to know about that?' His eyes held a certain coolness that struck at her.

'I was just curious, but it doesn't matter.' She pulled away from him.

He caught hold of her hand and drew her back before she could move too far away. 'Why are you curious? You don't usually ask me things.'

She allowed him to pull her back into his arms. She didn't ask him things because she was afraid that the closer she got to him, the harder it would be to ignore the fact that she was crazy about him. 'I don't know why I asked. It's just that I always see you in the impersonal surroundings of your hotel suites.'

He stroked her hair back from her face. 'I know, why don't I take you to my house in Crete for the weekend?' It would be the perfect place to propose to her, he thought suddenly. Plus it would get her away from her father, who would be arriving back soon.

'Don't be silly, Nicholas.' She pulled away from him with a frown. 'Why would you do that?'

'Why do you think?' He looked at her mischievously, one dark eyebrow raised.

'Because we can have an uninterrupted weekend of sex.' She supplied the words dryly.

'Plus you can check out my décor,' he teased. 'Find out if I favour the minimalist look or not.'

'Ha ha, very funny.'

He watched as she swung away from him and reached to pick up her shorts from the floor. 'Do you want a drink or something?' She flicked him a glance over her shoulder.

She was running away from him again. Why did she keep doing this? He'd never met a woman who was so passionate and yet so... hard to fathom and pin down.

'It's very warm in Crete at the moment—twenty-eight degrees. You can relax by the pool, recharge your batteries.' He made the tempting offer and then stared at her back in frustration when she didn't answer immediately.

'Actually, I'm busy this weekend.'

'Busy doing what?'

She looked around at him with a raised eyebrow. 'Just busy, you know. Catching up on work.' She opened a drawer and took out another T-shirt and pulled it over her head. 'But thanks for the offer.' She was heading for the door now. 'Did you say whether you'd like a drink or not? I'm going to put the kettle on.'

'I'll have a coffee.'

'OK.' She smiled at him breezily and then closed the door behind her.

Nicholas stared up at the ceiling. *Busy this weekend.* The words taunted him. What was she going to do—meet up with her father...meet up with the man from the photograph?

He threw back the sheet and reached for his clothes. She had to come to Crete and preferably for longer than just a weekend.

'Listen, Cat, I've been thinking—' As he strode into the other room he was surprised to see her sitting on the sofa, her head down between her knees. 'Are you all right?' He moved over towards her hurriedly.

'Yeah, I'm fine. I'm just tired and I was waiting for the kettle to boil.'

He crouched down in front of her to look at her. 'You don't look fine. You look very pale.'

'Really, don't fuss, Nicholas. I'm fine.' She pushed him away and went over to the kitchen to continue making their drinks.

He watched her with a frown.

'So what were you thinking about?' she prompted him firmly. She didn't want to talk about what could be wrong with her.

Her hand shook as she lifted up the jar of coffee. She was almost frightened to unscrew the cap again because a few moments ago the aroma had made her stomach suddenly heave.

'Are you sure you are OK?'

His voice seemed to be coming from a long way away.

'Yes—just tired.' It took all her willpower to get herself a glass of water from the tap.

'Do you want me to make the coffee?'

She nodded. 'Actually—yes, thanks, Nicholas.' It was a relief to get away from the situation.

Cat went into the bathroom and closed the door.

It was strange; she had always liked the smell of coffee before. But then she had heard that pregnancy could affect the senses like that. Surely she couldn't be pregnant? The idea pounded through her. Yes, they had made love once in Venice without any protection. But it had just been once! How unlucky would it be that the first time she made love she got pregnant? The odds against that would be high—surely?

She opened up the bathroom cabinet and found the pregnancy testing kit. She'd been too anxious to use it earlier but she couldn't put it off any longer—she needed to know the truth.

Nicholas put the coffee down on the lounge table just as Cat's mobile started to ring. He picked it up from the sofa and glanced at the screen. He could see that the call was from her father.

He quickly switched the phone off and then slipped it down under the cushions. Carter McKenzie could go to hell.

'I was thinking that we could make it a long weekend in Crete,' he said as Cat returned a little while later. She still looked very pale, he noted. 'You know you could do with a break. You do look a bit tired.'

'Yes, I think maybe you should go now.' She pulled a hand distractedly through her long blonde hair.

Was she agreeing to go to Crete? Was she even listening to him? He frowned. Maybe her mind was running ahead, thinking about meeting up with her father—thinking about a marriage of convenience?

'There are things we need to discuss,' he said firmly.

She gave him a strange look. 'Like what?'

'Like you taking some time off work next week.'

'It's too busy at the office right now to even contemplate taking time off.'

'I would have thought that discussing the Zentenas contract would give you complete freedom to be out of the office.'

'But we wouldn't be discussing the contract.' She shook her head. She couldn't think about this right now; her head was all over the place.

'We *could* discuss it,' he said softly. 'Amongst other things.'

She shook her head. He was teasing her now and she couldn't take it. 'Look, Nicholas—I'm really not in the mood for this right now.'

She wasn't in the mood to talk about work? He looked at her in perplexity.

Cat suddenly noticed the probing way he was watching her and tried to turn away from him, but he reached out a hand and pulled her back.

'Are you feeling ill?'

'No!' She tried to stop him but he pulled her closer and tipped her face upwards so that he could look at her closely.

'I'm fine.' She closed her eyes and then shivered with desire when he stroked his fingers over the side of her face.

'You've been putting in too many hours in that office.'

His voice was huskily concerned and her eyes flew open to meet his. He looked concerned as well—but it was an illusion, of course. He wasn't really bothered about her. He just had some free time at the weekend and thought he'd spend it making love.

'Come to Crete with me for the weekend, Catherine. I know you said you are busy, but surely whatever it is can wait?'

When she didn't answer him, he pulled her closer into his arms. She allowed herself to be held. It felt wonderful and she closed her eyes, trying desperately to think sensibly about what she should do.

What would he say if she told him she was pregnant? The question sizzled through her. He would probably finish with her immediately! But then she didn't know for sure how he would react, a little voice whispered insidiously inside her. She didn't even know for sure how she felt right now—she supposed she was in shock.

'A little time alone together would be fun,' he said softly as he stroked her hair back from her face. 'Don't you think?'

Maybe a weekend in his company would help her decide what she should do? And, if nothing else, it would give her a chance to recharge her batteries and think.

'I suppose it would.' Her voice was muffled against his chest.

He smiled. 'So, pack a bikini and I'll pick you up tomorrow morning, early—say seven.'

She was allowing him to take over. But really she didn't have a lot of strength left to argue. 'And we could talk about the contract?' she managed vaguely as he pulled away from her.

He smiled at that. 'On Monday we will talk about the contract.'

'I have to be back in the office on Monday.'

'We'll see.'

'No, I *really* have to be back by Monday morning.'

He nodded and reached for his jacket. 'Get some sleep and I'll see you bright and early tomorrow.'

CHAPTER TWELVE

HEAT danced like shimmering water on the tarmac road.

Ahead, through the haze, Cat could see the blue glimmer of the sea. She couldn't believe that she was back in Crete, that she was pregnant or that she was here with Nicholas Zentenas. As she sat next to him in the open-top Jeep, her mind was bouncing in much the same way as the vehicle had a few moments ago over some of the potholed lanes.

It was all happening too fast. She didn't know what to think. But she was already starting to regret coming here. As soon as the private jet had landed an hour ago on the runway, the memories of Crete had started and now they were competing for space along with everything else she had to reflect on.

'Here we are; this is my home.' Nicholas drove the car around the curve of the bay. Up ahead, a white villa gleamed bright in the sunshine; perched like a wedding cake in three tiers, it looked down over an olive grove towards a stunning white beach.

Pink oleander lined the driveway and the gardens were tropically lush, thanks no doubt to a robust sprinkler system. Red bougainvillea was twined over the carport and a turquoise pool sparkled against the greenery, sun-beds and parasols laid out in invitation.

'It's a beautiful place,' Cat remarked as they stepped out of the vehicle.

'I like it.' He took her overnight bag from the back of the car and led the way up to the front door.

No expense had been spared inside the villa and the furnishings were exquisite but to Cat's surprise it also had a homely lived-in feel with the trinkets of everyday life scattered around. She glanced at the family photographs as she followed him through towards the master bedroom and made a note to go back and study them in more detail later.

Like the rest of the house, the bedroom was luxurious but it was the spectacular views along the coast from large sliding glass doors that held her attention.

'Its lovely that the coastline is unspoilt.' She walked across to look out. 'So many scenic places seem to be turning into concrete jungles these days, with no regard for beauty or wildlife.' She reached to slide the door open. The air was hot and silent except for the distant sound of the waves breaking on the shore below. 'I hate the way some developers destroy our environments under the guise of progress.'

'So do I.' Nicholas watched her with a frown. He wanted to remind her that her father was one of those people but he bit the words back. Did she just lie to herself? he wondered. Or was she simply blinded by love for her family?

And, if that was the case, did that make her a bad person? Suddenly he didn't think so. He swept a hand through the darkness of his hair, wondering if once again he was looking for excuses to justify her behaviour. The trouble was that these kind of doubts had been plaguing him for a while now—in fact, ever since spending time with her in Venice he was finding it harder and harder to see her in any kind of cold and calculating light.

She turned and he quickly composed himself. 'I think it's time for lunch. Are you hungry?'

'Maybe—a little.'

He nodded. 'I'll go and throw something together in the kitchen. Make yourself at home.'

When he left the room Cat changed out of her jeans and put on a red bikini and a matching pair of shorts with a cropped white T-shirt. Then she padded barefoot outside to dip a toe into the turquoise water of the pool and admire the garden. When she walked back up towards the house she saw Nicholas through an open door that led through from the kitchen on to the terrace.

She leaned against the doorframe and watched him for a moment whilst he was unaware of her presence. It was strange seeing him in this domesticated setting; he seemed so relaxed, and even more attractive if that was at all possible.

'Need some help?' she asked as he turned and saw her.

'No, I was just making a salad.'

'What, without a chef?' she teased him. 'Are you sure you can manage without that team of staff who usually cater to your every whim?'

'Highly amusing, Catherine!' He smiled. 'If you are going to make fun, you may as well make yourself useful. Come in here and cater to a few of my whims.'

'Sounds interesting.'

'I can make it very interesting.' He caught hold of her as she stepped through the doorway and pulled her into his arms to kiss her. It was a hard yet intimately satisfying kiss and at the same time he was pulling her T-shirt off.

'Nice bikini,' he growled as he drew back to look at her. The ring of his mobile phone interrupted them. 'Damn!' He frowned. 'That might be important—I'm expecting to close a deal this weekend.'

'You'd better answer the call, then.' Cat smiled at him and broke away to carry on where he had left off making the salad.

She half listened as he talked in Greek to whoever was at the other end of the line. The conversation was about donating money for the building of a new orphanage. She remembered she had heard him talking about this before and had doubted her translation. But now it seemed she had been right the first time and Nicholas was involved with the charity in a big way.

He had to be a nice person to do something like that—a person who cared about people, about children, not just about the business of making money.

He finished the call and then went over to stand behind her as she rinsed some leaves under the cold water in the sink. He slipped one hand around her waist and kissed the side of her neck. She felt like melting against him.

It was nice being with him like this. It felt as if they were a real couple.

'I like having you here in my house.'

'Do you?'

'Yes, and you are good in the kitchen—you look like you really know what you are doing with that colander.'

'You're just getting your own back now for my earlier remark.' She laughed.

He kissed the side of her neck again. 'But I'm serious when I tell you that I like having you here.'

'You just like *having* me.' She tried to sound flippant but his hand was resting on the flatness of her stomach, stirring up all kinds of emotions inside her.

She allowed herself to daydream for a moment that she had told him about the baby and that he was delighted and excited and that they were going to prepare for the child together and that they would be a family.

She did want this baby. The realization was suddenly very strong. The emotional response to the tender way Nicholas was holding her, his hand resting almost protectively over her stomach, made her eyes blur with tears.

But she also wanted Nicholas. Throughout her relationship with him she had been wary—had feared putting her trust in him because ultimately her experience had taught her that men only let you down. But perhaps she hadn't given Nicholas a fair chance. Maybe she should have allowed her feelings full rein, because she had fallen in love with him. As hard as she tried to fight it, the truth was indisputable—she was head over heels about him. It was why she hadn't been able to finish with him; it was why she was standing here crying.

She blinked away the tears fiercely. Feeling emotional wasn't going to help. Maybe she should tell him about the baby and see what he said.

His mobile phone started to ring again.

'Sorry about this.' He pulled away from her.

'That's OK,' she said lightly. 'I had to leave without my phone this morning as I couldn't find it. Maybe it's a good thing.'

'Yes, they are a distraction.' He took the call and then moved out of the room to talk to whoever it was.

Cat laid the table outside on the terrace and then sat down to wait. The minutes ticked away and she helped herself to a few lusciously juicy black olives and poured herself a glass of iced water as she tried to work out exactly how to word her news. *Nicholas, I've got something to tell you…* No, maybe more direct. *Nicholas, I'm pregnant and I'm keeping the baby. If you don't want to be involved, then that's fine…I can manage on my own.*

She probably could manage on her own—somehow. But she didn't want to. And it wasn't the fact that money would be tight—it was far more than that. It was the emotional pull of her feelings for Nicholas. She longed for the intimacy they had shared today, standing in that kitchen. They had just been a few snatched moments within a web of moments but they had clarified something. She didn't want to be an island any more—she didn't want not to trust him. Life could be so much better than that.

What was taking Nicholas so long? Impatiently she scraped her chair back from the table and went to look for him. She could hear his voice; as usual, he was talking in his native tongue and the deep, attractive tone resonated down the hallway.

'Whether or not I use the inheritance money, I will still be funding the orphanage.'

The words made Cat's confident footsteps falter. Why was Nicholas talking about inheritance money? *He couldn't possibly be talking about her inheritance money, could he?* Confusion raced within her.

'I just want us to be clear about that,' Nicholas continued crisply. 'Time is of the essence now. I need everything in place before the end of the month.'

It was her birthday soon and Nicholas's words held the hallmarks of something her father and half-brother would say. Suddenly it was as if the cold from the tiled floor was striking through her, hitting her heart, draining all the warmth and life from her body. Did Nicholas know her family? Was he working in conjunction with them to get her inheritance? It wouldn't be the first time her brother had tried such an idea.

But why would a billionaire like Nicholas be interested in a scam like that? He didn't need money—it didn't make sense.

She must have got this wrong; there must be another explanation. Maybe her Greek was rustier than she had thought. Cat started to walk forward again and, as she rounded the corner, she could see Nicholas sitting behind a desk in a book-lined room. 'No, Demetrius, I'm going to play it safe, so I still want you to email the prenuptial agreement to me.' He smiled at her as she approached and just continued with his conversation. Obviously he presumed that she couldn't understand Greek.

'And as I said before, I want to marry her as soon as possible—preferably before the end of the month.'

There was no ambiguity about that statement and Cat felt the coldness inside her turn to the searing white heat of fury. There was a ringing in her ears and a surge of adrenalin that was truly scary. She didn't fully understand what was going on here but one thing was clear—Nicholas was setting up some kind of honey trap. He was using her—deceiving her. There was no difference between him and all the other men in her life. She felt sick with the knowledge.

'OK, Demetrius, I've got to go. I'll ring you later.' He put the phone down. 'Sorry to be so long, Catherine.' He switched to English with fluid ease.

She didn't answer him immediately—her brain was racing as she wondered how she should play this.

'Are you all right? You look a bit pale.'

The phoney concern was the last straw. 'Oh, yes, I'm fine, Nicholas.' Her voice was brittle.

'Good, well, let's relax and have some lunch—'

'Actually, why don't you just ask me now?'

'Ask you what now?'

'Ask me to marry you, of course, and get it over with.'

He leaned back in his chair and said nothing. Silence stretched between them, as tense as an elastic band drawn back as far as it could go and almost at breaking point. She could almost see his brain ticking over. 'What makes you think I'm going to ask you to marry me?'

'What makes you think that I don't understand Greek?' She switched to his native tongue and watched his expression darken.

'I didn't know you spoke my language,' he said quietly.

'Oh, I'm well versed in your language.' Her voice was

scathing. 'But I'm not talking about Greek now. I'm talking about the language of deceit. I take it you and my father and half-brother are in on this together.' Her voice held a catch that was painful. She suddenly wanted to cry but she was damned if she would do that in front of him. She hated him—hated him with a fervency that she had never known before. She wanted to smack his smug arrogant face. But she just stood there, her hands curled into tight helpless fists at her sides.

He frowned. 'Why would you think I'm in on anything with your father and brother?'

'You must think I'm really stupid.'

'I don't think that for one minute, Catherine. And I can assure you that I am not in on anything with—'

'Don't bother to try and lie your way out of this, Nicholas. I can see the resemblance. You are just like them. All my life I have put up with their deceit and their lies as they used me to get what they wanted—namely money. I've endured their cold-hearted scheming. I've tried to fix the dreadful scams they have pulled. I even came back here to Crete last year to try and pay back money that they had conned out of unsuspecting people!' Her voice splintered with feeling.

Something changed in the darkness of his eyes as he looked at her. 'I didn't know—'

'Oh, for heaven's sake, save it, Nicholas!' She cut across him fiercely. 'I was actually starting to think that you were different. I can't believe that you took me in; I can't believe that I haven't seen it before. Because in reality you are just like them.'

'I'm nothing like them.' His voice was vehement.

'Well, at least you are no longer trying to pretend that you don't know them.'

The contempt in her voice lashed over him and suddenly he felt utterly ashamed for all the times he had tried to convince himself that she was scheming and conniving and just like her family. One thing was suddenly abundantly clear—he couldn't have been more wrong.

'What I can't understand is why.' Her voice softened and for a second her anger receded like the tide, giving a glimpse of raw pain in the green depths of her eyes. 'You don't need the money and yet you were prepared to use me like…like some kind of pawn in a game.'

The knowledge that he had misjudged her and hurt her like this was almost unbearable. He stood up from his chair. He needed to take her into his arms; he needed to try and explain that what she had overheard wasn't what it seemed—yes, his affair with her had started out as just a plan for revenge—but his feelings for her had changed and grown so much that he hadn't wanted to go through with that. *He needed to make her see that he loved her!* 'Catherine, we can sort this out.'

'I don't think so!' Her anger rushed back with the force of a tidal wave and blindly she reached and swept the papers from his desk. Files and papers spilled at her feet and amongst them she could see photographs of her, photographs taken as she was shopping and as she was walking into the building where she worked.

She bent down to pick one up with shaking hands. It was a snap of her having coffee with a work colleague, taken almost six months ago, certainly well before she had met Nicholas.

'You bastard!' Her voice was no more than a whisper. 'You had me followed as you made your plans—or did Michael do that? It's one of his little specialities—selling unsavoury ideas with a colour photo or two. He's been hounding me for ages to get married, using tactics just like that.'

'Catherine, I am not in league with your family.' He started to come around towards her.

'Keep away from me.' She backed towards the door.

'Just let me explain.'

'Explain what? How you seduced me to get your hands on the McKenzie money? What were you thinking when you were making love with me? Were you closing your eyes and thinking about how you would dupe me into putting the inheritance money into a joint bank account once we were married?'

'No, I wasn't thinking that.'

She didn't believe him. 'I don't care anyway.' Her chin slanted up as she met his eyes fiercely. 'Making love didn't mean anything to me—*you* don't mean anything to me.'

But she was lying. Even as she looked at him and hated him she still felt her heart twist with desire—with feelings for him that were so deep that they cut. Tears prickled perilously close to the surface and she swallowed them down hastily, furious with herself. 'I suppose you asked me here thinking that the lure of beautiful surroundings would act as a smoke-screen when you asked me to marry you—would make up for the fact that you have no feelings for me whatsoever. Well it wouldn't have worked.' She almost spat the words at him. 'Because my answer would still have been no; I would never have married you. Never.'

'Catherine, let's calm down and talk about this.' His voice was unwavering and rational and somehow that just made everything worse. He didn't need to calm down—he was perfectly in control because he didn't give a damn.

'Go to hell, Nicholas.' She turned and headed blindly down the hallway towards the front door.

'Where are you going?'

She was vaguely aware that Nicholas was calling after her but she ignored him and kept on going out of the front door and down on to the drive. She had no idea where she was going. All she knew was that she had to get away from him before she broke down into a million pieces. She may have foolishly lost her heart to him but she was damned if she was going to lose her pride as well.

The sun seared down on her from a clear azure sky. The only sound was the waves on the shore and the insistent hum of the cicadas. She wore no shoes and she was just in her bikini top and shorts with no sunscreen, but she didn't care. The heat of the road was burning the soles of her feet so she walked instead along the rough parched grass.

The sound of a car coming along the road behind her made her quicken her pace and start to run; that was when she caught her foot on the uneven ground and tumbled down. The fall winded her and for a second she couldn't move.

'Catherine, are you OK?' She heard a car door slam and a few seconds later Nicholas was crouching down beside her. 'Have you hurt yourself?'

'Go away.' She rubbed at her ankle; her eyes were blurred with tears and she couldn't even look at him.

'Come on, let's get you back to the house.' He touched her shoulder and she flinched.

'Leave me alone, Nicholas.'

'I know you are angry with me and you have every right to be.' His voice softened. 'But I can't leave you here. You've hurt yourself. You are miles from even the nearest village.'

She bit down on her lip.

'Let me take you back to the house and we'll sort this out—we'll talk and—'

'We *can't* sort this out, Nicholas.' She looked up at him then and her eyes were shadowed with emotion. 'I'm not one of your business deals that's gone wrong.'

'If it's any consolation, I never thought of you as a business deal.'

'You're right—it's no consolation. And I don't want to go

back to your house. I wouldn't go back there if it was the last building left standing.'

Cat struggled to get onto her feet and that was when the world seemed to tip and tilt on its axis as dizziness set in. 'Nicholas…' She breathed his name in panic before the world just blacked out.

CHAPTER THIRTEEN

NICHOLAS'S voice seemed to be coming from a long distance away yet when she opened her eyes he was holding her close. She could smell the scent of his cologne, feel the heat of his body against hers.

She tried to think straight but the world felt fuzzy.

'Catherine, are you all right? Talk to me.' He stroked a hand along the side of her cheek and the tender touch made her recoil instantly.

'You passed out.'

'I know I passed out; just get away from me.'

He totally ignored her and the next moment he was scooping her up into his arms and carrying her back towards his car.

'Put me down, Nicholas!' Although her anger and the need to get away from him were strong, she felt too weak to struggle and she was forced to give herself up to the indignity of leaning her head against his shoulder. 'I don't want to go back to your house.'

'I'm not taking you back to my house.'

Cat was vaguely aware that she was in the passenger seat of his car but it was as if the journey was happening to someone else; she felt strangely detached and she just wanted to close her eyes and sleep.

She opened her eyes as he pulled up outside a white-washed house with blue shutters which were closed to the heat of the day.

'Where are we?'

'My cousin's house—she's a doctor. She can check you over.'

'I don't want to be checked over!' She felt panic and anger in equal measures now. 'Look, Nicholas, just take me to the airport. I want to go home.'

He ignored the request and instead came around to open the passenger door and lift her out. Once again she was forced to hold on to him as he strode down the path towards the front door.

The house was blissfully cool and dark inside. A woman appeared almost immediately and began talking in rapid Greek. Nicholas explained that Cat was a friend of his and that she had fallen and then blacked out.

A *friend*! The word clawed at Cat, inflaming her anger against him all over again.

They weren't friends—they weren't even lovers. Nicholas had used her. He was an enemy—a traitorous, calculating enemy who had tricked his way behind her defence mechanisms.

She pushed against his shoulder, her hands ineffectual against his powerful hold. 'I want you to let me go.'

'All in good time.'

'Place her on the sofa, Nicholas,' the woman ordered softly. 'Then you can leave us.'

As he put her down carefully and stepped back, perversely Cat felt bereft without his strength.

'Catherine?' The woman leaned closer. She spoke in English, her voice gentle and her manner soothing. 'Catherine, my name is Sophia Zentenas. I'm a doctor. Did you bang your head when you fell?'

'No. And I'm fine, really I am.' Cat struggled to sit up but as she tried the room felt as if it were spinning around.

'I think you should lie still, Catherine.' Sophia put a cool hand against her forehead. Then she checked her pulse rate. 'Your blood pressure is raised.'

'I'm not surprised,' Cat muttered wryly. 'Nicholas is enough to give anyone high blood pressure.'

Sophia laughed at that. 'You just lie still and I'll get my bag from the next room.'

Cat's eyes darted to Nicholas who was standing in the shadows. 'I want you to go now,' she told him firmly. 'I don't want you here.'

'I'm not going anywhere until I know you are all right.'

'It's over, Nicholas,' she told him calmly. 'Your little game has backfired. I suggest you take your phoney concern and tell my family that your plans have fallen through.'

'Catherine, I am not in league with your family.'

'I don't believe you.' She stared at him stonily. 'And anyway, you may as well be. You are as cold-blooded as they are.'

For a moment she thought she glimpsed a raw expression on his remote features.

'I didn't want to hurt you.'

'No, you just wanted to use me, steal the McKenzie money like they did—'

'I didn't need your money, Catherine.'

'Well, maybe that makes you worse than they are.' Her voice trembled. 'And that is stooping pretty low, believe me.'

There was a long silence. She could see a pulse moving on his jaw line.

'My father is a cheat and a liar and he has never really loved me.' She admitted the truth in a huskily broken tone. 'My half-brother is even worse, if that is possible. So I don't know what that makes you.'

'Catherine, why didn't you tell me this before?' He took a step closer and bent down beside her.

'Why would I tell you?' She practically spat the words at him. Her eyes blurred for a second. 'And anyway, would you want to admit to having a family like that?'

'Catherine, I'm so sorry,' He reached to touch her and she flinched.

'I want you to go.'

'I need to explain things. I wasn't going to take the money for myself. I was going to give it to a charity, to an orphanage—'

'I don't care what your plans were. I don't want to hear your explanations.'

'But I need to tell you—'

'Just leave me alone.' Her voice rose with distress. 'I don't want your excuses.'

'Nicholas, you'd better go.' Sophia's voice interrupted them gently. 'You are upsetting Catherine and I can't allow that. She needs to rest right now.'

For a second Nicholas hesitated and Cat thought that he was going to argue, but then he pulled back from her, his dark eyes shuttered. 'I'll wait in the other room.'

'No, I think it's best if you go home.' Sophia came closer. 'Catherine doesn't want you around. We'll ring you if you are needed.'

The curt dismissal wasn't something Nicholas would have accepted normally but, to Catherine's surprise, after a brief hesitation he nodded and with just a glance in her direction he strode out of the room.

As Sophia strapped a monitor on to Cat's arm to take her pulse they heard the sound of his Jeep starting up outside and then the roar of the engine as he sped away.

'There, feel better now?' Sophia asked softly.

Cat nodded and then bit down on her lip as tears flooded her eyes.

'My cousin has obviously hurt you a great deal, Catherine,' Sophia said briskly. 'And therefore he is not worth your tears—even if he is undeniably as handsome as the devil.'

Catherine smiled tremulously. 'Yes… It's just… I can't believe I've made such a terrible mistake. He's used me.'

Sophia frowned. 'I know it's not an excuse. But I sometimes think Nicholas has difficulty in trusting women. Certainly since his divorce he has avoided any deep and meaningful relationship. I think he's frightened of being hurt again.'

'Frightened?' Cat gave a bitter laugh. 'I don't think Nicholas is frightened of anything.'

'I know he does give that impression.' Sophia shrugged. 'But, believe it or not, he's been through a lot in his life. He's never taken things for granted the way I have.'

'What do you mean?' Cat asked curiously.

'Well, for instance, I always took for granted the unconditional love of my family but he never did. I think deep down he was always frightened that love would be snatched away from him. That hard outer shell he likes to present to the world is just a front.'

'You're right. I don't believe you.'

Sophia looked at her quizzically and Cat felt herself blush. 'Sorry—I know he's your cousin… It's just…' She trailed off helplessly.

'It's just that he's hurt you and you love him,' Sophia finished for her softly.

'No! I hate him.'

Sophia smiled. 'You blood pressure was slightly raised until I asked that question and then it almost shot off the scale.' She took the straps off Cat's arm. 'Try to relax. Tell me, have you any idea why you passed out?'

'No. It was hot and I was running.' She shrugged. 'I haven't eaten properly for a while. I keep being sick.'

'Are you pregnant?'

The direct question made Cat's blush deepen. There was a long silence and she made no reply.

'I'm a doctor, Catherine. Anything you say to me will be in confidence.'

Cat hesitated for a moment and then nodded.

'Right, if you've been sick a lot, you're probably dehydrated and your blood sugars are low. Combined with the heat, it could account for you passing out. I think what you need to do is drink lots of fluids and rest for a while.'

'I want to go home to London, but my passport and belongings are at Nicholas's house.'

'I don't think you are fit to travel anywhere today.'

'I can't go back to Nicholas!' Cat's voice rose slightly in panic.

'Don't worry. You can stay here. I have a spare room.'

'I can't impose on you like that!'

'Why not?' Sophia smiled at her. 'I'd say it was the least I can do after my cousin has upset you so much. Now, let's have a look at your ankle.'

Cat watched as Sophia knelt to carefully examine her foot. She liked this woman's no nonsense, but gentle approach. She was soothing to be around. She was probably about ten years older than Nicholas, but incredibly attractive. Her raven dark hair was shiny, her sloe-dark eyes warmed with laughter lines.

'I don't think you have broken anything, it's just a sprain,' she declared as she put Cat's foot down again. 'I'll get you a drink and then I'll help you to the bedroom and, when you're ready, I'll make you something to eat.'

The sound of children laughing woke Cat. She lay in the cool darkened bedroom listening to them playing in the front garden, and watched the floral curtains flutter as a breeze caught them.

Somewhere a church bell was chiming. It was early Sunday morning and she had surprised herself by sleeping through the night, even though she had been sure she would toss and turn.

Her mind went back to yesterday and the discovery of Nicholas's duplicity and once again her eyes filled with tears. He'd said he wasn't in league with her family, but she didn't know if she believed that or not—she couldn't get a handle on why he had deceived her. Hastily she brushed her tears away, it was her hormones making her cry, she told herself shakily. She didn't care why Nicholas had treated her so badly—the only thing that counted was the fact that she had found him out. And she now knew she could never trust him. Now she knew that he was another man just like Ryan Malone.

She pushed back the covers of the bed and reached for the clothes that Sophia had lent her. As she fastened the long skirt, her hand rested for a moment on her stomach and she remembered how Nicholas had held her yesterday, remembered the foolish dreams about telling him about the baby—about being a family.

Briskly she turned to make the bed. Thoughts like that had been crazy. She certainly had no intention of telling Nicholas about the baby now. What was the point? She didn't want him in her life and he didn't want her. He'd probably be horrified to learn she was pregnant and demand she had an abortion. A baby definitely wouldn't figure in the ruthless plans of a man who had deceived her so callously, who cared nothing for her.

Her eyes were suddenly blinded with tears again. He could go to hell, she told herself fiercely. Because she was glad that she was pregnant; she wanted this child and one loving parent was enough. She would give her baby all the love and support that had been missing in her own life—and she could do that without the help of any man.

The sound of a car pulling up outside made her hurry towards the window.

Outside in the blaze of the morning sun she saw Nicholas climb out of his Jeep. He looked tall and handsome and her heart twisted instantly with pain.

She saw Sophia's two little girls running down the path to welcome him; they whooped for joy as he swung them up in his arms and whirled them around, they clamoured for more as he set them down again.

'Not now, girls.' His voice drifted up to the open window. 'I've come to see Catherine. How is she today?'

'OK, but Mummy says we are not to disturb her.'

'Is that so?' Nicholas glanced up and suddenly their eyes connected and it was as if an electric current passed between them. She dropped the curtain and stepped away from the window, her heart racing.

Hurriedly she moved to open the bedroom door, just as Sophia rushed up the stairs.

'Nicholas is here,' she hissed. 'What do you want me to tell him?'

'Tell him I can't see him,' Cat implored. 'I can't face him, Sophia.'

'All right, but he might not take no for an answer. He's phoned three times already and—'

'And you're right, I'm not going to take no for an answer.' Nicholas's deep tone cut across the conversation. Cat glanced around. He was coming up the stairs, a look of determination on his handsome features.

'Nicholas, I don't want to talk to you.' She took an instinctive step backwards into the bedroom. Her gaze swung to

Sophia beseechingly but it was too late—Nicholas was sweeping past his cousin.

'Give us some time alone, Sophia,' he demanded curtly. 'We have things to sort out.'

The next moment he had stepped into the bedroom and closed the door behind him.

'Nicholas, I don't think there is anything more for us to say. I just want you to give me my passport so I can go home.' She was pleased at how cool and composed she sounded whilst inside her heart was turning over with sadness, with a longing for something that could never be—with anger like molten fire.

'You are not going anywhere until you've heard me out.'

'How dare you come barging in here, laying down the law like I owe you something?' She crossed her arms defensively over her chest as he moved closer. 'I don't owe you anything. And there is nothing left to talk about.'

'Well, I owe you something,' he said softly. 'I owe you an apology. I'm sorry I hurt you, Catherine—really I am.'

The softness of his tone made her defences waver alarmingly.

'The only thing that you are sorry about is the fact that I've found you out and you are not going to get your hands on the McKenzie inheritance.'

'This was never about money,' he said quietly.

'So what was it about, Nicholas?'

'It was about revenge—about the fact that your father cheated me in a business deal. He lied and deceived me in a most ruthless fashion and almost succeeded in ruining my reputation.'

Cat could feel her heart beating violently against her chest. 'So you thought you would bed me for your revenge?'

'When I found out about your inheritance, it did seem the perfect way to get revenge. I knew your father wanted to get his hands on that money—and yes, I'll admit I had no qualms at first about using you to get to him.' He watched how she flinched at that and he reached out to touch her arm.

'Get away from me.' She stepped back angrily, her eyes burning into his.

'I thought you were as bad as they were,' he continued softly. 'I thought you were in alliance with them when they worked their vicious scams. In particular I thought you helped in that con they played here in Crete. I had photographs from a private investigator backing up that assumption.'

'Yes, well, your private investigator got it wrong,' she blazed. 'In fact he couldn't have got it more wrong. I was as duped as the people here in Crete. I gave money in good faith to Michael for what I believed to be an honest business venture. He used it to set up a scam. By the time I realized what was going on, the damage had already been done.'

'But you bailed your brother out,' Nicholas stated firmly.

'No—I repaid what he had stolen, which is something totally different.'

'Yes…I realize now that I made a mistake about you. I'm sorry, Catherine.' His eyes held steadily with hers. 'Truly I am, sorry from the bottom of my heart.'

'You haven't got a heart.'

'That's where you are wrong.' He said the words quietly. 'The only problem was that I didn't trust myself enough to listen to it.'

'Don't try and sweet-talk me, Nicholas, because it won't work. I've met men like you before. Unbeknown to me, my brother set me up once before. I met someone I thought knew nothing about my background, someone who told me he loved me. I'd been going out with him for six months and I was starting to trust him—starting to have feelings for him—and then I discovered it was all an elaborate hoax, just so my family could get their hands on the McKenzie money. Do you know what a curse that inheritance is? Do you know what it feels like to have people lie to you, profess feelings they haven't got, just to get your money?'

'Surprisingly, yes, I do.' Nicholas's voice was grim and she remembered suddenly how Sophia had told her how difficult he had found it to trust women since his divorce.

'Well, then, maybe you should have been a little more careful with my emotions.' Quickly she shut out the feelings of sympathy.

'I never told you I loved you, Catherine.'

He noted how her complexion paled, how her eyes burnt like bright emerald fire.

'So what were you going to say when you got around to asking me to marry you?' She shot the question at him with a quiver in her voice. 'Come away with me so we can have red-hot sex on tap for ever?'

His lips twisted derisively. 'I don't know what I was going to say. To be honest, when I held you in my arms, revenge was far from my thoughts.'

'Liar.'

'It's the truth, Catherine. I started to have feelings for you that I didn't want to have—started to doubt my motives.'

'But you were still going to go through with your revenge until I overheard your little plan and ended it.'

'I was definitely going to ask you to marry me—yes. But whether I would have gone through with the revenge of taking the money—' He shrugged. 'I was having second thoughts about that.'

'It didn't sound to me as if you were having second thoughts. Why would you have asked me to marry you if you weren't going to take the money?'

He held her gaze steadily. 'That was a question I kept

asking myself over and over again and I kept ignoring the answer because, quite frankly, it scared the hell out of me.'

Cat stared at him as she tried to digest what he was saying to her, and then she shook her head. 'I don't believe that you were having second thoughts. You were having a prenuptial agreement drawn up when I overheard you talking on the phone.'

'Yes, I got my lawyer to draw up a prenuptial agreement as a safeguard. I wasn't sure I could trust my feelings where you were concerned. I admit that, having made a mistake once before in marriage, it's made me cynical and overcautious—it's made me doubt you when I really didn't want to doubt you. But I was sure that I wanted you. I still want you,' he said huskily. 'And I know now that I was wrong to ever believe for one moment that you are anything like your family.'

'I have to give you ten out of ten for being able to talk your way out of a situation, Nicholas,' she said fiercely. 'I suppose this is why you are so wealthy. You could persuade a person that the sun is made of butter and have them reaching to put some on their bread.'

'Well, good, because I'm asking you to marry me and I want very much for you to say yes.'

'You must think I'm very naïve.' Cat's voice trembled alarmingly. 'I wouldn't marry you if you were the last man left in the universe.'

'I'm asking you to marry me because I want you in my life, Catherine. I've fallen in love with you. The proposal has nothing to do with revenge,' he continued smoothly, as if she hadn't said anything.

Cat shook her head. 'I can't believe you've got the gall to go ahead with this proposal when I know you are lying.'

'I'm not lying. I don't want anything to do with the

McKenzie inheritance, Catherine—you've got to believe me. To be honest, it was only ever a drop in the ocean to me anyway. And the charity will still get its large donation from me.'

Cat turned away from him and stared out of the window. Her eyes were blurred with tears and she didn't want him to see her crying.

'I've behaved badly towards you, but I want you to know that my only real sin was not having the courage to believe my heart. I love you, Cat, please believe that.'

She didn't answer him—she couldn't—she was too choked up with emotion.

'And I do trust you,' he continued softly. 'I tore up the pre-nuptial agreement when it was emailed to me this morning. Everything I have is yours.'

'I don't want anything from you.'

'Cat, please forgive me.'

She shook her head and stood with her back resolutely to him.

'Do you see that land outside the window?' Nicholas asked suddenly. He reached past her to hold back the curtain.

Through the haze of her tears, she took in the gentle undulating landscape, the silver-green olive trees and the blaze of lemon groves against the backdrop of the sea.

'That land meant something to the people of this village. It meant something to the family who took me in. They trusted me to save it for them. I, in turn, trusted your father in a business deal. We had an agreement to preserve all of this. But he broke that deal. I went away and when I came back the land was torn up—the ancient trees that had been lovingly tended for generations had been torn apart—a way of life was under threat, with bulldozers and contractors everywhere. And people who had once treated me with respect—with love—looked at me once again as if I were a stranger.'

Cat wiped the tears from her cheeks. 'Well, I'm sorry, Nicholas—my father isn't a man to trust—it's a lesson I learnt a long time ago. He's hurt me too.'

'I realize that now.'

'At least you were able to put everything right again—the countryside looks unscathed—'

'Yes, but I didn't manage to do it before my adoptive father died. He didn't live to see how sorry I was. He died thinking I had let him down and that was the last thing in the world I would ever have wanted to do to him. My family here gave me everything and I'm not talking about money now—I'm talking about the important things in life like love and respect. I wanted so much to repay that debt.'

For a moment Cat remembered Sophia's words to her yesterday. About how Nicholas never took the love of his family for granted. That deep down he was always frightened that love would be snatched away from him. That the hard outer shell he liked to present to the world was just a front.

Things about Nicholas's character started to clarify in her mind. It had probably hit him very hard to think he had let down the family who had taken him in. 'I didn't know you were adopted,' she said quietly.

'It's not relevant.'

She brushed a shaking hand across her wet cheek and turned to look at him. 'It's obviously relevant. It was why you were giving that money to an orphanage—wasn't it? How long did you spend in one?'

'That's not important!'

Once more she could see the arrogant glint in his eyes, the proud tilt of his head. Nicholas had insecurities that he hid well. Sophia was right—she could see that now. Maybe he wasn't so different from her after all. They had both endured traumas in their childhood. They had both been hurt in adulthood and it had made them wary—too wary, perhaps. 'I'm sorry my father hurt you so much.'

The gentleness of her tone tore at Nicholas. 'It's not your fault. It was never your fault.'

Cat shrugged. 'I have a family I am ashamed of.'

'I'm ashamed of myself right now.'

'So you should be.' For a moment there was a gleam of humour amidst the pain in her eyes. 'But we can call it quits if you like,' she offered softly.

Nicholas raked a hand through his hair. He felt awkward—like a complete rat. 'It's more than I deserve.'

'That's true…' She smiled at him. 'But holding on to anger isn't good—we need to move on with our lives.'

He couldn't believe that he had ever doubted this woman's integrity. She was so gentle and honest and her family had hurt her so much in the past. That he had added to that pain was almost beyond endurance.

'Anyway, I need to get back to London, so if you would just bring me my passport…'

Nicholas watched as she tilted her head upwards, a determined look in her eyes.

He should have read the signs—should have known that she was nothing like them. But he had been so bound up in his quest for revenge—so tied up with guarding his heart in case he made another big mistake in marriage that he had almost made the biggest one of his life and let her get away.

'Cat, I don't want you to go,' he said quietly. 'I realize that it's going to take a lot to make you trust me again, but I'm willing to work at it. I meant what I said before. I love you very much and I want us to be together. No secrets—no hidden agenda. Just the two of us getting to know each other all over again.'

'I think it might be a bit late for that.'

'I don't accept that.' He moved closer towards her. 'You have feelings for me—I know that you do.'

The arrogance was back in his voice. 'Look at me and tell me honestly that you don't want me.' His voice was terse.

She looked up into his eyes and tried to find her voice but it seemed to have deserted her.

'You see you can't!'

'Nicholas, things aren't as simple as all that,' she breathed huskily.

'Things are as simple or as complicated as we choose to make them.' He reached out and pulled her into his arms and then he kissed her. It was a hard brutal kiss and yet so filled with passion that she found herself yielding to it immediately. It felt so good to be in his arms.

She still loved him…

'You see.' There was a gleam of triumph in his voice as he pulled back from her. 'You want me—it's as simple as that.'

'Not really.' She pulled away from him with a frown.

'Look, I know you are wary of me—I know I've messed up, but…'

'Nicholas, I'm pregnant.'

The words fell from her lips before she could stop them. 'It must have happened in Venice—that night—well…you know…'

There was a look of incredulity on his handsome features that would have struck her as amusing if she hadn't been so tense. This was the real test. It was all very well pretending to love her—whispering glib words about trust and want. But a baby—well, that wasn't something you could gloss over. It made everything real; it focused the mind and the emotions until there was no room for pretence.

'So you see it isn't just about you and me any more,' she carried on quickly. 'Which is another reason why we need to move on from anger and revenge and all of that. But don't worry. I don't want anything from you. I can manage on my own and—'

'How long have you known?'

'What?' She looked up at him in trepidation. 'Only a few days.'

'You should have told me…' He raked a hand through his hair. 'I've hurt you like this and you are pregnant! No wonder you passed out!'

'I'm all right now.'

'I'm so sorry, Catherine!'

The feeling in his voice and in his eyes wasn't something she could doubt. But she didn't want his sorrow.

'You are the best thing to happen to me in a long, long time.' He ran a hand tenderly along the side of her face, a look of wonder in his eyes. 'And now you are pregnant and, just when life couldn't be more perfect, I've nearly ruined it all.'

She frowned. 'Nicholas, you don't have to even pretend to want the baby—I said I can manage and I meant it.'

'What the hell are you talking about?' He grated the words out unevenly, his voice broken with the weight of his emotion. 'Of course I want the baby—and I want you. I can't think of anything I've ever wanted more in my whole life.'

She couldn't speak for a moment—she was too over-whelmed with the craziest feelings. Exhilaration—but also fear in case this too was some kind of test—some kind of cruel trickery—and that fate would snatch this away from her.

'Please give me a chance to prove my love to you and to our baby, Catherine… We can arrange a wedding for after your twenty-first birthday. I'm begging you not to walk away.'

And suddenly, as she looked up at his proud face, she knew in her heart that he meant what he was saying and that if she walked away from him without giving what they had a chance that she would regret it for the rest of her life.

'I love you, Nicholas,' she whispered softly.

'I love you too.' He pulled her into his arms, holding her tight, knowing he would never let her go.

THE GREEK'S
CONVENIENT MISTRESS

BY
ANNIE WEST

Annie West spent her childhood with her nose between the covers of a book—a habit she retains. After years preparing government reports and official correspondence, she decided to write something she *really* enjoys. And there's nothing she loves more than a great romance. Despite her office-bound past, she has managed a few interesting moments—including a marriage offer with the promise of a herd of camels to sweeten the contract. She is happily married to her ever-patient husband (who has never owned a dromedary). They live with their two children amongst the tall eucalypts at beautiful Lake Macquarie, on Australia's east coast. You can email Annie at www.annie-west.com

To Maureen,
for your wonderful generosity
in sharing so much.

To Karen,
for the tireless encouragement and hard work.

To Judy,
for advice on matters medical.

And to Dimitria,
whose Greek is much better than mine.

Thank you all.

CHAPTER ONE

COSTAS SWITCHED OFF the ignition and studied the house he'd crossed the world to find. A red-brick bungalow in suburban Sydney. It was plain and solid, but with an air of recent neglect. Junk mail spilled from the letter box and the lawn was overgrown.

He frowned as he opened the car door and got out, stretching some of the stiffness from his tall frame.

Despite the uncollected mail he knew she was home. Or she had been thirty hours ago, before he'd left Athens. He refused to consider the possibility that she wasn't here. There was too much at stake to countenance failure.

Unclenching fingers that had curled into fists, he shrugged, trying to relieve the rigid set of his shoulders. He'd flown in first-class luxury as usual, but he'd been unable to sleep. The tension that had gripped him for so long now had reached crisis point. He hadn't slept for three days, had barely eaten.

He wouldn't rest till he got what he needed from this woman.

It took twenty seconds precisely to stride across the quiet street, through the low gateway and up the cement path to the front door.

He jabbed the doorbell and cast an assessing gaze across the tiny, unswept patio to the lacy cobwebs blurring the corners of the front window. She was a lazy housekeeper. His lips curved in a cynical twist. Why didn't that surprise him?

He pushed the buzzer again, keeping his finger on for a few extra seconds.

He wasn't in the mood to be ignored. Especially by this woman. Impatience rose in a hot, flooding tide. He'd had enough of her ignorant selfishness. Now she would learn just who she was dealing with.

Stepping off the patio, he surveyed the side of the house. Sure enough, one of the windows was wide open, only the flyscreen separating him from the interior. But he'd be damned if he'd resort to illegal entry.

Unless he had to.

Returning to the front door, he pushed his finger down on the bell and kept it there. The incessant peal echoed through the house.

Good! That would shift her. No one could stand that appalling clamour for long.

Nevertheless it was several minutes before he heard the slam of an internal door. And even longer before someone fumbled at the latch.

Anticipation tightened his body. Once they were face to face, she'd do as he wanted. She'd have no choice. He'd cajole if he had to, though considering her behaviour he was sorely tempted to dispense with the niceties and go straight to threats. He'd use whatever tactics necessary. He took a slow breath and summoned his formidable control. He'd need it for this interview.

The door opened to reveal a woman. Obviously not the one he'd come to see but…*sto Diavolo!*

He froze, his composure splintering as sunlight illuminated her features.

His heart slammed against his ribs and sweat beaded his brow. His neck prickled as he stared straight at a ghost.

She had the same classically pure bone structure. The same wide eyes, elegant nose and slender neck.

For a heartbeat, for two, he was caught in the illusion. Then with a single, shuddering breath common sense reasserted itself. This woman was flesh and blood, not a spectre from the past come to haunt him.

Now he saw the subtle differences in her face. Her eyes were a lustrous honey-gold, not dark. Her mouth was a perfect bow, fuller than Fotini's lips had been.

He took in the knotted cloud of her dark hair with its hint of auburn. The creases along her cheek where she'd obviously lain. The crumpled blouse and dark skirt. She must have had an end-of-week celebration last night then crashed out in her work clothes. He took in her pasty colour and the dark rings under her vacant eyes and wondered if it was illicit drugs she favoured or just old-fashioned alcohol.

Did it matter? The sight of her disturbed him, stirring too many memories. But he had no time to concern himself with anyone but the woman he'd raced round the globe to find.

'I'm looking for Christina Liakos,' he said.

She stared up at him, blinking owlishly.

He frowned, wondering if she was sober enough to understand. *'Kyria Liakos?'* he tried in his own language.

Her eyes narrowed and he saw her knuckles whiten on the edge of the door.

'I've come to see Christina Liakos,' he tried again in deliberately slow, precise English. 'Please tell her she has a visitor.'

She opened her lips but no words emerged. Her mouth worked as if she was about to say something, then she shut it and swallowed convulsively. Her eyes were impossibly huge in her face.

'Oh, God!' Her whisper was hoarse, barely audible even from so close. And then in an instant she was gone, stumbling back down the corridor, leaving Costas to stare after her through the open doorway.

He didn't hesitate. A second later he was in the narrow hall, reaching out to pull the door shut behind him.

The young woman lurched into a room towards the back of the house. Her hunched shoulders, the hand clamped over her mouth, told their own story. She'd over-indulged last night and now she faced the consequences.

For a moment he experienced that horrible sense of *déjà vu* once more, sparked by her startling resemblance to Fotini. But he had no sympathy to waste on a stupid young woman who didn't respect her own body.

His senses were on the alert, ready for the confrontation with his quarry. Yet the house had an aura of emptiness. Already he sensed that he and the girl with the hangover were the only ones here. But he had to make sure.

It only took a couple of minutes to check the entire house, it was so small. The place was comfortably furnished and tidy, except for the shambles of a living room, with its litter of bottles, glasses and plates of stale food. And the kitchen, where someone had barely started on the mountain of washing-up.

It must have been some party, he decided, surveying the haphazard stack of platters and the left-over food spoiling on the counter, the glasses jammed into the sink.

And still no sign of the woman he'd come so far to find. The woman who held his future in her hands.

But there was one person who knew exactly where Christina Liakos was.

He turned and strode into the bathroom, only to pull up abruptly.

It wasn't the awful retching sound that stopped him. Or any sense of delicacy at the thought that she might prefer privacy.

To his horror it was the sight of her trim, beautifully rounded bottom in that tight black skirt as she bent over the toilet. And the shapely length of her legs encased in sheer black stockings.

Ridiculous, he told his suddenly alert body. No woman could be sexy while she vomited into a toilet bowl. Even a woman as beautiful as this.

Sophie's eyes streamed as she gulped another breath into her raw, aching throat. Her mouth tasted foul and she shook so hard she could barely support herself. The nausea was fading but her whole skin prickled uncomfortably in reaction. And it felt as if someone had wrapped a band around her head and constricted it till even the throb of her blood hurt.

'Here.'

She opened her eyes to see a damp flannel thrust in front of her. A man's hand held it. A large, square, capable-looking hand with long fingers. Olive skin. A sprinkle of silky dark hair. The sleeve of a finely woven suit. A flash of snowy white cuff. The subdued elegance of a gold cufflink.

Sophie stared but didn't have the strength to reach out.

'I…can't,' she croaked. She felt so weak that it took all her energy to stay on her feet.

There was a burst of sound behind her. Swearing, by the sound of it, but in incomprehensible Greek. And then an arm like hot steel wrapped around her waist and drew her upright till she sagged against the solid wall of his body. His intense heat was like a furnace at her back. But even that couldn't thaw the chill that gripped her.

He swiped the blessedly wet flannel over her brow, down her cheeks, along her mouth and chin and she silently gave thanks to this man, whoever he was.

She recalled looking up into a set face. Into eyes so dark they shone like jet, revealing nothing. Or maybe that illusion was due to the barely leashed anger she'd sensed in him. Even his arrogantly angled black brows lent fierceness to his brooding countenance. He'd had an aura of edginess, of danger, that belied his tailored suavity.

He was a complete stranger. No woman would forget a man like him—all hard, arrogant male and sexy as sin.

Her head lolled against his chest as the lassitude swept her again. She yawned so wide her jaw cracked. As soon as he left she'd go back to bed, she thought dully.

But then his hand was at her shoulder, fingers digging into the tender flesh so that she winced. He shook her and her whole body flopped, unresisting.

'I *said,* what did you take?' His voice was deep, with the hint of an accent, and Sophie felt a tug of feminine response to the timbre of it. 'Tell me!'

Hazily she realised he was speaking to her.

'Tell you what?' Her brain had fogged up. Now the nausea was passing she felt almost human, but everything was so vague.

Only his punishing grip on her shoulder and the way he held her in close round the waist kept her anchored in reality.

His lips were at her ear, his breath hot against her skin as her eyes fluttered shut.

'What have you taken?' His voice was slow and patient but it held a razor-sharp edge. 'Was it drugs? Pills?'

Pills. That was right. She'd taken two pills. Or was it three? She was sure they'd said two only. 'Pills,' she said, nodding. 'Sleeping pills.'

Another burst of cursing. This guy really had a temper problem. She plucked at his arm, trying to free herself. Suddenly she felt trapped rather than supported by his strength.

'Can you stand by yourself?' he asked.

'Of course.' But when he whipped his arm away, Sophie had to grab for the basin to stay upright.

She felt him move away and relief seeped through her weary bones. He'd helped when she needed assistance, but he was a total stranger. As soon as she'd had just a few minutes to gather her strength, she'd make him leave. Her grip on the vanity unit grew desperate as she forced herself to stand straighter.

Was that water running?

She swung round, then wished she hadn't when dizziness swept her. It was a fight to stay standing, even with the vanity unit to lean against.

It was his hands on her clothes that jerked her out of her stupor. The brush of his knuckles as he unbuttoned her blouse. She swatted at his hands but he was too deft. The blouse was already hanging open as he reached round to unzip her skirt.

With a surge of frantic strength she pushed him away with both hands, only to find it wasn't fine wool suiting under her hands, or crisp cotton, but the warm contours of a solid male chest.

What the…?

Dampness hazed his olive skin and his muscles rippled under her hands. She pushed again and felt the tickle of chest hairs against her palms, shooting sensations of pure pleasure through her body. But it was like pushing at a brick wall for all the impact she made. It was an impressive chest.

Right now she was scared, not admiring. Her breath caught on a harsh sob of fear as she tried desperately to thrust him away.

'Leave me alone!' Her voice was breathless, wavering. 'Get out of here now or I'll call the police.'

He ignored her completely, bending instead to tug her pantihose down her legs. His insistent pressure on first one ankle and then the other allowed him to strip it off. If only her coordination hadn't deserted her she might have put up a better resistance.

'I'm not going to hurt you,' he snarled when she aimed a clumsy punch at him and managed to graze his cheek as he straightened. His dark gaze raked her with such disgust that she almost believed him.

She was cradling her fist when he pulled her up and over his shoulder, knocking the breath out of her.

She slumped, disoriented against him, flesh to flesh. The room whirled around her, as dizzying as the blatantly masculine scent of his bare skin. She felt raw heat, rigid bone and muscle, the brush of his hair against her side as he swung her round.

Then, without warning, he slid her down his torso and onto her feet. Straight into a blast of water from the shower. The full force of it hit her back, then her head.

'What…?'

Wet hair streamed down her face, half-blinding her. The pounding water was so heavy it hurt. All that kept her there was the strength of his hands on her shoulders, holding her up and away from him. She swayed and his grip tightened, but he kept her at arm's length.

His dark eyes were unreadable, gleaming with an inner fire. His face was harsh, his jaw set like stone. It was a face Sophie didn't have the energy to deal with right now.

She sagged, her knees loosening, as the water slowly brought her body back to weary, tingling life. Her head fell forward, drooping under the weight of water and of growing consciousness.

This grim-faced stranger thought she needed sobering up, she realised with a fleeting twist of dark amusement. Maybe he thought she'd come close to overdosing. Why else would they both be in the shower in their underwear?

At another time, in another life, she might have thought this scene humorous or embarrassing. Or even provocative. She in white lace bra and panties. The Greek god with the inscrutable eyes and the magnificent body clad in nothing but black briefs.

But not today.

Today was Saturday, she realised, her mind clearing completely as the searing pain of remembrance tore through her chest. No wonder she felt like hell. Yesterday had been the worst day of her life.

'I'm all right now,' she mumbled. 'You can get out.'

Silence.

'I said I'm all right.' She lifted her head and met his stare. If it weren't for the blast of warm water sluicing down she would have shivered at the icy chill of his unwavering gaze.

'You don't look it,' he said brutally. 'You look like you need medical attention. I'll take you to the hospital and they can—'

'What? Pump my stomach?' She blinked at him through the water and wet hair plastering her face. Outrage warred with exhaustion, holding her motionless but for the tremor in her legs. 'Look, I took a couple of sleeping tablets and obviously they didn't agree with me. That's all.'

'How many exactly?'

'Two,' she said. 'Maybe three, I wasn't really concentrating. But not enough to OD, since that's what you're thinking.'

'And what else did you take with the pills?' His voice was sharp, accusing.

'Nothing. I don't do drugs.' Sophie shrugged against his hold and this time he released her. But he didn't move away, just stood there, arms akimbo, blocking the exit. He looked solid, strong, all taut muscle and unyielding bone. His expression was even harder. It made her shudder.

She swayed without him to prop her up. She could still feel

the imprint of his large hands on her upper arms and guessed she'd have bruises there later.

She counted to ten, then, when she managed to dredge up some strength, she turned and twisted the taps closed.

In the sudden silence she could hear his breathing. And the thunder of her own pulse in her ears.

'I didn't have anything else,' she repeated. 'No drugs, no alcohol. This is just a reaction to the pills.'

And to the unrelenting stress of the past weeks.

Slowly she turned back to face him. He looked about as understanding as Ares, god of war, with his flinty gaze and his wide, battle-ready stance.

'I'm sorry you were worried,' she said as she pulled her hair back from her face and looked past his shoulder at the steamy mirror. Anything to avoid staring at the vast expanse of taut masculine skin that scented the damp air with its hot, musky aroma. 'I appreciate your help, really. But I'm OK.' Or as OK as she was likely to be for a long, long time.

For a moment she thought he didn't believe her. Those penetrating eyes surveyed her slowly, clinically and comprehensively. If she'd been capable of feeling embarrassment she'd have shrivelled under that look.

But right now she was strangely detached, felt little except the welling ache deep inside.

At last he nodded tersely and stepped out of the shower. Immediately she sagged, relief slackening her exhausted muscles. He crossed to the cupboard and dragged out a couple of clean towels.

Dumbly Sophie watched him, her brain processing the series of images. The arrogant jut of his uncompromising jaw. His broad shoulders and sleek back: all gleaming-wet, toned muscle. The taut curve of his backside in briefs that clung now like a second skin. Heavy, powerful thighs.

She shivered and dragged in an unsteady breath.

He turned, scooped up his gear and thrust a towel at her. 'I'll get changed in another room.' His deep voice was devoid of emotion.

Was there anything soft about this man?

She watched him stride out the door. No, she decided. He was all adamantine hardness. From the steely strength of his body to his brooding face and cold eyes.

Sure, he had enough humanity to help her when he thought she needed it. Had gone to great lengths, in fact. But not because of kindness, or fellow feeling, she knew instinctively. He'd simply believed it necessary. He'd done what he thought had to be done—kept her conscious before calling medical aid.

She trembled, still holding the towel against her chest. The tremor grew to a shudder and, despite her flushed skin and the steamy fug of the bathroom, that bone-deep chill invaded her body once more.

Sophie stumbled out of the shower cubicle, wrapped the towel around her body and another round her hair, and escaped to her bedroom. Ten minutes later, dressed in old jeans and a comfortable, loose shirt, she went in search of the stranger who'd invaded her house.

Costas stood in the kitchen, sipping strong black coffee. Something to restore normality after his encounter with the girl who looked so much like Fotini.

At first the similarity had been stunning. Even now it was remarkable, despite the obvious differences. This girl was slightly built, more slender. Her face was less round and her cheekbones more pronounced.

He stared blindly into the back yard and swallowed another mouthful of searing liquid. He barely registered the heat. Instead he concentrated on the images that played alternately in his mind. First the sight of her opening the door, so like Fotini that he'd simply gawped in shock.

And second, the picture of her slumped in his hands. Water streaming down, accentuating her seductive curves. His mouth dried as he remembered the narrowness of her waist, the sensuous flare of her hips. Her lacy bra and briefs had been saturated. They had left nothing to his imagination, not the upward

tilt of her breasts nor the invitation of her nipples, revealed by
the delicate fabric. Nor the evocative shadow of feminine secrecy
between her legs.

He'd held her in his hands and immediately he'd wanted her,
desired her with a raw, aching hunger that told him he'd been far
too long without a woman. Just the feel of her supple, smooth
skin against his and he'd known an overwhelming compulsion
to have her naked beneath him.

He'd stood there, oblivious to the drenching spray, and wished
the circumstances completely different, just for an hour, or two.
For long enough to lose himself in the sweet temptation of her.
To forget his responsibilities and worries in the mindless bliss
he knew he could find in her siren's body.

Costas sipped the scalding coffee and tried to ignore the
heavy tension in his lower body. His mission was too urgent.
No matter how delicious the enticement, he wouldn't be distracted from his purpose.

The sound of a shuffling footstep made him spin round. She
stood in the doorway, apparently steady now on her own two feet.
She looked about sixteen in those clothes, and with her hair
combed down to her shoulders. But her eyes and the purple
shadows beneath them belied that illusion.

Costas frowned as his mind superimposed an image of her,
almost naked in her sexy, pristine lace underwear. The baggy
shirt failed miserably as camouflage. He'd stripped her, touched
her bare skin with his hands. The experience was printed indelibly on his brain.

'There's coffee,' he said abruptly, gesturing to the steaming
mug on the table.

She didn't meet his eyes as she sank into a chair and slowly
lifted the mug in both hands.

'Thank you,' she said. Her voice was like water: cool, devoid
of colour, slipping away to nothing. He felt a moment's burgeoning curiosity then crushed it.

'I need to see Christina Liakos immediately,' he said yet again,
curbing his impatience with iron control. 'How do I contact her?'

'You don't.' This time there was something in her tone. Emotion so strong her voice cracked. 'And her name's not Liakos any more,' she added abruptly. 'It's Paterson.'

Her eyes met his and he endured once again that unwanted, unstoppable sizzle of sexual need.

'Who are you?' she asked.

'My name is Costas Palamidis.' He paused, waiting for her reaction but her face remained blank. 'I have an urgent matter to discuss with Ms Paterson.'

'Palamidis,' she muttered. 'I know that name.' Her brows drew together. But clearly last night's excesses hampered the effort of recollection.

Costas shifted his weight, tired of this nonsense. He was getting nowhere.

'I've just stepped off a plane from Athens. It's imperative that I talk to Ms Paterson immediately.' He refrained from adding that it was a matter of life and death. This was too personal, too private to disclose to strangers.

'Athens?' Her eyes narrowed. 'You were the one on the phone.' He watched her perplexity morph into anger. Her coffee mug thumped onto the table. 'You left messages on the answering machine.'

He nodded. 'Messages that were never returned—'

'You bastard,' she hissed, scrambling to her feet so fast her chair crashed to the floor. 'Now I know who you are! You can leave right now. I want you out of here!'

Costas didn't budge. The girl was clearly unhinged. Her eyes were wild and her fingers curved like talons against the edge of the table.

But she was his one lead in locating Christina Liakos. And he'd deal with the devil himself to reach that woman. Deliberately he leaned back against the kitchen bench, crossing one foot over the other.

'I'm not going anywhere. I've come to talk to Christina Liakos or Paterson as she is now. And I'm not leaving until I do.'

Fascinated, he watched the emotions race across her face. Her snarling frown blanked out into staring shock. Then her features seemed to crumple into a mask of pain. She laughed, an ugly, hysterical sound that filled him with a sense of foreboding.

'Well, unless you're clairvoyant you'll have a long wait, Mr Palamidis. I buried my mother yesterday.'

CHAPTER TWO

THROUGH THE SEARING glaze of unshed tears, Sophie glared up at him.

Hell! If she'd known who he was when she opened the front door she'd have slammed it in his good-looking face.

How dared he show up here the day after her mother's funeral and make himself at home? She stared at the mug he held and wanted to smash it right out of his hand. There'd be satisfaction in a violent outburst. She imagined vividly the splash of hot coffee on his snowy white shirt, the look of outrage on his face.

Pity it took all her strength just to stay upright.

Furiously she blinked. She wouldn't let him see her cry. Her grief was too raw, too overwhelming to share, let alone with a man as coldly unfeeling as he was.

She wanted to shout. To rage. Damn it, she wanted to pummel him with her fists till he felt just a fraction of the pain that was ripping her apart.

But what good would that do? Her mother was gone. Nothing would bring her back.

Sophie drew a shuddering breath and lifted her eyes to meet those of her unwanted visitor. His black gaze wasn't quite so unreadable now. Maybe it was the way his eyes had widened, brows raised in surprise.

No, not surprise. Shock. He looked as if he'd just got the shock of his life. In fact, he looked ill—his face suddenly drawn and his complexion paler. A muscle in his hard-set jaw worked, pumping frenetically. It was the only sign of animation in him. He didn't even blink.

Over the sound of her pulse thundering in her ears, Sophie caught the hiss of his indrawn breath. His chest expanded mightily as if his lungs had emptied and he'd only just remembered to breathe.

Then she saw a flicker of emotion in his eyes. Something so fierce that she almost backed away.

'I'm sorry,' he said at last. 'If I'd known…' Again Sophie saw that shadow of turbulent emotion in his gaze and trembled at the force of it. 'If I'd known,' he continued, 'I would not have intruded on you today.'

'You wouldn't have been welcome at any time,' she said bluntly.

He had a nerve, offering her condolences, now when it didn't matter. It was too little and far, far too late.

'Pardon?' His wide brow pleated in a frown just as if he hadn't understood exactly what she'd said.

'I don't want your apologies,' she said. 'I don't want anything from you.'

'I understand that you are grieving. I—'

'You understand *nothing*,' she snarled. 'You with your superior air and your apologies. You make me sick.' She gulped down a raw breath. 'I want you out of my house and I never want to see you again.'

Silence gathered as he returned her gaze, his brows drawing together in a straight, disapproving line.

'If I could, I would leave now as you wish. But,' the word fell heavily between them, 'I cannot. I come here on a matter of great importance. A family matter.'

'A *family* matter?' Her voice rose and broke. How could he be so callous? 'I have no family.' No siblings. No father. And now her mother…

'Of course you have a family.' He stepped close. So close that his warmth insinuated itself into her chilled body, sending tendrils of heat skirling through her. The invasion of her space was strangely shocking.

But she didn't move away. This was *her* home, *her* territory. No way was she backing down.

'You have a family in Greece.'

She stared into his grim face. A family in Greece. For how many years had she heard that? The stubborn mantra of her mother, a woman who'd had to make her life in a new country, far from home. A woman who had refused to be cowed, even by her own father's rejection.

The irony of it. Sophie's mouth twisted in a lopsided grimace at the unbelievable timing. Her mum had waited a quarter of a century to hear those words confirmed. Now, just days after her death, they were being offered to Sophie like a talisman to keep her safe.

'Stop it!' he barked, his hands closing around her shoulders, digging into her flesh.

Sophie jumped, startled out of the beginnings of hysterical laughter. She felt branded by his touch, contaminated. She shrugged, tried to shove his hands off her. Finally he let her go.

'I have no family,' she repeated, staring into his furious gaze.

'You are upset,' he countered as if explaining away her emotions. 'But you have a grandfather and—'

'How *dare* you?' she snapped. 'How can you have the gall to mention him in this house?' Her heart raced so fast she thought it might burst right out of her ribcage. Again she felt the white-hot rage, that savage need to lash out in fury and smash something.

She'd got through the past few days only by refusing to dwell on what she couldn't change, by telling herself that it didn't matter. It was all over now anyway. Old history. No one, not even the cruel patriarch of the Liakos family, had the ability to hurt her mother any more.

And now this family henchman appeared on the scene and dredged it all up again. All the pain and the lacerated hope. The regret and the smouldering hate.

She trembled. But not with weakness this time.

'Do you think there's any place in my life for a man who completely disowned his daughter?' she hissed. 'Who ignored her year after year? Pretended she didn't exist?'

Sophie's chest ached with the force of her hurt, with the gasping breaths she inhaled. Her hands shook with a palsy of repressed fury.

'Who didn't even have enough compassion to contact her when she was dying?' The accusation echoed between them, ebbing away into a silence thick with challenge and pain.

She stared into a face devoid of all emotion. Yet he couldn't conceal the flicker of surprise in his eyes. So this was news to him. And not welcome news, judging by the way his brows drew together.

'Nevertheless, we *must* talk.' He raised a peremptory hand as she opened her mouth to speak. 'I am not your grandfather's emissary. I don't come on his business, but my own.'

Sophie shook her head, confusion clouding her tired brain. His business? It didn't seem likely. Should she believe him or was this some ploy?

'But your phone calls. They came just a few days after I'd contacted my grandfather. I left a message asking him to call.'

Begging him to ring and speak to her mother.

Sophie steeled herself against the memory of those hopeless days. Of the doctor saying there was nothing more they could do to counter the virulent strain of influenza her mother had contracted. Of how Sophie had swallowed her pride and tracked down a phone number for Petros Liakos, the tyrant who'd disowned his daughter, Sophie's mother.

But still the old man hadn't called.

Sophie felt the hatred, the searing pain flood her once more and cursed this arrogant stranger for making her relive it all.

He spoke, his deep voice cutting across the whirling turmoil of her memories. 'I knew of your mother, but not where she was or how to contact her. I needed to speak with her urgently.'

Something about the tension in him, the harsh lines around his mouth, snared her attention, broke through her impotent rage.

'When you rang Petros Liakos,' he said, 'I was able to get your phone number. I called all this week.'

But Sophie hadn't answered the messages from the Greek

stranger that had filled the answering machine. What was the point, when they'd commenced the very day she'd made the funeral arrangements? It was too late for her mother to forgive her family's neglect. And Sophie had no intention of ever forgetting the way the Liakos family had treated her mother.

The messages had become more imperious, more urgent, but Sophie had trashed them. And taken satisfaction in slamming the phone down the one time the Greek stranger had reached her at home.

Now he was no stranger. She looked up into his impenetrable eyes, felt again his aura of implacable power. A shiver of apprehension feathered down her spine.

He claimed not to be her grandfather's lackey.

'Who are you?' she whispered. 'What do you want?'

Costas stared into the sparking, troubled eyes of the girl before him and wished he could leave her to grieve in peace. She was wound up tighter than a spring.

He'd released his hold on her reluctantly, on his guard in case she lashed out. If there'd been a knife to hand she'd probably have swept it up and plunged it straight into his heart. She'd looked like a Fury, eager for vengeance. But the next moment she was heartbreakingly vulnerable.

He felt her grief as a palpable force, heard it in the savage, scouring breaths she took. He exhaled slowly, schooling his face against the pity he knew she wouldn't want to see.

Not for the first time he wished he'd never become entangled with the Liakos family. They were nothing but trouble. Had always been trouble for him. And for her, this girl with the fine lines of pain dragging her mouth down and etching deep around her eyes.

He thrust his hand through his hair and silently cursed this appalling mess.

But he couldn't walk away. He had no choice but to continue. Even though it meant forcing his problems onto a distraught girl.

A pang of guilt pierced his chest. He should give her time. Respect her need to mourn.

But time was the one luxury he didn't possess.

She was right to be cautious, Costas decided grimly as tension hummed through him. This situation had never been simple. And now, since he'd met her, it had become even more complex. Dangerous.

He needed this woman. She was his only hope of diverting the monstrous disaster that loomed ever closer.

But now, to his horror, there was more.

He could barely believe it, didn't want to believe it. It should be impossible. But he couldn't ignore the sheer potency of his physical craving for her. *Of all women!*

It was unique. Inappropriate. It was a complication he didn't need. He didn't have time for lust. Especially not for a grief-stricken girl who saw him as some sort of ogre.

Especially not for a girl from the house of Liakos.

He'd learned that particular lesson long ago.

Look at her! She wore paint-smeared jeans and a baggy shirt. Her trainers were stained and worn and her hair had probably never seen a stylist's scissors.

Yet he couldn't drag his ravenous gaze from her. The elegance of her delicate bone structure stole his breath. Her wide-as-innocence honey-gold eyes, her ripe mouth. Beneath the cotton of her shirt he could see her proud, high breasts. Hell! He could almost feel them against his palms, firm and round and tempting. And those ancient jeans clung to her like a second skin, showing off long, slender legs.

He couldn't believe it. Where was his honour? His respect for her grief?

His sense of self-preservation?

'Who are you?' she whispered again and he saw a spark of fear in her expression.

'My name is Costas Vassilis Palamidis,' he said quickly, spreading his hands in an open gesture. 'I live in Crete. I am a respectable businessman.' In other circumstances he'd have found the novelty amusing, being forced to present his credentials. But there was nothing humorous here.

'I need to speak with you. Is there somewhere else we can talk?' He looked around the room, realising that the untidy remains must be from a large post-funeral gathering.

Damn. It was brutal, forcing this on her now, so soon after her loss. But what choice did he have? There was no time for compassion if it meant delay.

'Outside perhaps?' He gestured towards the back yard. Anywhere away from the claustrophobic atmosphere of mourning that pervaded the house.

She looked at him with wary eyes, clearly unconvinced.

'It's been a long journey and some fresh air would be welcome,' he urged. 'It will take a little time to explain.'

Eventually she nodded slowly. 'There's a park just around the corner. We'll go there.'

She looked so fragile he doubted she'd make it to the front door, let alone down the street. 'Surely that's too far. We could—'

'You were the one who wanted to talk, Mr Palamidis. This is your chance. Take it or leave it.'

Her chin notched up belligerently and faint colour washed her cheeks. Animation, or temper, suited this passionate woman. It was a pity that, given the circumstances, he would not be exploring a more personal acquaintance with her.

Finally he nodded. If she collapsed and he had to carry her back, then so be it.

'Of course, Ms Paterson. That will suit admirably.'

Five minutes later Sophie settled back on the weathered park bench and stifled a groan. He'd been right. She should have stayed at home rather than pretend to an energy she didn't have.

But at least here they were in a public place. And the crisp autumn air felt good in her lungs.

The thought of staying in the house, where this man's presence dominated the very atmosphere, had been unthinkable. It wasn't just his size. It was the way he unsettled her. The indefinable sense of authority that emanated from him. And made her want to put as much distance between them as possible.

Surreptitiously she shot a glance at her companion as he stood a few metres away, answering a call on his phone. From the top of his black-as-night hair to the tips of his glossy, handmade shoes, he was the epitome of discreet wealth, she now realised.

He turned his head abruptly and met her eyes. Instantly heat licked across her cheeks. Yet she read nothing in his expression, not a shred of emotion. His face might have been carved from living rock, a study in masculine power and strength with that commanding blade of a nose and those arrogant eyebrows.

So why had her pulse begun to race?

'My apologies, Ms Paterson,' he said as he snapped the phone shut and sat down. 'It was a call I had to take.'

Sophie nodded, wondering why she should feel so uncomfortable with him sitting almost a metre away.

'My name's Sophie,' she said quickly to cover her nervousness. 'I prefer that to Ms Paterson.'

He inclined his head. 'And, as you know, I am Costas.'

'You haven't really answered me. Who are you?' His height wasn't typical of the Greek men she'd known. And his aura of brooding mastery, of carefully leashed force, set him apart. His features were severe, harsh, but more than handsome. He was unique, would stand out in any crowd.

Why was he here? Her life, and her mother's since settling in Australia, had been ordinary with a capital O.

'Did you know your mother had a sister?' he countered.

'Yes. She and my mum were twins.'

'Your aunt had one daughter, Fotini.' Something in his tone made her watch him intently. His lips had compressed tautly, curved down at the corners. His eyes were bleak.

'A few years ago Fotini and I married, which makes us, you and I, related by marriage.'

'Cousins-in-law,' she whispered, wondering why she found the expression on his face so disturbing. She'd never seen this man anything but controlled. Yet something about his set jaw and the desolation in his eyes told her he clamped down hard on the strongest of emotions.

'Your wife, Fotini, is she here with you in Sydney?'

'My wife died in a car smash last year.'

Now she understood the expression of repressed pain on his face. He was still grieving. 'I'm sorry,' she murmured.

Sophie wondered how she'd feel about her own loss in a year's time. Everyone said the pain would be easier to bear later. That the happy memories would one day outweigh the ponderous weight of grief that pinned her down till sometimes she felt she could barely breathe.

She looked at the man beside her. Time didn't seem to have healed his wounds.

'Thank you,' he said stiffly. Then after a moment he added, 'We have a little girl. Eleni.'

She heard the love in his voice as he spoke and watched his features relax. His lips curved into a fleeting, devastating smile. Gone was the granite-hard expression, the grimly restrained power. Instead, to her shock, Sophie saw a face that was... handsome? No, not that. Nor simply attractive. It was compelling. A face any woman could stare at for hours, imagining all sorts of wonderful, crazily sensual things.

Sophie snagged a short, startled breath and looked away, letting her feet scuff the grass.

'So you do have a family in Greece,' he said. 'There are second cousins. There's little Eleni. And me...'

No! No matter what he said, Sophie would never be able to think of this man as a relative. She frowned. The idea was just too preposterous. Too unsettling.

'And there's your grandfather, Petros Liakos.'

'I don't want to talk about him.'

'Whether you want to discuss him or not, you need to understand,' Costas said.

Sophie refused to meet his gaze and stared instead across the park, watching wrens flit out of a nearby bush.

'Your grandfather isn't well.'

'Is that why you came?' Anger rose, constricting her chest. 'Because the old man's sick and wants his family at long last?'

She shook her head. 'Why should I care about the man who broke my mother's heart with his selfishness? You've come a long way for nothing, Mr Palamidis.'

'Costas,' he said. 'We're family after all, if only by marriage.'

She let the silence grow between them. She didn't trust herself to speak.

'No, I'm not here for that. But your grandfather's condition is serious.' He paused. 'He had a severe stroke. He's in hospital.'

Sophie was surprised to feel a pang of shock at his words. Of…regret. Could it be? Regret for the man who'd turned against her mother all those years ago?

Sophie's lips thinned as she dredged up the ready anger. She wouldn't allow herself to feel anything like pity for him. He didn't deserve it.

'Do you understand?' Costas asked.

'Of course I understand,' she snapped. 'What do you want me to do? Fly to Greece and hold his hand?'

She swung round to face him, all the repressed fury and despair of the last weeks fuelling her passion. 'It's more than he did for my mother. For twenty-five years he pretended she didn't exist. All because she'd had the temerity to marry for love and not in some antiquated arranged marriage! Can you believe it?'

She glared up at him. 'He cut her out of his life completely. Didn't relent with the news that she'd married. Didn't care that he had a grandchild. Was probably disappointed I was only a girl.'

She drew a rasping breath. 'And when she's *dying* he refuses to call and speak to her.' Her voice broke on a rising note and she turned from his piercing gaze, dragging a tissue out of her back pocket and blowing her nose.

'Do you have any idea how much it would have meant to my mother to be reconciled with him? To be forgiven?' She stuffed the tissue away and blinked desperately to clear her vision. 'As if she'd committed some crime.'

'Your grandfather is a traditionalist,' Costas said. 'He believes in the old ways: the absolute authority of the head of the family, the importance of obedient children, the benefits of a marriage approved by both families.'

She looked into his give-nothing-away eyes and his hard face and suspected not much had changed. Costas Palamidis was a man who wore his authority like a badge of identity. Of his blatant masculinity.

'Is that how you married into the Liakos family?' she asked, trying to sound offhand. 'The Palamidis and Liakos clans decided there was benefit in a merger?'

His eyes blazed dark fire and for a moment she felt as if she'd stepped off a cliff without a safety rope. She shivered, for all her bravado, acknowledging an atavistic fear at the idea of rousing this man to angry retaliation.

'The marriage had the blessing of both families,' he said eventually, tonelessly. 'It was not an elopement.'

Which didn't answer her question. Sophie stared into his face and saw the warning signs of a strong man keeping his temper tightly leashed.

That was answer enough. Just looking at him, she knew Costas Palamidis wouldn't settle for anything, especially a wife, unless it was exactly what he desired. He'd get what he wanted every time and be damned to the consequences. The idea of him needing help to get a bride was laughable.

Sophie would bet her cousin, Fotini, had been charming, gorgeous and utterly captivated by her bold, devastatingly masculine husband. No doubt she'd been at his beck and call, deferring to him in everything, like a good, traditional Greek wife was apparently supposed to do.

'Thanks for coming all this way with your news,' she said at last, 'but as you can see I…'

What? Don't care?

No, she couldn't lie. There was a part of her that felt regret at the old man's pain. A sneaking sympathy for him, looking death in the face and deciding, far too late, that he had done the wrong thing by his daughter.

The realisation made her feel like a traitor.

'It's too late to build bridges,' she said quickly. 'I've never been part of the Liakos family and there's no point pretending now that I am.'

She was her own person. Sophie Paterson. Strong, capable, independent. She didn't need some long-lost family in Greece. Instead she had friends, an address book full of them. And she had a career to start, a life to get on with.

Yet right now she wanted nothing more than to lean against this silent stranger and sob her eyes out till some of the pain went away. To let his obvious strength enfold and support her.

What was happening to her?

This weakness would pass. It must, she decided as she bit down hard on her quivering lower lip.

'You've made your feelings abundantly clear.' His deep voice scraped across her raw nerves so she shivered. 'But it's not that simple to disconnect from your family.'

'What do you mean?' She swung round on the seat. For all his calm composure, there was an inner tension about him that screamed its presence. Immediately she shrank back, suddenly aware of how very little she knew about him. Of exactly how much larger and tougher he was.

'Don't look like that,' he growled. 'I don't bite.'

She shivered at the immediate, preposterous idea of him bending that proud head towards her and scraping his strong white teeth over the ultra-sensitive skin at the side of her neck.

Where the heck had that come from?

Her breathing notched up its pace and her heart thudded hard against her ribcage. Sophie whipped round away from him, horrified that he might have registered the flash of awareness still rippling through her.

She squeezed her eyes shut. She was off balance. The funeral, the lack of sleep, were taking their toll.

'Sophia—'

'Sophie,' she corrected automatically. She'd rejected the original version of her name as soon as she was old enough to realise it belonged to the world of that far-away family who'd treated her mother so appallingly.

'Sophie.' He paused and she wondered what was coming next. He sounded as if he had the weight of the world on his shoulders. 'I came to find your mother because it seemed she was the only person left who might be able to help.'

'Why her?'

'Because she's family.' He sighed and from the corner of her eye she saw him thrust his hand back through his immaculate hair.

'My daughter is very ill.' His voice now was brusque to the point of harshness. 'She needs a bone-marrow transplant. I hoped your mother might be a match to donate what Eleni needs.'

The words, so prosaic, so simple, dropped between them with all the finesse of a bomb.

Appalled, Sophie felt the words sink in. She found herself facing him, aware for the first time that some of his formidable reserve must be a product of his need to clamp down on an unbearable mix of anguished emotions.

'You're not compatible yourself?' she asked, then realised the answer was obvious. He wouldn't be here if he'd been able to help his little girl.

But she wasn't prepared for the wave of anger that swept through him. His hands clenched dangerously and his whole body seemed to stiffen. There was no mistaking the expression in his eyes this time. Fury. And pain.

Silently he shook his head.

'And no one in your family—?'

'No one in the Palamidis family is a suitable donor,' he cut across her tentative question. 'Nor are any of your relatives.' He paused, dragging in a deliberate breath that made his chest and shoulders rise.

He must feel so helpless. And there was no doubt in her mind that Costas Palamidis was a man accustomed to controlling his world, not being at its mercy.

Sophie's heart sank as she realised how dire the situation was.

If the girl's own father wasn't a match for her marrow type, how likely was it that she would be?

He might have read her mind. His voice was grim as he continued. 'Nor did we have luck finding a match in the database of potential donors. But your mother and her sister were identical twins. So there's a possibility.'

'You think I might be able to donate bone marrow?'

'That's why I'm here.' He spread his fingers across his thighs, stretching the fine wool of his dark suit. 'Nothing else would have dragged me away from Eleni now.'

Sophie felt the weight of his expectation, his hope, press down on her, even heavier than the burden of grief she already carried. She had a horrible premonition that he was doomed to disappointment.

How desperate he must have been to fly to Australia, not even knowing if her mother was here. And how distraught when she'd hung up on him and deleted his messages. No wonder he'd looked like an avenging angel when he'd stormed the house and demanded to see her mother!

She shivered and wrapped her arms tight round her body as a sense of deep foreboding chilled her.

All his expectations, all his dark, potent energy, had shifted focus. He wanted her.

CHAPTER THREE

COSTAS FORCED HIMSELF into a semblance of patient stillness as the girl beside him digested the news.

Admitting that the chance of success was slim had brought the black fear surging back. The inescapable truth that for all his power and authority, this was one thing he couldn't make go away.

He'd give anything to save his daughter. Do anything. He wouldn't hesitate a second to take the illness into his own body, if only it were possible. Anything to save Eleni.

Instead he'd been forced into a role of unbearable powerlessness. He'd demanded the best medical attention, engaged the top physicians and bullied Eleni's distant relatives into testing their compatibility to donate bone marrow. All to no avail.

If the doctors were to be believed, this girl beside him was the only hope his daughter had left.

It was the smallest of chances. But hope was all they had left, he and Eleni. He'd bargained with God and would tackle the devil, too, if it meant they could overcome this disease.

Why didn't Sophie Paterson say something? Why not answer his unspoken question?

His hands fisted so tight that pain throbbed through them. The muscles of his neck and shoulders stiffened into adamantine hardness as he fought the impulse for action. He wanted to shake her into speech. Bellow out that she was their last hope. She had to take the test. *She had to.*

What was she thinking?

He reviewed the material the private enquiry agency had just phoned in about her and her mother. A pity they hadn't reported before he'd arrived at her house. He winced, remembering his demand to see Christina Liakos.

Sophia Dimitria Paterson was twenty-three, had just finished her course in speech pathology, an only child. Her father had died in an industrial accident when she was five. Her mother had worked as a cleaner to support them.

He wondered how Petros Liakos would feel, learning his once-beloved daughter had spent years working double shifts to keep food on the table. Such a far cry from the pampered life she'd led in Greece.

Sophie had worked as a waitress part-time while she studied. She liked to party. Was outgoing and very popular, especially with young men.

Educated but no money. In fact, according to the financial report he'd just heard, Sophie Paterson had inherited a substantial debt from her mother.

Why didn't she say something, damn it? Wasn't it obvious what he wanted from her?

Or was she waiting for him to persuade her?

He darted a measuring glance her way. Surely not. She didn't seem the type.

But then he had personal experience of exactly how acquisitive and devious women could be. It wasn't a lesson he needed to learn twice.

Unable to contain the urgent need for a physical outlet for his tension, he shot to his feet, towering over her as she stared into space. He shoved his fists into his trouser pockets, hunching his shoulders against the hollowing pain he refused to admit into his consciousness.

For an instant her eyes met his. Then quickly she shifted her gaze.

In that moment Costas felt the last of his hard-won control tear apart. The social niceties, the veneer of the civilised world were

stripped away, like a long, uncoiling ribbon, leaving him free of
everything but his desperation.

'If it's money you want there's plenty of that to sweeten the
choice for you.'

Her head swung round and she stared up at him, eyebrows
arched. As if she didn't already know just how wealthy the Liakos
family was.

And their riches were nothing compared to his. Would she do
what he wanted for money? He'd met too many people, including
beautiful young women, who'd sell their integrity, much less some
bone marrow, for a tiny fraction of his material wealth. And she
was a Liakos. He knew exactly what that family was capable of.

Still, the idea that she could be bought sickened him. He
swallowed down hard on the sour taste of disappointment and
swung away from her.

'Your grandfather set aside a legacy for Eleni. Money and
company shares.' His tone was clipped. Anything to get this over
with. They'd strike a bargain and settle it.

He sensed her involuntary movement and knew he had her
hooked. He heard her breath catch.

'If the doctors say you're a match and you go through with the
procedure,' he continued, 'I'll arrange to have that legacy passed
to you instead. There'll be no argument from your grandfather, I'll
guarantee it.' He paused, letting her wait for the clincher. 'I haven't
had it valued, but I guarantee it totals well into seven figures.'

Silence.

No doubt she was imagining what she could do with several
million dollars. Already in debt, she'd be eager to take up the offer.

'Is that all?'

'What?' He swung round. She stood at his shoulder. Colour
tinted her cheekbones and washed across her slender neck. Her
eyes were brighter too.

Again he experienced that shaft of molten desire straight to
his lower body. But now he felt contaminated by it. Even in lust
his taste was usually more discriminating. Gold-diggers had
never held any appeal for him.

'Is that the last of your offers?' she asked.

He ignored her attempt to bargain for more and cut to the chase. 'You'll agree to be tested and take my terms?'

'I'll agree to nothing, you arrogant bully.'

He stared down, shocked to realise the gleam of avarice in her eyes was instead a flare of blatant fury. No sign here of a grasping, money-hungry opportunist. She looked as if she'd like to tear his eyes out.

Could he have got it wrong?

'You might think you're a big man but you're just a hollow sham.' She shoved her mass of riotous hair back behind her shoulder and squared up to him, toe to toe. Her head barely topped his shoulder. Her chin jutted at an impossible angle as she glared at him.

'What gives you the right to assume that I'm some heartless, avaricious monster?' She jabbed his chest with her index finger. 'Who'd take *money*,' jab, 'to help a sick child?' Jab and twist.

'I bet you didn't put this proposition to any of your relatives back in Greece, did you?'

He opened his mouth to argue. But she was right. They were family. They'd be mortally offended at the very idea. But Sophie Paterson... She was Eleni's family, yet she was an unknown quantity.

He refused to question the way his mind shied from the idea of her being part of *his* family.

'Of course you didn't,' she almost spat at him. 'You wouldn't offend your daughter's *real* family.' Again that jab into his chest. 'But we Australians...we were never up to scratch, were we? You'd expect the worst from us.'

Her voice rose in strident accusation yet he saw the glitter of unshed tears in her eyes. Her soft mouth quivered and she bit down so hard he feared she'd draw blood.

Burning shame seared out from the accusing point of her finger, through his torso, right to his heart. It wasn't an emotion he was used to. And he didn't like the sensation of guilt one iota.

'Enough,' he growled, clamping one hand round hers and pressing her open palm across his shirt.

His heart leapt at the contact, thudding an uncontrollable tattoo, and he fought the impulse to drag her into his arms and stop her voice with his mouth. Her lush lips were open now, in a circle of surprise that made him want to dip his head and discover the taste of her on his tongue. She'd be sweet as honey. Hot as flame. Heat burst across his skin, just at the thought of it.

Anger. Guilt. Lust. They rushed through him in a feverish swirl that escalated into raw desire. So savage it slammed through him with a force that almost made him reel.

He dragged oxygen into his air-starved lungs and stared down at her, wondering. He knew desire—had no trouble assuaging it. But he'd never felt anything like this before. Ever.

What the hell had he got himself into?

Sophie blinked up into his glittering black eyes and felt the blaze of fury that had buoyed her through the outburst dwindle and fade.

He was so close she could see that, for all the severe planes and angles of his face, his skin was fine-grained and smooth but for the rough shadow along his jaw. Her nostrils flared as she detected and instinctively responded to his scent: heat and musk. One hundred per cent pure masculine pheromones.

'Enough,' he said again, his voice a husky growl that sent all her nerves into alert.

For an endless space their eyes met and held, an indefinable heat pulsing through the crackling silence between them. If she could have broken his hold she would have backed away, put some distance between them till she felt safe again. When he looked at her like that she couldn't think. And she didn't want to feel.

'You have my apologies,' he said at last. He shook his head decisively when she would have spoken. 'In the extremity of the situation, I leaped to the wrong conclusion. I saw your silence in the worst light.'

He paused and dragged in a breath so deep that his chest almost touched hers.

'I have experience in dealing with people who are not so…unaffected by material wealth as you.' His eyes, darkly mesmerising, held hers. 'I regret the offence my words caused you.'

His heart drummed beneath Sophie's fingers, the encompassing heat of his body surrounded her. His eyes seemed to gaze right into her soul. If she could have looked away she would. But the intensity of his scrutiny held her in thrall, as surely as if he'd bound her physically to him.

This was dangerous. She had to end it. Now.

'I accept your apology,' she said, wincing at the stilted sound of her voice. 'I was hurt that you believed…' She shook her head. What did it matter now? 'It was a misunderstanding,' she said as graciously as she could.

'Thank you, Sophie.' His voice was a low burr, brushing across her skin.

And then he did something totally unexpected. He lifted her hand, raised it to his lips and, gaze still meshed with hers, pressed a slow kiss to the back of it.

A jolt of sensation speared through her and her eyes widened. For a moment she saw the reflection of her own shock in his ink-dark eyes, and then they turned blank, giving nothing away. But ripples of awareness raced through her body, awakening dormant senses into stirring life.

It scared her.

She tugged her hand away, rubbing it with her other thumb, as if that would erase the burning sensation of his mouth on her flesh. He stepped back and she released the breath she hadn't known she'd been holding.

For the first time she looked, really looked, at Costas Palamidis. Trying to see beyond the stereotype she'd assigned to him.

He was more than the epitome of ruthless machismo she'd first thought him. More than a father fighting against the odds for his daughter's life. He was clearly used to dealing with wealth and power, and from what he'd said, with the sort of people she'd prefer to avoid.

The grimness of his face had seemed bone-deep when they'd

met. But was it simply the overlay of despair on a man protecting his family against the worst possible odds?

And there was more to ponder over. Now she'd seen that spark of undiluted sexual energy in him, felt its potency in her own crazily jangling nerves. It set off every alarm bell in her brain. But she couldn't simply walk away from him. Not now she understood why he was here.

She was no closer to understanding who Costas Palamidis was. And, she realised, she was torn between wanting to have nothing more to do with him and the disturbing need to find out everything.

Sophie drew in a slow breath, acknowledging that she was in deep trouble.

Something had happened in that short, violent storm of emotions. Some barrier had been breached, some internal barricade splintered, leaving her feeling wide open and defenceless. She hadn't a clue how, but now, instead of feeling only grief at her loss and fury at the thought of her grandfather, a new mix of feelings swirled within her. They threatened the iron-hard control that had kept her going through the last few weeks.

Something about this man, this stranger, had reached straight out to her, unsettling her in ways she didn't comprehend.

He wasn't her type. Not at all. Big, bossy, take-charge guys weren't her style. So how could she explain this feeling of linkage, of a bond between them?

She couldn't.

'Now we understand each other.' His voice was low, vibrant, making her aware of her body's immediate response of shimmering excitement. Just to the sound of him!

She nodded, not trusting her own voice.

'And you'll help?' There was unmistakable urgency in his controlled tone.

'Of course I'll do what I can,' she said. 'I couldn't ignore your little girl.'

His smile was taut, perfunctory. Already he was planning his next move; she could see it in his eyes, in his ready-for-anything stance. He was probably deciding how best to manage the logistics of the test.

'But don't forget,' she warned, reaching out a hand as if to restrain him, then losing her nerve and letting her arm drop to her side, 'there's no guarantee it will work.'

His look told her what he thought of her caution. 'It's got to work. There's no other option.'

He made it sound simple. As if the outcome were assured. Sophie shivered. The bleak reality was that she probably wouldn't be able to help his daughter.

But she didn't voice her caution again. She understood too well the desperation of watching a loved one wither away before your eyes. The eagerness with which you snatched any hope, no matter how tenuous. The constant prayers, the belief that somehow you might *will* them to survive.

She'd been like that as her mother lay in hospital, unable to fight the disease that robbed her of life far too early. And it was like that now with Costas Palamidis.

He might look hard as nails. In fact, she was sure he *was*. But the weary lines fanning from his eyes, the carved lines bracketing his mouth, revealed a pain that was no less real for being savagely hidden behind his formidable reserve.

That must be why she felt this unique connection to him. As if there was far more between them than their status as cousins-in-law.

Sophie breathed a deep sigh of relief. That was it. Of course there was a rational explanation. Fellow feeling for someone suffering the trauma she'd been through.

She looked up into his severe face and told herself it would be all right. She didn't need to worry any more about the inexplicable fusion of awareness and fear that he evoked in her. It had an explanation after all.

Steadfastly she ignored the trickle of unease that slid down her spine as her eyes met his. Fire sparked again deep within her.

'I'll make all the arrangements,' he was saying, and for the first time his gaze was warm with approval.

The trickle disappeared as a wave of heat washed over her.

She nodded, trying to concentrate on what lay ahead and ignore her physical response to that look.

'Can you be ready tomorrow?' he asked.

'Sure.' The sooner the better.

'Good.' He took her elbow and turned towards her house, pulling her along with him. His hand was hot through the sleeve of her shirt and his warmth at her side enfolded her. Her chest constricted strangely, as if all the air had been sucked from her lungs.

'I'll organise our flight for tomorrow,' he said.

Sophie faltered to a stop. 'Sorry?'

'Our flight.' He sent her an impatient glance and started walking again, guiding her beside him. 'I'll call you with the details and drive you to the airport.'

'I don't understand.' She frowned. 'It's just a medical test, isn't it? A blood test or something?'

'That's right,' he said. 'A blood test, and if that's compatible the doctor will take a bone-marrow sample.'

'Wait!' She planted her feet wide on the ground so this time he was forced to stop and face her. 'What's this about a flight?' she demanded. 'Surely the tests can be done in Sydney?'

His dark brows arrowed down in a V. 'They can be done anywhere. But this way you'll be on hand if the doctors say we can go ahead with the transplant.'

Again Sophie felt that stab of unease at his presumption this would work. That she would be Eleni's donor. But what if the news wasn't good?

'You're taking a lot for granted. It would be easier if I come to Greece once we know if this will work.' That would be time enough for her to face her mother's relatives. The very idea of that made her stomach churn.

His hand curled tighter round her elbow and he drew her up against his body. She stared into his face, so implacable, so determined that for a single, startled moment Sophie's breath stopped.

Out of nowhere surfaced the mind-numbing idea that he wasn't going to release her. Ever.

* * *

Costas stared down into her dark-honey eyes and told himself to slow down, to be patient. And, above all, to ignore the searing realisation of just how good it felt to touch her. To feel her body against his.

She was grieving.

She was off-limits for all sorts of reasons.

But she felt so right, tucked here against him. Her fresh scent had teased him from the moment he'd pulled her close, awakening long-dormant senses. Old needs.

He wanted…

Carefully Costas released his hold and stepped away, putting some space between them. Her chest rose and fell with her choppy breathing and he could see the reflection of his own puzzled response in her face.

No. This wasn't about what he wanted from her. That could never be. This was about what Eleni *needed* from her. Nothing else could be allowed to cloud the issue. Nothing.

He stepped back another fraction and let his hands drop to his sides.

'It will be simpler and faster this way,' he said. He refused to voice the superstitious fear that if he let Sophie out of his sight, left Australia without her, this opportunity to save Eleni might slip through his fingers. That something would prevent Sophie from coming to Greece. He clenched his hands together behind his back.

'I could go to a clinic here in Sydney—'

'We can be in Athens in a day,' he interrupted. 'And when I ring ahead the doctors will be waiting for you. You can have the first blood test the next day.' He held her gaze with his, willing her to agree. Then he forced himself to spell out what he'd left unsaid before. 'This is my daughter's last chance.'

The words echoed between them, appalling, unbearable.

His body was tense with the effort of control, aching with the stress of it. He broke eye contact and stared into the distance, not seeing the unfamiliar Australian scene, or the slim woman before him. Remembering instead his little Eleni, so brave and uncomplaining. So innocent. What had she done to deserve this?

Couldn't Sophie understand his need to get this done *now?* As soon as humanly possible?

He flinched when she touched him, so unexpected was it. And so shockingly familiar to his hungry senses.

He looked into her upturned face. The sympathy he saw there would have broken a lesser man. Her eyes were huge in her pale face and she stared at him as if she understood just how desperate he was.

In all these nightmare months there'd been no one to share the anger and the fear, the horror of fighting the temptation of despair. He hadn't realised till this moment just what a difference that would have made.

And now here was this girl offering him sympathy and understanding. And all the while her body spoke to his, tempting with its heady promise of ultimate physical release.

For an instant he teetered on the brink of reaching out and grasping what she offered. But he didn't need anyone. He'd learned to stand alone long ago.

'I understand,' she said, the knowledge of his pain there in her husky tone. 'And I promise if I'm compatible then I'll be on the first plane to Athens.'

'No!'

That wasn't good enough. He'd exhausted every other avenue. He couldn't afford to let her stay behind. A thousand things could happen, even in a few weeks, to prevent her trip to Greece.

'No,' he said again, striving for a normal tone. 'You'll come now. I'll make the arrangements. And if,' he forced himself to go on, 'you're incompatible, you'll have lost nothing by it. You won't be out of pocket. You'll be my guest, of course.'

He watched her open her mouth as if to protest, and then close it again.

'A short break from here won't hurt. You haven't any pressing engagements, have you?' He knew from the investigator she had nothing, neither study nor work, scheduled.

Slowly she shook her head.

His spirits rose as he scented victory. 'Look on it as a short holiday,' he said, using the low, coaxing tones that always got him what he wanted with women.

She met his gaze and he felt something deep inside stir, unsettling him again. She was just a young woman, like so many others he'd known. Why did he have the gut-deep sensation that she saw into his very soul?

Sto Diavolo! Maybe the strain was starting to tell on him after all.

'I'll pay my own way,' she responded, her soft mouth setting in a mulish line that brought back a flood of memories when he least expected it.

Practice helped him to curb his temper and persuade instead of order. 'You'll be visiting Greece to help my daughter. It will be my pleasure to have you stay with us.'

The girl had such pride! He knew she couldn't even afford the airfare to Athens, would have to organise a loan for the trip.

'It's not Liakos money,' he added. 'You would not be obligated to your grandfather.'

For another long moment her gaze locked with his. Then she nodded once. 'All right. I'll come to Greece. And I'll pray the tests turn out the way you hope.'

There was deep sadness in her voice. Her eyes were shadowed and he guessed she was remembering her mother. How she'd been unable to save her.

He reached out and took Sophie's elbow. He moved slowly, his touch on her arm light, knowing how much she must be hurting. She'd never guess the sudden violent surge of adrenaline that shot through him at her words. The immediate, searing lightness that flared in the recesses of his mind.

This was going to work.

They were going to save Eleni.

CHAPTER FOUR

SOPHIE STEPPED THROUGH the airport's sliding doors.

She was here, in Crete.

She took a deep breath, wondering how the air in Greece could be just the same as home, but somehow different enough to send a quiver of emotion through her. She bit her lip. She wasn't going to cry, was she?

It wasn't as if this place meant *anything* to her.

But it had meant so much to her mum. Despite the painful memories, her mother had been an optimist. She'd planned to bring Sophie here. A girls' trip, she'd said, badgering Sophie into organising a passport in anticipation of the day when they'd have money saved to travel. And if they weren't able to visit family, there were lots of other things to see in Crete.

Sophie blinked rapidly against the bright light. She'd planned to surprise her mum and buy their tickets after she'd been working professionally for a year.

It would never happen now.

Nearby people milled and talked, called out greetings and embraced each other. Welcomes and departures.

And Sophie had never felt so alone in her life.

'Are you all right?' A hand touched her elbow, guided her forward.

A *frisson* of awareness snaked through her at the sound of that deep voice, the fleeting warmth of his hand. She sucked in a breath and schooled her features into what she hoped was a bland expression.

Costas hadn't touched her since their conversation in the park back in Sydney. He'd been scrupulous in keeping his distance. And she'd convinced herself she'd imagined her response to him.

But this was frighteningly real. Instantaneous. Devastating.

'I'm OK,' she said, scanning the bustle of activity, rather than turning to look up at him. 'Maybe a little tired.'

'You can rest when we reach the house.' He dropped his hand and Sophie felt as if a constricting weight lifted off her chest, allowing her to breathe freely again.

'We'll soon be on our way. And it's not too far along the coast to my home.' He gestured to a limousine parked straight ahead. It was long, dark and gleaming.

She should have expected no less. Obviously she'd stepped into another world: one of wealth and privilege. There had been the assiduously helpful airline staff, the VIP treatment through Customs and the discovery that, far from spending the long flight to Athens with hundreds of other economy travellers, Costas had obtained the whole first-class cabin for them alone.

That had astounded her. But anything was possible to the man who owned the airline, she'd discovered.

Had this been the world her mother had given up for love? No wonder Petros Liakos had been shocked at her choice of a penniless Australian for her husband.

Sophie walked slowly towards the limousine, suddenly dreading the idea of what awaited her at the end of this journey. How would she ever live up to Costas Palamidis' expectations? What if she couldn't help?

But she hadn't been able to refuse him.

She'd almost been convinced that if she didn't leave Sydney willingly, he'd scoop her up into his arms and bring her here by force. The grim, absolute determination in his face, in his battle-ready stance, in his piercing dark eyes, had spoken of a man who stood outside the civilised conventions of polite request and negotiation. He'd looked as if he welcomed any excuse for action. As if he was prepared to bundle her over his shoulder and smuggle her away to his private lair in Greece.

The fantastical notion still sent a shiver of appalled excitement through her.

But what had decided her to come was the vulnerability she could only guess at, hidden behind his obstinate determination and aura of aggressive, macho power. She'd caught a glimpse of it in his eyes when he'd spoken of Eleni. She knew it was there, deep inside him. The love for his daughter, the fear for her. Sophie could relate to it far too well.

'Here we are.' Costas gestured her towards the rear door of the vehicle. A young man in uniform stood smiling, holding it open for her.

The discreet buzz of a phone sounded and Costas stopped, frowning at the number displayed. 'Excuse me a moment,' he said. 'It's a call from the house. I'd better take it.'

Sophie sensed the immediate tension in him as he stepped aside, saw the grimness around his mouth as he lifted the phone to his ear. He was expecting bad news.

Sophie paused, couldn't help but watch. Just how bad could the news be?

Then she saw his lips curve up in a smile. His tender expression stole her breath away. 'Eleni,' he said. And what she heard in his voice made her turn back to the car and the waiting driver, feeling like a voyeur. It didn't matter that the conversation was in rapid Greek, too quick for her to follow. It was far too personal for her to intrude.

Costas stared up at the vivid blue bowl of the open sky, heard his little girl's chatter in his ear and thanked the lord he was home again at last.

And with such excellent news! The hope he'd been searching for so frantically.

He listened to Eleni's story of the kittens she'd seen just yesterday, and of how useful a cat would be, to keep the non-existent mice at bay. He almost laughed aloud at her transparent tactics.

There was a grin on his face as he promised once more that he'd be home soon and said goodbye. He swung around towards the car, eager to be on his way.

There was Sophie, the embodiment of their last hope. He quickened his step. She wasn't in the car, but stood, talking to Yiorgos. The driver had lost some of his professional aloofness and was standing close, gesticulating as he spoke. As Costas watched, Sophie smiled, then started to laugh, a light sound that teased at his senses.

He paused, watching the play of expression across her face. The shadows of grief lifted from her face and he saw her as she must have been before her mother's illness. Carefree, happy… stunningly beautiful. Her vibrant loveliness tugged at him, stirred deep-buried feelings into life.

Yiorgos said something and Sophie laughed again, her eyes smiling appreciatively at her companion. Costas' breath hissed between his teeth as a stab of sensation speared into his chest.

Discomfort. Annoyance.

Jealousy?

No. That wasn't possible. He barely knew the woman. Had no claim over her. No interest in a personal relationship. The idea was ludicrous.

He shoved the cellphone into his pocket and strode over to the car. 'Ready?' His voice was brusque.

Yiorgos immediately snapped to attention and into position beside the door. Sophie's smile faded and she looked away.

Costas felt disappointment percolate through his elation at being home.

What more did he want? He had what he'd sought: the chance to save Eleni. That was all that mattered. There was nothing else he needed. Not this woman's smiles nor her company.

This persistent awareness, his physical response to her, was damned unsettling. Especially to a man like him, who relied on no one but himself. Who had learned to doubt rather than to trust. To be cautious rather than impulsive.

He waited for Sophie to settle herself into the car, then sat in the far corner of the wide back seat.

Avoiding her gaze, he began explaining their surroundings, giving her a tourist's guide to Heraklion. Detailed, informative and totally impersonal.

It reinforced his role as host and helped him erect the barriers that weakened whenever he looked at her. Barriers that were essential if he was to get through the next few days.

Sophie leaned back in her corner of the seat and listened to Costas describe the bustle of Heraklion harbour and some of the city's history and traditions. He really did love the place.

But despite his enthusiasm for his home town, she sensed a change in him. The man beside her didn't meet her eyes. He spoke with the clipped, precise tones of a professional guide.

Had she done something to offend him?

Not that she could think of. Despite her long sleep on the plane she was probably jet-lagged, imagining things. And after all, wasn't this distant Costas Palamidis easier to cope with than the man she'd faced in Sydney? With his raw passion that both scared and fascinated her? She'd felt almost powerless against the force of his personality and his dark emotions.

She told herself she was glad of the change in him.

They drew up before a sprawling, modern house twenty minutes later. A house unlike any Sophie had ever seen, let alone entered. One glance confirmed what she'd already discovered: this man had more money than she'd ever dreamed of.

As the car pulled to a halt in the turning circle, the large front doors opened and a woman stepped out. A tall, grey-haired woman, holding a small child in her arms.

Costas flung open his door and was out of the car as it stopped. Sophie watched through the tinted glass as Costas strode across the gravel, arms open to take the tiny child in his arms. She must only be about three or four, Sophie decided, her heart wrenching as she took in the little girl's pallor and her bald head, evidence of her medical treatment.

A lump the size of Sydney Harbour settled in her throat and she blinked back tears. *Oh, lord, let it be all right. Let me be able to help her.*

Her own door opened and she looked up into the smiling face of Yiorgos, the chauffeur.

Now or never.

Sophie took a deep breath and swung her legs out of the car, registering but ignoring the sudden onset of exhaustion as she stood up. It had been a long trip. And now she felt every kilometre of it: the weariness of travel and the burden of expectation. She walked slowly towards the house, unwilling to interrupt the family reunion.

There was a trill of laughter from the little girl in response to Costas' deep murmur. Then he turned and Sophie stopped dead, anchored to the spot by the change in him.

The shadows had fled from his face. There was love in his eyes as he hugged his daughter, a softness about his mouth. He looked younger, sexier, more vibrantly alive. A grin a mile wide transformed him from the brooding man she'd known into someone new. Someone who had the power to knock her off balance even at a distance of ten metres.

Then, as Eleni moved in his arms, Sophie's gaze turned to her, taking in her tiny, fragile form and her huge dark eyes, so much like her father's.

The little girl stared at her for a long moment. Then she wriggled in Costas' embrace and held out her arms towards Sophie.

Clearly, unmistakably, she called, *'Mamá.'*

CHAPTER FIVE

GRATEFULLY SOPHIE SIPPED the scalding coffee. It was too sweet for her taste, but it was just what she needed. The coffee traced a welcome trail of heat that counteracted the deep chill of shock still gripping her.

She listened to the retreating sound of high heels tapping across the polished floor in the foyer. To the soft stream of rapid-fire Greek as Costas' mother spoke to her son on her way out.

For the first time in years Sophie wished her language skills were better. She'd rebelled early, refusing to attend Greek classes as soon as she was old enough to understand the rift between her mother and her family in Greece. But now she'd have given a lot to understand what Mrs Palamidis said to her son. And more to know what his murmured responses were. Even from here, the sound of his deep voice made her stomach muscles clench in awareness.

Mrs Palamidis had been so welcoming. So understanding and sympathetic, apologising for the shock of Eleni's words, ushering Sophie in here to the elegant sitting room to recuperate while Costas went to settle his daughter for an overdue nap.

But now she'd left and Sophie would be alone with Costas. And later, with little Eleni.

That moment when Eleni had looked at her with such excitement and called her *Mamá*…

Sophie shuddered. She'd been horrified. She felt as if she'd stepped straight into her dead cousin's shoes. Her stunned gaze had turned from the little girl to Costas and she saw in his face a flash of emotion so strong and tortured that she knew without doubt he was remembering his wife. And the knowledge had been like a knife twisting in her breast.

Why hadn't he told her that there was a family resemblance between her and her cousin? Had he been afraid she wouldn't agree to come to Greece?

She couldn't escape it, could she? Everything came back to family. Costas' driven determination to save his daughter. The precious DNA linking Sophie to Eleni. The uncanny physical similarity to a dead woman she'd never met. The bond that bridged half a world and still couldn't be denied, despite the high-handed rejection by her grandfather.

No wonder the very air had seemed alive with tension and old remembrances when she'd stepped out of the airport.

Sophie's eyes filled with burning tears as she thought of her mother. How much she'd have loved to reconnect to the family she'd left behind.

Her mum would have taken it for granted that Sophie would take the first plane to Greece in the circumstances. She wouldn't have thought twice about the pain of reopening old family wounds if it meant helping a child.

Inevitably Sophie thought of her grandfather, recovering from his stroke somewhere on this very island. But her sympathy didn't extend that far. The man who'd disowned her mother could be on another planet as far as she was concerned.

A shadow of movement at the far end of the massive sitting room caught Sophie's eye and she looked up. There, filling the doorway with his broad shoulders, stood Costas. She couldn't read the expression in his eyes at this distance, but there was a watchful quality about his stance that made the hairs on the back of her neck stand up.

She shivered and straightened in her seat. 'Your mother has left?'

'That's right,' he said, and the timbre of his deep voice was like the brush of fine sandpaper across Sophie's nerves, stirring life and awareness where before there was chilled numbness. 'My parents live several kilometres away.'

So they were alone. She and Costas Palamidis. Why did the idea send a skitter of anxiety through her?

He strode across the room to stand near the end of the sofa where Sophie sat. He seemed to invade her personal space and she had to make a conscious effort not to tuck her feet back away from his.

She knew from the glint in his eyes that he recognised her discomfort. There was a slightly mocking arch to his black brows as he returned her look. Then he frowned and settled himself on the long leather sofa opposite her.

'I apologise,' he said, 'that your arrival should be so…difficult. If I'd guessed how Eleni would react to the sight of you I would have warned my mother, asked her to explain to Eleni before you arrived.'

His expression was deeply brooding, his regret obviously genuine. And she felt her indignation drain away, despite the appalling situation he'd put her in.

The joy that had lit his face as he'd held his daughter in his arms was a faded memory. Back instead was the dour stranger burdened by care.

It disturbed Sophie to realise how much she wanted another glimpse of that other Costas.

'It's all right,' she murmured. 'There's no harm done. It was just a surprise.'

'More than that, I'm sure. You looked white as a sheet when Eleni called out to you. I should have—'

'It's over,' she interrupted, then paused as a horrible thought penetrated her weary brain. 'You *did* explain to her, didn't you? She doesn't think—?'

'No. I explained that your resemblance to her mother is because you are cousins. Eleni understands now that you are a very special visitor, who has travelled around the world to see her. She was so excited I'm surprised she went to sleep. She can't wait to play with her long-lost cousin.'

'But surely—' Sophie began.

'You're not scared of spending a little time with her, are you?' he challenged, his frown deepening. 'She's only a child, and a very lonely one. She hasn't been able to mix with other children as she normally would, because of her treatment. And now, for obvious reasons, she's curious about you. Is it too much to ask?'

'I was just going to say that I may not be here long, so it might be better not to interfere with her routine.'

But it was more than that, Sophie admitted to herself. There was something that made her want to hold back from this family, from Eleni and her father. Perhaps the superstitious desire not to tempt fate by believing she really could help the child, despite the odds. Or maybe it was a primitive fear of taking a dead woman's place, even if only for a short time. And that instantly made her think of Costas, not Eleni.

She shot him a glance under her lashes and found him watching her intently. There it was again. That sense of compelling force, drawing her towards him, as if she had no will of her own when he was around. It scared the living daylights out of her, this awareness, this attraction. And she wasn't ready to cope with it.

'I'm sure a little change in routine won't harm Eleni in the least. We must make the most of you while you're here with us.'

Sophie's breath jammed in her chest as his gaze dropped to her lips, lingering there for a moment too long before flicking back to her eyes. It felt as if her ribs were constricting in against her, making it hard to breathe. Her heart drummed to an increasing tempo that echoed in her ears.

The room seemed full of the heavy awareness strung like a tangible weight between them.

Sophie leaned forward abruptly and put her cup on the coffee table between them with a click. Her hand was trembling. And the way he looked at her only exacerbated the tremor. She shot to her feet.

'You have a magnificent home,' she said, determined to steer the conversation to a subject that was simple and impersonal. Something to break the uneasy connection building between them.

'I'm glad you approve, Sophie.' Even his voice was different:

a rich, caressing burr that vibrated through her, drew her skin tight and shivery.

Late-afternoon sunlight slanted through the huge panoramic windows, highlighting what she could have sworn was a trace of grim amusement on his features. Surely not. There was no way he could guess at the unholy mix of trepidation and excitement she felt, knowing she was alone with him.

She spun on her foot and walked towards the enormous curving line of full-length glass that comprised one wall. She guessed it was an expensive, architectural masterpiece. But she barely registered it. Her mind was fully occupied with the man she felt watching her.

'I've never seen anything like it,' she said at last, cursing the way her voice emerged: light and breathless. 'It's so modern, so unique, yet somehow it fits its surroundings.'

Brilliant, Sophie. I bet he really wanted that incisive commentary on his home. The place had probably featured in prestigious architectural digests.

'A friend designed it,' he answered. 'Someone I went to school with. He knows me and what I wanted so that made the job simpler.'

Below her stretched a silver-green vista: an ancient olive grove surrounded by a dry packed stone wall, sloping down towards the sea. Beyond it glinted the dark water of a cove, enclosed on two sides by headlands. It was peaceful. Enticing.

She guessed the place had looked like this for hundreds of years. Possibly thousands. And there was no other sign of habitation in sight. But then if you had Costas Palamidis' fortune you wouldn't want to share this slice of paradise with neighbours.

'That's a big sigh.' His voice came from just behind her and she froze. 'Are you sure you're all right?'

'Yes.' She made herself turn towards him, but didn't meet his gaze. 'I'm just tired.'

'Of course. It's been a long journey. If you come with me I'll show you your room.'

There was nothing in his voice now to alarm her. Nothing at

all. His tone was bland, as if the searing look he'd sent her before had been the product of her imagination.

Sophie chanced a peep at his face. It was set in the harsh lines of control she recognised from their first encounter. He looked as hard as flint and just as unfeeling.

The speed of his change from feverish intensity to chilly reserve threw her completely off balance. She would never be comfortable with this man.

The silence as they made their way through the luxurious reception rooms was almost oppressive. Taut with the strain of undercurrents that set her nerves on edge. Tinged with the unsettling awareness that they were alone except for the child sleeping upstairs.

'Why didn't you tell me I looked like my cousin?' she blurted out as they ascended a sweeping marble staircase.

It was a relief to break the humming silence.

His wide shoulders shrugged beside her, but he continued up the steps without breaking his stride. 'It wasn't important.'

Not important? Sophie stopped, clutching the banister with one hand. Not important that she looked enough like his dead wife to convince the woman's own daughter?

Ahead of her he halted, turned and looked down at her. His eyes had that awful blank look she remembered from their first meeting. As if he was clamping down on every vestige of emotion.

'I should have told you. But, as I explained, it didn't occur to me that Eleni would react as she did. I can only apologise again.'

Sophie read his tightly compressed lips, the rigid tilt of his jaw, and suddenly wondered how *he'd* reacted when he'd first seen her. Had he immediately thought of his dead wife?

He must have, of course. And perhaps that accounted for some of his searing anger that first day. To be confronted by someone who so closely resembled the woman he'd loved and lost must have been a terrible shock.

'It's all right,' she lied. Eleni's reaction had rocked her. She released her stiff fingers from the metal railing and started forward again.

She reached the stair where he waited for her with his unreadable eyes, his closed expression.

'Are we so alike, then? Fotini and I?'

There was no mistaking the flare of emotion in his eyes at her question. The spasm of quickly controlled movement through his big body.

Perhaps she shouldn't have asked, should have respected his obvious grief for his wife. But she had to know.

His night-dark eyes held hers as he shook his head. 'No,' he said brusquely. 'At first glance there's a superficial similarity, but the differences are much stronger.'

Oddly, instead of reassuring her, the knowledge that she was unique, not a mirror image of Fotini, didn't comfort as it should have. Or perhaps it was the dismissive way he brushed aside the resemblance. She supposed in his eyes no one could compare to the woman he'd loved.

Sophie drew a slow breath and started up the stairs beside him. What did she want? For him to look at her and see his wife? For him to respond to her as he had to Fotini? As if she were the woman he loved?

No! Of course not.

'I hadn't realised Eleni would remember what her mother looked like so well,' she said. 'But then I don't know much about small children. If it's been a year since—'

'Ten months,' he said as they reached the top of the stairs. 'Ten months almost exactly since the accident.'

Sophie cursed her tongue as she heard the pent up anger, the fierce emotion in his tone. She wanted to reach out to him and…

And what? Soothe his pain?

Who was she to ease another's grief? She could barely contain her own. Couldn't begin to understand what it would be like to lose a spouse, a partner you thought would be yours for life.

'Eleni has a photo of her mother in her room,' he said, interrupting her thoughts. 'I put it there when Fotini died. It seemed to help Eleni when she missed her mother.'

Sophie wondered if photos had helped Costas deal with his

own loss. Looking at the rigid set of his shoulders, she thought not. He was obviously a man still very much in love with his wife.

'Here we are,' he said briskly, standing aside and gesturing to a pair of doors. 'This is your suite. Your bags have been unpacked for you.' His smile was perfunctory as he added, 'I'll leave you to rest and settle in.'

He turned then and walked away, his whole frame rigid. With disapproval or pain?

Sophie wondered why it mattered so much to her. Why she wanted to run after him and try to comfort him.

Just as well she had too much sense for that.

The rest of the evening passed in a blur that Sophie hoped was due to jet lag. By the time she'd showered and changed and eaten the meal Costas insisted she have on a tray in her room, she was exhausted.

A maid bustled out, wishing her a good night. And Sophie even managed to laugh at her earlier sense of claustrophobia, at the idea of being alone here with Costas. She hadn't been thinking clearly enough to realise that a house this size must have a full-time staff on the premises.

Her room alone would have swallowed up at least half of her home in Sydney. And the bathroom! A cleaner's nightmare with all that gleaming marble and the massive mirrors on two walls.

She shrugged into her old cotton wrap and padded across the thick carpet to the glass doors. Just one more look at that magnificent view and then she'd sleep. She stepped outside into the darkness, letting her eyes adjust to the silvery light of a half moon and the jewelled panoply of stars. They were away from the city here and it was quiet. So quiet she could hear the soft shushing of the waves in the cove.

Sophie drew a deep breath of fresh night air, registering the unfamiliar scents. Salt of course, from the sea, but something else too. Herbs? It smelt like oregano and thyme, rosemary and something else, spicy and sweet.

She approached the corner of the long curving balcony, only

to pull up abruptly as a darker shadow detached itself from the gloom and blocked her way.

'Can't you sleep, Sophie?' His voice slid like heavy silk against her skin, right down her spine. And heat flared in the secret, feminine core of her.

Costas thrust his hands deep into his pockets, feeling them curl into tight fists as he caught her delicate scent on the night breeze.

He'd come out here to think, to gather the tatters of his control in preparation for another day of desperate hope and unspeakable fear. He'd begun to find solace in the still darkness.

And then she'd appeared, ripping at the shreds of his self-possession like a blade.

It was torture being so close to such temptation. Craving the numbing, mindless ecstasy that he knew he could find in her body. Yet knowing he couldn't afford to act on his primitive instinct to take, to hold, to tame.

She was off-limits for all sorts of reasons. Not least that she was his guest. He had a duty to protect her, even from himself.

'I just thought I'd get a breath of fresh air,' she explained, her voice so high and light he knew with a deep, visceral certainty that she felt it too, this force that drew them inexorably together.

She half turned, as if to leave, and the light behind her silhouetted the luscious upthrust curve of her breasts.

His indrawn breath hissed between his clenched teeth and her head swung round.

For a frozen instant neither moved, his galloping pulse the only animation. Then he forced himself to speak. 'Don't leave on my account.' His throat was raw with the effort of control, making his voice a grumbling murmur. 'I was just going in.'

In the darkness he felt her eyes on him. It was a touch that heated his skin to fever pitch.

'No! Don't go. I didn't mean to intrude on your privacy.' She sounded breathless, distressed.

His mother's warning this afternoon came back to him again. *She could be so easily hurt, Costa. Treat her well.*

Caution didn't come easily to him. But he wasn't reckless enough to give in to this beckoning temptation and cross the demarcation line that kept them apart. Anyone could see that disaster lay that way. For both of them.

'It's all right, Sophie. I was going in to check on Eleni anyway.'

He forced himself to move forward, passed her so close that her body heat warmed his side. Her enticing fragrance filled his nostrils and his fists clenched so tight that they throbbed. Tension gripped his neck and shoulders in a vice.

He kept his eyes fixed on the door to Eleni's room further along the balcony and made himself keep walking. 'Enjoy the peace for a little longer. Then get a good night's sleep.'

She'd need it for tomorrow.

Yes, that was what he needed to concentrate on—the blood test, the options for Eleni's treatment. The long discussion he'd have with the medics tomorrow. Anything but Sophie's lithe body, warm and inviting, just metres away.

'Goodnight.' Her voice was a light whisper that made him falter. Then he hunched his shoulders and strode on.

CHAPTER SIX

IT WAS LATE IN THE MORNING when Sophie woke and her head felt thick and heavy. She'd slept through the night but disturbing dreams had plagued her. Fortunately for her peace of mind, she couldn't remember them. But she suspected they'd featured a pair of probing black eyes.

She ate her solitary breakfast in a sunny parlour while another maid explained that the *kyrios,* the master, was busy conferring with his daughter's doctor. Her meal finished, Sophie took the opportunity to explore.

The French windows on this side of the house led to a wide flagged terrace, then down to an immaculate lawn. She strolled across it, feeling the warmth of the sun on her face, hearing the unfamiliar birdsong and, in the distance, a dog barking. There were scents here too, from the border of bright flowers that edged the lawn, from fruit blossom somewhere near, and inevitably from the waves that she could just hear rolling in to shore in gentle rhythm.

Sophie closed her eyes and breathed it in. The sounds and warmth and smell of the place.

A sense of peace settled on her. Perhaps because she was so far from home and her real life. From the pain and drudgery of the everyday. She felt that, just for now, she could relax and enjoy the moment.

A gurgle of laughter caught her attention and her eyes

snapped open. There, rounding a path at the end of the garden, was Eleni, pedalling unsteadily on a bright orange tricycle. Behind her followed a young woman, close enough to ensure she kept her balance.

Sophie watched as, inevitably, Eleni looked up and saw her. She didn't understand it, but she felt almost guilty. As if she shouldn't be here, strong and healthy, when such a tiny child was battling the odds for survival. As if somehow it would be *her* fault if the transplant couldn't take place.

But it was too late to slink away.

The laughter died away as Eleni saw her, her eyes widening. She stopped pedalling and planted her feet on either side of the tricycle.

Her face was grave as she said, *'Kalimera sas.'* Good morning to you.

'Kalimera, Eleni.'

Immediately the little girl's eyes brightened and she tilted her head to one side as if to get a better view of her new cousin. Then she launched into a hurried spate of Greek that Sophie had no hope of following.

'Siga, parakalo,' Sophie said, smiling. Slow, please. *'Then katalaveno.'* I don't understand.

Eleni's mouth rounded in astonishment and the girl with her bent to explain that Sophie didn't understand Greek.

'I speak a little,' Sophie said. 'But it's been a long time since I used it.' They'd spoken English at home.

'Unfortunately Eleni doesn't speak English,' said the girl, who introduced herself as Eleni's nanny.

But the language barrier didn't deter Eleni. She climbed off her trike and headed straight over to Sophie, barely pausing before she reached up for her hand.

Sophie felt the tiny, warm fingers close round hers. She looked down at Eleni's pale, serious face, at her dark eyes, old beyond their years, and something, a hard, cold knot deep inside her, shifted suddenly and began to thaw.

No wonder Costas had been so adamant that she come to Greece. Life was too precious to waste. And, looking down into that pinched little face, Sophie had an inkling of the protective love he must feel for his daughter. The desperation to find a way to save her.

'*Ela,*' said Eleni insistently, pulling her hand. Come.

Out in the garden, he'd been told. But where? Costas scanned the pool, the lawn and all the areas closest to the house. As long as Sophie hadn't decided to go for a long walk along the shore. The doctor was waiting inside, ready to take her blood sample for the initial compatibility test.

Costas strode past the formal gardens and headed for the path that led through fruit trees to the olive grove and then to the beach.

The doctor would wait, that wasn't a problem. But he, Costas, wanted it done *now*. He had to know what chance there was for this to work.

He had to—

His head shot up as he heard laughter, lilting and evocative, ahead. His steps slowed as he rounded a hedge. And then he stopped.

Bright sunlight illuminated two heads, one bare and pale, the other dark, with a thick mane of hair that gleamed with the tiniest, seductive hint of auburn.

Eleni and Sophie. Cross-legged in the grass of the old orchard, bending over something in the meadow grass.

'Beetle,' said Eleni in Greek.

'Beetle,' said Sophie.

'Green beetle.'

'Green beetle,' mimicked Sophie.

His daughter was teaching Sophie Greek. Behind them, on the stone wall, sat her nanny, making a daisy chain.

'Nose.' Eleni placed her finger on Sophie's nose.

'Nose.' Sophie copied the gesture and then gave Eleni's button nose a tiny tweak, making Eleni giggle.

Costas swallowed down hard on the lump that rose in his throat. He'd heard his little girl laugh so rarely in recent months. It was the best sound he'd heard in ages.

He must have moved then. Something made the pair of them

look up. Immediately Eleni clambered to her feet and raced across to wrap her arms around his legs. *'Papa!'*

He'd never grow tired of her embraces. Even if, the good lord willing, she grew to be a mother herself.

He bent down and swung her up high in his arms and around till she squealed with delight. Then he tucked her close against his torso, inhaling her sweet, fresh soap scent. Felt her tiny, warm body wriggling against his.

And over her shoulder his eyes locked with Sophie's. The laughter had faded from hers and now he saw there the welling emotion he battled so often himself.

A shaft of heat pierced his chest, warming places that had been frozen against the pain. The knowledge of her understanding did that to him. It promised so much.

But it also threatened his control.

'Come,' he said, turning abruptly away. 'There's someone to see you.'

Costas stood on the front steps, watching the doctor's car disappear down the driveway. The warmth of the sun was on his face, the light sea breeze tickled his collar. He registered the physical sensations but that was all.

He didn't feel anything else. Not excitement, not the fervent hope of yesterday. Not even the impatient anticipation he'd expected.

His emotions had shut down.

Or was he lying to himself? Pretending he didn't feel anything so he wouldn't have to face the yawning chasm of fear that might suck him down if he let it? Fear that the test result would be negative.

'Costas?' The voice was soft, tentative.

He'd never heard his name on her lips, he realised. And he liked it. Liked it too much for a man whose emotions were supposed to have shut down.

'Costas, is everything all right?' Closer now, Sophie's voice came from just beside him. Her hand settled on his sleeve, feather-light, tentative, and immediately fire sparked in his bloodstream. He clenched his fists to prevent his instinctive response: to cover her hand with his own and keep it there.

He turned to find her looking up at him. The sun caught the highlights in her hair, illuminated the purity of her classically beautiful features. But they were nothing to the impact of her gold-flecked eyes. She returned his gaze openly, with such candour and sympathy, that he felt the warmth of her compassion like a caress.

How had he ever, even for an instant, thought she looked like Fotini's mirror image? There was no comparison between the two.

Fotini had been so alive, so full of passion, but there'd been precious little generosity in her. She'd been too wrapped up in herself. She'd been vivacious, but never, not once, had she connected with him the way Sophie did with just this single, heartfelt look.

A shudder rippled up his spine, a presentiment of destiny drawing close.

No! He didn't believe in such things.

Sophie didn't understand him. How could she? He barely understood his own feelings. There *was* no connection.

He thrust away the desire to lean down and draw whatever comfort he could from her. She tempted him to forget how fickle women could be. However sweet the illusion, experience had taught him well.

Yet it disconcerted him to realise how much he wished the illusion were real.

'Yes, everything is fine,' he said, surprised to find his voice had dropped to a gravelly murmur. He stepped back, felt her hand fall, and knew it was better that way.

'The doctor said he'd ring as soon as he could with the results,' she said. 'It won't be a long wait.'

Costas experienced a sudden, futile wish that the results might be delayed. What would he do if the news was bad? If a transplant wasn't possible? How would he face Eleni? The thought of it scared him as nothing else had.

He needed to get away, do something to fill the next few hours, he suddenly decided. Waiting here for news would drive him crazy

'It's almost time for Eleni's lunch,' he found himself saying. 'Then she has a long nap. Would you like to do a little sightseeing? Or are you too tired from the journey?'

He watched her intently, waiting for her response.

He *wanted* to spend time with this girl, he acknowledged. Despite the way she got under his skin, challenging his composure and his expectations. Despite the turmoil, the confusion he experienced whenever they were together, something about her drew him every time. And it wasn't just sex.

Maybe, if he got to know her, he could work out what it was—that indefinable something that set her apart from other women he'd known.

'Thanks,' she was saying, not quite meeting his eyes. 'I'd like that. If you've got the time.'

'Of course.' He'd already put in several hours' intensive work this morning on the phone and the email. An afternoon off wouldn't hurt. 'It will be my pleasure.'

An hour later he strode out of the house. Eleni was tucked up in bed, asleep after a story on his lap. He'd postponed his afternoon teleconference and he was eager to get away.

Just a sightseeing drive, he told himself. Simple, uncomplicated. A host's duty. But that didn't prevent the sizzle of anticipation he experienced as he remembered Sophie's warm gaze meshing with his. The subtle temptation of her body when she stood close.

He slid on his sunglasses and turned towards the garages. Strange that Yiorgos didn't have the limousine waiting at the front door as instructed.

Her voice alerted him first. Automatically his step quickened. Sure enough, there she was, deep in conversation with his driver. The pair had their heads together over a map spread on the bonnet of the limo. Yiorgos was tracing a finger along some route, all the while leaning closer than necessary towards the woman at his side.

But Sophie didn't mind. She was laughing, flicking her hair

back over her shoulder in a gesture obviously designed to encourage the driver's attention.

Déjà vu.

It slammed into him with nauseating brutality.

In the shadows of the garage it could have been Fotini standing there, flirting. That siren's smile, the provocative angle of her head, the ripple of laughter. The two women were so alike in that moment.

Fotini had never done more than flirt with anyone else after their marriage—he'd made sure of that. But when the mood was upon her she'd found a perverse delight in flaunting herself with other men, teasing Costas with the sight of her sharing an emotional intimacy she denied him.

A cloud blocked the sun and Costas registered a sudden chill in the sea breeze.

Yiorgos said something and Sophie leaned forward, peering over the map. The movement stretched her jeans taut, emphasising feminine curves in a way that made the muscles in Costas' belly spasm tight and his throat dry. His hands itched to reach for her.

Silently he cursed himself for his inevitable reaction. And for being so disappointed in her. Hadn't he told himself she was no different?

'Ready to go?' His tone was carefully even, revealing none of his simmering anger.

Yiorgos jumped, clear evidence of a guilty conscience, and put a decent distance between himself and Sophie.

She swung round, a tentative smile on her lips. The look of welcome on her face made it seem as if she'd been filling in time, waiting for Costas' arrival. Unbidden, answering warmth flared in his belly.

But he wasn't fooled by her.

'Not the limo today, I think.' He gestured curtly to one of the other vehicles. 'We'll take the Jaguar. No need for you to drive us,' he said over his shoulder to Yiorgos.

Minutes later they were heading along the coast road, Costas describing the local highlights. That should have distracted him from the unreasoning disappointment that had taken hold when he'd seen her amusing herself with Yiorgos.

Why was he surprised? It must be second nature to her, as it had been to Fotini, to seek male attention. Hadn't the investigator's report specifically mentioned Sophie's popularity with the opposite sex?

The knowledge should make it easier for him to resist the temptation she represented. After all, he had discriminating tastes. He didn't share his women.

Yet still he burned for her. And that made him furious.

'You do not mind driving alone with me?' Costas asked. 'I should have asked if you'd prefer the limousine.'

'No, this is lovely. It's a beautiful car.' Sophie smoothed her hand over the seat—she'd never felt leather so soft.

'I'm glad you like it.' Costas' deep voice thrummed across her skin, drawing it tight. She looked up and for a moment met his eyes, dark and glowing with an intense emotion she couldn't identify. Then he turned his attention back to the road and she let out a slow breath, wondering how he managed to affect her so with just a glance.

'Some women prefer not to be alone with a man who is not a close friend or family member.'

Sophie frowned at the edge in his voice. He was showing her the local sights—what was there to object to in that? 'In Australia no one would think anything of it.'

She turned and stared at the coastal development they were approaching. It was modern and brand-new. But her attention was caught by the figure of an old, black-clad woman, leading a laden donkey down a narrow lane right beside the massive new structures.

'I suppose the customs here are different from those at home,' she murmured.

'Things have changed, but some of the old ways linger. We still have a strong tradition of protecting our women.'

Her mouth pursed at the idea. Much good it would have done her or her mother to wait for their male relatives to protect them! 'In Australia we're independent. Women look after themselves.' It came out as a challenge. But then he'd hit a raw nerve. Far from looking after his womenfolk, Petros Liakos had shunned them, left them utterly alone to sink or swim. If that was an example of Greek male protectiveness she wanted nothing to do with it.

Her mother had made her own way, against the odds, in a new country. Sophie remembered how exhausted her mum had used to be after her long shifts and how that never stopped her putting in a few more hours, taking in ironing for extra money. Never once had she complained.

'You never felt the need for protection? Not even from unwanted male attention?'

Why the sudden interest? He wasn't thinking of setting himself up as some sort of male guardian, was he? Instantly she rejected the disturbing idea.

'I find there's safety in numbers.' It was much better having a large group of friends.

He sent a piercing stare her way. 'So, you have many male friends? Doesn't that make life complicated?'

She frowned. 'Not at all. Sticking with one guy isn't all it's made out to be.' Her one serious boyfriend had turned out to be a disappointment. And after that experience Sophie wasn't eager to rush into intimacy again.

Now she found it easier to be part of a group. There was no pressure to pair off and she could go out and enjoy herself without worrying about sexual politics. Simpler. Safer.

Sophie felt Costas' scrutiny and turned to meet his brooding look. His expression had settled into grim lines that accentuated the stern set of his face.

His disapproval was obvious.

So, he didn't think women should take charge of their lives? She tilted her chin and looked out at the view, surprised at her disappointment.

For a while there she'd felt as if she and Costas were devel oping a tentative understanding. She was dismayed to discover how strongly she felt his rejection.

Why should it matter so much to her?

CHAPTER SEVEN

SOPHIE LEANED BACK against the trunk of an old pine tree and felt her body relax, muscle by muscle. It was so peaceful here, so quiet. She didn't ever want to move.

Only Costas' presence, so temptingly close, marred her contentment. He was silent, absorbed in his own dark thoughts, staring up at the snow-covered peaks where Mt Ida caught the clouds.

He couldn't see how hungrily she followed the crisp line of his profile against the sky. The angle of his jaw, the curve of his lips, the lean strength of his broad shoulders.

If only he'd…what? Turn and talk to her? Share his thoughts?

Or look at her again the way he sometimes did—so that her blood seemed to thicken in her arteries, beating slower and harder as excitement dried her mouth.

She needed to get a grip, cultivate some distance from the man. That was what common sense told her. But if she was honest with herself she'd admit common sense had little to do with the growing feelings she had for Costas Palamidis.

She'd seen him battling fear and despair. His elation when that first test had shown positive and she'd gone to hospital for a bone-marrow sample. The demons of doubt that rode him now, days later, as he waited for news. She'd seen him so heartbreakingly gentle with Eleni and couldn't help wishing he'd share some of that tenderness with her.

She had no business wanting more from a man who'd recently lost his wife. But she did.

These past days in Crete Sophie had let herself be lulled into hoping something…meaningful was developing between her and Costas.

Each afternoon, while Eleni slept, she and Costas drove out, exploring the countryside. These trips were a source of secret anticipation and intense disappointment. Sometimes she felt as if she and Costas connected in a way she never had with anyone. There was a warmth of shared understanding, a spark of something special between them, that made her blood sing and the shadows fall away. And then, in the next instant, it disappeared. She could feel his withdrawal.

Did she imagine their growing understanding? Sometimes she'd swear it was real. And others…

The one constant was the undeniable thread of simmering attraction that bound them. Even when Costas' expression was dark, almost disapproving, the magnetism drew them, like polar opposites, together.

He threatened her peace in ways no man ever had. Her mind turned to mush if ever his suddenly hot gaze trawled over her face, or he drew so close she could inhale his scent. Awareness, expectation, excitement were a constant throb in her blood whenever he was near.

Nothing had prepared her for it. Her one intimate relationship hadn't been even a poor reflection of these intense feelings.

How she wished her mother were here to advise her. To share her experience and wisdom. But Sophie was on her own.

Abruptly she turned away. Perhaps if she stared at the ruins spread out before her she could imagine it as a thriving city. Anything to take her mind off Costas and this see-saw of emotions.

But ancient Phaestos stubbornly remained a confusion of stone foundations. Not nearly as fascinating as the man beside her.

'Have you thought any more about your grandfather?' he asked so suddenly that she jumped. She felt her eyes widen as she swung round to meet his gaze.

Of course she'd thought about him. How could she not when she knew he was so close, on this very island? She nodded.

'But you're not willing to let the feud go?'

'It was *his* feud, not mine!' She felt the familiar, instant surge of hot fury. 'It was up to him to end it.' Her chest rose and fell with her angry breathing. 'And I did *try,* remember? I rang him and never got a response.'

She read sympathy in his expression and something else. Something that made the hairs rise on her nape. 'Why do you ask?'

'I think perhaps he does want to end it.'

'What do you mean?' Her eyes narrowed suspiciously.

'I've heard something that may change your views.' He paused. 'According to his housekeeper, Petros Liakos intended to call your mother.'

A jolt of something—shock? Disbelief?—slammed into her.

'You mean that's what he says now?' So he'd changed his tune now it was he who lay in a solitary sick bed.

Costas' expression grew severe. 'No. He hasn't spoken about it. When the housekeeper told him of your call, he asked her to bring the letter from your mother. Apparently when she first wrote he instructed his staff that any mail from her should be set aside and not delivered to him.'

'Unfeeling bastard,' Sophie murmured, her heart clenching at the memories of her mother enclosing a photo with the letter she wrote to Petros Liakos each year on her daughter's name day.

'The point is,' Costas' words broke across the painful recollections, 'he hadn't realised she'd written again. Apparently he was shocked to discover how many letters there were.'

Sophie said nothing. She refused to have any sympathy for the old man.

'The housekeeper left him in his study.' Costas paused. 'When she returned later he'd collapsed across the desk. There were letters and photos spilled onto the floor and his arm was stretched out towards the telephone.'

Sophie could see the image so vividly she couldn't see

anything else for a moment. Not the bright sky, nor even the man so close beside her.

'You think the news precipitated his stroke?' Nausea swirled in the pit of her stomach, rose like a tide, engulfing her.

'I've no idea,' he said. 'But I felt you should know.'

'I… Thank you.' Sophie shook her head, trying to clear the whirling thoughts that bombarded her. If her grandfather *had* been trying to call, how tragic that he hadn't succeeded. For her mother and for him.

Sophie shot to her feet and took a few faltering steps away, breathing deeply to counter the shock of this news. For it *was* a shock. It didn't change the essentials—her grandfather was obviously an arrogant, domineering old man, too proud for his own good. But still…

'You would prefer I hadn't told you?' Costas' voice had a rough edge that sent a tremor of reaction racing across her skin.

'No. You did the right thing.' Sophie stared out over the stones of the old city, her vision blurred, her throat closing. She wrapped her arms round herself, trying to hold in the pain of conflicting emotions. Grief for her mother was a constant. But now it melded into something more complex and confusing.

'But the pain is still raw,' he murmured. 'Almost too much to bear.' The words came from just behind her, feathering the tender skin of her neck. She spun round, automatically stepping back so that he stood at arm's length. Even so his dark gaze mesmerised her, filling her vision.

The yearning for his touch, for the comfort of his embrace, was almost overpowering. She had to force herself to stand rigidly still, not stumble closer as she so desperately wanted to do.

'You are strong, Sophie. Stronger than you think. Eventually, one day, the hurt will ease.'

She looked up into his sombre face, letting his words wash over her. It was his expression that held her attention, the fierce concentration on his proud features as he watched her.

She felt the tension between them spike, the still afternoon air was thick with it. His gaze had never been so unfathomable or more tantalising.

'Whatever your grandfather's mistakes, they are in the past, they're behind you.' he said.

But it wasn't that simple. It seemed she had unfinished business with Petros Liakos.

And now, here, right this minute, she *had* to find out if she was imagining the unnerving intimacy between herself and Costas. The need to know was a driving force that overwhelmed caution.

Were his words simply trite encouragement from an acquaintance? Or did he feel what she felt—a strengthening bond of understanding between them?

She took a single step, closing the gap so that the heat of his body encompassed hers. She shivered, feeling as if she'd stepped into danger. Her nostrils flared as she recognised the warm scent of his skin. It sent a jolt of desire right through her. She tilted her head up towards his. Her heartbeat raced as she saw his mouth just a whisper of breath away from hers.

Anticipation hummed through her, her body swayed infinitesimally closer. She *willed* him to reach for her, to tell her he'd felt it too—the sense of rightness when they were together.

That was what she wanted—wasn't it? To put an end to this suspense? She'd imagined his embrace so often these last days, the need for it had consumed her, keeping her awake well into the long nights.

Yet still he stood, looking down at her, neither encouraging nor discouraging. His lips had parted slightly as if ready for the taste of her. Excitement twisted ever tighter in her belly, urging her on. She could kiss him if she just reached up and pressed her mouth against his.

He expected it too: the gleam in his eyes told her that, as did the throbbing pulse at the base of his neck.

But he wouldn't take the initiative. Sophie understood that with sudden, devastating clarity that halted her instinctive move towards him.

Why? Why wait for her to make the first move? He must read the invitation in her eyes.

She hesitated on the brink of committing herself.

And then the answer came to her, like a bolt out of the clear sky, stabbing straight to her heart.

A shadow stood between them, a shade of the past. Costas looked at her but, she realised, he didn't see her, not really. He was attracted to her because she reminded him of the woman he'd loved and lost just ten months ago. Her cousin, Fotini.

Sophie stumbled back a pace, horrified at what she'd almost done. The acrid taste of disappointment filled her mouth.

'What is it?' He took a step forward and she raised her hand to stop him. The soft linen of his shirt grazed her palm and she dropped her hand as if it burned. She couldn't touch him. Not now.

'It's Fotini, isn't it?' she whispered. 'You look at me like that because you're thinking of her.'

Costas met her stunned, hurt gaze and felt as if the ground had opened up beneath his feet. If it weren't for the pain in Sophie's eyes, the hurt in her trembling lips, he might have laughed at the absurd idea.

His body *ached* with the effort of repressing his desire for her. He'd struggled not to follow his instinct and kiss her senseless as he'd wanted to ever since she'd sat down on that bed of pine needles.

Vivid images of him and Sophie, together on that soft carpet, had kept him fully occupied. So much so that he hadn't been able to look at her—had turned instead to stare out into the distance. But the scent of her, the whisper-soft echo of her breath, the knowledge of her being *there,* so close to him, had tested his self-control beyond all reasonable limits.

Him pining for Fotini! For the woman who'd destroyed his belief in the possibility of marriage as a partnership. Who'd viewed their wedding simply as a stepping stone to more wealth she could squander. Who'd cruelly rejected her own daughter and taught him a bone-deep distrust of women. Beautiful women in particular.

He grimaced. He supposed he owed Fotini some thanks. She'd stripped the scales from his eyes. It was that experience alone that kept him sane in the face of the temptation Sophie offered.

He knew Sophie was no Fotini. Few women could be that self-absorbed and destructive. But since his marriage he understood that what he felt for Sophie was best dealt with in a bedroom: no strings attached.

Even so some part of him wanted to believe the fantasy he felt when he looked at Sophie—the illusory promise of a real partnership. But that was impossible.

Physical passion was all he trusted a woman to give him now. And his desire for Sophie had reached such combustible levels.

If only she weren't so vulnerable from her mother's death he'd have suggested a temporary liaison for their mutual pleasure. That was all he would ever offer another woman.

But he couldn't in all honour seduce a girl whose grief for her mother was so fresh and painful.

It had been hell resisting her. And never more so than just now, when she'd stepped close and he'd had to summon every atom of will-power so as not to sweep her close and do something she might regret later.

'You've got it wrong.' His voice emerged as rough as gravel.

'Have I? I've seen the photo of your wife in Eleni's room. I know how similar we are.'

'No!' He paused, shocked by her mistake, searching for the words to explain without revealing the past which he and his daughter had to live with.

'At first glance, yes, there's a similarity. But not after that single, initial moment.'

Her eyes were wary and he wanted to reach out and fold her close, kiss her till the pain went away and the spark of desire ignited in her eyes.

He wanted this woman as he'd never wanted before. With a savage, gnawing hunger that threatened his pretensions to being a civilised man.

Sto Diavolo! She needed protecting from *him*.

'Fotini will always have an important place as the mother of my daughter,' he said slowly, choosing his words. 'But ours was not a love match. We both wanted marriage and it was expected that love would grow with time.' As it might have done if Fotini had been a different woman.

'But believe me, Sophie,' he looked down into her drowning, golden-brown eyes, 'when I look at you it's only you that I see. I can assure you *absolutely* that I'm not seeking a replacement for Fotini. And I never will.'

CHAPTER EIGHT

SOPHIE PUFFED AS she strode up the path to the house. The walk had been long and tiring but it hadn't brought the peace she craved.

She kept replaying in her mind that scene at Phaestos. How close she'd come to making an utter fool of herself. She'd been so needy, reaching out to Costas like that. So sure he felt the spark between them too.

She stumbled as she recalled his words—his vehemence when he'd declared he never wanted a replacement for Fotini.

In other words, he didn't want another woman in his life. He didn't want *her.*

Sophie cringed at the memory, but still she couldn't let it go. Try as she might to stop it, her mind kept circling back to that confrontation, trying to make sense of what had happened between them.

He'd been adamant that Sophie didn't remind him of Fotini and in that, at least, she believed him. The dawning horror on his face at her words had been unmistakable.

He'd said the marriage wasn't a love match, but in the next breath had told her no one could replace his wife.

There was more to this, surely. Something he hadn't explained.

But what right did she have to pursue it any further? Her heart squeezed tight in her chest as she faced the fact that she had no rights at all where Costas Palamidis was concerned.

But Costas was a hard man to ignore and those persistent daydreams, of her held close in his arms, kept intruding no matter how hard she fought them.

He was a devoted father, spending much of the day with Eleni. As far as Sophie could tell he stayed on the estate, dealing with urgent business by phone and email. Which meant she had to work hard to avoid him.

With every cool glance and formal smile he sent her way he made it clear that he didn't want or need her sympathy or her company. That she was here for one thing only, the precious bone marrow which, if all went well, she'd be able to give his daughter.

Sophie blinked back the ready tears that were inevitably close these days. It was as if she'd somehow lost an outer protective layer that had muted her emotions during the traumatic weeks of her mother's illness.

Now, without its shield, she felt vulnerable, scraped raw by the strong currents of pain and need that tugged her this way and that.

Her time with Eleni was special, as was the tenuous, but real relationship that was building between them. Eleni was a little darling, full of pluck and with a cheeky sense of humour that Sophie envied.

As each day passed, she had to fight harder against her feelings for Costas. Back in Sydney it had been anger she'd felt for him, and a touch of fear too, if she was honest. Then had come a reluctant fellow feeling, when she realised what pain he hid behind his iron-hard exterior.

And through it all a potent awareness unlike anything she'd experienced before.

Now there was more. A growing tenderness as she watched him battle his inner demons and focus all his energies on his daughter. The sight of the pair of them together, one so big and tough and capable, and the other so fragile, yet so feisty, never failed to wring her heart.

Her every sense went on alert when he came near. The deep rasp of his voice sent a thrill through her. And, despite his rejection, she knew she'd do anything she could to smooth away the worry lines on his brow and the stiff, unyielding set of his shoulders that told her of the grief he carried. For his daughter. And for his wife.

Sophie sighed and took the path up to the house.

She didn't understand all that he felt for Fotini but of course he still grieved for her.

What a fool Sophie was. Wanting to help him through the pain that only time could heal.

As if she had some secret remedy for grief!

Her own sense of loss was a tangible thing, a deep, still well of pain that woke her early each morning. Yet here in the Palamidis home there was peace too, a sense of purpose that helped her day by day.

She shook her head. This situation was fraught with emotions and needs she barely understood. All she knew for sure was that she'd stay as long as she was needed.

Darkness was closing in as she entered the house but it would be a while yet before dinner. She didn't meet anyone as she crossed the ground floor and headed for the stairs. Evening settled like a blanket on the house, deepening its shadows, as she emerged into her corridor on the first floor.

Something made her pause, a muffled sound she couldn't identify. It came from the other wing, where Costas and Eleni had their rooms. Sophie hesitated a moment, then swung round. If Eleni had gone to bed perhaps she was having a bad dream.

There was no repeat of the noise, just silence as she slowed her steps and stopped outside Eleni's room.

Sure enough, there she was, tucked up with a teddy bear in a canopied bed with gossamer hangings that was every little girl's dream. A night-light glowed already in one corner and a tumble of toys on the huge window-seat was testament to a late play hour.

Sophie stood in the doorway, one hand on the jamb, as she watched Eleni's chest rise and fall. Her mouth wore a tiny smile and she'd hooked her plush bear up under one arm so it nestled beneath her chin.

Something caught in Sophie's throat as she stood there. A fierce, protective surge of emotion held her still.

That was why it took a few moments to realise she wasn't alone. The barest of movements caught her eye and she turned her head to see Costas hunched in a chair behind the door.

His elbows were on his splayed knees and his head was in his hands.

He made no sound. Didn't move. And in the soft light she could almost have sworn that he didn't even breathe, so still was he.

But not at peace.

There was despair in every line of his large frame. In the fingers tunnelled through his shining dark hair, in the slump of his broad shoulders. And in the droop of his neck.

He looked like a man defeated. A man who'd lost all hope. Not at all like the Costas Palamidis she knew.

And she couldn't bear it.

Softly she took a step towards him, and another. After a bare moment's hesitation she let her hand fall to his shoulder, moulding the hard ridge of wide muscle above the bone. Its rigidity confirmed what she'd seen. He was close to the end of his tether.

His head shot up at her touch, his dark gaze fixed on hers with an intensity that made her throat close, her breath catch. There was such fierce pain in his expression.

She let her hand slide along his broad shoulder to the stiff muscles of his neck, as if she could stroke some of the tension away. The heat of his flesh against hers seemed shockingly intimate.

She opened her mouth to speak but he put his finger to his lips.

She glanced across at Eleni, still sleeping soundly. In that moment he moved, clamping his hand over hers and dragging it to his side as he rose from the seat to tower above her. His hand, hard and unyielding, engulfed hers.

He pulled her out of the room, into the dusky corridor where the shadows lengthened. He didn't stop till they reached the curve in the hall that turned towards her room. Then he halted abruptly and stood, staring silently down at her.

His eyes glittered dark as night but she couldn't discern his expression.

'Are you all right?' she asked before she had time to think twice. 'Can I get you anything?' She took a tiny pace closer, tilting her chin up and trying to read his face, but it gave nothing away. Even his eyes were blank. She could have been looking into chips of pure obsidian for all the emotion she could find there.

What could she get him anyway? How would a cup of coffee or even a shot of alcohol help a man watching his daughter fight for her life?

She was foolish even to try reaching out to him. He'd made it abundantly clear that he didn't want her understanding. Or her presence.

It was time she left.

She tugged at his hand to release his hold. But his fingers didn't loosen their grip.

'Forget I—'

'Yes, there is something,' he murmured, his voice a low, dark thread of sound that sent a shard of tension through her.

Sophie stared up at him, saw the moment when his eyes lit with a flash of life. Like fire in a frozen wasteland. But the sight of that blaze brought no comfort.

Something very like fear trickled inch by inch down her spine as she watched his expression change, his lips curve up into a wolfish smile.

'What—'

'This,' he hissed as his head plunged down and his lips took hers.

Fire. Flaring need. A maelstrom of sensations assaulted her. His lips so soft yet so demanding. His searing breath, burning like an invader's bombardment.

And deep within her a quivering awareness that *this* was what she'd wanted from him. This frightening, glorious passion.

He cupped her face in his big hands, holding it still while he turned his head and slanted his mouth hard over hers. And then he was inside. His tongue boldly seductive, inviting her to respond to his flagrantly erotic invitation.

And of course she did.

Swirling heat roared through her, loosening her muscles and her inhibitions. A sweet, yearning ache began deep in her womb and her skin prickled all over. Her nipples tightened.

She pressed into his kiss, drunk on the taste of him, dark and strong and erotically addictive.

Sophie welcomed him with her lips, her tongue, as if he was no stranger, but the centre of all her yearning, all her secret dreams.

His kiss was bold, unrepentant. Yet there was an underlying tenderness, a sensitivity to her own responses, that lulled her into surrender.

If she'd been thinking straight she would have pushed away from him. Denied the tell-tale excitement she felt at his touch. But Sophie wasn't thinking. She was drowning in sensations, floating on a tide of glorious passion. Excited by the aura of his severe strength, tightly leashed.

His hands threaded through her hair and his lips trailed down to the corner of her jaw, to the erogenous zone beneath her ear, and she sighed.

Giving in to the inevitable, she let her hands slide up his chest, revelling in the way his breath hitched in his throat at their slow, delicious progress. Ribbed muscle, solid chest, up to the hot skin of his neck and his dark, silky hair. Her fingers splayed on the back of his skull and she sought his mouth again.

Heaven!

This time the thrust of his tongue was more insistent, blatantly demanding.

And still she couldn't get close enough to him. The edgy, unsettling sensation in the pit of her stomach intensified. She shifted her weight, trying to ease that indefinable ache, even as she returned his kiss with a passion equal to his own.

His thigh brushed hers. He stepped closer. Sophie felt his body lean in towards hers. His heat pressed against her from shoulder to hip.

And then, on a surge of energy, he crowded her back against the wall, trapping her with his weight so that she couldn't move, even if she'd sought escape. Her breasts were crushed against him. Her breathing shallowed, but she didn't want him to move away.

The feel of him, solid and hot along the length of her body, evoked a passion she'd never known before. She wriggled nearer. Immediately he pushed one heavy thigh forward, holding her still. And then he jammed closer, so close she could hardly breathe, nudging her legs aside so that he could anchor himself within the cradle of her hips.

Right where the fire he'd stoked flared brightest.

Every inch of her burned. Burned for him. It was as inevitable as the ceaseless motion of the waves down on the shore. Nothing had ever felt so perfect, as if her body had known him before and was impatient to welcome him home.

It should have scared her. But Sophie was lost. There were no warning bells clanging in her brain, only the certain knowledge that this was *right*. And that it still wasn't enough. The musky scent of him, of powerful, uncompromising masculinity, should have made her pause, so blatant was it now as he clamped her body against his. But it only incited her starved senses. And when his hand swept down her side so knowingly, pressing into the curve of her waist, the swell of her hips, and back to tease the side of her breast, she was only aware of the sinuous push of her body into his touch, of her longing for him.

She stretched up against him, eager to match the demands of his mouth as it plundered hers.

Then he gripped her torso in both hands and lifted her higher, pinning her against the wall with his lower body. She gasped at the intimacy of his touch, his erection unmistakable between her legs, against her belly. And the need grew in her there, the restless, empty yearning for physical fulfilment.

His kiss became more potent, devastating in its ruthless sensuality, as he took her mouth, possessed it utterly. His heart pounded against her breasts, its rhythm like a racing train. Matching hers.

And then his hands slid round and cupped her breasts. Sophie sighed into his mouth. Darts of electric energy tingled from her nipples at his every caress and spread burning devastation along her nerves. To her womb. To her legs. To the juncture of her thighs that softened like warm butter against the press of his strength.

When he broke the kiss to press his lips to her throat, she gasped for air in huge, frantic mouthfuls. She was out of control, far beyond any mastery of her own body. She shuddered convulsively as he nipped her ear lobe, sending delicious tremors of awareness through her.

'You like this, Sophie?' His voice was a rasping, air-starved murmur that weakened her even more. Through the cotton fabric of her shirt he tweaked her nipple, creating another jolt of blazing excitement.

'Yes,' she breathed, her hands busy with their restless exploration of his muscled shoulders, so wide and so tense.

He lifted his head then to stare at her. His eyes glittered with a savage excitement that should have frightened her. Except that it matched her own. The laboured sound of their breathing echoed in the still hall.

'Good,' he said, his chest still heaving. 'Because that's what you can give me, Sophie.' He slid his hand down to her waist, insinuating it between them to brush across the front of her jeans, lower and lower, till she shuddered at the explicit contact.

She stared up into a face ravaged by raw need. No evidence of softness, of gentleness there. Only stark lust.

She shivered, but this time it wasn't with carnal excitement. Finally, too late, she realised she was dealing with a man who didn't give a damn for anyone or anything right now except the need for release.

'Sex, Sophie,' he breathed. His dark-as-sin eyes locked with hers. 'That's what I want. That's *all* I want from you.'

She watched his lips move, heard the words, yet somehow she couldn't take them in.

But if she sought something else, some shred of tenderness, some deeper emotion from this man, she was doomed to disappointment. His eyes were febrile with lust. And nothing else. His face had a tightly drawn quality that proclaimed the extremity of his need. Pure physical desire. Nothing else.

What else had she expected?

Cold, hard, unwanted reality doused the roaring inferno that had held her spellbound.

She slumped, her hands still grasping his shoulders for support. He let her slide down the wall so she could stand on her own two feet.

Yet she would have collapsed in a heap if not for his possessive hold on her. Her knees shook as if she'd run a marathon.

'Nothing to say, Sophie?' His lips twisted in a humourless smile that finally eliminated the last trace of burgeoning excitement that had grown inside her during their kiss.

All her desperate desire was extinguished as suddenly and completely as a candle snuffed out in a strong wind. She felt hollow, as if something vital had been scooped out of her at his words, and at the emptiness she read in his features.

An emptiness that echoed inside her.

She'd been a fool. A blind, unthinking fool.

There was nothing here for her. She knew it now, without his words. Yet he said them anyway. And each syllable was like a nail hammering into her vulnerable, foolish heart.

'I don't want your sympathy,' he said. 'There's no place in my life for that.' He drew in a mighty breath and paused.

'But I'll take your body, Sophie. Every gorgeous centimetre of it. I want to lose myself in your softness. I want to forget the world for an hour. For a single night. But that's all. It's oblivion I want, Sophie. Sex and ecstasy and simple, animal pleasure. Nothing else. Not feelings or tenderness. No relationship. No future.'

He swiped his thumb over her nipple, once, twice, deliberately, while he stared down at her with a face darkened by pure need. She shuddered in unwilling response to his touch. Her body was so weak. She was appalled not by the ferocity of his stare, but by the shameful realisation that she still wanted him, still responded to him, even though he'd made it unequivocally clear that he didn't want *her*. That any warm, willing female body would satisfy him right now.

And she felt ashamed of what she'd done. Of how she'd responded to him so uninhibitedly.

'So, Sophie. Will you give me what I want? What I've craved ever since I saw you? Will you give me sweet oblivion?'

Sophie opened her mouth. Tried to find the words. Any words that would end this. But nothing came. She gaped at him, still feeling the echo of desire thrumming through her body, remembering the ecstasy of their mutual need.

But now she felt cheapened by it. He'd made her feel like a whore.

She'd reached out to him, wanting to help, to ease his pain and share his burden. And, she realised with brutal honesty that cut through all her instinctive excuses, she'd craved his affection, had wanted to build a relationship, however fragile, with this complex, difficult man who'd taken control of her life from the moment he stalked into it a mere week ago.

Yet all the while he'd seen her as nothing more than a convenient female body. Lips and breasts and hips to be enjoyed for a moment's pleasure then discarded.

He didn't want *her*. Didn't need *her*. Not her brain or her heart or the person she was, still trying to come to grips with her life.

She drew a shuddering breath, ignoring the bone-deep pain that lanced through her chest.

At least he was honest. She should be thankful he'd spelled it all out for her now, before she'd been swept away by his ardour and by her own longing. A longing for love, she now realised, turning her head away, unable to meet his piercing stare.

His hands tightened around her ribs, their span heavily possessive. 'Is that a no?' he drawled. But she heard the urgency behind his contempt.

And, lord help her, it wouldn't take much for her to give in and offer him what he wanted. Not when her body responded to his as if they were soul mates. She didn't doubt for an instant that physically it would be glorious.

And then how would she feel? It didn't bear thinking about.

Sophie slid her hands down from his shoulders and shoved with all her might. She had to get away. Now.

For a few fraught moments he didn't budge. She didn't have the strength to shift him, despite her growing desperation.

And then, abruptly, he stepped back, his eyes shadowed and unreadable. Her hands fell to her sides.

She didn't remember running down the hallway to the sanctuary of her room, of locking the door, or stripping off and standing under a shower so hot surely it must cleanse her.

All she knew was that she'd left her self-respect behind with Costas Palamidis.

CHAPTER NINE

COSTAS PACED THE sitting room, flicking another impatient glare at his watch. Where was she? The sun was already riding low in the west and still she hadn't returned.

Sophie had been out since early morning. Surely she should be back by now?

He paused in front of the picture window, scowling as he stared out at the silver-grey olive grove and the glitter of the sea.

She'd sneaked down for breakfast almost before the staff was awake. Slipped out of the house and told the housekeeper merely that she would be out for the day.

And she'd taken Yiorgos with her. He didn't know whether to be glad she wasn't alone or furious with jealousy.

It was no good. He had so little control where Sophie was concerned. She intruded on his thoughts all the time. She was there in his mind when he carried Eleni on his shoulders down through the orchard to the sea. And there as he'd tucked his daughter in for her nap, fielding her interminable, sulky questions about where Sophie was today and why she hadn't come to play.

He'd known the answer to that. And his flesh crawled as he thought of it now.

She was avoiding him. It was a wonder she hadn't disappeared completely, not just escaped for a day. Not after what he'd done to her.

He spun on his foot and strode the length of the massive

room, along the corridor and through the door that led outside. He stood on the stone steps in the warmth of the late sun, breathing hard as if he'd just sprinted a couple of kilometres. He scrubbed his hand over his face and up to tunnel through his hair.

But he couldn't hide from it. The guilt that had dogged him since last night. Since he'd kissed Sophie. Since he'd almost ravaged her with a hunger more befitting a beast than a civilised man.

He'd deliberately taken advantage of her worry and sympathy, allowing his needy, selfish desires to drive him. When he'd felt her hand on him, her gentle, soothing touch to his shoulder, and when he'd seen the answering pain in her soft eyes as he'd sat beside Eleni's bed, his control had finally snapped.

In one writhing, overpowering, unstoppable wave, his need had risen and consumed him. Consumed them both. All he'd known was that he had to get her away from his daughter's room. That they needed some vestige of privacy for what was between them.

But he hadn't even made it further than the open hallway!

Costas swallowed down the bitter taste of self-loathing and stepped away down the path, striding out as if he could somehow escape the knowledge of his own guilt. But of course that was impossible.

Hell! Even now he could see the distress in her eyes. The horrified recoil as he'd told her exactly what he wanted from her. At every deliberately brutal, cruel word she'd winced, her pupils dilating with pain. He'd taken her charity and thrust it back at her, making it a tainted thing. As tainted as his own lust for her.

No matter that his body had been rock hard with wanting her. And with the effort of control needed to prevent himself from taking her then and there, without preliminaries, in the corridor. No matter that his soul ached for the comfort he knew she alone could give him, for the touch of her soft hands against his flesh. He'd known that touch intimately every night in his turbulent dreams. And in his waking fantasies. He craved the reality of it as the parched earth craved soft, sweet rain at the end of the long summer drought.

No matter that she tasted like an angel. So miraculously sweet that he was addicted after just one kiss. Or that she responded to him so completely, so ferociously that his soul cried out in wonder and delight.

His woman. Those were the crazy, impossible words that had pounded through his numbed, awed brain as he drank in the taste of her, imprinted her soft curves against his rampant body. That was the knowledge that had throbbed through his pulse and made his hands quiver.

His.

Even now the primitive, potent need to possess her lay barely suppressed. He wanted to reach out and take her. Hold her fast. Claim her for his own. It was a certainty that defied logic, but resided bone-deep in his body, soul-deep in his psyche.

He emerged from a thicket onto the bare top of the small headland, came to a stop on the edge of the cliff that dropped down to the shallow curve of the bay. The tang of salt was on his lips. The sound of waves rolling in was heavy and more regular than his own heartbeat.

He strove for cool logic. The fire in his blood, the proprietorial instinct…they'd clouded his brain. It was simply a volatile surge of lust he experienced.

She was no more his woman than he was the man of her dreams.

He owed all his allegiance to his daughter. He had no time for anyone else in his life. Much less a girl with her own life far away in Australia. A girl grieving for her mother, wounded by the memories of family conflict and rejection.

A girl so passionate and independent that he felt more alive just talking with her, arguing and debating and finally finding common ground, than he had in a long time.

He shook his head. He was deluding himself. They were strangers brought together by circumstance. That was all.

That was why he'd been so brutally frank with her last night. Describing his aching need in blatant physical terms, each word designed to shred their growing intimacy and make her shun him. For he knew one thing: he'd lost his own battle to retain his honour.

That was why he'd deliberately provoked her disgust of him.

It was the only barrier left between them. But even as he'd done it, giving her every excuse to hate him, he'd teetered on a knife edge, almost wishing she wouldn't care. That she'd lead him to her room anyway and take him to paradise.

No decent man would seduce a guest in his house, a young woman already battling her own pain with a grace and inner strength that must draw respect. No honourable man would take advantage of her empathy to force himself on her.

Yet he would have taken her last night, grateful for the solace of her body, the sweet sensuality of her response. Even hating his weakness, he would have had her. Not once but right through the long, aching hours of darkness.

His body hardened at the memory of her against him. He should be grateful that she'd shown the will-power he lacked and removed herself from his vicinity.

Yet he couldn't stifle his restless unease. Her absence was even worse than the torment of having her close at hand.

'Not far now,' Yiorgos said with a quick smile.

The words were like a douche of chill water to Sophie's spirits. Soon they'd be back at the Palamidis villa and she'd have to face Costas.

She chewed on her lip, wondering how she was going to brazen it out. How could she see him again after what had happened last night? Now he knew just how weak she was. She'd almost crawled up his body, so impetuous in her need to get close to him. He'd kissed her, held her in his arms, and she'd lost all control. Had offered herself to him, there in the hallway, without thought.

It had only been his words, pounding into her desire-numbed brain, that finally brought her to her senses.

And even then, even when he looked at her with the easy contempt of a man who knew she was his for the taking, it had been an almost insurmountable struggle to tear herself away. Despite his words, despite the pain they inflicted, she'd still wanted him.

What sort of woman did that make her?

'*Thespinis?* Are you all right?'

She turned to Yiorgos, noting the genuine concern in his flashing eyes. He'd been a pleasant companion all day, even though she hadn't been able to convince him to call her by her name. The boss wouldn't like it, he said. And that settled the matter, of course. The boss obviously got whatever he wanted.

Except her.

'I'm OK,' she said, dredging up a smile. 'Maybe just a little tired.'

He grinned then, flicking her a mischievous glance. 'I don't see how that could be. After all it was only the markets you visited. And then the archaeological museum. And Knossos. And—'

'You've made your point,' Sophie said, and this time her smile was real. 'It's been a wonderful day. Thank you.'

'It was my pleasure. Any time. You just ask and I'll drive you wherever you want to go.'

Sophie watched as he concentrated on a tight curve in the road. He really was remarkably good-looking. Gorgeous even, with those large, laughing eyes. And he was close enough to her own age for her to relax in his company and enjoy his jokes.

So why didn't she feel even a spark of attraction to him?

Why did his handsome face leave her unmoved, when just the memory of Costas' hard, passionate features and dark, probing eyes made her feel as if something had unravelled in the pit of her stomach?

And why did eagerness mix with her trepidation at the prospect of seeing him again?

Fortunately Yiorgos chose that moment to regale her with another of his stories, distracting her from thoughts she'd rather avoid. And soon she was laughing so much that she didn't even notice that they'd swung through the security gates to the estate.

It was only as they rounded a gentle curve in the long private road and the house came into view that she realised they were back.

And that Costas was waiting for them.

He stood, arms akimbo, at the head of the steps. A forbidding figure that dominated the scene.

Sophie's grin morphed into a rictus stretch of taut lips, all laughter fled. Would she ever see the man and not experience that desperate, melting awareness deep inside?

He was down the steps and opening the passenger door even as the limousine drew to a gentle halt.

'Where have you been?' His hand fastened on her elbow, drawing her from her seat as soon as she'd released her seat belt.

'Sightseeing,' she said, raising her eyes to his. They were unreadable. Pure, impenetrable black. But the scowl on his face needed no interpretation. He was furious. His brows tilted down at a ferocious angle and the grip on her elbow was more than supportive. It was like a vice, clamped hard round her arm.

She shrugged, but he didn't break his hold. Instead he bent low to the open car door and snapped a barrage of staccato Greek at his chauffeur. It was too rapid for her to understand, but she could tell by the suddenly sombre look on Yiorgos' face that it was far from pleasant.

What was Costas' problem?

'I'm sorry,' she interrupted, 'I didn't know you needed the car today.'

Costas straightened to stare down at her. A flash of dark emotion in his eyes made her shiver. The controlled energy he projected made her hackles rise. She sensed he was waiting for the right moment to pounce.

'I didn't,' he cut in succinctly. 'And I have more than one car, should I need one. But I would have appreciated knowing where you were. I expected you back hours ago.'

What? He'd been worried about her? Surely not. Not when he glared at her so disapprovingly.

'I didn't know I had to report my movements to you.'

She was damned if she'd apologise again. He'd offered the use of the car and now he was annoyed she'd used it. Was he worried his precious bone-marrow donor might disappear off the island if he didn't keep tabs on her?

'Why did you switch the cellphone off? What were you up to all that time?' He thrust his head close to hers. She could see the tic of a rapid pulse at the base of his clenched jaw; smell the natural, masculine scent of him in her nostrils.

And feel the traitorous weakness of her reaction to him. The recognition of it was like a betrayal. How could she?

'We went into the mountains this afternoon, *Kyrie Palamidis*,' Yiorgos said from inside the car. 'We lost the signal.'

'And you could always have left a message,' she interrupted, 'if it was anything important.'

Costas flicked her a momentary glance then said something curtly dismissive to Yiorgos and slammed the car door shut. He still held her arm in a tight grip as the engine purred into life and the car headed round the corner of the house towards the garages.

'Did you know that Yiorgos is engaged to be married?' he said in a lethally quiet voice.

She frowned. What had that to do with anything?

'Did you know?' His fingers bit into her flesh and she winced. Immediately he loosened his grip. But he didn't release her.

'No, I didn't.' She glared up at him, wondering what the hell was going on.

He nodded once. 'Then perhaps I should tell you that his fiancée is a very possessive, very jealous young woman.'

For a couple of seconds Sophie stared at him, her jaw sagging as the implications of his words permeated her brain. He was warning her off? What did he think she was, some sort of seductress who'd gone straight from the boss to the chauffeur?

Nausea churned her stomach, welled in her throat. His tone was as icy as his eyes were hot, and she felt as if he'd just slapped her, hard.

In that instant she realised just what sort of woman Costas thought her.

'Get your hands off me!' she hissed.

Surprisingly, this time he complied, leaving her free to escape up the stairs, almost stumbling in her haste to seek sanctuary.

Well done, Palamidis. Costas watched her scramble inside as if the hound of Hades himself were after her.

Sto Diavolo! He couldn't have done worse if he'd tried!

He planted his feet wide, refusing to give in to the instinct that told him to race after her and gather her close. The last thing she needed was him invading her space. Not when he'd hurt her again, insulted her out of sheer, bloody, dog-in-the-manger jealousy.

It had taken just one glance at her smiling face, the carefree laughter in her eyes as she responded to Yiorgos, and the look on his driver's face as he watched her, and Costas had lost it.

Jealous of his driver!

She was so beautiful when she smiled like that, all vestige of strain disappearing from her face, that it had struck him like a blow, deep and devastating in his chest. It hurt, knowing she'd never look at him in that way, smile so freely and approvingly. He'd sacrificed that last night when he'd behaved like a thug.

But no man could fail to recognise the male appreciation in Yiorgos' eyes as he turned on the charm for her. More than appreciation. There'd been speculation. And it was that look that had drawn Costas' simmering anger to the surface, making him lash out indiscriminately.

He shook his head. He should have saved his anger for Yiorgos. Hell, the guy was a practised womaniser with a reputation envied by half the local men.

Costas would have a few choice words with him soon.

And in future he, Costas, would drive Sophie wherever she wanted to go.

He straightened his shoulders and started up the steps. In the meantime he had an apology to make.

Eventually he located her, emerging from a downstairs powder room. Her shoulders were hunched and her eyes skittered from his. Her mouth was a taut line of pain in her overly pale face.

He'd done that. Damn his possessive masculine ego!

'Sophie…' He reached for her hand but she jerked away, retreating a step till she'd backed up to a wall.

Sick to the stomach, he let his hand drop to his side.

'What do you want?' Her tone was weary. She stared at a point somewhere near his chin.

'I need to apologise.' The words were rough, dragged from him by the sight of her hurt.

Fleetingly her eyes met his and her lips curved in a surprised circle that tightened the curl of need deep in the pit of his stomach. He drew a long breath.

'I was annoyed with my driver, not you,' he said. 'He should have known to keep in contact. In future you have only to ask and I'll take you wherever you wish to go.'

Silence.

'I'm sorry you thought I was implying—'

'What? That I was a tramp?'

She met his eyes now and the turbulent mix of emotions he saw there, the anguish and the shocked fury, seared his conscience.

She hurried on before he could formulate a response. 'That because I'd decided not to go to bed with you last night, I must be eager for a little fun and games with someone else?' Her voice was a searing, agonised whisper. 'What do you think I am? A bitch on heat?'

'Sophie, I—'

'Keep away from me.' She slapped away the hand he hadn't even noticed he'd held out to her.

There were tears in her eyes and her lower lip trembled. Pain twisted deep inside him as he watched her obvious distress. He'd done that to her, damn his black soul. He wanted nothing more than to kiss her hurt away.

'I said, stay away,' she hissed, as he closed the distance between them, reaching out to bracket her with his hands, flat on the wall beside her head. The tantalising shimmer of liquid gold in her eyes ensnared him. Her delicate, fresh scent encompassed him, and the warmth of her luscious body drew him like a magnet.

He hefted one massive breath and struggled against the compulsion to reach out and claim her. To brand her as his own.

'That's the problem, Sophie. I can't keep my distance. Not

any more.' He dragged in another juddering breath. 'Don't you understand?'

He stared down into her wide stunned eyes and knew he was lost.

'Why do you think I was so furious with Yiorgos?'

'Because you thought I was seducing him,' she said flatly.

He shook his head.

She shifted her weight and shot a glance over his shoulder. 'I need to go and—'

'Why, Sophie?' he demanded.

Slowly, as if she fought with every ounce of her strength, she lifted her eyes to his. She looked impossibly weary. 'Because you don't want me out of your sight,' she whispered slowly then looked away.

He nodded, acknowledging the surge of ravening hunger that even now tore at the frayed remnants of his self-control. A good thing his hands were planted firmly against the plaster. It helped him resist the desire to use them to shape her face, her fragile neck, her delicate curves.

'And why is that?' he whispered, focusing on her convulsive swallow, on the way she tugged at her lower lip with her teeth.

'Because I'm the only person who might be able to help Eleni,' she murmured at last, still refusing to meet his gaze.

'Wrong.'

Her gaze shot up again at the single word. The instant connection between them was like a jolt of electricity, charging the air with pulsing anticipation.

'It's because I'm jealous,' he admitted, stripping his soul bare. His voice was a low animal growl that matched perfectly the savage possessiveness welling inside him. 'I'm jealous of anyone who has you to themselves when I don't.'

Her eyes widened and her mouth gaped and he wanted, more than anything, the ultimate luxury of taking her lush, enticing lips with his. His whole body trembled with barely repressed desire. Sweat hazed his skin at the effort it took to keep still, keep from sweeping her into his embrace and burying his face in her sweetly scented hair.

'Do you understand, Sophie?' His voice was raw, all pretence at civilised gloss scoured away by this elemental hunger. 'I was jealous of my driver because he spent the day alone with you. I didn't think for a minute you might be seducing him.'

He paused, gathering his courage.

'I wanted you to be seducing me.'

The stark admission reverberated in the still air between them. Blatant. Inescapable. Overpowering.

He'd never felt so driven, so desperate for a woman's touch. And even more, for her understanding.

He saw the warm colour flood her face, accentuate the high contours of her cheekbones. And he felt an answering heat, pooling low in his groin. Her eyes were wide, so clear and enticing that he felt he could lose himself in their promise, just as he wanted to lose himself in the heady temptation of her body.

He inhaled the scent of her, like beckoning spring after a long, cold winter. Enticing, promising, seductive.

He heard her soft breaths, short and rapid. And he could taste her already on his tongue. After last night he'd craved that taste with a frenzied longing that appalled him.

He had only to lift a hand, cup her face as he closed the distance between them and—

'Kyrie Palamidis.' The quiet voice of his housekeeper shattered the stillness.

The world tilted and shifted into focus again.

Till that moment it had been as if nothing else existed. There was only this space where he and Sophie stood, bound by a passion so strong it eclipsed all his puny self-control.

He blinked, drew himself up and turned.

The housekeeper stood at the end of the hall, near the door to the servants' quarters. She held a cordless phone in her hands and her eyes were wide with astonishment. Hastily she looked away.

In all the years she'd worked for him she'd never seen him with any woman other than Fotini. Even before his marriage, he hadn't been in the habit of seducing guests in his home.

'It's the hospital on the phone,' she explained.

Costas' heart leapt right up into his throat at her words.

The moment of reckoning had arrived. Something—fear—clutched at his chest, squeezing so tight that for a moment he couldn't breathe.

He felt Sophie's eyes on him and pushed back his shoulders, forced himself to move, to accept whatever news awaited.

He'd done what he could. Now he had to summon the strength to endure what he must.

He paced over and took the phone with a brief word of thanks. Then he turned and met Sophie's stare across the room.

'Costas Palamidis speaking,' he said, automatically switching to Greek.

'We have the result, sir.' He recognised the voice of Eleni's doctor. 'We'd like you to bring your daughter in for treatment as soon as possible. We believe the donor you found is compatible. We'll proceed with the transplant.'

CHAPTER TEN

COSTAS STARED THROUGH THE glass wall panel and felt a lump the size of a football lodge in his chest. He swallowed hard and forced down the welling emotion.

He'd coped with the trauma of the transplant procedure and the hard days that followed, helpless to do more than stay with Eleni through her discomfort. Through her raw, aching tiredness and the inevitable tears and upsets.

He'd done what he had to. Kept his emotions in check. He'd cajoled, encouraged, consoled.

And he'd been astounded at his little girl's strength and determination. She was so tiny. So incredibly fragile. Yet she had the heart of a lion. Possessed a fearlessness that far outstripped his own strength.

Through the long weeks since the transplant he'd held it all together: delegating control of his business empire, fending off Press intrusions, fielding endless queries from friends and relatives, doing what had to be done.

So why suddenly now did the sight of his daughter strike him so hard that it felt as if someone had grabbed his heart and tried to rip it out?

He braced himself against the wall, dragging in a tortured breath that sawed painfully into his lungs.

His palm was slippery with sweat. His arm trembled as he fought to brace himself. The cold, bitter taste of fear filled his mouth.

Even now no one knew if the transplant would save Eleni.

He raised his head and looked again into his daughter's hospital room. She was propped up against a bank of pillows, her tiny frame pathetically thin. Yet a smile lurked at the corners of her mouth and her eyes danced. She looked down at the huge picture book spread before her and said something he couldn't hear.

It must have been a joke. Even through the glass he heard the woman beside her give an answering laugh.

Sophie.

He couldn't see her smile—it was hidden by the surgical mask she wore. But he saw the way her eyes crinkled in delight at Eleni's comment. The way she tipped back her head, laughing with her whole body.

The ache inside him deepened, twisted. His pulse ratcheted up a notch, as it always did when she was near.

Sophie and Eleni. Eleni and Sophie.

He shook his head, as if he could clear the whirling tumble of emotions and half-formed thoughts bombarding him.

He'd seen them together before. Sophie visited every day. Eleni wanted her there, so she was one of the few people allowed into the quarantined room.

The pair of them had grown ever closer. That was obvious even though Sophie tried to time her visits to avoid him: for the rare occasions when he was snatching a nap or meeting with doctors.

Not that he could blame her. They hadn't been alone together since the afternoon he'd confronted her with his jealous rage.

After that it was a wonder she hadn't left. Technically there was nothing to keep her in Greece. Yet she hadn't taken him up on his offer of a flight to Sydney. Instead she'd stayed on.

For Eleni.

She certainly hadn't remained in Crete to be near him. Costas knew he'd been a brute. An unreasoning, foul-tempered lout. Yet he knew that, faced again with the same circumstances, he'd probably behave exactly the same.

'Costa?'

He swung round to see his mother hurrying towards him down the corridor.

'Has something happened? You look so—'

'Nothing's happened,' he reassured her. He straightened and turned his back on the wall of glass. 'There's no change. She seems to be doing reasonably well.'

'Then what's wrong?' She allowed herself to be drawn into his embrace and kissed him soundly on both cheeks.

'Nothing's wrong,' he lied.

His mother glanced into Eleni's room and smiled. 'It's good to see them together—they have a real bond. At first glance that girl is so like Fotini it's astounding. But the differences are strong beneath the surface.'

'We won't go there,' he murmured, but even to his own ears it sounded like a growl. He turned to the glass panel, seeing Sophie close the book and look up to find him watching her. Her whole body stilled.

He wished he could read her expression. Not just the blaze of molten gold in her widening eyes. They held his for a heartbeat, for two, so long that he almost forgot about his mother, standing there beside him.

'Hiding from the truth won't make it go away.'

He watched Sophie put the book down beside the bed, then turn to talk to Eleni.

'Believe me. I'm not hiding from anything.'

'Aren't you? Yet you scowl whenever you look at Sophie. And you still freeze out any conversation about Fotini.'

He swung round to stare at his mother. 'This is neither the time nor the place.'

'Then when *is* the time? You've avoided talking about Fotini ever since the accident.'

'There's nothing to discuss. But don't worry, I'm aware of the differences between Sophie and her cousin.' His body responded vigorously and constantly to those unique differences. 'Sophie is no spoiled heiress and she wasn't brought up to be shallow or selfish.'

'Costa! That's not what I meant. And it's not like you to be so harsh. Not after the way you supported Fotini. You did everything a husband could to help her. More than many men would have done.'

And what had that achieved? Despite his vigilance, his eternal patience, he hadn't saved her from herself.

Costas felt the familiar helpless anger in the hollow of his gut. Perhaps if he'd truly loved her—

'She had severe post-natal depression,' his mother said. He felt her hand on his sleeve and looked down at her neat fingers against the dark fabric. 'It was no one's fault that her condition escalated so uncontrollably.'

'I disagree,' he countered. 'My wife chose to disregard her medical advice and shun her family. If she hadn't tried to drink and party her way out of her illness she wouldn't have lost control and smashed her car.'

If only he'd been with her that night. He should have ignored Eleni's slight fever and left her to her nanny's care. He could have postponed the late teleconference to Singapore. He should have—

'It was *no one's* fault, son. You weren't responsible.' He heard the words as if from a distance.

'And Eleni's illness is no one's fault either.'

Yet he felt the flare of guilt deep inside. The fear that he'd failed his daughter.

The silence was punctuated only by the harsh sound of his breathing as he fought a vice-like grip around his chest. It was as if iron bands constricted his lungs, cutting off his oxygen.

'Don't blame yourself, Costa. You need time to heal. To learn to trust again.'

Sharply he lifted his head. So, they were back to Sophie.

He wondered what his mother would say if she knew precisely how much his body wanted to *trust* Sophie Paterson. How completely she'd got under his skin, dominating even his troubled sleep. How impossibly strong was the connection he felt with her.

But he'd learned his lesson well. Trust and partnership were illusions he could do without. He knew not to fall for their spurious promise.

No matter how much he was tempted to believe.

After his marriage the last thing he needed was a new relationship. Especially with another girl from the house of Liakos.

His mother shook her head then turned away and began the ritual of hand-washing and donning mask and gown ready to visit Eleni.

Costas stood rock-still, trying to salvage the tattered shreds of his control.

His mother had dredged up memories he'd tried so hard to bury. And tenuous, seductive hopes that had no place in his life. He was off-balance, teetering on the brink of a black abyss of turbulent emotions.

What was happening to him?

He was always in control. That was how he operated. This sudden uncertainty—the wretched, unfamiliar feelings—he hated it.

Almost as much as he hated this waiting game, waiting to see if Eleni would live or die.

He shrugged back his shoulders and lifted his head, disgusted with himself. This was no time for weakness.

He watched his mother enter the private room. He wouldn't follow her just yet. Eleni might pick up on his tension. Instead he'd go and check if the doctor was in. So far the medical staff had been cautiously optimistic, but noncommittal about Eleni's long-term recovery. It drove him crazy. He needed something more concrete.

He was moving down the corridor when he heard the door open behind him. He heard a murmur of voices then footsteps. It was Sophie.

He stopped, unable to help himself.

Sophie avoided his intense stare as she removed her mask and gown. It only took a few seconds. She wished it took longer—anything to delay their inevitable conversation.

She was a coward, she knew.

Especially when Costas Palamidis stood there, as imposing and as unapproachable as a stone idol.

She wondered what he was thinking. She hadn't missed the speculation in his eyes when he'd found her sitting with Eleni.

She should be furious with him for the way he'd treated her. She *was* furious.

But that insidious longing was stronger than ever. Shamefully so.

Even now, after so much time to pull herself together, to perfect a semblance of nonchalance when he was near, she felt the skitter of awareness, that thrill of self-destructive excitement under her skin.

And it was far worse now. For this time they were alone. No Eleni, no medical staff, no hovering relatives to fill the room and break the tension between them.

The tension was there all right. A taut awareness that vibrated like a wire humming between them. It made her movements choppy, uncoordinated. Her breath came in short, jagged gasps till she found the strength to regulate it.

Now wasn't the time to try to fathom Costas or the extraordinary hold he exerted over her. There'd never be a right time for that. She wasn't a masochist.

She needed to concentrate on something else. Like the duty she had to discharge. Just thinking about it made her nervous.

'Hello, Sophie.' His voice was as deep as ever, like the soft, low rumble of thunder in the distance.

'Costas.' She inclined her head, trying to seem unfazed by his liquid dark eyes and the way he loomed over her. 'Eleni seems a little brighter this afternoon,' she offered. 'She was laughing and there's colour in her cheeks.'

He nodded but his brooding gaze didn't leave her face.

'I'm about to go and check whether the results of the latest tests are back,' he said and she read fierce control in the grim lines bracketing his mouth.

She wished she could offer to go with him. To support him when he got whatever news was awaiting him.

How stupid was that? He didn't want her help, her sympathy. He'd made it abundantly clear that he didn't need anything from her except the use of her body for a night.

And yet, idiotically, she couldn't stop the surge of empathy for him as he stood alone, facing the dark, uncertain future.

She'd lain awake night after night wondering if that was the real reason she'd stayed in Crete. Not just because of little Eleni. But because Costas Palamidis needed someone.

Needed her.

She shook her head. How mind-blowingly pathetic could she get? The man had turned independence into an art form. And as for truly needing anyone as ordinary as her...

'Sophie? We need to talk. I—'

'I was wondering if you'd help me,' she burst out before he could continue. Anything to stop him. Whatever he was going to say, whatever trite apology or explanation he was going to make, she didn't want to hear it.

'I need to find another one of the private wards,' she said quickly. 'And I need to convince the nursing staff to let me in.'

'Your grandfather.' It wasn't a question.

'Yes.'

Her grandfather. The man she'd vowed never to forgive.

'You've decided to see him, then.' Costas' dark eyes bored into her, penetrating her defences, her would-be careless posture.

She shrugged. 'It seemed appropriate.'

The information Costas had given her about the old man and the discovery that he was here in this very hospital had irrevocably altered her daily visits. Knowing that she passed so close to the tyrant who'd shaped her mother's life. Gradually, almost imperceptibly, the guilt had come. It had been compounded by the vague feeling, after watching a valiant child struggle through each new day, that perhaps life was more important than old grudges.

An uncomfortable suspicion had grown inside her. However right she was in her judgement of Petros Liakos, life was too precious for feuds. Was she was growing into someone just as stubbornly cruel as he'd been to her mum?

She didn't intend to forgive him for what he'd done. But she couldn't be as pitiless as he'd been.

Maybe he wouldn't want a visit from her. That wouldn't be a surprise. But if he did, then she'd swallow her resentment and see him.

'Sophie?'

She looked up, wondering if she'd missed something Costas had said.

'Are you ready?' he murmured. 'I can show you the way, I've visited him myself.'

Of course. She'd forgotten Petros Liakos had been his wife's grandfather too. Costas would take such family obligations seriously, even after Fotini's death.

'Yes. Thanks.' She wasn't about to admit that she didn't think she'd ever be ready to face old man Liakos. That the thought of meeting him made her want to turn tail and run. Instead she fell into step beside Costas.

There was something strangely soothing about his easy, deliberate pace. His tall presence beside her generated a welcome heat that counteracted her sudden chill.

She was glad of his company. After avoiding him for so long, trying not even to think about him, she felt better just having him beside her as she went to face the man she'd hated and resented most of her life.

Surreptitiously she watched Costas. So aloof, so impenetrable. He stared ahead down the corridor and she saw strength etched in his profile, in the way he held himself.

She knew without doubt that his was a different strength to her grandfather's. He had no need to prove himself by manipulating people weaker than himself. By playing vicious games with their lives.

Costas was a man who allowed himself to be tender with those he loved—his daughter and his mother. She'd seen it in his amazing gentleness when he was with them.

For one soul-searing, painful moment she let herself wish he'd extend that loving protectiveness to encompass her.

But that would never happen.

She and Costas were doomed to rub each other up the wrong way—to strike sparks. From the first he'd awakened reactions so intense that she'd known at some primitive level he was dangerous. She'd been fighting him one way or another ever since.

So how could she be drawing strength now from his presence?

Sophie gave up trying to fathom that conundrum. Nothing about their relationship was logical or moderate. It was all high emotion and raw passion—running hot in her blood. It had nothing to do with her mind.

Even now, as he led the way to another floor, passing ward staff and visitors, the two of them were essentially alone, cocooned in a private world where everything else faded into a background blur. He didn't touch her. Yet she was aware with every alert nerve of his lithe form beside her, the swing of his arm so close to her own, the way he tempered his pace to match hers.

They rounded a corner and stopped in front of a nursing station. Sophie clawed for mental control as she realised they were here, at Petros Liakos' ward.

She couldn't face the old man with her mind fixed on Costas. She needed her wits about her, and every ounce of self-assurance she'd learned at her mother's knee.

Sophie straightened her shoulders, only half listening to the conversation between Costas and the nurse. She knew that facing this one, sick old man would test her resolve to the limits. But she owed it to her mother to be calm. To show him that her mother's daughter was a woman to be reckoned with, not brushed aside as unworthy.

She shouldn't care what he thought, but deep down she knew she did.

Her heart raced at a staccato beat. Dampness bloomed at her palms and she swiped them down the back of her jeans.

'Sophie?' Costas stared down at her. 'It's supposed to be one visitor at a time, but I'll come in with you.'

'No!' She shook her head. 'No, that's OK. I'd rather see him alone.'

She couldn't even begin to imagine facing both Petros Liakos and Costas together. She'd be a nervous wreck! And more than that, this confrontation was far too private, too personal, to be shared.

'It will be easier with me there,' he persisted. 'The stroke—it's affected his speech.'

She nodded. 'You forget I'm a trained speech pathologist. I'm used to working with speech impediments. And,' she hurried on before he could interrupt, 'as long as he speaks slowly I'll understand simple Greek.'

'You won't need to. Your grandfather speaks English.'

Now, that surprised her. She'd imagined him such an old-fashioned patriarch that he wouldn't concede the value of learning any language other than his own.

'*Kyrie Liakos* will see you now,' said the nurse, emerging from a room near by. Her eyes were fixed on Costas. She didn't even glance in Sophie's direction.

'Thank you,' Sophie said, walking towards the room.

'Sophie—' Costas sounded as if he'd like to say more.

'I'll see you later,' she said before he could continue and slipped into the private ward, letting the door close behind her.

It felt different from Eleni's bright hospital room.

Immediately the familiar too-sweet scent of sick-room flowers filled her nostrils, making her stomach churn. The intense, distinctive quiet that accompanied the gravely ill enveloped her.

For a long, awful interval the memories of her mother's deathbed rose to swamp her. Bitter nausea made her reel, her hand outstretched to the door behind her for support. Her skin prickled hotly and she swallowed down bile.

Then she blinked and the *déjà vu* eased. The resemblance between this suite and her mother's spartan room were few. Every inch here attested to a luxury unlike anything the Paterson family had been able to command.

But despite that it was a hospital room. The nearby oxygen tank, the drip, the panel of emergency buttons and dials beside the bed—they were all familiar.

Despite Petros Liakos' wealth, he was as powerless against illness as her mother had been.

There was complete silence as she concentrated on getting her breathing under control.

A curtain hid the head of the bed. Was he even awake? There was no movement, no rustle of sheets.

But the nurse had said he'd see her. He must be lying there now, waiting for her. Perhaps guessing she was too nervous to face him.

Sophie tilted up her chin and clenched her fists at her sides. If Petros Liakos could bear to look her in the eye, she wouldn't deny him the opportunity.

Slowly she paced towards the bed. Ridiculous to feel so nervous. She had nothing to be ashamed of!

The bedcovers shaped feet, long legs, a thin body. A big, gnarled hand lay on the coverlet, curled into a claw.

Tingling heat seared her skin as she paused, imagining how the owner of a hand like that, once strong and capable, could bear his body's incapacity. It must be hell.

She walked closer, to the end of the bed, and then she saw him. Petros Liakos, her mother's father. Patriarch of the Liakos family.

The man who'd disowned his flesh and blood because he'd refused to relinquish control over his daughter's life.

Glittering dark eyes met hers and she felt the force of his will-power, the surge of energy, even from where she stood. His heavy brows jutted low in a ferocious scowl. His nose was a prominent, commanding beak, just what you'd expect of a power-hungry tyrant.

Thank heaven she hadn't inherited that nose, Sophie thought hysterically, her mind shutting down against the turmoil of desperate emotion deep within.

Movement caught her eye. A clumsy, abrupt gesture from that useless fist on the bedclothes. She heard the hiss of his indrawn breath, recognised the savage sound of pure frustration. A man as proud as him would hate being seen like this.

Sophie looked up to his face again. This time she saw the rest, not the power she'd looked for and found the first time, but the frailty. The old man's cheeks were sunken, the skull too prominent beneath his skin. His mouth was distorted into a lopsided grimace.

A twist of sympathy knotted her stomach.

'Come to…gloat.' His voice was laboured, barely intelligible with its slurred consonants. She had to lean forward to hear it.

'No.' She stared straight back into his eyes. They seemed the only thing about him still alive.

He drew a deep, shuddering breath that racked his frail body and scoured her conscience. Maybe she should leave. He was in pain.

'Come…for my…money,' he mumbled.

'No!' She stood straighter, anger driving out unwilling sympathy.

She glared at him, feeling the hurried beat of her pulse as long moments passed.

'I was curious,' she said at last when she could control her voice.

Again that stifled gesture with his useless claw of a hand.

'Closer,' he whispered. 'Come closer.'

Sophie stepped up to the head of the bed, looking down at her grandfather propped against the mountain of pillows. This close his eyes looked febrile, glittering. It took her a moment to realise it was moisture that made his eyes so bright. Tears.

She stared, dumbfounded at the thought of this man crying. He must have seen the shock on her face, for he blinked and turned his head away, towards the window.

Sophie stared at his grizzled, still curly hair, and wondered if that had been genuine emotion she'd seen or simply the effect of his stroke.

'Look like…her.' He struggled to get the words out, as if the impediment of an almost useless tongue had got worse.

Silence throbbed between them, beating down against her like a weapon.

She felt numb. No, not numb. She felt *everything*. Fear, resentment, despair, grief. And something else, a grudging link she couldn't explain.

'Look…like…Christina.'

Her breath snared in her throat at his words.

He turned his head to glower at her, his eyes fiercer than ever.

But now she suspected that look was a mask designed to hide whatever emotions he felt as he stared back at her.

'Sit.' It was an order, despite his weak voice.

Sophie held his gaze, knowing that they were both remembering her mother.

She reached out a hand and drew forward the visitor's chair. Then she sat down beside her grandfather.

CHAPTER ELEVEN

THE SUN HAD dropped out of sight, leaving only the pellucid afterglow of twilight to show the cliff path.

Sophie breathed in the salty air, drawing the aromatic scent of wild herbs and the sea down deep into her lungs. So different from the antiseptic smell of the hospital.

She wrapped her arms tight round herself, hugging back the pain, dismayed at the welter of confused emotions that bombarded her. Each day they grew stronger.

Today had been no different from any other. An early walk along the shore and then her hospital visit. A few minutes' polite, stilted conversation with Costas as she left Eleni's room. Nothing extraordinary. And yet…today she felt raw, rubbed bare by intense emotion.

She should feel optimistic. Eleni looked brighter by the day, was making steady progress. Even her grandfather had gathered strength since her first visit. And a relationship of sorts was developing gradually, almost grudgingly, between them.

Sophie turned her face towards the sea breeze and shut her eyes, seeking peace from her confused thoughts.

Inevitably she saw him. *Costas.* His wide-shouldered frame and smouldering eyes filled her mind as always.

There was no escape, even though they worked hard to avoid each other. He haunted her waking hours as well as her sleep—an edgy, demanding presence that she craved, despite her efforts to be sensible.

He was pure temptation. He couldn't give her what she longed for and she couldn't settle for the little he offered. But the strain of resisting him was almost unbearable.

Especially when he'd tried to make amends. Not just with easy things like the bouquet of ice-white roses and a written apology after their confrontation. Or the offer of an Aegean island tour on his yacht, no strings attached.

No, what she appreciated was far more intangible. The first time she'd visited her grandfather she'd left feeling hollowed out, shocked by the depth of her inner turmoil. She'd emerged from the room to find Costas waiting. Tall, silent and surprisingly comforting. She hadn't even objected when his hand, hard and hot, encircled her elbow and he wordlessly led her away.

They'd walked in silence through the hospital. Costas' expression had been unreadable. But something about his taut features as he'd looked back at her spoke of understanding. Strength and sympathy.

Ever since, whenever she left her grandfather, Costas was waiting. And his solid presence, his unquestioning support, meant more than she'd thought possible.

Sophie opened her eyes, determined to clear it of his disturbing presence. She turned and headed down the steep track to the cove below the Palamidis villa.

There were so many thoughts and fears crowding her mind: Eleni's progress; her feelings for her grandfather; and the dilemma of when to go home. It was time to pick up her life in Sydney. But somehow she couldn't make the decision to leave.

She'd told herself she stayed for Eleni. She'd come to care for her and knew the little girl loved having her around. She refused to dwell on the possibility that it was because of her likeness to Eleni's mother.

Then too, she wanted to explore the tenuous bond with Petros Liakos. She'd told him she must leave soon and he'd welcomed her idea that she return for another visit to Crete.

But above all there was Costas. The man tied her emotions in knots and her mind into a syrupy pulp of yearning. And her body—hell! He only had to come close and all pretence of control left her. It was as if something in her body, and in her soul, came alive only when she was with him.

The light was almost gone when she reached the beach, but the sand was still warm and inviting. She dropped to her knees as the emotions she'd tried so hard to suppress bubbled up.

How she missed her mum! How much she needed her love and guidance. She'd give anything to wake up and find her mother's death had been a nightmare. If only the doctors had diagnosed the illness sooner. If only her mother had listened to her when Sophie had told her to rest. If only the drugs had worked. If only…

Her head and shoulders bowed. She pressed her hands to her eyes, feeling the wetness there as tears streamed down her cheeks. Her mouth slackened, lips quivering till the sobs welled up from deep inside her and she gave in to the force of her grief.

It was dark when she finally raised her head, bereft now of tears. Evening had fallen, like the sudden drop of a curtain. But early stars already bloomed.

The storm of weeping had left her boneless, curiously empty as she huddled there. Eventually she braced her hands on the ground to lever herself up. But her right hand didn't touch sand. It fastened on something soft.

In the gloom she could make out the large, pale shape beside her. A towel.

Clutching the cotton towelling with both hands, she stumbled to her feet, then swayed as the circulation returning to her legs prickled her.

This was a private estate with high-tech security. No tourists allowed here. She turned and stared out into the cove. She'd have seen anyone swimming when she arrived. Wouldn't she? Or had she been too caught up in her own miserable thoughts to notice the quiet stroke of a swimmer? There'd been no one in the shallows. But further out…?

The steady shush of waves on the shore was loud in her ears, she couldn't hear anything else. But then she became aware of movement. A black shape in the sea. It headed straight in to the beach. And now she could make out the faint echo of sound, the splash of a body forging its way through the velvet dark water.

Her eyes had become accustomed to the darkness and she saw the precise moment he reached the shallows and found his footing. His wide, rangy shoulders emerged and he shook his head. Water sluiced, streaming over his massive chest, broad and heavy, down his narrowing torso to a lean waist.

And yet Sophie couldn't look away. Her breath snared somewhere in her chest as she watched Costas—it could be no one else—rise from the lapping waves.

She should call out, warn him that he wasn't alone.

She should turn her back, give him the privacy she'd demand herself.

For even in the deep gloom of early evening she could see that he was nude. No shadow of a swimsuit marred the perfect, athletic lines of his body.

Her breathing faltered, even her pulse stuttered as she stared, transfixed.

He was perfect. Every taut, ultra-masculine inch of him.

He'd seen her. He stopped in mid-stride, still knee-deep in water.

Go. Now!

Drop the towel and disappear as fast as you can.

Her mind screamed at her to run. To take herself off before it was too late. They'd been through this before—the searing physical attraction, the driving need.

It was all he wanted, all he needed from her. He'd never offer her anything more.

Sophie swallowed hard, trying to summon the strength to ignore the potency of her response to him, her own needs. The longer she stood, transfixed by his presence, the weaker grew the voice of self-preservation. Till it became only a blur of white noise buzzing in her ears.

Out of the morass of painful emotion, out of the guilt and grief and doubt, only one thing was absolutely clear to her. How much she wanted this man. Wanted him body and soul. Needed him with a desperation that was beyond understanding. Beyond right and wrong or fear for the future.

She remembered the bliss of his mouth on hers, his hands on her body, his heat against her own. And she wanted that again.

This craving for comfort, *for Costas,* was self-destructive. Foolish. But right now it was beyond her to do anything but stand and wait for him.

She'd been strong for so long. She just couldn't do it any more.

'Sophie.' His voice was as hypnotic as the susurrating waves.

He strode forward till he stood on dry land. Starlight limned the well-defined ridges and curves of his muscled body. The stark angle of his jaw. The bunch of his fists. The heavy fullness of his muscled thighs. His complete maleness.

Sophie gripped the towel tighter in her clenched fingers, feeling the now familiar burst of heat ignite within her. She was trembling hard as she stared back at him unable, unwilling, to look away.

'Sophie.' Her name on his lips was a groan this time, long and low and pained. 'Go away.'

She knew he was right. That in the bright light of day she'd run a mile from the dangerous undercurrents swirling around them.

But, heaven help her, she couldn't fight any more. All she felt was need. Pure, driving need. Nothing else mattered. Not the memory of his brutal words when they'd kissed, nor the pain she'd felt afterwards. She'd lived with loss and hurt so long now that she didn't care about tomorrow. Didn't care about anything but the extraordinary completeness she felt only with him.

He stalked up the beach, silent and sure-footed. Sophie swallowed hard, trembling at his aura of potent energy. He looked bigger than ever. Impossibly masculine and exciting. Some atavistic part of her wanted to flee before him—the embodiment of the primitive, dangerous male hunter.

She could smell the heady scent of musk on his wet skin and wondered how it would taste to her tongue.

Just that wayward thought sent her temperature soaring.

'Don't you hear me?' he growled. 'Go back to the house.'

He was so close she could feel his hot breath against her face and tilted her chin up towards it, closing her eyes. Even straight from the icy Aegean, his skin burned like a furnace. She could feel the heat of his bare flesh.

His breathing sawed heavy and stertorous, louder even than her galloping pulse.

'*Sto Diavolo.*' His voice was a hoarse rasp of despair. 'You would try the patience of a saint! Don't you have any sense at all?' He sounded desperate.

He couldn't be any more desperate than she.

She swayed towards the sound of his voice and his hands clamped on her shoulders, sure and possessive. She sighed at the thrill of anticipation that shot down through her arms, her torso, at his touch. Her nipples peaked in immediate, agonising sensitivity.

'No, Sophie.' Costas' voice rumbled from above her. 'No, we can't.'

But his fingers spread over her shoulders, surreptitiously massaging an erotic message into her flesh. His body communicated directly to hers, and there was no mistaking his intent, despite his verbal denial.

She lifted her hand, reaching out till she felt his chilled, wet, burning flesh beneath the pads of her fingers.

His breath hissed violently as his hands spasmed tight then splayed wide over her shoulders.

Slowly, deliberately, she planted her whole hand against him, skin to skin, and a world of sensation exploded across her palm. She traced the solid ridge of his collar bone, paused at the clavicle and rose to the pulse point beneath his jaw. The life blood throbbed violently there. It raced in a frenzied tattoo that echoed her own heartbeat thudding so hard against her ribcage.

'You mustn't touch—ahh!' His words died as she let her hand slide down over the firm strength of his broad chest, finding the crisp, enticing silk of hair, the thud of his heart hammering deep inside.

His hands slipped then, from her shoulders to her arms, round her back, returning to her neck, her face, pushing into her hair and holding her still.

His kiss was ruthless—his mouth urgent and hard. His tongue aggressively proprietorial as it explored, dominated, demanded her unstinting response.

If she'd had any shred of will-power left to resist him it would have melted at the first erotic, knowing lap of his tongue against hers. At the sensation of his searing breath filling her mouth.

She wrapped her arms tight round his wet torso, pulling herself flush against his blazing heat, his slick flesh. Feeling his solid, unyielding muscles against her skin. His erection pressed long and hard against her. His thighs braced wide enough to encompass her.

It was so exactly *right*. Instinctively Sophie knew this was what she'd wanted from the very first. She and Costas together. That was what she'd craved. What she'd pushed into a dark corner of her consciousness, as if she could hide it away!

The surge of possessiveness that filled her numbed brain was so strong it rocked her. It was even more powerful than the pulsing, urgent need, the wild yearning for more. More sensation. More feeling. More…

'Sophie.' She felt rather than heard him speak her name between their frantic kisses. The sensation of his deep voice thrumming through her, hoarse with passion as he groaned out her name, erased the last tiny vestige of fear that it might be Fotini he was thinking of.

Costas was with *her*, truly wanted *her*.

And there was no doubt in her mind they belonged together.

'Tell me to stop, Sophie.'

How could she send him away when his kisses set her on fire? When his body beckoned hers with such irresistible promise and shivered in response at the very touch of her hands? How could she send him away when he was hers?

Whatever logic said, or the law, or cold common sense, Sophie recognised it now with absolute certainly. Costas was *hers*. This was right.

She sighed into his mouth. This was perfect.

* * *

Costas heard her sigh. Felt it in her warm, fresh breath mingling with his own. Tasted it, sweet and conquering, deep in his mouth.

And he knew he was lost.

He let his hands slide from her silky hair, rove her delicately moulded body as he'd longed to ever since he'd seen her standing there, waiting for him in the twilight.

He'd thought he was seeing things. An apparition come to seduce his waking mind just as she'd come to him every night in his tortured erotic dreams.

But she was real. He lashed his arms tight round her, pulling her against him, imprinting every gorgeous, seductive centimetre of her body against his. She felt too good to be true. Too perfect.

Like Circe, the sorceress who enslaved men with her magical beauty.

No woman had ever been this perfect. Ever.

He shuddered as she smoothed her hands down his back, into the curve at the base of his spine and out, fingers edging over his buttocks.

Instantly his whirling half-formed thoughts blacked out. He was incapable of thinking coherently now. Instead it was instinct that drove him. He kissed her so comprehensively that she bowed back over his arm. Tucked her lower body in against him.

He moved automatically, taking her down with him as he knelt, finding the beach towel with one hand and shaking it out to spread on the sand.

He didn't even break their kiss as he prevented her automatic movement to lie down. Her breath still seared into his mouth as he worked the buttons on her shirt undone, dragged her hands away from him so he could strip the top from her. The bra took only a single, tearing wrench and then his hands found her breasts. Firm, pouting, ripe breasts that she pushed into his palms as she sighed her delight into his mouth.

Oh, lord. He was going to die. She was killing him.

He was never going to restrain himself. Even as he fondled the soft, tantalising fullness of her, palmed and squeezed her hard nipples, his whole being focused on the effort it took *not* simply to strip away her jeans and thrust himself into her like some marauding barbarian.

She pulled away, stunning him with the loss of her soft warmth. Instinctively he followed, finding himself on all fours as she lay back on the towel. Her eyes were unreadable in this light but they were fixed on him.

His heart gave a single, enormous thump that juddered through him.

Then his eyes dropped to her hands, busy tugging down her jeans. Her panties. Revealing a dark triangle of femininity. The tender curve of rounded hips. Slim, shapely thighs.

He'd reach out to help her pull the denim from her legs but he didn't dare. If he touched her…

He shut his eyes, summoning desperate control. Willing himself to exercise some restraint.

But even in the dark he could see her naked before him. Feel again the impossibly soft texture of her breasts filling his hands. Taste her, warm and generous, in his mouth.

Their breathing was loud in his ears. That and the thud of his racing pulse.

He braced himself. Even the sound of her uneven gasps was seductive music to his bewitched senses.

And the scent of her. The fresh, always enticing perfume of her. It was overlaid now with a tangy, musky invitation. Female scent. His nostrils flared and his arms, braced hard against the ground, trembled.

'Costas.' It was the merest sigh of sound. And yet it was charged with the same need that drove him.

He opened his eyes to the woman lying before him. She reached out one slim arm and he felt her fingers trail across his chest.

He surged over her. Covering her completely so that the magic sensation of her warm, soft female flesh greeted him, tantalised him even more.

His breath was expelled in a huge sigh. The fit of their bodies was magnificent. Mind-numbing.

She moved her legs, shifting them outwards so that he felt the smooth skin of her thighs against the outer edges of his own. He let her take just a little more of his weight, allowing his lower body to sink against the feminine core of her.

There was a hiss of breath, his or hers he didn't know. And movement. Friction, deliberate invitation. Had she lifted her hips or had he thrust against her?

He was too dazed by the onslaught against his senses to be sure. All he knew was that he had to concentrate on not moving. Not doing anything. Just till he—

She shifted her legs, sliding her thighs up and around his, encircling him. She reached up, linking her arms round his neck, tugging him down. And of course he went, leaning into her, kissing her feverishly, knowing he could never get enough of her.

The more he got the more he wanted. He was a doomed man.

He drew back slightly, brushing his hand lightly across the juncture of her thighs, slowing to explore the delicate folds there.

Sophie moaned into his mouth and the blood rushed faster in his arteries. The tension in him so immense he trembled with it.

There. His questing fingers struck gold and her whole body jolted. And again.

And then she was urging him nearer. Her legs tight round him, her hands clutching him, her lips fretful against his.

No man could withstand the temptation.

He pressed forward, found her slick and welcoming, pulling him closer, deeper, further. Then with a single uncontrollable thrust he joined them so completely that there was no ending and no beginning.

The shocked, shattering silence held for just a second and then he felt Sophie tremble in his arms. From the inside out it started, until the trembling became her shuddering, rocking climax. And the inevitable, answering motion began in him, so that he withdrew then pushed even further, tighter, faster into her. Till the world shattered in a blur of roaring flames and dazzling light.

CHAPTER TWELVE

ECSTASY.

That was what this was, Costas thought dazedly as he wrapped Sophie against him. Starlight silvered her lithe curves as she sprawled across him—a living, breathing, sensuous blanket.

He knew he should take time to assess the situation, engage his brain. Something nagged at him, some hint of trouble.

His conscience? He should be appalled that he hadn't found the strength to push her away.

The litany of reasons he shouldn't get involved with her: her strained emotional state, her status as a guest and as Eleni's relative and benefactress…the taboos had crumbled to dust when he'd found her waiting for him on the shore.

She'd been pure seduction. Inviting him. Enticing him. *Wanting* him—as much, it seemed, as he wanted her.

He should have resisted, should have been strong for both of them, but it had been impossible.

And there was no turning back now. No help for her, or him, once that first barrier had been breached. One touch and his control had vanished.

And, the good lord help him, he could think of nothing but how miraculous it had been. How miraculous Sophie was. His instinct had been right. They were explosive together. Sex had never been so earth-shattering.

He dropped a leaden hand to the soft spread of her hair across her shoulder.

Mine. All mine.

At least for tonight, he hastily reminded himself. That was all he wanted, all he needed—a night of bliss to counteract the burden of his days.

But was that enough?

He frowned and his hold on her tightened a fraction. She murmured, her warm breath hazing the hollow of his neck and he froze, stunned to discover his body wasn't quite as sated as he'd thought.

He smoothed his hand over her bare skin, savouring the delicious sensation, and his mouth curved into a smile so wide it felt as if it might split his cheeks. Anticipation hummed in his blood.

The night was still young.

He had her now—exactly as he'd imagined so many times. She'd come to him at last, of her own volition, made it clear she understood and accepted his terms. Sex, physical release, comfort—exactly what they both needed.

And it had been worth the wait.

He felt alive again. More alive than he'd felt in years. Than he'd ever felt.

No wonder lightning crackled in the air whenever they were together. The sensual charge between them was unbelievable. Unique. And that made for mind-blowing sex.

His grin grew impossibly wider.

He felt as if he'd been through cataclysm and fire. Death and rebirth. His very bones had dissolved in the intensity of their passion.

But now he was looking forward to the next time. He stroked a hand over her back. She was exhausted. Sleeping. It wouldn't be right to disturb her. Not yet.

But she was getting cold, he realised as he felt goose-pimples on her shoulder. He had no idea how long they'd been lying here in each other's arms, but the night was cooling.

Time to get his lover inside.

This time he knew his grin was smug. The thought of Sophie in his bed, where the lamplight would illuminate each glowing centimetre of her body and reveal every nuance of her response to him…

It was the work of a moment to wrap her in the towel and hoist her into his arms. He strode towards the track up to the house, grateful for the starlight to guide him.

'Costas?' The word feathered across his bare chest, low and tentative.

'Just relax,' he murmured. 'I've got you.'

And I'm not going to let you go.

Even carrying her in his arms came naturally, as if she were designed precisely for him.

'Our clothes—'

'Are safe where they are.'

She was silent a moment and then he felt her palm against his chest, hot like a brand.

'No. I need to get my clothes. I—'

'They're unimportant, *glikia mou.* You won't need them again tonight.' The words heightened the anticipation already humming through his taut frame. He lengthened his stride.

'No!'

His pace faltered at her vehement denial.

'No,' she repeated. 'Someone might see.'

He laughed, relief lightening the sudden tension in his chest. For an instant he'd thought she meant to deny him. 'No need to worry, Sophie. I have my own private entrance. The servants know not to intrude on my privacy unless told to.'

Her hair teased his flesh as she shook her head. Her hand pushed harder against him.

'No! I don't want…' She paused. 'Put me down.'

'No need for that.' He hugged her tight. Revelling in the smooth softness of her body against his where the towel had slipped. 'I know this path like the back of my hand. You don't.'

Already they'd reached the olive grove, a shadowed glade where the darkness was thicker.

'I *said* put me down!' The rapid rise and fall of her breasts told him as much as her words. He stopped, barely preventing an impatient sigh.

Why did women have to get so hung up about inessentials

Hadn't he already promised no one but he would see her? And she couldn't be worried about a pair of jeans! No one was going to steal them.

'Please.'

He could resist her, barely, when she argued with him, when she fought and challenged and defied him. But when she whispered in that low, honey-sweet voice, he had no defence.

He shifted his hold, trying and failing abysmally to ignore the sensation of her bare skin against him. There was minuscule comfort in the sound of her indrawn hiss of breath, telling him she felt the same excitement that held him rigid.

Slowly he lowered her, deliberately letting her slide centimetre by centimetre down his body. The towel dropped away, leaving only the two of them, naked flesh to naked flesh, on fire again with the most primitive of needs.

Blood pulsed loud in his ears, a counterpoint to their ragged breathing. Sweat broke across his skin as he felt her silken body press intimately against him.

Maybe stopping here in the olive grove wasn't such a bad idea. The grass was long and soft, still scented with the day's perfume of wild flowers.

He splayed his hands over her back, down, down, to cup her buttocks and draw her close against him. She shuddered, her hands tightening her hold on his shoulders.

He grinned into her hair.

No, stopping here wasn't a bad idea at all.

Sophie caught her breath on a sigh of abandonment. Of raw pleasure.

Why did Costas' touch excite her so? The feel of his gaze on her? The awareness that they were alone, naked and wanting?

She'd felt desire before. Had some limited experience of it before Costas Palamidis had erupted into her life.

She thought she'd known…

Sophie shook her head. She'd known nothing.

She swallowed a moan of pure pleasure as his big hands

swiped low over her body, pulling her close to his flagrant, heavy erection. The sensation was exquisite.

It seemed only a few minutes ago that they'd had each other, consumed by a need so long repressed it had been combustible.

Yet already he wanted her again. As she did him.

Surely now he recognised it too—the remarkable *rightness* of them together. It was physical desire but it was so much more too. She felt it deep in her very soul.

Something wonderful had happened between them.

Despite the tension drawing heavily at every muscle, her mouth curved up in a smile that grazed the damp skin of his chest. She tasted the salty tang of him on her lips.

There was something heady, something exciting, about having all that raw male power, all that potent energy focused on her. She could get used to—

'Sophie.' His voice was a throaty rumble in her ear as he bent to press his lips to her neck, feather-light kisses up past her jawbone. The tug of his teeth against her ear lobe had her knees buckling and it was only his arms wrapped round her, the strength of him supporting her, that stopped her from falling.

And then she *was* falling. Gently tugged off balance, to tumble forward and land sprawled against him as he lay back on the grass. Her heart raced as she recognised the scent of desire in the air. Her breasts were crushed against his massive chest so she felt the rapid thump of his heart beating time with hers. His hands slid over her, fast, restless, hungry.

And Sophie knew the hunger that had woken in her at the sight of him emerging from the sea hadn't been assuaged at all. The yearning for completion, for fulfilment was far stronger now than before.

Then she hadn't known how it could be. Now she did and she craved it with every cell in her body. That sense of sharing, of bonding, had been so complete it was pure ecstasy.

'Kiss me,' he demanded, dragging her up the length of him. His glorious, hard, aroused body lay beneath her. The friction of flesh against flesh, of teasing body hair against smooth skin, made her gasp. And when he pulled her head down to his, it was for an erotic kiss, tongue laving tongue.

He tasted like every dream come true. Potent and strong and sensuously, darkly sweet. Sophie cupped his face in her hands, loving the slightly abrasive temptation of his jaw, the hint of a tremor in his hard hands as she kissed him back.

'Yes!' The single sibilant word hissed in her ear as she moved to kiss his chin, his cheek, nuzzle his neck, nip at the sensitive flesh of his ear.

Costas' hands slid down, shaping the indent of her waist, slowing at the curve of her hips, grasping her bottom and pulling her against him, hard and blatant in his need for her. Against her ear he whispered a stream of Greek, of words she barely registered. But she understood enough to know he was describing her power over him, his need for her, and exactly what he wanted to do with her.

His voice was the most exciting thing she'd ever heard, urging her on as his hands tightened on her hips, his thighs nudged hers wider, till she felt soft meadow grass beneath her knees. And at the centre of her was him.

He waited. Let her choose her own pace. Only his deep voice, throbbing low and sensuous in her ear, his hands clamped possessively on her hips, told her of the urgency of his need. And the feel of him, hot and hard beneath her.

She levered herself up with her hands on the ground near his shoulders. She gasped as he took her breasts in his hands, petting them gently, then not gently at all, till she cried out at the exquisite delight that shuddered through her, so close to yet so different to pain.

And then he was suckling her. He made her squirm against him, her head thrown back so she could gulp down shuddering breaths of meadow-scented air.

'I can't get enough of you, Sophie,' he murmured against her breast. 'Never enough. You make me burn like I've never burned before.'

She looked down at his dark sculpted face, strong even in the deep shadows. Saw him take her nipple in his mouth, felt the sweet pang of delight spear through her, and felt the trembling begin in every part of her body.

It was the sight of him. The feel of him. But more, there was something else, some powerful connection that drew her to him, linked her invisibly but inexorably to him. That met his need with answering need, desire with desire. And melted the brittle barrier of icy grief around her heart.

Emotion swelled within her. She wanted to cradle him, hold him, pleasure him.

Love him.

She felt protective, possessive and more turned on than she'd ever been in her life.

'Costas…' She needed to tell him, make him understand how she felt. This was so momentous, so extraordinary.

Then he was kissing her, plundering her mouth with a raw hunger that sent fire shimmering through her veins, urgency pounding in her brain.

It took all her strength to break their kiss and draw back. He lay below her, dark eyes fixed on her, his massive chest heaving. As desperate, as wanting as she was.

Sophie reached down to slide her fingers round him. Her eyes widened as she realised just how well-endowed he was. He'd felt stupendous before, but now…

His hiss of indrawn breath was loud in the stillness. 'Don't Sophie!'

The power she felt was exciting. She was heady with it. He throbbed in her hands and something clenched deep inside her. The sight of Costas, obviously at the edge of his control, was intoxicating.

'Why? Don't you like it?'

For answer his hands cupped her bottom and he pulled her closer, until all thought of games fled her mind and there was only need. His hands were urgent, his body thrust against her and she sighed at how good he felt.

'Do it!' he growled, his voice hoarse. 'Now!' He lifted her up, urging her against him.

For a moment she strained, poised above him, delighting in the sensation of him watching her with hooded eyes, knowing he was as excited by the sight and feel of her as she was by him.

And then she couldn't wait any longer. She sank down slowly. Deep inside she felt him. Tighter, fuller, impossibly more than even the last time.

'Costas?' Her voice trembled with doubt.

'Sh, *Sophie mou.* It's all right,' he whispered. 'I'll make it all right.'

And he did. His hands swept over her, came up to cup her breasts, squeezing gently in a way that loosened every tensing muscle in her body. And from beneath her he pushed up steadily, deliberately, creating waves of erotic sensation that swamped her senses.

His rhythm increased and automatically she matched it, rising and falling against him in a quickening pace that pounded relentlessly in her blood. She felt the muscle-packed strength of him beneath her, surging into her. The callus-hard caress of his hands on her. The sound of his breathing, as laboured as her own. And his eyes. She felt their heat on her as she moved above him.

She felt like a queen. Powerful, commanding. She felt…

Her breath snagged as the surge of sensation caught her suddenly, overpoweringly. Each movement was exquisite torture, pushing her higher and closer. She grabbed for Costas, her hands grasping his wrists as he held her breasts. He bucked up harder against her, the heavy weight of his thighs pure power against her legs.

And then she exploded. Reality came apart in one shattering, shuddering moment that rolled on and on, prolonged by the insistent rhythm of his body.

When at last the sensations eased he pulled her down hard against him, expelling her breath with his force.

She lay over him, his heart throbbing beneath her, his hot breath riffling her hair, his body so powerfully alive beneath her, within her. The smoky musk aroma of aroused male filled her nostrils. His arms wrapped tight round her as if he'd never let her go. Even when she felt his tempo increase to fever pitch, he held her close. He pulsed, warm and throbbing within her, exciting her with a primitive satisfaction.

Suddenly, out of nowhere, the tension spiralled in her again, drawing her with him into a shared experience of fulfilment.

They were so close they were one. His climax was hers. His body belonged to her. *He* was hers.

She loved him, she realised.

She loved Costas Vassilis Palamidis. The arrogant, caring, tender, proud man who'd taken over her life in every way.

Should she feel shock? Disbelief?

Drowsily Sophie smiled, delighting in the feel of his hot, silky skin against her lips. She didn't feel anything right now except a sense of rightness.

Bliss.

Sophie half opened her eyes and protested. Costas still held her close, his heart beating steadily beneath her, his arms holding her. She wanted to snuggle in against him, stay like this forever, but something had changed.

She had it now, the steady rhythm that lulled her, kept her in a lazy haze of well-being. It was the feel of him striding, cradling her in his arms.

She fought to lift her eyelids, to check where they were. There was a light somewhere, making her slit her heavy lids against its brightness. He shifted his hold, pressing her face in against his collar-bone, where she caught the salt scent of the sea and man. Drowsily she pressed her open lips against his skin, loving the tangy taste against her tongue.

He shuddered, holding her tighter till she was consumed by the sense of him all around her. He muttered something she couldn't catch.

Then there was a sudden whooshing sound behind her, making her blink her eyes wide open.

They were in a room, the lights concealed around the rim of the ceiling as she looked over his shoulder.

A bathroom, a massive bathroom, warm with the glow of

rosy tinted marble, glittering from the light reflecting off enormous mirrors and gold fittings.

'Shower with me, Sophie.' His voice rumbled beneath her ear. He leaned forward and she felt a haze of warm spray sprinkle her shoulder.

That woke her from her lethargy. She opened her eyes wide, staring straight into Costas' gaze. This time she had no trouble reading his thoughts. Mischief danced in his black eyes just as surely as it curved his strong, sensuous mouth in a smile that stole her breath.

Her heart seemed to swell as she stared back, mesmerised by his male beauty, and by sheer delight.

It was too much.

These feelings, the wondrous knowledge of this new emotional bond between them, of love…it was too much. Surely her heart would burst out of her ribcage.

She loved him so. Adored him. Even down to the smug anticipation lighting his expression.

He was definitely a man with but one thing on his mind. She took in his expression. Lust. Anticipation.

Out of nowhere fear jagged through her brain. Remembered pain.

Her body tensed as insidious doubt wormed its way into her brain. Could she be wrong? Was it possible she'd made a mistake? That his passion was, after all, only skin-deep? As shallow as a simple desire for a bed partner.

Could it be that he hadn't experienced the revelation she had?

Goose-pimples rose on her arms as a sudden chill encompassed her.

As she watched, his smile faded. His face grew serious, as if he could read her doubt and fear.

'Sophie,' he murmured. 'You're like a light in the darkness.' His voice was hoarse with emotion. A mirror to her own overwhelming feelings. His eyes held the same wonder. 'I can't imagine what I've done to deserve you.'

He leaned down, pressed a lingering, tender kiss against her lips.

Sophie shut her eyes, knowing that here, in his arms, she'd come home. She hadn't made some terrible mistake.

This was where she was meant to be.

Hungry for his caresses, even more for his love, she linked her arms up round his neck, tugging him to her.

The kiss escalated from gentle to lush. From lush to languorously seductive. And then to passionate. Desperate.

It only ended when he stepped into a huge shower compartment and warm jets of water sprayed across them.

'You can put me down,' she spluttered, wiping a lock of wet hair back from her face.

He did, lowering her slowly to her feet, and then keeping his hands on her arms, holding her steady as she swayed.

She watched the water sluice down, plastering his dark hair to his head, glistening on every curve and angle of his hard chest, highlighting every masculine plane and curve. She sucked in her breath on a sigh of sheer wonder.

Costas lifted a hand and smoothed her hair back over her shoulder, his hand lingering to curve around her neck, splay-fingered in a possessive hold.

Sophie couldn't stop the smile that shaped her lips as she leaned close to his touch. She was acting on instinct and instinct told her this was the most wonderful experience of her life.

He stepped closer, reaching round behind her then holding out a cake of soap in his hand.

'I've been wanting to do this ever since the first time I saw you,' he said, his voice husky.

She remembered him that first day. All soaking-wet muscle and barely suppressed impatience as he'd forced her under the shower. Even then, sick and grief-stricken, she'd barely been able to take her eyes off his magnificent body.

And now…she had the right to do more than look.

Mesmerised, she watched him lather the soap between his hands, slowly, methodically, and then reach behind her to put it down. His breath was warm against her face as his hands, slippery with soap bubbles, skimmed across her collar-bone.

down the curve to her breasts, where he slowed and circled, till she bit down on her lip to stop from calling out. She reached for his shoulders, needing his strength to stay upright as the slow, erotic swirl of his hands weakened her knees.

'There are so many things I've been wanting to do with you, Sophie.' His voice was a low rumble and his smile was taut as his hands smoothed a path down her ribcage, into the indentation of her waist, out across the flare of her hips and then lower.

CHAPTER THIRTEEN

SOPHIE NEVER WANTED to move. She could stay like this forever.

She was sprawled in the largest, most luxurious bed she'd ever seen. The rich cotton sheets were soft against her skin. Her body felt light, almost weightless, but at the same time ultra-sensitive, after hour upon hour of lovemaking.

Even now she felt a warm curl of satisfaction deep in her belly at how well-loved she'd been.

No wonder she didn't have the strength yet to raise her head or open her eyes.

Last night Costas had been so voracious in his need for her. Under his tutelage she'd responded uninhibitedly. They'd taken each other to peak after peak, as desire was rekindled time and again.

He'd been boldly demanding. Outrageously seductive. Fiercely passionate. And incredibly tender.

He'd brought tears to her eyes more than once. And the way he'd watched her so intensely, refusing to turn out the light precisely, he said, because he needed to see her. She shivered, remembering the intensity of his regard. At first she'd been reluctant, preferring to hide her responses to him. But then she'd discovered just what he meant, as she watched him lose control for her. Just for her.

That was the reason she felt so good.

It wasn't just the sex. It was the bond, so strong now between them that she *knew* he felt it just as much as she did.

Maybe this time when he woke there'd be time for conversation, for declarations.

She wriggled, snuggling down beneath the sheet.

It took her a while to realise that for the first time since she'd seen Costas stalking out of the sea towards her, she couldn't feel him. All night he'd been close, touching, embracing, stroking. Teasing. As if he couldn't bear her as far as arm's length from him.

Which had suited her just fine.

Sophie swiped her foot across the bed.

Nothing.

She frowned and dragged her hand across the sheet till her arm stretched across the centre of the mattress.

It was cold.

She frowned. The bathroom? She couldn't hear anything. But the rooms were soundproofed. Heat scorched her throat and cheeks as she remembered Costas reassuring her last night that she could be as loud as she liked and no one but he could hear.

She opened her eyes and saw it was morning. Not only that— it was late. The glare of full sun rimmed the curtains. She rolled onto her back and found herself alone.

A cold weight settled in her stomach, pressing down.

Ridiculous. There was nothing wrong. Costas was probably in the shower, maybe even waiting for her.

She threw back the sheet and crawled to the end of the bed, aware now of the dull, delicious ache of muscles rarely used. She was a little self-conscious by the time she reached the door to the *en suite* bathroom. But that was ridiculous. After all that had happened between them there was no need to be.

Nevertheless she paused and knocked.

No answer.

She rapped harder with her knuckles, waited for the door to swing open and Costas to smile down at her, his eyes glittering with secret promise.

Eventually she opened the door and walked in. The bathroom was empty.

Again she felt that heavy, plunging sensation in her stomach.

Not foreboding. Just a need for food. She'd have it as soon as Costas returned. He'd probably gone onto the balcony for some fresh air.

Sophie crossed to the bedroom window and opened the curtain enough to see the large balcony. It was empty too. She repressed a frown. He'd gone downstairs to get some food for them. That was all.

She swung away and turned towards the bed. And stopped.

On the floor beside where she'd lain was a neat pile of clothes.

Slowly she paced towards it, recognising a T-shirt and a pair of jeans that had just been washed—they'd only been put in her wardrobe yesterday. Undies, bra, even a pair of flat-heeled sandals and her hairbrush.

Suddenly Sophie found herself sitting in a club chair near the bed. These weren't the clothes she'd worn yesterday. Costas had dressed, gone to her room and found something for her to wear then left the bundle by the bed. All without bothering to wake her.

What sort of message was that?

Blankly she stared, trying to work out what had happened. Trying so hard not to jump to conclusions. She wasn't well-acquainted with the rules for dealing with the morning after.

But then she hadn't thought of this as a *morning after*. She'd been so sure it was a new beginning. Not an ending.

She sucked in a breath, holding her palm against her ribs where a stitch caught her. A dull ache started up somewhere deep inside.

Eventually she moved. Took her time showering, dressing, brushing out her knotted hair. All the while waiting for the sound of a door slamming open, the quick, decisive stride she'd come to know so well. The deep, sensuous voice that had urged her to ecstasy.

Costas' room remained stubbornly empty. As was hers. As was the whole upper floor.

He's gone to the hospital, she told herself. That must be it.

Anxiety bloomed in the pit of her stomach. Had Eleni taken a turn for the worse? Was there a crisis?

She shook her head, striving to control her breathing. No. If it was serious Costas would have told her, or left word. She knew he would have.

So why hadn't he woken her? Told her he had to leave? Or even scribbled a note? Why leave her to wake alone and wondering?

She frowned as she stared at her watch. It wasn't breakfast she'd missed. It was lunch too. She'd been so exhausted she'd slept more solidly than she had in weeks.

Which meant Costas had probably been gone for hours.

By the time she descended to the ground floor Sophie felt unseasonably chilled, as if the cold had gone bone-deep despite the bright sunshine outside.

No one in the dining room, or the sitting room, or—

'*Kalimera, thespinis.*'

Sophie swung round to see the housekeeper emerge from the servants' quarters.

'*Kalimera sas,*' she responded, her smile shaky.

'You have slept well, yes? Would you like some food?'

'I'll wait, thanks,' she said. '*Kyrie Palamidis* and I had some things to discuss. I'll wait and eat with him.'

The housekeeper tilted her head, her expression puzzled.

'But the *kyrios* left the house hours ago,' she explained. 'He visited the hospital first. Then he rang to say he'd decided to take some business meetings. He won't be back until this evening. You take a seat and I'll bring you a nice meal, in just a few minutes.' She smiled and nodded and turned back the way she'd come.

Which was just as well. Otherwise she'd have known something was terribly wrong when Sophie stumbled blindly to a hard-backed chair and collapsed onto it.

One shuddering breath. Another.

Sophie forced the air down into her lungs. She felt the excruciating stab of pain straight to her heart.

She knew now why Costas had slipped away. And stayed away all day. As far as he was concerned nothing had changed. And there was nothing more to be said between them.

Sex. That's what I want. That's all I want.

She slammed her hands over her ears but nothing could stop the hateful memory of those words echoing in her head.

I want to forget the world for a single night. Sex and ecstasy and animal pleasure.

Scalding tears welled in her eyes as she remembered how ferociously he'd responded to her last night. Just how much *animal pleasure* he drawn from her willing body through the long hours of darkness.

When she'd stupidly thought they were making love.

No relationship. No future.

The words were a death knell to her fragile hopes.

She'd been a fool last night, carried away by the strength of her need. By her *love* for him.

Stupidly she'd believed that because she felt far more than lust, Costas must now too. But nothing had changed for him.

She choked back the bitter taste of despair.

She knew exactly where she stood with Costas Palamidis.

CHAPTER FOURTEEN

COSTAS MANOEUVRED THE car around another swooping curve on the road home. He kept the powerful engine at a moderate speed, unwilling to follow his inclination and floor the accelerator. There was no need to hurry, he assured himself. That would be a sign of weakness.

He was a man who'd always prided himself on his strength of character. And he would not weaken now. No matter how great the incentive.

But he permitted himself a smile at the thought of the delicious temptation awaiting him at home.

Sophie.

Generous and ripely seductive. A revelation even to a man of his experience. Never had he possessed a lover who turned night into glorious, dazzling day for him. Who made his blood sing and his senses swim. Who stripped him bare of all civilised refinement and reduced him to mindless ecstasy.

Was it any wonder he'd been careful to keep his distance today?

A man needed to retain some control, some perspective. He couldn't allow a love affair, however delightful, to cloud his judgement. He had responsibilities. A daughter to care for. A multinational business to direct.

No. He needed to remember that a lover could not be permitted to take over his life.

He'd woken to the pearly dawn light and to a sense of such

fulfilment, such peace and such fizzing anticipation, that it alarmed him.

Hell, it had *terrified* him! He could admit that to himself at least.

He'd felt the smooth curve of Sophie's waist beneath his palm, smelt the love-scent of her, heady in his nostrils, and knew he never wanted to leave her.

Hell! What sort of nonsense was that?

An illusion left over from the starlight when she'd come to him like a goddess out of the darkness. When she'd been the lover he'd yearned for. Absolute perfection.

He shook his head, to clear it of the fantasy that even now clouded his thinking.

She'd played havoc with his thought processes. With his self-control. For a while there she'd even tempted him into thinking he needed more from her. Something other than sexual satisfaction and the blissful, mindless release it brought.

The woman was too dangerous.

So he'd left her. A tactical withdrawal.

He shrugged. He hadn't exhibited any finesse, or even his customary good manners. Instead he'd left her to wake alone. He'd been more brutal, perhaps, than strictly necessary. But he didn't want her harbouring illusions. He wasn't after a permanent relationship.

But an affair—mutually satisfying—now, that was something completely different.

He felt the unfamiliar stretch of facial muscles as his mouth curved into a smile.

Time and again today he'd found himself succumbing to temptation: reaching for his keys, calculating how long it would take to drive home, race up the stairs and find her. Perhaps she'd even be in bed, waiting for him, as eager for his touch as he was for hers.

But no. It was late afternoon. She'd have vacated his bed hours ago.

He'd deliberately kept away long enough to ensure there was no misunderstanding between them. He didn't want her expecting more from him than he was prepared to give.

His nights would be hers, as long as it suited them both. But by day he had other duties. He ignored the fact that he'd just cancelled his last meeting so he could hurry back to her. He was a man, after all, not a machine. And no sane man would opt for a late-afternoon meeting when he could have Sophie instead.

He ignored too the guilty suspicion that he'd made his point too blatantly. He could have called her earlier and explained he'd be away all day. He could have left her a message this morning. In fact, he could have woken her when he left their bed. Except he'd been scared that he might be tempted to remain there, heedless of all else.

Costas had never experienced a craving that could compare with his appetite for this one woman. He didn't know how to handle it.

Had he been a coward? Had he hurt her?

No. He'd been decisive, sensible. He'd started as he meant to go on. He knew Sophie, so open and honest, would appreciate that in the long run.

And after all, she'd waited for him on the beach last night. Clearly she now accepted his terms: no emotional ties, no plans for the future.

If she was disappointed this morning, well, he'd found it hard to leave her too. And he'd make it up to her.

Anticipation clenched his stomach muscles as he slowed for the electronic gates to open then nosed the car onto his private road.

Fleetingly this morning he'd felt guilt that he'd taken advantage of a guest under his roof. But he hadn't been able to sustain the remorse, not as the memories flooded back of the incredible night they'd shared.

It had been debatable who had seduced whom down on the shore. She was a natural siren, luring him to forget his scruples, his hesitation, everything but the need for her in his arms.

His breath snagged in his chest. He imagined her lying in sated abandonment in the centre of his bed. Waiting for his touch to bring her to passionate life again.

His foot slid forward on the accelerator as he pictured himself igniting her passion with his hands, his mouth, his body. He wanted her again. But then he'd wanted her all night and all day. Had been aroused time and again by the scent of her arousal, the magic of her flesh against his and the slumberous eroticism of her heavy-lidded eyes when she woke to his caresses.

Her absolute responsiveness had stunned him, urging him on to want, to take more than he ever had from a woman before. And she'd revelled in it, answering his desire with her own urgent need, provoking him to love her longer, harder, more completely than he'd thought possible.

He ached as hunger, unabated and white hot, took hold again.

He'd received excellent news today from Eleni's doctors. The best news. And he knew just how to celebrate it.

'Yes, *kyrie,* she went out some time ago, towards the sea, I think.' His housekeeper paused, frowning. 'She didn't look well. She was so pale, and she hasn't eaten anything, not even a morsel.'

Foreboding slammed into him, carving a hollow in his stomach. He'd *known* something was wrong. Had sensed it as soon as he'd failed to find Sophie in the house.

'Ah, here she is now,' said the housekeeper, tilting her head. Then he heard it, the sound of the front door and Sophie's light step across the foyer. 'Shall I—?'

'No. It's all right.' He was already turning away, ignoring the speculative gleam in his housekeeper's eyes.

He strode down the hallway, but Sophie had disappeared from the entrance hall. He took the stairs two at a time, an atavistic presentiment of trouble urging him to hurry.

He pushed open her door and there she was, wearing the clothes he'd chosen for her this morning. And somehow that fact was even more intimate than all last night's desperate loving.

Home. I've come home at last.

Something warm and tender, a stunning new sensation, curved tight in his chest as he looked at her. It held him spellbound for one long moment.

Then common sense reasserted itself and he breathed again.

Lust. That was what he felt. Simple. Uncomplicated. Easily assuaged.

Her hair fanned round her shoulders as she spun to face him.

He remembered the scent of those tresses, the impossibly soft texture of them sliding through his hands, teasing his flesh.

His automatic step towards her ended abruptly and he pulled up short, surveying her drawn face. His hand dropped to his side and a different sort of tension clamped his body into immobility.

Her face was a rigid mask. Her mouth clamped hard as if in pain. And her eyes—they were huge and shadowed.

'Sophie? What's wrong?' A piercing shard of fear sliced into him as he looked into her eyes. She was hurting, surely. He could barely believe it was the same woman he'd left warm, willing and satisfied in his bed.

'Nothing's wrong.' Her voice was light and high, but brittle as glass.

She opened her wardrobe door and bent to deposit a pair of sandals inside. When she turned round there was a wash of colour high on her cheekbones. It only accentuated the unusual pallor of her face.

What on earth was going on?

'Where have you been?' he demanded. Something must have happened in his absence.

'Just down to the beach.' She spun on her foot and headed for the bathroom, a bundle of clothes in her arms.

He'd taken just two paces when she came back, her hands empty this time.

'I was collecting my clothes from last night.'

Now the sweep of colour extended down her throat. She didn't meet his eyes but stood alone, staring blankly over his shoulder as if the sight of him pained her.

He frowned, trying to ignore the urgent clamour of his senses that urged him to march over and sweep her into his arms. He wanted to comfort her, for something was clearly, awfully wrong. Yet the way she held herself, as if a single touch might shatter her, held him back.

'You're back early,' she said at last and he heard the faintest echo of something—sarcasm—in her tone.

Ah, that was it. She objected to being left alone all day—was feeling neglected.

Costas brushed aside the voice of his conscience—the voice that agreed with her. That insisted he'd behaved appallingly.

This was no hard-edged business rival he faced, nor was it the immature, self-centred woman he'd made the mistake of marrying. This was Sophie: sweet, honest and caring.

But that didn't matter, he told himself again. He'd done the right thing. He didn't have time for emotional entanglements. He was simply being honest with her, making sure she didn't read too much into their intimacy.

Perhaps in his haste to get away, to put the situation in per-spective and make sense of his intense reaction to her, he'd been brutal. But that could be remedied.

His pulse quickened at the prospect of soothing her ruffled ego.

'I had a lot to do,' he began.

'Of course.' She nodded. 'The hospital. And your business. You must have work to catch up on after all the time you've spent away from it.'

His brows pulled together in a frown as he tried to read her blank expression. An uncomfortable sensation clawed at him.

Guilt? After all, he'd manufactured those meetings this after-noon—seeking an excuse to keep away. He didn't do business personally in Heraklion any more. He worked from offices in Athens and New York, or here at home, where the latest telecom-munications equipment allowed him to keep in touch with his worldwide enterprises.

He wasn't accustomed to using subterfuge. The feeling made him uncomfortable.

'You're not annoyed?'

He scrutinised her reaction, strangely piqued that she should accept his neglect so easily. Where was her fire? Where was the passionate, intense woman who'd captured his…interest… from the first?

'Why should I be annoyed?' She stared straight back at him and shrugged, wide-eyed and with palms spread towards him.

'You're a very important man with a commercial empire to run. And I...' She swallowed suddenly and blinked. 'I was tired. I slept for hours.'

Something wasn't right. Despite her direct look, despite her words, something was definitely amiss. He took a step towards her.

'But I must admit,' she said quickly, jutting her chin, 'where I come from it's customary at least to thank the woman you've spent the night with.' Her eyes blazed now, scorching him where he stood. 'To do it in person is best. But a note or at least a phone call would suffice. It's considered bad manners to lope off without a word.'

Her words rooted him to the spot. Not because of the searing temper he read behind them—that was almost welcome after her unnatural calm. But the implication of what she'd said—*where I come from...*

She was lecturing him on post-coital etiquette—with the insouciance of a woman who knew just what she was talking about.

A surge of white-hot jealousy rocked him. It was so intense and immediate that he clenched his fists against the need to find a violent outlet for his feelings.

How many men had shared her bed in Australia?

Did she care for any of them? Even one of them?

The thought of Sophie, *his* Sophie, with another man, *ever,* was untenable. He shook his head, trying to clear the red fog of rage that blinded him.

'That's not something you'll need to worry about again,' he growled, closing the distance between them with a single stride. 'There'll be no more men in your bed.'

'Are you including yourself in that?' Her brows arched haughtily as she tipped her head up to meet him head-on.

'Don't play games, Sophie. You know what I mean.' He gathered in a huge, sustaining breath. The depth of his jealousy, and its suddenness, made his head spin. He reacted instinctively. 'You're mine now. There won't be any other men in your life, much less anywhere near your bed!'

She glared back at him, her eyes flashing gold fire. Her nostrils flared and her hands fisted on her hips as she stood, toe to toe against him.

What a woman she was! Beautiful and strong and passionate. The sexiest woman he'd ever known.

His woman, intoned the possessive voice that had echoed in his ears all through the night.

'I don't think that's any of your business,' she said, her words slow and deliberate.

He scowled. What sort of nonsense was this? 'Of course it's my business. You and I—'

'What makes you think you have exclusive rights over me?' Her brow pleated in mock-concentration and her head tilted to one side as if to reinforce her point. 'I don't remember any discussion of that last night.'

'There was no discussion last night. We didn't—'

'Then perhaps I should make it clear to you now,' she said, just as if he hadn't spoken. 'I'm my own woman, Costas Palamidis. I don't belong to you. Or to any other man.' She stared past him, at a point somewhere over his shoulder. 'Last night doesn't entitle you to determine anything at all about the way I live my life.'

The blood pounded loud in Costas' ears, a deafening roar that almost obliterated the last of her declaration. Almost, but unfortunately not quite.

She was exerting her independence.

From him!

He gritted his teeth against the primitive howl of rage that welled in his throat.

This woman drove him crazy, awoke the most barbaric of impulses in him. He could fully understand the urge of less civilised men to keep their women cloistered at home. Preferably tied to the bed.

'Surely,' he said at last in an unsteady voice, 'you're not trying to convince me you're promiscuous.'

He caught the horrified expression in her eyes and repressed a satisfied smile. 'I'd find it hard to believe you're the sort of woman who keeps a couple of guys on a string.' Despite what he'd originally thought.

There, he'd called her bluff and it had worked, that was obvious from the sag of her shoulders and the way she bit her lip. He wanted to reach out and brush his fingers over that luscious bottom lip, ease the hurt with the caress of his own mouth. And then perhaps lead her a step or two back towards the mattress, so conveniently located just behind her.

'You're right,' she said, but her voice was tight. 'That's not what I meant.'

Her gaze slid from his. She took a slow breath and he watched her breasts rise with it. He wanted her naked. Now. His eyes flickered to the bed. He was already planning how he'd have her when her voice jerked him back to the present.

'You made it plain what you wanted from me. A single night, you said.' Her eyes met his again and something slammed hard into his solar plexus at the expression he saw there. 'You wanted sex. That's all. Sex and release.' Molten gold burned in her eyes, brighter with each word.

'Well, you've had your night and now it's over.'

'You must be joking. *Glikia mou!*' He spread his hands in a gesture of amazement. 'After last night you can't expect this to stop so easily. The way we were together…it was incredible.'

A perfunctory smile curved her lips for an instant then disappeared. 'I'm glad you thought so. But nevertheless it's over.'

Costas shook his head, dumbfounded as never before. Sophie was *rejecting* him? After all that had passed between them last night?

It was impossible. Unbelievable.

His eyes narrowed as he took in her wary stance, the rapid rise and fall of her breasts. She was hoaxing. That was it. She was trying to bargain for more. He'd wounded her pride with his clumsy behaviour this morning and now she wanted him to grovel.

He wouldn't grovel, but he'd apologise. After all, she deserved it. He'd behaved like a lout.

'*Sophie mou.*' He lifted his hand towards her and was stunned when she stepped away from him.

He frowned. There was no need to play hard to get. He was a reasonable man, after all.

'I apologise for leaving you the way I did this morning. I should have woken you, or rung earlier in the day. I—'

She shook her head. 'There's no need to apologise,' she interrupted, though the over-bright glitter of her eyes belied her words. 'Last night was wonderful, but now it's finished. As you said, we both needed the release. And now we can go our separate ways with no regrets.'

Slowly the words penetrated his stunned brain. And then *déjà vu* cannoned into him, like a blow to the gut.

The expression on her face, the challenging stance and jutting chin. Just so had Fotini looked when he'd confronted her with his concerns about her safety. About her late-night celebrations with dubious new friends, about his suspicions that her herbal 'pick-me-up' tablets were something far more dangerous. She'd been defiant, amused, uncaring.

He swiped a hand over his face, trying to dislodge the memories and the devastating seed of doubt they planted in his mind. Two girls from the same family. Two women from the house of Liakos.

Was the independent spirit he'd so admired in Sophie a blind for something less palatable?

No! He didn't believe it. This was Sophie, sweet and caring. Not Fotini.

'It's over,' she reiterated. 'And now it's time to move on.' And with the words she turned away from him, as if to leave.

His hand shot out and circled her upper arm before she'd even taken a step. Her smooth flesh was warm beneath his fingers, soft as silk. But not as soft as her belly, or the indescribably tender skin of her inner thighs.

'No!' He stopped, trying to get control over his voice. 'It's not over, Sophie.'

She lifted her face and for an instant her expression was vivid, bright, like the sun in summer. And then a shutter came down, hiding her thoughts.

Costas groped for words, tried to get his brain into gear. But all he could think of was that she'd done the impossible—had rejected him, decided she wanted no more from him than a one-night stand.

The seductive, feminine scent of her skin made his nostrils flare and his blood quicken. It only fed his confusion and anger.

'What if you're pregnant?' he bit out.

He saw the flicker of shock in her face. Felt her stiffen beneath his hands. For an instant her eyes blazed with golden light, and then she turned her head away.

'And that would change things?' Her voice had an oddly muffled quality.

'*Sto Diavolo!* It would change everything. A child…' He paused, dragging in a deep breath. He'd said the first thing that had surged into his numbed brain. But now the idea had lodged there.

How could he want another child when he had Eleni? How could he face the possibility of such trauma again? But despite the fear, he recognised excitement tremble to life in the pit of his stomach.

A child. His and Sophie's. An invisible hand squeezed his heart. What a gift that would be.

'You know I take my family responsibilities seriously.' Somehow he managed to keep his voice even as he looked down at her.

'Then it's just as well that's not a possibility.'

'Of course it's a possibility,' he thundered. 'We had unpro-tected sex, not once, but several times last night.'

That was what had been at the back of his mind down on the beach, the vague notion of something not right. But it hadn't stopped him. Lord help him, even if he'd realised at the time, he doubted he'd have been able to pull back from her. His need for Sophie had been elemental, unstoppable.

He looked down into her staring eyes. Had she been too caught up in their mutual passion to realise he hadn't used a condom? Inevitably the idea pleased him, softening his temper into something else. His iron hard grip on her arm loosened and he slid his fingers down her tender flesh, stroking. She trembled under his touch as she always did.

Abruptly she tore herself away and paced over to the windows, presenting him with her hunched shoulders. Something—pain—twisted deep inside him at her rebuff.

'There's absolutely no chance I'm pregnant,' she said in a cold, precise voice that speared him like a knife.

Bright sunlight blurred her outline, and for an instant it was another girl who stood there. Another bloodless voice that echoed between them, taunting him.

Memories again. Stronger this time.

He'd married Fotini because he'd decided he needed a wife. But the marriage had held none of the peace, the trust or even companionship that he'd expected would grow with time.

And now he'd ignored his better judgement, shoved aside every caution and succumbed to the temptation of this woman, Fotini's cousin. She was like fire in his blood, destroying his logic and his self-control.

Two girls so different.

But could there be similarities as well?

Nausea churned in his stomach at the possibility.

'What if you're mistaken, Sophie?' He forced the words out, sickened by the fact that he even had to ask. 'What if you *are* pregnant? Would you expect me to pay for the abortion?'

CHAPTER FIFTEEN

SOPHIE HAD THOUGHT an hour ago that she could bear the truth. Just. But this was torture. Listening to the man she loved. Yes— the man she *loved,* lashing her heart with his blatant contempt.

What more did he want from her?

He'd taken her body. He'd taken her trust, her love, her tentative hopes and dreams and trampled them underfoot.

Oh, it hadn't been his fault. He'd warned her, had been totally honest. He'd told her in no uncertain terms that his need for her was at the most basic, physical level only. He'd left her under no illusion that he wanted a relationship with her.

It had been her own naïve fault that she'd succumbed to him with such self-destructive passion. Hurting as she was, needing comfort and overwhelmed by feelings she'd never before experienced, she'd turned to him.

And then, when it was too late, she'd assumed that the situation had changed, that he felt it now too—the bond between them.

How could he *not* feel something so powerful?

She'd given herself joyfully, loved him with her heart and soul, not just her body.

And today she'd woken to the harsh truth. She'd deluded herself. He simply didn't love her.

So she'd gathered the tatters of her self-respect about her and decided not to let him see how much she was hurting. Her plan was to escape, soon, with her dignity intact if possible. She'd remove herself far from his vicinity in the hope that time might heal her battered heart.

She'd been coping, just, with the trauma of seeing him again. It had been virtually impossible but she'd hidden her emotions as best she could.

But now he'd turned into a vengeful stranger and she didn't think she could keep up the pretence of indifference much longer.

'Answer me, Sophie! Would you come to me to fund an abortion?'

'That question doesn't deserve an answer.' Stubbornly she stared out the window, eyes blinking at the bright blue cloudless sky. The serene, blazing Greek sun half-blinded her—mocking her pretensions in ever hoping for a future with this man.

A large hand grabbed her elbow and Costas swung her around so abruptly she almost fell. But he was so close, his other hand already supporting her, that she merely stumbled. The inevitable tremor spread from his touch along her arms, reminding her of those hours not long ago when his caress had been searingly tender, heartbreakingly gentle.

And she hated her weakness in remembering.

His eyes fired with unholy anger as he thrust his belligerent face towards hers. Every plane, every angle was harsh and unforgiving.

'Answer me!'

Fear scudded through her, now she was up close to such potent rage. She could feel his fury in his hands, clamped so hard on her arms that she had pins and needles from the restricted blood flow. She could smell it in his blood-hot masculine scent, taste it in the heat of his breath on her face.

But she refused to be cowed. His anger fuelled her courage. How dare he talk to her like that?

'And which part of that scenario would bother you most, *Kyrie Palamidis?* The abortion itself or me asking you to foot the bill?'

'*Christos!*' He shook her once, twice, as a flurry of fierce Greek split the air.

Sophie's head swam as she stared up into his dark face. She

didn't recognise the man she saw. He looked as savage, as dangerous as a predator, moving in for the kill.

'You will not dispose of any child of mine as if it were some inconvenience,' he snarled.

'And you will stop making insulting assumptions about me,' she gasped between strangled breaths. Fruitlessly she tried to wrest herself from his punishing hold. Now, before the emotion clogging her throat welled into shameful tears.

She'd done nothing wrong. She didn't deserve his contempt!

'I am *not* pregnant with your precious baby,' she spat at him. 'And even if I were, I wouldn't consider a termination.' She stopped to drag down air into a chest so tight she couldn't seem to fill it with oxygen. 'More than that, you're the last person I'd ever accept money from.'

Her hair swirled round her face as she struggled to break his grip. She was so frantic to escape she didn't notice the way he shifted his weight, crowding closer.

'Enough! You will hurt yourself if you don't calm down.'

Inexorably he drew her arms back so he could shackle both her wrists in his hands. She was no match for his strength. She couldn't prevent him from bowing her back over his other arm.

She was helpless against his power. And against the savage determination she read in his eyes.

'Let me go—' Her protest ended in muffled outrage as his mouth blocked hers.

Savagely he kissed her, like some rapacious thief, plundering so thoroughly that she could barely breathe. He bruised her lips, invaded her mouth with a blatant, masculine possessiveness that stamped his domination on her.

Shock held her in its grasp and she almost choked on a sob. There was no tenderness here. No shred of the magic that had enthralled her last night. This time the hard length of his body was a weapon, crushing her into absolute submission.

After her hopes and tender dreams last night, she felt defiled. The pain of her disillusionment was so raw she thought her heart would bleed.

'Sophie.' The unrelenting pressure abated a fraction and his words feathered across her swollen lips. 'You make me wild. I can't believe…'

Hot kisses trawled down her chin, her neck, to her collar-bone. He pressed his mouth to the tender flesh there, sucking gently till she shuddered in unwilling response. He knew every erogenous zone on her body—he'd spent the night learning each one.

To Sophie's horror she felt the familiar electric charge of excitement skitter through her. She was trembling, but not solely with outrage.

He took her mouth again, but gently, so tenderly that she might have been some fragile, breakable treasure. He slid his lips along hers as if seeking permission to enter. His tongue flicked out, drawing her opposition from her.

His hand came up to hold her breast, squeeze it, sending another heated, frantic response through her nerve-endings. Dimly she registered the hollow feeling between her legs. The wanting. His caress slowed as he circled her nipple, just as his tongue stroked her mouth.

She moaned and felt the caress of his arm at her back, cradling her against him.

Suddenly desire was a swirling, dazzling force within her, loosening every taut muscle, leaving her body defenceless, willing, even when she *knew* she had to resist. Feebly she fought the onslaught against her senses.

'*Glikia mou,*' he whispered, his voice so deep she felt the words as much as heard them. 'You make me mindless, Sophie.' His fingers tightened on her breast and sensation juddered through her. 'I want you. Now.'

If he hadn't spoken he might even have got what he wanted. She was aroused, eager, panting for him.

After all he'd said and done!

The realisation shamed her with the knowledge of her appalling weakness. But his words penetrated her numbed brain even as her body responded ecstatically to his caresses. That was when she discovered he'd released her wrists.

Adrenaline surged through her, stiffening her resolve and her body. She shoved with all her might, bringing her knee up sharply in a vicious thrust that should have crippled him.

But his assault on her senses had weakened her. Either that or he could read her mind. He side-stepped just as her knee slammed up. She was off balance and would have fallen if it weren't for his hands pulling her upright.

'Don't touch me!' She shrugged out of his hold and stumbled back a few paces. 'Don't come near me,' she gasped, chest heaving for breath. Her heart hammered like a set of pistons.

'Sophie.' He paced towards her and she flinched.

'Stay away!'

'You don't mean that.' His voice was a low, persuasive murmur. It made her skin prickle, eager for the delights he could bestow.

'I mean what I say. I don't need some arrogant male to tell me what I want.'

'Sophie, I know you're upset. But it doesn't have to be like this. You know how good it is between us.'

She shook her head. He saw her as a convenient lay. Better than a sleeping tablet to get him through the long nights.

'I don't want you to touch me. Ever.'

He crossed his arms. His legs were already planted wide apart and he looked impossibly big and powerful. What hope did she have if he refused to listen? She didn't trust her treacherous body not to respond if he tried to seduce her again.

There was a knowing glint in his eyes and his mouth twisted up at one side. 'I know how much you want me, Sophie. How you burn for me.'

He stalked closer as he spoke, the words rolling off his seductive tongue in a murmur that made her body tighten. 'I've never had such an eager lover.'

She gritted her teeth. 'How do I get through to you? One night was enough and now it's over.' She stared hard into his glittering eyes and deliberately played her last card. 'Unless you intend to use force.'

'What are you talking about?' His brows dipped into a ferocious scowl. 'You must know I would never use force on a woman.' He drew himself up to his full looming height and looked down his nose at her. As if she'd dared to insult him!

'Then what do you call this?' She thrust her arms out in front of her, silent witness to the power he'd unleashed to hold her still. Red marks encircled each wrist. There was no pain. Not now. But there'd be bruises soon.

His face froze and his golden skin paled. She watched his convulsive swallow as he realised what he'd done.

'I must apologise,' he said in a stifled voice. 'It is no excuse to say that I didn't realise how tightly I held you. But be assured you have nothing to fear. It will never happen again.'

She let her arms drop to her sides, curiously drained. 'Let it end,' she pleaded, feeling the weight of emotional exhaustion descend onto her shoulders. 'It was…nice, while it lasted. But I don't need a relationship any more than you do. Not now. It would be too messy.'

She turned away, hoping he wouldn't call her bluff. Not now her eyes had filled with useless tears.

'We've both been through a rough time and last night—just happened,' she said, whispering to conceal the wobble in her voice. 'But now I need to get on with my own life.' She wrapped her arms round herself, squeezing as if she could force back the pain welling up inside her.

If she could just hold on until he left her alone.

'You're right, of course.' His words were clipped, precise, his voice a stranger's. 'Since neither of us is in a position to want more than physical release from a partner, it's best if we put last night behind us.'

Each word bit into her, carving away the last of her defences. She'd been right. Absolutely right. How foolish of her to cling to that final, stubborn hope that Costas would object. That he'd swear it was more than lust between them. That he felt tenderness for her, even love.

She squeezed shut her eyes and bit her lip, praying for the strength to see out this scene without giving herself away.

She had nothing left. Nothing at all but the remnants of her pride.

The silence was so loud it pulsed between them. But she didn't dare turn round. She knew her anguish would be obvious in her face.

And then she heard it—the sound she'd been praying for. And dreading. The sound of his measured pace crossing the room. The quiet, definite click of the door behind him.

Costas Palamidis had done what she asked and walked out of her life.

CHAPTER SIXTEEN

LEAVING THE NEXT DAY was harder than Sophie had expected.

Not that she'd had to confront Costas again. By mutual consent they'd avoided each other yesterday evening. The house was big enough to accommodate them both in perfect isolation. And she hadn't sought him out today after she'd packed her suitcase and organised a lift into town.

She'd wondered if he might try to prevent her leaving, persuade her to stay. Her pulse had raced at the possibility, wondering if she'd have the strength to resist his persuasion if he exerted himself. But he'd already taken an early-morning flight to Athens to deal in person with some urgent business. His housekeeper had been flustered, concerned at her departure while the *kyrios* was away.

But to Sophie it was a tremendous relief. She could pretend she was glad not to have to face him again. That it would be easier this way. No embarrassing farewells, no regrets.

A pity she didn't really believe that.

Instead, as the villa disappeared behind her, she felt stretched too thin, as if she'd left some part of herself behind. The part she'd left with Costas.

And then she had to face the hospital farewells. Her grandfather already knew she was only in Crete for a short time. He said nothing when she explained about the flight today. But she'd seen the disappointment in his eyes. Which only made her feel worse.

Despite his treatment of her mother, and his antiquated views, he was family. She couldn't turn her back on him completely. Her eyes prickled as she squeezed his hand and promised to visit again when she'd tidied up her mother's affairs.

She'd be back. But under her own steam this time. And she'd make a point of steering well clear of Costas Palamidis. Might even take her grandfather up on his gruff offer to stay with him when he was released from hospital.

The farewell to Eleni was no easier. Sophie hadn't realised how close they'd become until she had to say goodbye. And the little girl's stoic smile, just a little wobbly, was almost Sophie's undoing.

But what could she do? It was impossible to stay in Costas' home any longer. And the thought of seeing him every day, as she would if she continued to visit Eleni, was untenable.

She'd planned to leave soon anyway. She couldn't put her life on hold forever, even for such a little sweetie as Eleni. The parting had always been inevitable. But that didn't make it any easier.

She wondered if she'd be able to see Eleni again when she returned to Greece, and yet avoid Costas.

Hell! What a mess this was.

Yet she had no doubts about what she was doing. For her own sanity she had to leave. Now. She couldn't afford to torture herself, being so close to the man she loved and couldn't have.

She'd done the right thing, pushing him away. Of course she had. She wasn't cut out for an affair. She wanted a future. The chance of lasting happiness with someone who cared for her as much as she loved him.

Another night in the Palamidis mansion might just destroy the final tatters of her self-respect. Even now she couldn't risk the temptation to be alone with Costas. She was so weak-willed when it came to him.

'*Thespinis?* Are you all right?'

Sophie blinked back hot tears at the sound of Yiorgos' words and fumbled in her bag for sunglasses.

'I'm OK, thanks. The sun is so bright, isn't it?' She turned her head and watched the outskirts of Heraklion slide by. Soon now she'd be at the airport. But she wouldn't relax till she was off the island. She had enough money to get to Athens. Then she'd visit the embassy. Find out how she could finance the flight to Sydney. Surely they'd lend her the money? And she could pay it back when she got home.

Home.

That empty house didn't feel like home any more. The sooner she sold it and found a little flat the better. She could organise another trip to see her grandfather and then look around for permanent work. Speech pathologists were always in demand.

The car slid to a halt at the airport entrance. By the time she fumbled her way free of the seat belt, Yiorgos had collected her bag and held the door open for her.

'Are you sure, *thespinis,* that you're all right?' His handsome features puckered in a concerned frown.

'I'm fine. Thanks.' She dredged up a smile and held out her hand for her bag.

'No, no!' He was horrified. He clasped the suitcase close then gestured for her to precede him. It was unthinkable, apparently, for her to be left alone to enter the airport.

Yiorgos remained with her through the flight check-in and would have stayed longer, she was sure, except for a peremptory summons on his cellphone. The way he snapped to attention convinced her it was Costas on the line. Her heart lurched, realising this was the closest she'd ever come again to the man she loved.

She pushed back her shoulders and walked away to find a seat while she waited to board the plane.

The wait went on and on. Too nervous to sit for long, she paced continually, but the time crawled by. Eventually she looked at her watch and realised the flight should have been called. Had she missed it?

No. It was there on the board. Delayed.

Sophie bit back a frustrated oath.

So there was a slight delay. It didn't matter. It wasn't as if she had a connecting flight booked. All she had to do was get into

Athens and find a cheap *pension* for the night. Then tomorrow she'd visit the embassy and everything would be settled.

'Miss Paterson?' There was a discreet cough behind her and she swung round. Two men stood there. One in uniform and the other in a grey suit that strained over his rotund form.

'Yes? I'm Sophie Paterson.'

'Excellent,' said the man in the suit. She saw a flash of gold as he smiled. 'Would you mind coming with us, please?'

'What's wrong? My flight is due—'

'Nothing is wrong,' he assured her, gesturing for her to accompany them. 'The flight is delayed but not for much longer. In the meantime,' he led her across the waiting area towards an unmarked door, 'there is a message for you.'

'For me?' She swung round. Who could have left a message for her? She gazed at the plump little man beside her but got only an unctuous smile. And the uniformed guy behind him looked so serious she felt a thrill of fear skitter up her spine.

'Are you sure there's not a problem?'

'No, no.' The man beside her opened the door and gestured for her to precede him. 'As I said, just a message.'

He ushered her into what was clearly an interview room. Furnished only with a table and a couple of chairs. Automatically Sophie wondered what was wrong.

She swung round just as the door closed behind her. The guard hadn't come in. She assumed he was stationed outside the room. The idea made the hair prickle on the back of her neck.

'If there's a difficulty with my papers—'

'No, no. Nothing like that.' Again the stranger smiled, spreading his arms wide. 'Please, take a seat.'

'I'd rather stand, thank you.'

He tilted his head to one side. 'As you wish. I will just be a moment.' And with that he let himself out of another door. One she assumed led into the airport offices.

The room must be soundproofed. She couldn't hear anything. Not the people waiting for their flights nor the hum of engines. The realisation chilled her. She didn't know why she was here.

Or for how long. What if she missed her flight? It was the only one to Athens this afternoon. She didn't want to stay on Crete another night.

Sophie bit down on her lower lip. Panicking wouldn't help her. Whatever the problem she'd sort it out. She hadn't done anything wrong, after all.

The door opened and she swung round.

Her heart leapt into her throat and she would have stumbled if she hadn't grabbed on to the back of a chair.

Costas stood framed in the doorway.

'Sophie.' He paced towards her and the walls of the small room seemed to close in around her. His face was unreadable but the tense set of his shoulders was eloquent.

'What are you doing here?' Her voice sounded rusty.

'I need you.'

His dark velvet eyes held hers and the world tilted. He needed her?

'No.' She shook her head, holding the chair in a death grip.

But his gaze was so intense she felt as if he delved into the very heart of her, reading the secret she tried so desperately to hide. Her knees trembled as she looked up into his stark face.

'Yes.' Something pulsed between them. Raw and desperate. 'We need you Sophie.'

'We?'

'Eleni—'

'She's worse?' Sophie swallowed down the hard knot of anxiety that blocked her throat. It had only been a few hours since she'd left the hospital. Eleni had been fine then, though upset about Sophie's departure. Had she taken a turn for the worse?

Costas' face was grim as he held out his hand. 'She needs you. Now. You wouldn't deny her, would you?'

'But I can't. I have a flight.' She gestured helplessly to the other door.

Costas' hand sliced through the air between them. 'That means nothing. I can book you onto another flight when this is over. If you want.'

She stared up at him, noting the drawn look around his mouth, the stiff set to his jaw. Whatever had happened was life-and-death serious. Her anxiety notched up another level. Poor, brave little Eleni.

'You promise?'

'When you want a flight I will personally see you on board.'

She believed him. Whatever else he might be, Costas was a man of his word. He'd been straight down the line with her. No prevaricating, no dressing up the truth with convenient euphemisms. He said what he meant.

'But why me—?'

'It's you she needs.'

Sophie frowned. Eleni had grown attached to her—it had been mutual, after all. But surely Eleni's father, her grandparents, were the ones who should be with her now?

'It's time we left.' He stepped close, stretching out his hand as if to take her arm. She felt the fierce heat of his body reaching out to her, but then his hand dropped to his side. He maintained a small but telling distance.

And she was grateful for it. Even this close the tension seemed to shimmer between them, the air charged with a force that she couldn't hope to ignore.

'I'll have to make arrangements for my luggage.'

'It's been taken care of.' He motioned for her to lead the way out of the room. 'It's all in hand.'

'In hand?' In the act of walking out the door she stopped and spun round to stare at him. 'You did that without even asking me?'

'Sophie.' She'd never heard this dreadful urgency in his voice before. 'It was necessary. Believe me. This is an emergency.'

His face was set hard. But something about his eyes told her this really *mattered*. More even than her heartbreak. Or her pride. Pain radiated from him. And more than that—uncertainty. That was so remarkable it convinced her as nothing else could.

Eleni's condition must be serious.

His pain tore at her already lacerated heart. She shook her

head, wondering helplessly how she could feel so much for a man who didn't want her. How had *his* pain become hers?

But so it was. Despite everything—her anger and her hurt—she didn't want him to suffer. Not with the raw agony she saw staring back at her from his proud features.

His arm wrapped round her shoulders and he propelled her towards the door. His hold was light, but she sensed the steel behind it.

Her body reacted predictably. A tremor started somewhere deep inside her, spreading out until she was weak with barely suppressed longing.

The short man in the grey suit was in the corridor, waiting for them. 'Everything is all right, *Kyrie Palamidis?*'

'Yes.' Costas reached out and shook his hand, but kept his left arm around her. 'Thank you for your assistance. I regret the inconvenience.'

'But that is nothing. Nothing at all. It was a pleasure to assist in such circumstances.'

'And it was greatly appreciated.'

The other man beamed.

'Now we must leave.' Costas was already ushering Sophie down the hall.

'What inconvenience?' she asked as they emerged near the airport entrance.

The muscles in his arm bunched around her as they walked rapidly towards the exit. 'Holding up your flight.'

'What?'

'It was easier to have you and your luggage taken off the plane before it departed than having it turn around.'

She stumbled to a halt and stared up into his face. He wasn't joking. 'You'd do that?'

He shrugged and somehow the action pulled her closer to him, close enough to recognise the hard, tantalising strength of his superb body. For his natural scent to tease her nostrils and ignite a flare of forbidden desire in her feminine core.

'Of course. If it was necessary.' The commanding tilt of his head, the arrogant line of his nose and the decisive glint in his eyes told her he wasn't joking. This was a man to whom power was a natural extension of his will. He wouldn't baulk at using it when it suited his needs.

She'd known he was influential. But would he really be able to have a jet turn around in mid-flight?

'*Ela*. Come, Sophie. This is not the place.'

Of course not. Eleni needed them.

'OK. Let's go to the hospital.' She stepped forward, shrugging to remove his hold. For a moment she thought he wouldn't let her go. His arm clenched tighter round her. Then, to her immense relief, it dropped away. She breathed easier, glad of even this minimal space between them.

Yiorgos was waiting beside the limousine, his face anxious. He broke into a strained smile as they both appeared.

'The luggage?' Costas prompted as he ushered her into the spacious back section of the vehicle.

'Already in the boot, *kyrie*.'

And within seconds they pulled away, leaving the airport behind. The privacy screen slid up, blocking them off from Yiorgos, emphasising the empty silence in the vehicle. Sophie slid to one corner of the wide back seat, well away from the daunting presence of the man beside her.

Her emotions were a confused jumble. Fear for Sophie. Numb horror that she had to face Costas again after what had passed between them. And, could it be? Yes, relief that she wasn't leaving Crete just yet.

From the moment Costas had appeared in that bare little room and demanded she accompany him, it had been so unreal. For one cruelly short moment she'd really thought he'd come because he needed her himself. Because he couldn't bear to let her go. The idea had brought a fizz of searing excitement to her bloodstream.

But she'd known, as soon as he mentioned Eleni, that it was his daughter who needed her. That was why he'd brought her to Greece after all. Her disappointment had been so acute that for an instant she'd even thought of refusing to go with him. But she could never turn her back on Eleni. She loved the little girl. Almost as deeply as she loved Eleni's father.

Sophie's heart sank at the idea of an emergency severe enough to recall her from a flight to Athens.

She turned her head towards the window, blindly staring out at the passing scene.

Costas sat back in the opposite corner, watching Sophie. His heart still pounded from the adrenaline in his bloodstream. He'd barely been in time to prevent her departure. It had been so close it scared him.

Now she was here, secure in his car. He waited for the sense of satisfaction to come. After all, he'd got what he wanted. Almost. She'd followed him like a lamb once he mentioned Eleni.

But he felt no lessening of the tension that gripped him in its vice. There were no self-satisfied congratulations.

For Sophie looked miserable, hunched like a prisoner in the corner. Exhaustion etched shadows in the contours of her face and her shoulders slumped heavily. His gaze dropped to her hands, clasped tight in her lap, and he shuddered.

On one arm she wore a wide, beaded bangle. But her other arm was bare and his stomach lurched at the sight of the bruise ringing her delicate wrist. Nausea welled in him.

He'd done that. He'd hurt her—used his physical superiority to try controlling her.

Costas drew a ragged breath, stunned at the evidence of his barbaric behaviour. In all his life he'd *never* used force on a woman. The very idea was anathema. Even in those darkest days, when Fotini had driven him to despair and lashing fury, he had never come close to touching her in violence.

How could Sophie ever trust him after such a disgraceful act? No man of honour would do such a thing.

But then his honour was a tainted thing, wasn't it? He'd taken advantage of her in the worst possible way. She'd been so vulnerable. So deserving of his protection. A guest. The donor who was saving his daughter's life. A member of Eleni's family. A woman grieving her own terrible loss and far from home.

Any one of those considerations should have ensured he treated her with absolute courtesy and care.

But none of it had mattered enough to stop him.

Guilt slashed him. He'd been no protector. He'd been insane, consumed by his own rapacious need and his determination to have her on *his* terms.

He'd been ruthless, so desperate in his craving for her that he'd thrown away his honour to possess her. He'd subjected her to the risk of pregnancy without a second thought. In fact, some deep-buried part of him exalted in the possibility that she might be pregnant to him.

No wonder she hadn't waited to say farewell in person but had taken the opportunity to sneak away while he was absent. He should never have—

'What's going on?' Sophie swung round from her contemplation of the scenery to fix him with accusing eyes. 'This isn't the way to the hospital.'

Even in her confusion, with a frown marring her features, her beauty made his throat constrict.

'No, it's not,' he said, relieved that it was time to sort this out, once and for all. 'I'm taking you home.'

CHAPTER SEVENTEEN

HOME? THE WORD echoed in her ears. Home was an empty bungalow on the other side of the world.

And this was the coastal road leading to the Palamidis villa. The place where she'd known such hopes and such appalling disappointment.

Sophie stared into Costas' eyes. They were almost black—a sign, she'd learned, of strong emotion. And the way he looked at her—hungrily, so intensely that she should be frightened.

Her breath caught. Sensation shivered down her spine.

Just so had he gazed at her two nights ago when he'd loved her so wondrously.

'What's going on?' Suspicion flared as she took in his utter stillness. He was tensed, completely focused on her, like a predator watching its prey.

'You're not taking me to the hospital, are you?' Realisation came in a rush. But even so she couldn't quite believe what her brain was telling her.

'Not yet.'

'How is Eleni's condition?'

He hesitated infinitesimally. 'Physically she's doing re-markably well. She'll be coming home to us soon. But she was terribly upset about your plans to leave.'

'You lied to me.' The accusation was a whisper. Even in the face of the evidence Sophie couldn't imagine Costas telling an untruth. 'You deliberately made me believe Eleni's condition was worse.'

'All I said was—'

'I know what you said, damn you,' she gasped. 'How could you be so cruel? You made me think…'

Suddenly he seemed much closer, his wide shoulders and his dark, compelling face filling her vision. He reached for her hand, his fingers hard and warm, but she wrenched out of his grasp.

'I told you that we needed you.'

'And you lied.'

'No, I spoke the truth. We need you. Both of us.'

She shook her head, denying the flicker of hope in the chilled recesses of her heart. She was tired, so tired she couldn't cope with this right now. But one thing she knew without doubt: Costas Palamidis did not need her.

'Don't lie to me. I won't play your games.'

'It is no game, Sophie. Only once have I told you an untruth.' His gaze held hers and she couldn't look away. 'When I said I wanted you for a single night only. Do you remember?'

Oh, she remembered all right. Heat scorched her cheeks at the memory.

'It wasn't true, Sophie. I want more. So much more.'

Now it began to make some sort of crazy sense. Costas wanted more. And what Costas wanted Costas got. He'd decided one night wasn't enough. She supposed she should feel complimented that he found her so attractive.

But she didn't. She felt…sullied. It was her body he wanted. Not *her*.

He leaned close, his scent and his heat and his aura of energy encompassing her. But she had no difficulty pushing him away. Hard.

'Stay away from me,' she panted. 'I don't want you near me.'

'Sophie.' He reached out a hand and she slapped it back. The contact made her palm sting.

'Stay away!' Her voice rose. 'If you think I want anything more to do with you, you're wrong.'

Despite its luxurious size the limousine felt claustrophobically small. There wasn't enough air for them both in the charged atmosphere. And though he didn't touch her, Costas' very presence crowded her. His energy was a palpable force.

Suddenly he reached away from her, to a control panel on his side of the car. The screen between them and the driver slid down and Costas shot out some orders in rapid-fire Greek. Then the screen slid into place again and Costas turned back to her.

The car slowed and turned. But instead of swinging round in the direction they'd come from, it slid to a halt off the road. Dazed, Sophie stared out the window. She recognised this place, a little glade on the edge of an ancient olive grove. They'd left the main road and were already on Costas' estate. She hadn't even noticed them slow to pass the security system on their way in.

She heard Yiorgos get out and automatically reached for the door. She didn't know why they'd stopped here rather than at the house, but the sooner she got out into the fresh air, where she could put some distance between herself and Costas, the better.

Even as her fingers closed round the handle there came the soft, decisive click of the door locks engaging.

She swung round. Costas had his hand on the control panel.

'Unlock the door.'

'Soon. When we've talked.'

'We have nothing to discuss. It's all been said. We both know where we stand. And now I'd like to leave.' Her heart pounded against her ribs and her breathing shallowed as she fought to maintain an appearance of calm.

'There is still much to discuss, Sophie, before we both know where we stand.' His voice was deep and smooth but she heard the strain in it. 'You will be free to leave once we've discussed what's between us.'

She shook her head. 'You can't do that. You can't hold me against my will!'

'Only until you hear me out.' He reached for her hand and held it between both of his. She didn't bother to struggle—she knew his strength would win out. So she concentrated instead on pretending to ignore the barrage of sensations flooding her at his touch. The heat, the sizzle of delight, the ravenous need.

How could she respond so mindlessly? And to such a casual caress? She tilted her chin high. 'Then I hope you're prepared to face trial for abduction.'

He ignored the threat.

Horrified, she watched him raise her hand to his mouth, felt the caress of his lips against her flesh and almost closed her eyes at the memories evoked by the sensation. How her body still craved him.

'I mean it! I'll lay charges. And then what about your reputation? Think of the talk, all the rumours. The stain on your good name.'

'You must do as you think appropriate, *after* we've talked,' he murmured against her wrist and turned her hand over to kiss her palm.

Darts of fierce desire shot along her arm, arrowing straight to the hollow, aching core of her need. Her taut muscles loosened as his tongue lapped, rough velvet against her sensitive skin.

She struggled to focus. 'I don't want you. Don't you understand that? Where is your pride?' Surely that, if anything, would get through to him.

He looked up, his head still bent over her hand. His eyes were so hot she felt their incendiary heat burn deep inside as he met her gaze.

'*Agapi mou,* you need me as much as I need you. I was a fool yesterday to think I could ever walk away from you.'

He leaned closer, looming over her, and she fought the absurd impulse to bury her head on his shoulder and wrap her arms tight round him.

'Yiorgos will see us.' She was desperate for anything that would stop his inexorable assault on her senses. On her self-control.

'Yiorgos is already walking to the house.' His breath was hot on her face as he leaned closer still. 'We're on my private property. No one will disturb us. And anyway, the tinted windows give us privacy.'

Privacy for what? Her mind raced as she read the raw desire in his stark features.

'No!' Frantically she shoved against the rock-hard wall of his chest. But it was like pushing against unforgiving granite. 'I don't want—'

His mouth on her lips stopped her voice. His tongue stroked against hers, inviting the response that shivered just a breath away. He leaned into her, pressing her back into the soft corner of the padded seat, his hands roving, skimming her body as if frantic to rediscover her.

He didn't use force. If he had she would have been able to fight him.

But the devious brute used gentle, erotic persuasion. And that weapon, in this man's hands, was unstoppable. Sophie didn't have a hope.

She tasted him in her mouth, inhaled the tangy scent of him, felt the shiver of delight wherever his hands caressed. The fiery heat of his body was like a magnet, drawing her closer, inciting a passion so strong it overruled every last remnant of her will-power.

Their night of intimacy had merely set the seal on the emotion that had been growing inside her over the past weeks.

This was the man she loved. The man who'd stolen her heart. So bold, so strong. Handsome, tender, protective. The most sensitive, daring, passionate lover a woman could wish for. Her weak body, even her mind, worked against the memory of the devastating pain he'd inflicted on her.

No matter how far she ran. Even if she escaped back to Sydney, she'd never be free of her feelings for him.

He only had to take her in his arms, seduce her with the incredible tenderness he wielded so easily, and all her defences shattered.

She sighed into his open mouth as his hand brushed her breast, teasing, tempting, till she pressed forward and felt his palm close round her.

Her hands locked round the back of his neck and she didn't protest as he pushed her down against the seat. She sensed the urgency in him as his breathing changed, the rhythm of his heart hammering against hers quickened. His hands grew heavier, more urgent as they stroked her, lingering on the buttons of her shirt.

Sophie knew what he wanted. Here, in a parked car in broad daylight. And, lord help her, she wanted it too. Just one last time.

She'd regret it later. But she had no more lies left inside her. She couldn't pretend any longer.

He'd won.

She turned her head and nuzzled the hollow of his neck, breathing deep of the masculine scent of his arousal. His skin was steamy with the energy of sexual excitement.

'Sophie?' He lifted a hand to her cheek, his thumb brushing the skin below her eye.

'Ah, *Sophie mou.* Don't cry. Please don't cry.' His voice was a hoarse groan of pain.

She blinked and registered the scalding tears spilling down her cheeks. Tears for her discarded hopes.

There was a surge of movement. Strong hands, an even stronger body against hers. And then she was sitting up. But not on the luxurious limousine seat. Instead she was cradled on Costas' thighs, sitting sideways across him, pulled in close against his massive chest, her head resting on his shoulder and his arms wrapped tight around her.

He was trembling, his whole body tense and shivering beneath hers.

'I hurt you.' His words were a whisper against her hair. 'I'm sorry, Sophie. I've been a monster. I don't ever want to cause you pain again.'

She felt a hard sob well inside her at the sincerity in his husky voice. He might not want to hurt her but he couldn't help it. It was inevitable when she craved so much more from him than he could give.

Wordlessly she shook her head and leaned closer to him. Ridiculous to find comfort in the embrace of the man who was at the core of her unhappiness, but so it was.

'I want to take care of you, Sophie. If you'll let me.' She felt the deep breath he drew into his lungs. 'I don't want you to leave. I want you to stay, with Eleni and me. Always.'

No. It wasn't true.

'Marry me, Sophie?' His hand stroked her hair, gentle and almost tentative. 'Marry me and live here, with us?'

For an instant she felt burgeoning joy. And then it was quenched as she registered the implication of his words.

For a single, glorious moment she'd forgotten that Eleni was the sole reason he'd brought her to Greece. Eleni had to be the only reason he was proposing now. He loved his daughter and he'd do anything, even marry, to make the little girl happy.

'No,' she whispered when she found her voice.

'No!' His voice was a muted roar. So much for his unaccustomed humility. 'What are you saying?'

'There's nothing between us,' she said and pulled herself away from him. He loosened his hold a fraction so she could sit up straight, but he wouldn't let her go. Typically stubborn. Well, she could be stubborn too.

'Nothing but sex.' She stared straight into his night-dark eyes as she said it, hoping he'd believe her.

'How can you say that?' His brows furrowed in a savage frown that highlighted the severe angles of his face.

'It's the truth.'

'You're lying, Sophie.'

Her gaze slid from his, down to the clean line of his jaw. 'You can't keep me here against my will indefinitely.'

'And what about Eleni? You would just leave her, because you are angry with me?'

'I…care for Eleni, very much. But you'll find someone else to look after her. You don't need me to do it.'

'You think I want to marry you so you can take care of Eleni?'

She shrugged, her eyes dropping from his jaw to the precise knot in his dark silk tie. 'It's convenient. Eleni likes me. And I remind her of her mother.' She let her glance skitter to his and then away again. Each word was bitter in her mouth as she forced herself to continue.

'No doubt I remind you of your wife. It's a neat solution from your perspective. But it's not what I want.'

Silence throbbed between them. Sophie held herself taut, perched on his lap, wishing against all common sense that he'd haul her close and tell her she was the only woman for him.

She really had a self-destructive streak where Costas was concerned.

'I should have told you about Fotini before,' he said in a deep voice that echoed hollowly between them.

'No!' That was the last thing she wanted to hear. 'There's no need to tell me.'

'There's every need.' His arms encircled her, hauling her close again. And, against her best intentions, she felt the heady delight of being held in his embrace. One last, tiny piece of paradise to enjoy before she left.

'That first day when you opened the door to me, it was as if I saw Fotini's ghost. The resemblance was remarkable.'

Sophie squeezed her eyes shut, pain slicing through her as he confirmed her fears.

'There were differences between you too. But in my mind I saw you as just like her.' He dragged in a deep breath, his chest pushing against her. 'That's why I refused to trust you at first.'

What? Sophie struggled to sit up straighter and meet his eyes, but his arms tightened like warm steel about her, locking her against his chest.

'I jumped to the conclusion that you'd been taking drugs. And when I told you about Eleni, when I offered you her legacy as payment to help her, that was my prejudice showing again.'

He'd been prejudiced *against* her because she reminded him of his wife? Sophie's mind buzzed with questions.

'It was only as I got to know you that I realised how wrong I was.' One hand circled her shoulder, caressing spiralling warmth into her rigid body. 'I found you were generous, caring. And honest.' He sighed, his breath a ripple of warmth through her hair.

'You were nothing like Fotini except in the most superficial of ways. And even that physical similarity faded as I yearned for you. Only you. For your bright eyes so fierce and passionate. For the touch of your hand.'

Dazed, Sophie heard the emotion in his voice, felt it in the tremor that ran through his body and in the brush of his hand on her shoulder. But she couldn't take it in.

'The night we kissed. *Christos!* That night I was terrified at how completely you made me lose control. I would have taken you right there in the hallway. I'd never experienced anything like it. I didn't trust myself not to ravish you. Every argument I'd used to keep my distance disintegrated once I held you in my arms. I had no defence against you. So I behaved brutally to push you away.'

His hand curled round the nape of her neck and pulled her in even closer. 'It was all I could do to prevent myself taking advantage of you.'

Taking advantage? That was how he'd seen their blaze of mutual passion?

Sophie struggled to loosen his embrace enough to sit back and look into his face. It was sombre, eyes dark with turbulent emotions.

'You insulted me, made me feel like a cheap tart, just because you didn't trust your libido?'

He winced as her words burst out. 'I couldn't trust myself to protect you any longer.'

'*Protect me?*' Her voice rose with outrage at the memory of her pain.

'And were you *protecting* me when you used me then shoved me aside later like something shameful? Were you protecting me when you accused me of planning an abortion? When you wanted me as a convenience in your bed?'

'You are right,' he said in a voice deep with shame. 'I am a man without honour. I have treated you appallingly.'

He drew in a tremendous breath and met her gaze. The emptiness, the ingrained despair she saw there, chilled her to the bone.

'I couldn't believe what I felt for you,' he said. 'It was beyond my experience and I reacted badly. I didn't want to believe what I felt. Tried to pretend I didn't believe in love.'

Love!

Was this some cruel joke?

'It was only after you rejected me yesterday, after I began to realise how much I'd hurt you and how much I needed you, that I began to understand.'

Sophie stared at his stern, commanding features, into his lost eyes, and felt her icy outrage disintegrate. He was hurting so badly. And she knew with absolute certainty that pain was not new to him. It was etched with the strength of years.

'Tell me about Fotini,' she whispered, realising at last that the past was the key to so much. She needed to understand what had happened to make Costas so distrustful.

He hesitated and she read the reluctance in his expression, the tight control.

'She was beautiful, spoiled, full of life,' he said in a low voice. 'It was a marriage of convenience, not love. I wanted a wife and she was pleased to accept me.'

His lips curved in a mirthless smile. 'There are some women who see me as a catch.'

Sophie ignored his last statement and shook her head, amazed at such a cold-blooded approach to choosing a life partner. Apparently her grandfather hadn't been alone in his belief that marriage and love had nothing to do with each other.

'It seemed enough at the time, Sophie,' Costas murmured. 'But then I hadn't met you.'

Dazed, she stared back at him. Her body reverberated with the force of the electric connection that sparked between them when he looked at her like that.

Hope surged within her.

'Fotini liked being the centre of attention. She was used to parties and fun. To an extravagant lifestyle.'

Sophie watched his brow furrow deep as he remembered. She wanted desperately to ease his hurt.

'When Eleni was born I thought it would help Fotini to settle into married life, give her a purpose that had been lacking in her life: someone other than herself to care for.'

And what about her husband? She hadn't cared for him?

Sophie found herself wondering why her cousin had married. Originally she'd assumed it was because Fotini was in love. Costas was sexy, overwhelmingly masculine, the sort of man any woman would want for herself. But he was also mega-wealthy. Now she wondered if that had been a factor in Fotini's decision to wed.

'But Fotini suffered from severe depression. And she didn't want our daughter.'

Costas turned his head to meet her gaze as her gasp of indrawn breath stretched between them. 'Her condition was so serious she was hospitalised. And when she came home, despite the medication, her moods were unpredictable, her behaviour extreme. The highest of highs and the darkest of lows.' He paused, nostrils flared and jaw set.

'The only constant was that she steadfastly refused to have anything to do with Eleni unless forced to.'

Sophie's heart clenched. For a little motherless child. For Costas, coping with a baby and a wildly unstable wife. And for her cousin, Fotini. What must they all have suffered?

'It turned out that Fotini's condition was exacerbated by the alcohol and the drugs her friends had been secretly supplying.'

'You're joking!' No one could be that foolish, surely.

He shook his head. 'I don't think they realised how serious her condition was. Fotini could be the life and soul of the party when the mood took her. But the night she died they found a mix of alcohol and illegal drugs in her bloodstream. That was why she ran off the road. We were just lucky no one else was with her at the time.'

'Oh, Costas.' Sophie curved her palm around the clenched tension in his jaw, wishing she could ease the pain that throbbed in his voice. The regret.

'It's over now,' he said, looking into her eyes. 'But you need to know I wasn't attracted to you because of any resemblance to Fotini. I want you for yourself, *glikia mou*. Everything about you is unique. You fill my heart in a way I never believed possible before.'

She met his eyes and saw the blaze of raw emotion there.

His hands cupped her face. She felt them shake. Those big, capable, powerful hands, trembling against her skin.

'I love you, Sophie. That's why I can't let you leave me. I want you with me always. I need you. You're part of me, part of my soul.'

Sophie closed her eyes for an instant against the hot, bright welling emotions that seared her. She was almost too scared to believe this was real.

'*Agapi mou.* I hurt you, I know. It was unforgivable. The act of a beast.' His ragged voice broke through the last of her barriers. 'What I feel for you—it scared me. Can you believe that? So like a coward I tried to run away, to pretend it was only lust between us.'

His thumb brushed her cheek in a soothing caress at odds with the searing fire in his eyes.

'I didn't believe in such a love between a man and a woman.' He shrugged. 'Perhaps it was the experience of an unhappy marriage. Or maybe it was fear of losing control, of total dependence on a single woman for my happiness. I don't know, Sophie. All I know is that I refused to believe what I felt. I lied to you and to myself, pretending it was something I could contain. But it was too late. And when you rejected me—' his voice deepened in pain and his hold on her tightened '—I lashed out at you. Unforgivably.'

Her eyes were brimful of tears. He was a dark blur filling her vision. She shook her head, too choked to speak. But her hands spanned his jaw, slid lovingly over his cheeks, his lips, his brow, needing the sensation of his hot flesh to anchor her in this spinning world of sudden, blazing happiness.

She leaned close. 'I love you too, Costas. So much. I tried to hide it from you—it was tearing me apart to leave you.'

'Sophie!' His voice, like black velvet, caressed her. 'We'll never be apart again, I promise.'

And then she couldn't speak, but this time because his lips were on hers, tenderly urgent. She opened for him and the world spun away.

It was an age later that she surfaced, panting as she dragged in oxygen. She felt so different. As if the shadows of the past had been banished by the magic of what she and Costas shared.

She smiled up into his face and he responded with a blazing grin that lit his features in a way that sucked the newly acquired oxygen straight from her lungs. He really was gorgeous when he looked at her like that.

'You've sealed your fate, Sophie. You're mine now.' There was no doubting the possessive gleam in his eyes. And Sophie didn't mind one bit.

She stroked the hard angle of his jaw, revelling in the sensation of his warm skin against hers.

'And you're mine.' She smiled and watched him swallow as she feathered her fingertips over his mouth.

'Sophie? There's something else you need to know.'

She experienced a moment's dread as she read uncertainty in his dark eyes. Then she squared her shoulders. Whatever it was, she could cope, now that she knew he loved her.

'What is it?'

'Eleni. She—'

'You said she was making a good recovery!'

'She is. The doctors are astounded at how well she's doing. The prognosis is very good.' He paused and she saw the pulse at the base of his neck quicken.

'The reason you were the only compatible donor we could find…' He hesitated and Sophie curled her fingers around his hand.

'When we did the initial blood tests the doctors discovered that no one in my family would be a match. Fotini was pregnant before we married. Eleni is no blood relation of mine.'

His dark gaze met hers and she read the question in it. 'Nevertheless I am her father. I love her and she will always be my daughter.'

For a long moment Sophie sat in stunned silence, absorbing the implications of his words. The story of deceit, betrayal and, above all, love.

What a man her Costas was! How strong. How generous and loving.

'All that matters is that you love me, *Costa mou,* just as I love you.'

'And you'll marry me? You'll even take on another woman's child?' There was an anguished edge to his voice and she knew it was uncertainty that held him so unforgivingly in its grip. Sophie slid her hands to his broad shoulders, massaging at the tightness there.

'Eleni will be *our* daughter,' she corrected.

He stared back, his face a sombre mask of slashing, powerful lines, his eyes burnished bright by emotion.

'I don't deserve you, Sophie. I know that. But I will spend my life making you happy.'

He smiled slowly, in a way that sent a skitter of excitement through her. She read mischief in the sudden twinkle of black eyes. 'And I will take enormous care to ensure you never change your mind. Starting immediately.'

He slid his hands round to the front of her shirt, his fingers deft and quick as they flicked open each button in turn.

'Costas—no!' She darted an appalled glance over his shoulder, fearful of seeing someone, Yiorgos maybe, outside the car. But the glade was deserted, except for some bird trilling in the shadows of the ancient olive trees.

Costas grinned as he slipped her shirt from her shoulders in a single, easy move and reached for the clasp of her bra.

'Sophie—yes!' He nuzzled at her breasts as he stripped her bra away and took her warm flesh in his hands. 'Yes and yes and yes!'

0411/05b

...Make sure you don't miss out on these fabulous stories!

3 in 1 ONLY £5.99

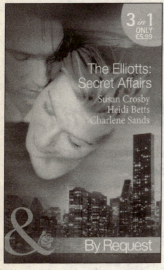

3 in 1 ONLY £5.99

The Elliotts: Secret Affairs

Susan Crosby
Heidi Betts
Charlene Sands

& By Request

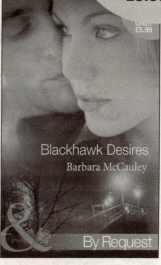

ONLY £5.99

Blackhawk Desires

Barbara McCauley

& By Request

featuring

THE FORBIDDEN TWIN
by Susan Crosby

MR AND MISTRESS
by Heidi Betts

HEIRESS BEWARE
by Charlene Sands

featuring

by Barbara McCauley

BLACKHAWK'S BETRAYAL

BLACKHAWK'S BOND

BLACKHAWK'S AFFAIR

On sale from 6th May 2011

*Available at WHSmith, Tesco, ASDA, Eason
and all good bookshops*

www.millsandboon.co.uk

BAD BLOOD

A POWERFUL DYNASTY, WHERE SECRETS AND SCANDAL NEVER SLEEP!

VOLUME 1 – 15th April 2011
TORTURED RAKE
by Sarah Morgan

VOLUME 2 – 6th May 2011
SHAMELESS PLAYBOY
by Caitlin Crews

VOLUME 3 – 20th May 2011
RESTLESS BILLIONAIRE
by Abby Green

VOLUME 4 – 3rd June 2011
FEARLESS MAVERICK
by Robyn Grady

8 VOLUMES IN ALL TO COLLECT!

www.millsandboon.co.uk

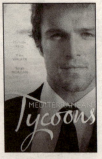

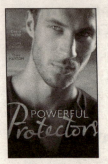
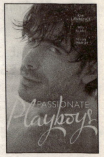